CONSUMED BY EVIL

a sequel to
THE CURSED AMONG US

JOHN DURGIN

Crystal Lake Publishing
Tales from the Darkest Depths
www.crystallakepub.com

BY JOHN DURGIN

Consumed By Evil

The Cursed Among Us

Inside The Devil's Nest

Sleeping in the Fire: A Collection of 9 Horrifying Tales

Blank Space

Kosa

COMING IN 2025

Suffocating Skies

(in the *Dark Tide* series)

WELCOME
TO ANOTHER

CRYSTAL LAKE PUBLISHING
CREATION

To Newport, the town responsible for inspiring the curse...

PROLOGUE

WINTER OF 1979

Bill Burke didn't hear the screaming until he killed the chainsaw. Cries of agony whipped through the surrounding forest, intertwining with the frigid winter air. At first, he thought maybe his ears were just playing tricks on him after a full day logging. But as soon as he removed his ear protection, it was clear something was wrong. Terribly wrong. He squinted, trying to decipher where the screams were coming from. It was all but impossible to see more than twenty feet as the snow continued to fall in the waning daylight. He set his old Husqvarna chainsaw on the ground and walked around the front of his logging truck, closer to the wall of trees blocking the commotion.

What the fuck is happening out there?

Whatever it was, the cries were getting closer. Instinct told him he needed to get out of there, and right fucking now. He decided to do just that, but first he needed to pack up his equipment as quickly as he could. The last thing he needed was to lose his chainsaw or skidder because he got spooked out of the woods. This was his livelihood.

He hurried back to his truck and opened the exterior cubby next to the driver's side door. He grabbed the chainsaw off the ground and set it inside, followed by the gas can. Then he jogged over to his skidder, pulling the keys out of his pocket as he went. He wouldn't be able to get both the truck and skidder out of the woods in time, but he could at least lock the rig before leaving and pray nobody fucked with it.

Bill tore off his work gloves and tossed them to the ground, fumbling for the proper key. The cries were getting louder by the second—a mix of women and men screaming for their lives. His breathing intensified, sending clouds of warm air swirling into his field of vision. When he got the key he needed, he locked the door on the skidder, double-checked to make sure it was locked, then turned back to retreat to his truck.

He'd promised his fiancée, Sheila, that he would come home earlier tonight after a week of working straight from sunup to sundown, busting his ass to save enough money before the baby came. She worried when he was gone too long, telling him he needed to be careful. Logging was an extremely dangerous career and one that paid shit on top of that. But after his dad passed a few years back—no tears were shed there after a life of physical and mental abuse—Bill had no choice but to drop out of high school and use his dad's old equipment to try and get by. Someday he hoped to go back to school. At least that's what he told himself. The more time that passed, the less likely that seemed a reality. One thing that *would* be a reality, he promised himself, was that he wouldn't be an abusive asshole to his baby like his dad was to him.

He hopped up into the cab and shut the door. His window remained open about an inch from earlier, as the inside of the truck always felt hotter than dragon shit, even in the dead of winter. With the window cracked, he heard the disturbance of branches snapping as panicked footsteps approached. He glanced at his watch and sighed. He should have left at least an hour ago, and he would've never been in this mess. Now, Sheila would be wondering if something happened to him out here.

Thank God it's fucking dark out.

Regardless of the lack of light, Bill still felt fully exposed with his red Peterbilt truck sitting in the middle of the man-made open field surrounded by trees on every side. It was as if nature was pointing right toward him saying, "Come this way." He didn't dare start the truck yet as more footsteps closed in. Hopefully if he stayed quiet, whoever was approaching would either move past the log site without finding him or just assume nobody was in the truck and get on with their business. Loggers did that all the time, right? He always gave his friend, Tommy, a.k.a. Tummy, shit for leaving his equipment in the woods overnight.

Muffled voices came into earshot. He couldn't hear what they were saying, so he leaned his head beneath the slightly open window to try to pick up any of the conversation.

"Go! She's...need...warn them..."

"What the *hell*?" Bill whispered to himself.

More disturbances in the woods. Screams. Branches breaking. Snow crunching beneath rattled steps. Bill wished he'd started his truck a few minutes ago so it would be ready to take off by now. Big rigs needed time to warm up, and his truck needed even *more* time with its engine having seen better days. Every day that passed without his truck shitting the bed was a blessing.

He couldn't get away on foot, not with his bum knee and the extra weight he carried around these days. He'd promised Sheila he would cut out junk food and get back to the weights, but all the hours in the woods left him exhausted at the end of the day.

The talking outside had stopped. So did the distant screams. Maybe whatever the hell was going on had passed? Some winter party in the woods to get away from the cops? Lord knew the new cop in town, Officer Miller, could be quite the prick.

Bill sat up slowly, peering out the window into the open space between his truck and the forest. At first, he didn't see anything. He prepared to open his door, considering himself a fool for being startled by a bunch of teens, when he spotted movement between the trees. At least two people were crouched behind the wide base of a towering maple tree, hiding from someone. *Something*. Everything appeared to freeze in time. The sounds of the forest were absent. Even the snow that had been falling the past few hours seemed to flee the area to get away from whatever it was these people were so scared of.

After what felt like minutes, the two unidentified figures stood from their crouch and ran toward the clearing. Toward his truck.

Shit!

He ducked again, this time simultaneously looking for anything to defend himself. All his tools were in the cubby on the truck's exterior. The gloomy sky that came with the storm commingled with the early hours of nightfall to create less than optimal visibility in the dark cab of his truck. He located his Maglite, which Sheila got him for Christmas last year, saying if he was going to be out in the woods at all hours of the night working, he at least needed to have a heavy-duty flashlight. He had no intention of turning the light on and giving away his location, but the weight of it made for a nice makeshift club if anyone decided to get too daring and approach his truck.

The muffled voices returned, this time right outside the truck. If not for the cracked window, he wouldn't have been able to hear a single word.

"We have to get out of here, now. She's coming!"

"Keep it down," a second voice said.

That second voice…it sounded familiar, but Bill didn't dare sit up to get a better look.

Before they could say another word, more screams erupted from the woods where they'd just exited. They were bloodcurdling. Bill lifted his head and looked toward the darkness between the trees. A middle-aged, red-faced man came sprinting into the opening wearing a black robe. *Robe? Fuck me.* He should have known. Those robes, he knew who they belonged to.

"Go! Now! She's right behind—"

His warning was cut short as something tore through his upper body, right beneath his collarbone, splashing the snow in crimson. His eyes went wide as he looked down at his chest in disbelief to see a clawed hand pushing through the wound, gripping the cloth on the front of his robe to hold him upright. The other men screamed as their friend's body twitched, being held up by whoever was behind him.

"Al, no!" shouted one of the men.

They took off from the truck, finally coming into view. Their attire matched that of the impaled man. With their hoods on, Bill still couldn't see who they were, not that it mattered at the moment. Fleeing for safety, they sprinted toward the makeshift road Bill had created with his skidder earlier in the day. With them out of sight, Bill brought his attention back to the man—Al—who still appeared as if he was floating a few inches in the air, grabbing at the hand that poked out of his chest. His attempts were weak.

"Ahhh!"

The man screamed, and at first Bill couldn't tell why the sudden intensity behind the cries. But then the man dropped to the ground in a heap, revealing a figure behind him. A woman in a matching black robe stepped forward, staring down at him. He whimpered, trying to crawl away. From the truck, all Bill could make out were parts of the woman's narrow face beneath the hood to go along with her slender build.

How the hell does she have the strength to lift this guy up with ease like that?

It was as if she was toying with the guy, walking slowly behind him as he continued crawling toward the road. He lifted his head and coughed up bloody phlegm, smearing the snow in front of him.

"Please... We didn't mean to do it!"

The man was now only fifteen feet from Bill's truck, getting far too close for his liking. Bill gripped the flashlight tightly, ready to strike. The woman kneeled and grabbed the man by the robe, flipping him over to his back.

"No...no, please. I have a family. Don't do this!"

Ignoring his plea, she dropped to her knees, mounting his wide chest. For a second, Bill thought it was some sadistic sexual act about to go down. The man tried to break free, but her strength was unnatural for a woman her size. He might as well have been trapped beneath a black bear. All Bill could do was watch in awe, hoping she didn't see him peeking out the window.

She lifted her bloodied hand and slowly pulled back her hood. Her hair hung over her face, hiding her features. And then she drove the hand through his chest with the force of a cannon; the sound of meat tearing apart mixed with bodily fluids squirming between her fingers cut off the man's pleas. Bill jolted back at the unexpected attack, immediately hoping his sudden movement didn't create too much noise. He leaned his head against his seat and closed his eyes, taking a deep breath. He could hear the man coughing up more blood, moaning incoherently.

After a second, the sound of fabric being torn interrupted his coughing. Bill dared to look again, then wished he hadn't. It wasn't fabric being torn; it was the man's skin. She had ripped a hole in his chest and was digging through it like a surgeon on coke. Bill thought the man was looking right at him, discovering that he was hiding in the truck and too much of a coward to try and help. Then he realized the eyes weren't moving at all. Instead, it was the blank stare of a dead man looking back at him while his body continued to be ravaged.

What is she doing?

He didn't have to wait much longer to find out. The crazed woman stopped digging, twisted her arm clockwise, then tore the heart from the dead man's chest. Blood splashed across the white ground like an abstract painting.

She lifted the heart toward her face.

No. God, no.

She opened her mouth. Then, before Bill could look away, she bit into the organ like it was an overripe apple. Bill's body went cold. The woman lowered her hood, revealing her full face for the first time, and he couldn't believe what he was seeing. He *knew* her. There wasn't time to register what was going on as two giant beams of headlights spotlighted her. She snapped her attention toward them and jumped off the man. Bill's heart slammed against his chest as she got closer to his truck, but then she moved away from the lights, returning to the forest.

A vehicle approached, its tires crunching over the fresh powder. Sporadic snowflakes painted a false beauty in their descent, catching the beams before hitting the ground. The headlights sliced through the frigid air, displaying more trees ahead but no figure.

Where the hell did she go?

The vehicle came to a stop somewhere along the side of his truck. He didn't reposition himself to look in his driver's side mirror. Maybe the fleeing men ran for help? He wasn't so sure they could have reached anyone that quickly, as the drive through the trail was close to a mile before they would've hit the main road. Even running for their lives, not enough time had passed for them to get there.

A car door shut.

Something crossed through the headlights, briefly casting a towering silhouette over the trees ahead.

"Bill! Bill, where are you?"

Oh fuck. Sheila. Go, Sheila, get out of here now!

She must have come to check on him, worried about it getting so late. He wished he'd never told her where the jobsite was today, but she always insisted he let her know so she could send for help if he didn't come home. She had genuine fears of a widowmaker falling on him or an accident with the chainsaw. One thing she never mentioned was a fear of a heart-eating psychopath terrorizing the woods.

He was about to open the truck door when a flash of movement ran between the trees spotlighted by the headlights. Sheila saw it, too, because she picked up speed as best she could at eight months pregnant.

"Bill! Is that you?"

The woman in the robe burst out of the woods, sprinting toward Sheila. Bill wanted to help, but his eyes were glued to the scene, his body paralyzed in a state of shock. Part of him thought there must be an explanation for what was going on because it wasn't just a random female eating the man's heart, it was Sheila's best friend. Jessica Black.

"Jessica? What are you doing out here?" Sheila asked, hugging herself from the cold.

Jessica stopped running when she realized it was Sheila.

"Why are *you* here, Sheila? You shouldn't have come."

"I'm looking for Bill. He's usually home by now but—" Sheila stopped when she looked down at the snow and spotted the excessive amount of blood. Bill watched her follow the trail until her eyes landed on the body of the dead man. "What..."

Get out and help her, damn it!

"You shouldn't be here. I can't stop it," Jessica said.

Her voice was full of pain, like someone was holding a gun to her head, forcing her to do something horrible. Jessica took a step toward Sheila, but instead of concern or happiness at the sight of her friend, what filled her eyes was a ravenous hunger that had a glint of orange in the beams of the headlights. Sheila took a step back.

"Jess, what are you doing? Who's that man? Where's Bill?"

"I haven't seen Bill. I... No! She's my friend!"

Jessica's voice shifted, turning to a deep growl.

Is she arguing with herself? Bill wondered.

"Are you okay, Jess?" Sheila asked, fear gripping her words.

"You should go. Go before I can't stop it, Sheila. Save yourself and the baby."

"Wha-what are you talking about?"

Something rippled beneath the skin on Jessica's face, the contorted shadows amplified by the headlights. Her eyes now glowed orange, giving off a supernatural spark. Bill knew he needed to act now. He reached for the door handle, squeezing his Maglite tight with the other hand—

But he was too late.

Jessica lunged at Sheila, driving her down to the ground. They landed with a loud thump and Sheila screamed. Bill pushed his door open, prepared to jump down on top of Jessica, but he was worried he'd land on Sheila and hurt the baby. Instead, he hopped down onto the snow behind them, and his ankle landed awkwardly on the uneven terrain. He fell to the ground, pain shooting up his leg. The flashlight landed in the snow next to him, and he quickly rolled to his hands and knees and crawled to it. As he went to retrieve it, he heard claws tearing apart Sheila's clothing behind him.

"Bill!" Sheila forced out.

Jessica paid no attention to him, focused on her prize buried in his fiancée's chest. Sheila screamed for her life. Jessica dug. And dug. They were only a few feet from Bill, but they might as well have been fifty feet away. Everything happened so fast. He limped over, lifting the Maglite, prepared to strike.

As he stood over Jessica's shoulder, Sheila's shocked face stared back at him. Blood dribbled down her chin, sliding onto the snow. She reached for him. Her skin already turning as white as the fresh powder she lay on top of. Bill swung with everything he could, the unyielding metal cracked against the back of Jessica's skull. She fell to the ground, rolling off Sheila, revealing a nightmare of blood and gore beneath Sheila's torn shirt.

"No!" Bill got to his knees and lifted his fiancée's head to his lap.

She was looking at him, but at the same time, looking *through* him. She was fading.

"I should've stopped her... I'm so sorry," he whispered.

"Bill... s-s-save the baby."

Tears poured down his face. He moved his eyes to her ravaged chest, then lower...to her stomach. He held the vomit down at the sight. No matter how bad it was, he couldn't tell her.

"Sheila..."

But he didn't have to lie. When he looked back at her face, she was gone. Her once beautiful eyes, full of energy and life, had diminished to two hazy orbs. He cried uncontrollably, squeezing his fiancée tight. Everything else around him meant nothing in that moment. He was a coward. And because of his hesitancy to help, his family was dead.

Distant shouts from the forest broke the silence. Still, he kept his eyes on Sheila. This was his fault. If he had just left the jobsite when he was supposed to ...

Multiple figures entered the clearing, wearing robes. He looked up at them, all staring at the scene in terror, and his blood boiled. They had something to do with this. Whoever the hell these people were, they made Jessica this way. Except he knew exactly who they were. *What* they were. They were part of the coven. And they caused Jessica to take the lives of his fiancée and unborn child. Something snapped inside him, never to change again.

Jessica began to stir.

"Get her, now!" a tall man wearing a black, featureless mask ordered the others.

As Bill eyed each and every one of them, he recognized many. They were residents of Newport. They swarmed toward Jessica, prepared to restrain her. Jessica lifted her head and saw them coming. She screamed in their direction, an octave that blasted through the forest, rattling the tree branches. The townspeople froze for a second, covering their ears. Jessica got to her feet, observing the situation. They all carried some form of weapon—sticks, shovels, one had a gun—and then she sprinted deeper into the woods. They followed. The man with the gun fired in her direction as the tall man in charge continued to shout orders.

And just like that, everyone was gone. Everyone except Bill, holding his dead fiancée and child in his arms. He knew in that moment, he would never allow himself to love again.

CHAPTER 1

NOVEMBER 1, 1999

"Ken Kincade here for WMUR News. I stand before you at the scene of one of the most gruesome massacres this country has ever seen. As you can see, a few days after the events at the school's Halloween homecoming event, crews are still hard at work getting the destruction cleaned up. The death toll continues to rise as more bodies are discovered, now totaling thirty-six deceased. A mix of students and faculty lost their lives here this past weekend. Newport police have worked countless hours to question survivors and get to the bottom of what happened. Vice Principal Cathy Ellis announced last night that school would remain shut down at least through Thanksgiving break, if not longer. She also stated that grief counseling is available to any students and teachers who need it during this difficult time. It's still unclear exactly what happened here. In the twenty years since the Black Heart Killer—Henry Black—was captured, Newport had returned to normal, with people living their day-to-day lives in peace and quiet," Ken turned to let the cameraman scan the parking lot to add some dramatic flair to the broadcast, and then he continued.

"Town officials believe it was Henry's missing wife, Jessica, who after going missing in 1980, returned to seek revenge for her husband who died in New Hampshire State Prison more than a decade ago. Eye-witnesses are reporting that a few key students aided in taking down Jessica, saving the town in the process. Students Howie Burke and Cory Stevens were said to end her reign of terror at the top of the school's ski jump behind me, while fellow student Bethany Carver helped get many classmates to safety. The families of these heroes have declined to speak to us at this time, but we will be sure to report any updates. I ask each and every one of you to keep the town of Newport in your thoughts and prayers as they cope with this tragedy. This is Ken Kincade signing off."

The cameraman, Brennan LaFaro, set the heavy camera carefully on the ground and stretched his back, revealing the bottom half of his bulging belly, which poked out of his shirt for all the world to see. Ken tried to hide his disgust, but he knew Brennan didn't care much for him anyway, so who gave a fuck if the overweight shitstain got offended? Ken worked hard to stay in impeccable shape. If he was going to be blasted across the entire New England region—and hopefully someday, nationally—he planned to make damn sure he looked good doing it. A cameraman didn't need to worry about their looks, but that didn't give him the excuse to be a fat slob.

"You get the shot of the ski jump behind me?"

"Yep. You only told me to get it, what, fifteen times before we went live? I don't understand all the theatrics. Don't you think people just want to know the facts?"

Jesus Christ, he's even dumber than I thought.

"And that's why you're *behind* the camera. The only people who want straight facts are the two thousand people in this shithole town. Well, the one thousand nine hundred and sixty-four that are left," Ken smirked. "The rest of the world wants a story, Brennan. They want to be drawn in, to feel the pain through the screen so they don't have to feel it in real life. Don't you get that? Do you wanna be working for these rinky-dink networks your whole career? This could be what we need to go big."

Not that you need to get any bigger, he thought.

"You're sick, you know that? I'm happy where I'm at. I have a wife and baby at home. I can't be moving to New York just to make more money."

Ken already regretted acting like he gave a shit what Brennan wanted. He was ready to go to the local hole-in-the-wall bar in this town and do some digging. He wanted to talk to those damn kids. Whatever he needed to offer, he would do it to get that interview—whether he intended to give it or not was another story. Most of the local news anchors didn't have the drive he did. They'd wait outside the Burke house for a few hours and then give up and try again the next day. Ken was in it to win it; WMUR was just a steppingstone to a bigger network and a bigger payday.

"Well, that's enough for tonight. I'll meet you back at the motel in a bit. I'm going to hit up the bar at the bowling alley and see what I can come up with," Ken said.

"Righto, boss. Drink one for me," Brennan said, then rolled up the cords, grabbed the camera, and stuck everything in the news van. He slammed the back door shut and got in the driver's seat. "You know, these are just kids you're trying to talk to. Maybe you should cut them some slack considering they just lost a ton of friends a few days ago."

Before Ken could respond, Brennan started the van and pulled out of the school parking lot. Brennan was so self-righteous when it came to kids. It didn't bother Ken in the slightest to do what he was doing. It was his job. Meanwhile, Brennan would go back to the motel and drink a two-liter of Pepsi while watching *WCW Nitro* like wrestling was a real sport, dreaming of the beer his alcoholic ass wasn't allowed to have.

Ken shook his head at the thought and scanned the school parking lot. It really was like a war zone, the asphalt still stained with dried blood in numerous spots, police tape surrounding most of the parking lot, and the smell of a stale bonfire that had previously meant pride for the town. Now as Ken stared at the towering pile of the bonfire's carcass, he imagined that smell would sicken the citizens for decades to come.

He glanced toward the hill near the ski jump and considered making a trip to the top to snoop around a bit but decided against it. It was almost dinnertime, which meant most of the town would be getting off work, and a good percentage of them would be heading to the bar. While the bowling alley and most of the businesses were shut down following the massacre, the bar was still open. People needed to drink in times of grief. He wanted to be there when those people started to pile in around him and to pry whatever information he could from the drunks.

Ken walked around the front of his silver Porsche 911 GT3 and opened the door. He kneeled to get a good look at himself in the driver's side mirror, not that he needed to worry about appearance in this hillbilly town. When he determined his frosted tips were perfectly tousled, he hopped in the car and started it up. With one last look over at the school sign reading *Home of the Tigers*, he sped out of the parking lot. He planned to be the only tiger in town tonight, and the drunk yokels would be his prey.

CHAPTER 2

Howie peered out the window overlooking his driveway, wishing the reporters would all just leave. Most of them *had* left, but a few stragglers still hung around, desperate to catch one quick interview with him about the "massacre." That's what the news was calling it. He couldn't argue with the title, but this wasn't some horror movie he and the guys watched every weekend. This was real life.

He stepped back, letting the curtain shut, and slouched down on his bed. The past few days had been a rollercoaster of emotions. Most of the time he just felt numb, unable to comprehend the reality of the situation. While other times, he'd struggle to keep himself from a complete breakdown.

One of those breakdowns was on the verge of making an appearance, so he picked up the most recent issue of *GamePro* to distract himself, reading the big headline on the front of the cover: *The Dreamcast Is Here*. The thought of the next-gen video game system releasing brought his thoughts back to his friends, who he'd never get to play games with again. To Ryan, who owned every game known to man, yet forced them to continue playing *GoldenEye* two years after it was released. To Todd, who routinely went for it on fourth and long, then threw the controller down in frustration every time he lost a game of *Madden*. These thoughts brought newfound tears to Howie's eyes, something he thought he was out of at this point. He tossed the magazine on the floor and closed his eyes.

After everything they had been through to rid the world of Jessica Black, he couldn't help but feel like nothing else mattered afterward. Even coming home to confront his dad, which normally brought on severe anxiety, didn't so much as cause his heart to skip a beat faster. He figured that would wear off eventually and everything would go back to normal, but all he wanted to do right now was stay in bed and watch movies or listen to music. So far, his parents hadn't bugged him much about coming out of his room unless it was mealtime. His dad, who typically searched for any excuse to put Howie to work, trying to "make a man out of him," had actually backed off since the events at the school. Howie wouldn't go as far as to say his dad was a changed man, but the look in his eyes when Howie walked through the front door after the massacre was one he'd never seen from his dad before.

Relief. Happiness. *Love*? His dad had never once said he loved Howie, or even let him know he was proud of him, but this new mood at least hinted it might be somewhere buried inside. When it should have warmed Howie's heart, it instead made him uncomfortable. Like it was the calm before the storm. Before his dad realized he'd let his guard down for a few minutes and needed to put his tough guy mask back on and teach Howie a lesson for going into the woods and breaking one of the most important rules he was supposed to obey.

The last few days had been strange, for sure. The hardest part, though, was every time Howie forgot to keep himself busy, he'd find his mind wandering off to the ski jump again, climbing the rusted rungs until he towered over the school grounds. He'd picture Jessica, her body burnt to a crisp, climbing the side of the structure after them, intent on ripping out their hearts. And then he'd see Ryan, with his half-melted face, staring up at the stars as he said his last words.

They were memories no one, especially a teen, should ever have to relive. Then there was Todd, who after everything, tried to help his friends in the end. Jessica had controlled his mind, forcing him to kill for her, but he fought through it when he was needed most. Todd was the real hero, dying to make sure everyone else was safe. Watching Jessica throw him over the top of the ski jump was an image Howie would never forget.

In the span of a few days, Howie had lost almost everyone he was close to. Mr. B, his film teacher who saw a bright future for Howie, was gone. Ryan and Todd were gone. That left Cory. In their crew of friends, they were the only survivors. He wanted to reach out and talk with Cory but knew his parents, as well as the police, wanted him to wait to call his friend. Cory had to cope, too, and even though they were best friends, they both lost many people they cared about dearly. He would have to wait until Ryan's funeral to talk with Cory.

The services for Ryan were going to be held at the funeral home, and Howie wasn't so sure he could handle all the emotions that were bound to come with it. Ryan's mom had insisted his life be celebrated. Not just *his* life, but the lives of his friends he admired most, because their group meant the world to Ryan. As if Howie needed another reason to feel guilty for Ryan's death. They had treated him like shit, taking jabs at his weight and nerdiness any chance they got. While Howie always thought of it as nothing more than friends ribbing friends, it didn't make him feel any better knowing Ryan died without realizing how much they cared about him.

It would be good to see Cory and make sure he was okay. That was the only silver lining in any of this. People kept tossing around the word "heroes" like that was supposed to make them feel any better. Little did they know, it was Howie and his friends who unleashed the evil in the first place. And now, he had this constant feeling of being watched. They hadn't only unleashed evil on the town, they'd uncovered the long-buried secrets of the coven that still existed in Newport—one being that the coven was responsible for Jessica evolving into the monster she had become. Mr. B warned the boys to be careful who they trusted, and now they had to navigate through conversations wondering if they were talking to someone associated with the coven.

While Jessica Black was gone, it felt as if Howie's problems were far from over. He'd already learned that Officer Miller and Principal White, among others, were part of the coven responsible for getting Jessica possessed back in the seventies. They were dead, but who knew how many remaining coven members lived in town, or how he would find out who those members were? He really wanted to talk with Cory and see if he shared the same fears. Who knew? Maybe everything would be buried in the past now. With Jessica gone, there was always a chance the coven would stay in hiding and die off. He still planned to make sure. By the time they went back to school after Thanksgiving break, he intended to have some more answers. And if he was being honest with himself, he needed this to keep his mind off his dead friends. The only way he found to cope with their loss was to keep busy and distract himself. He just needed to find a way to get around not only his parents' strict rules, but also the reporters who continued to camp out in their driveway day after day.

"Howie! Supper's ready!" his mom yelled from the kitchen.

Howie sighed. It was time to pretend he was okay and hope that dinner wasn't as awkward as it had been the first few nights back home. Not that he wanted the angry, abusive version of his dad to show his face again, but the version he'd seen the last few days was just *weird*. It made him uncomfortable to talk with his dad about things they had never talked about in his entire life. He got up from his bed, gazed into the mirror above his dresser to make sure his eyes weren't too bloodshot, and headed to the kitchen.

CHAPTER 3

Cory sat on the couch of his dimly lit living room, clenching his teeth as the sickness continued to eat away at his insides. He spent the first night after the massacre in the hospital, getting his wounds assessed and treated. While his body was banged up, the doctors and nurses said he was extremely lucky to escape the night with minor injuries. They sure as hell didn't *feel* like minor injuries. After numerous stitches and bandages were applied, they sent him home the next day with cracked ribs and a prescription for pain meds. If they would kick in any time now, he'd be thrilled. At the moment, he couldn't even walk to the bathroom without wanting to cry out in pain.

Jessica really did a number to his chest and torso. But it was what she did to his *mind* that had him most concerned. When they were struggling in the devil's star on the ski jump, Cory jumped on her back, holding her down for Howie to make the killing blow. While it had worked, and the bitch's head was cut clean off, Cory felt something during the scuffle. It was only a brief second, but while he was on her back, he was hit with a sensation like his skin catching fire. As if thousands of tiny little bugs were crawling beneath his skin and biting him from head to toe.

And then the feeling was gone. Just like that.

He assumed it was shock, his brain full of so much nervous energy that it didn't know what sensory feelings to push out to the rest of his body. After being laid up for the better part of the last few days, he quickly realized that wasn't the case. Something was wrong. *Very* wrong. His body wanted to sleep it off, but every time he closed his eyes, he saw countless corpses sprawled across the school parking lot like litter. Not only was he seeing terrible images from the worst night of his life, but he was seeing things that didn't exist as well. Odd shadows following him along the wall, as if they were simply monitoring his condition, waiting for it to evolve into something bad enough to fully reveal themselves. There was one shadow in particular that stalked him through every single room, every minute of the day. A faceless figure with elongated limbs that ended with claws sharp enough to slice through the thin barrier protecting his sanity. And then there were the strange noises he heard everywhere he went. Whispers constantly buzzing in his ears like a swarm of mosquitos that just wanted blood.

His dad was currently stationed in Iraq, and his mom had taken the first few days off from work to be with him, but today was her first day back at the wool factory. While most businesses agreed to shut down for at least a week, the factory was pretty strict on time off requests, so even though Cory almost died, his mom was lucky to get two days off. She tried to plead for more, but Cory told her he'd be okay at home while she was gone. He wasn't so sure that was true. And to make matters worse, his bedridden grandfather was currently living with them, and with his mom at work, it was up to Cory to bring the old man food and his meds and to clean any messes his grandfather made.

At least the factory was right down the street from their house. His mom said she'd come home on her lunch break each day to check on him. But she worked the second shift plus overtime, so her lunch break occurred when Cory was heading to bed. Which meant he had to get his own meals, and right now, he was starving. As much as he wanted to grab something to eat from the pantry, the thought of walking to the kitchen didn't appeal to him at all. Instead, he spread out on the couch and stared at the ceiling, wondering what Bethany was up to. If there was any positive to come from the massacre, it was that Bethany got to see him help save the town. He couldn't help the selfish thought, even after losing so many people he knew.

"She wants your little cock!"

He sat up, startled. The thought was in his head, but it wasn't his own. *What the hell is happening to me?*

Except, he knew exactly what was happening to him. While he could pretend it was fatigue, his body had been attempting to warn him ever since he got in the ambulance at the school. Whatever evil force was in Jessica was now trying to dig its way into his body. She was gone. But *it* wasn't.

He lay back down, closing his eyes to try and catch up on some rest and shake the intruding thought. The nightmares had come full force, and even a fifteen-minute nap could do him wonders right now. In a matter of seconds, he was asleep, traveling frantically through his troubled mind. A constant weight pushed down on his chest, and he knew it to be the anxiety that had troubled him ever since that day they went into the woods and found her grave.

Even though he sensed the impending nightmare coming, he forced himself to stay asleep. At least for now, he was still in control of his thoughts. Something tickled the top of his head. He assumed it was his dog, Dolly, licking his hair. She was the sweetest, always showering him with love. But then he remembered Dolly had died a few years ago. In his groggy state he thought she was still here with him. Then something fell on his face, jolting him awake. He glanced down at his shirt to see a large spider the size of a golf ball crawling across his chest. With a quick swat, he sent it flying across the living room to the dark corner behind the entertainment center. The one thing he hated more than snakes was fucking spiders. It was one of his least favorite things about living so close to the woods. No matter what time of year, they always seemed to find a way to sneak into the comfy confines of the Stevens's home.

Cory kept his eyes glued to the corner, waiting to see if the eight-legged little shit showed its face again. With his attention focused on the television, he didn't notice when another fell on the arm of the couch behind his head. Then something dropped on his chest again, and he glanced down to see a third spider. Again, swatting it away. He then glanced up at the ceiling and screamed. Hundreds of spiders scurried above him, frantically spreading across the entire space. The once-white Sheetrock was now a blanket of shimmering darkness. They were everywhere. Cory jumped to his feet, too afraid to take his eyes off the arachnids, worried if he did, they would all take the opportunity to swarm him and wrap their webs around him like a giant, tightly knit cocoon.

A scratching noise from the second floor drew his attention away. It sounded like it was coming from his grandfather's room. When he looked back to the ceiling, the spiders were gone. The space was clear, showing off the crisp paint job he and his mom had done together a few months ago. He squeezed his eyes shut and opened them, just to make sure they were really gone for good.

"What the fuck…"

Jumping off the couch turned out to be a huge mistake. A sharp, pulsating pain swam from his chest down to his abdomen, like a snake lined with fishhooks along its body, circling around his insides. He grimaced, grabbing at his side, and sat back down on the couch. *Deep breaths. Take deep breaths,* he thought. He closed his eyes, breathing slowly, and the pain slowly faded.

"Cory!"

Cory forgot all about his grandfather upstairs. When was the last time he checked on him? And was that him scratching a second ago? Had he fallen out of bed? It had to have been hours since he last popped in to see him. He needed to make sure Gramp took all his meds on time. Panic set in and he forced himself to his feet again, this time carefully. The stairs looked like a daunting task in his current condition, but he grabbed hold of the railing and forced himself up one at a time.

"Cory!" the old man yelled again.

"I'm coming, Gramp. Hold on!"

He reached the top step and approached the spare bedroom his grandfather had been living in for the last few months. Preparing himself for any possible scenario behind the closed door, he pushed it open.

His grandfather lay on the floor, facing the door, his eyes glossy. Cory ran to his side, ignoring the pain.

"Gramp, is everything okay? Let me help you up," Cory said, carefully lifting the old man back to the bed. He grabbed his bruised legs, feeling the bulging veins beneath the aged skin as he put a pillow beneath them.

A violent, heavy cough rattled inside the old man's brittle chest. He lifted a trembling hand and pointed to the tray Cory's mom had prepared with his medication for the day.

"My...pills, I couldn't reach them."

"I'm so sorry. I can't believe I forgot."

His grandfather waved away the comment like it was no big deal, but it sure felt like a big deal. How far past due was he for his meds? Cory grabbed the bottles in the order his mom had shown him and popped out two pills. He attempted to set the pills in his grandfather's wrinkled palm, but one of them dropped to the floor.

"Damn it. Sorry, Gramp."

Cory bent over to pick up the pill, and a sharp pain greeted him on the way down. His head was now just beneath the height of the mattress, right in earshot of his grandfather.

"It won't stop until it consumes all of you..."

Cory fell to his backside and stared up at his grandfather. The old man continued staring at the door, just like he had when Cory entered, like nothing abnormal just came from his weathered lips. There was the hint of a smile, although his eyes didn't move, just the corners of his mouth shifting upward ever so slightly.

"What? Gramp, what did you just say?"

Those glossy eyes flickered just a tad but never moved enough to focus directly on Cory. Cory waited a few minutes, wondering if any follow-up to the cryptic message would come. Instead, it felt like he was staring back at a corpse. Goose bumps infested his skin, and he shook off the chill they brought as he got to his feet with the pill in hand.

"Here you go. I'm sorry I was late getting them to you. Do you need help taking them?"

His grandfather lay still, and if it wasn't for his chest gently rising and falling like a boat in a calm sea, Cory would've thought he was dead. Finally, the old man's eyes shifted to meet his grandson.

"Thanks, sonny. Ol' Gramp needs his meds."

He leaned on his side, grabbed the pills, and dry swallowed them down, then slowly rolled to his back to face the television. Now that he had what he needed, he ignored Cory and continued watching his program, some old-timey show that would bore anyone below the age of sixty.

A sharp pain sliced through the inside of Cory's head, almost dropping him to the floor.

"Kill him... Shove the pillow over his ugly, wrinkled face and suffocate him. You know you want to."

"Stop it! Get out of my head!"

"Quiet down, son. I can't hear my show," his grandfather snapped, ignoring what his grandson just said.

Cory shook his head and backed out of the room, unable to pry his eyes off his grandfather the entire way. His mind was playing tricks on him, so he needed to just go to bed a few hours early. At least that's what he kept telling himself. Go to sleep, wake up tomorrow, and go to Ryan's funeral.

Once he was through the doorway, he shut the door and stood in the hallway taking deep breaths. It wasn't just the voice that scared the shit out of him. What scared him more than anything was that he wanted to listen. He *wanted* to kill his grandfather.

CHAPTER 4

Howie felt sick to his stomach as his dad pulled into the parking lot of the funeral home. News vans lined the street, along with police cruisers and a swarm of town residents all dressed in black. The line of families wrapped around the corner of the old brick building like they were waiting to get into a sold-out concert instead of visiting hours. While the thought of so many people wanting to pay their respect to one of his best friends was nice, it was all very overwhelming. He could feel the faces of everyone in line burning into him with a mix of support, pride, and sorrow as they drove by.

He was also trying to mentally prepare himself for all of the hero talk again. If they had stayed out of the woods like they were told, none of these people would be dead. It was guilt, not pride, that constantly sunk its teeth into Howie. How was he supposed to look Ryan's mom in the eye and not feel like a big piece of shit? At least he *could* look Ryan's mom in the eye. Todd's mom and dad were brutally murdered, leaving the house vacant with the entire family now dead. So many memories of sleepovers at Todd's place, where they would stay up late at night in his tree house and spy on the neighbor across the street with binoculars, making stories up about the man being the original suspect questioned for the murders before Henry Black was taken into custody.

Howie missed the days when they were just pretending to watch the killer from a tree house. Instead, they got to live a nightmare with the real-life killer that all the town lore was birthed from.

His dad was lucky to find a spot and parked the truck in the full parking lot. After a silent ride where the only sound was the country music playing on the radio at low volume, Howie's mom turned to him in the back seat. She had that stereotypical sad mom look, with her lips stuck in a frown and her eyes holding back tears.

"Hon, are you sure you're okay doing this? We can skip it and just hold off for the celebration of life."

"No. I want to do this. I haven't seen Cory since...since that night."

"Okay. But if the reporters start to bug you, let us know. We can get out of here if we need to," she said.

"I'll break their fucking neck if they even try their bullshit," his dad said.

"Bill!" his mom scolded.

"Sorry. You know I hate these things. And those peckerheads lurking around us like a bunch of damn vultures trying to pick our carcasses is the last thing I want to deal with today."

Howie's mom patted his dad on the shoulder, and the small gesture of love weirded Howie out. If almost dying was all he needed to do to bring his family closer together, he would have done it years ago. The only four-letter words that got passed around the Burke household were the ones Howie was forbidden to say. *Love* was not one of them.

"Let's get this over with. I won't stay the whole time. Just long enough to show our respect and then leave," his dad said.

They got out of the vehicle and approached the crowd. Howie had long ago stopped getting embarrassed about his dad's lack of respectable apparel, but as he scanned the crowd, seeing everyone with ties and dress clothes, he found himself falling a step back as his dad walked in the lead with his jeans and John Deere hat on. At least he wore a collared shirt for once instead of his typical stained flannel or old, worn T-shirts. The line was even longer than Howie realized, as the tail of it wrapped around the corner, hidden from the main road. The thought of waiting in that and having to mingle with the townsfolk filled him with anxiety. As they headed toward the end of the line, Howie's dad muttered something under his breath.

"There he is! One of our heroes. No waiting in line for you guys. Let's get you inside to the families," the funeral director, Burt Rollins, said as he rushed over to them.

The old man smelled of stale moth balls and mint-flavored Life Savers. He was completely bald and had a graying beard that hung six inches below his chin like a hairy bib. He always walked around town in his black suit, with the collar tight around his neck like he was still on the clock.

"Appreciate it, Burt. These fucking reporters are just waiting to catch us with our pants down," Howie's dad said.

Burt let out a nervous laugh. "Right this way, Bill. Hope all is well with the family."

We're at a funeral for one of my best friends. How well do you think it's going?

Howie felt every set of eyes from the line on him as they walked by. They weren't angry eyes for skipping the line but instead, it was admiration. The golden child had arrived.

"Howie! Spunky owes you free haircuts for life!" a lady standing next to Spunky, the town barber, yelled from the crowd. The barber didn't laugh, likely not wanting to give up any small profits he might get from Howie's future haircuts.

This got some laughter from everyone else, though, including Howie's dad, surprisingly.

"Spunky's butcher jobs should be free anyway," someone said, followed by another roar of laughter.

I'm glad you can all be in such happy moods during this.

Up ahead, a few reporters stood chatting with their camera crew. They noticed Howie and his family approaching and got to work. A female reporter, who on any other day Howie would have found quite stunning, walked toward them with her cameraman in tow.

"Howie! Trish Wilson, WHMG out of Bangor. A word?"

Maine? Reporters are coming here from out of state?

Trish wasn't waiting for an answer. She walked as fast as her high heels would allow, clicking off the asphalt in rapid-fire succession.

"Lady, beat it. Now's not the time for this," Burt snapped.

"Just a moment, please. Howie, what was it like taking down the lost wife of a decades-old serial killer?" she asked, holding the mic in his face.

"I suggest you take that mic out of my son's face before I take it myself and shove it up that cameraman's ass," Howie's dad said.

Burt's face turned red. Howie held in a laugh seeing his dad's anger issues directed toward someone else for once.

"I'm sorry, ma'am, but you need to leave," Burt said, then turned his back on her and guided the Burke family through the back door of the funeral home.

Once inside, the scene hit Howie like a freight train. A brown casket was displayed up front under two dim spotlights. He froze in place, staring at the large photo of Ryan on the easel beside the casket, fighting back tears. Howie's mom put her hand on his shoulder.

"I'm so sorry, Howie." It was all she could say.

Howie's dad walked over to a few of his friends and struck up a conversation, the raw emotion coming from his son apparently too much to handle. Howie scanned the room, taking in each person who sat in seats, mingling in the corner, all of them talking quietly. Vice Principal Ellis talked with some of the other teachers. The owner of Plaza Pizza, Aba, his eyes bloodshot, sat reading the pamphlet handed out to all guests as they walked in. A few of the adults who worked at the concrete factory carried on a conversation, complaining how they still had to go in and monitor the concrete slabs the business was molding for the construction of the dam down by the train track. How it wasn't fair that the place was shut down for the week, yet they had to make regular rounds to monitor the curing process. Even at a funeral, people still complained about their daily lives. Howie couldn't help but wonder which of them knew more about the coven, or worse, were part of the group. The new police chief, who took the job when Miller was slaughtered by Jessica, stood in the corner talking with another cop and a few adults. He could only imagine what they were talking about.

As he continued to search for familiar faces, his eyes fixated on Father Grimes. Not because the priest appeared out of place at a funeral, but because he was staring directly at Howie. At first, Howie thought he was just being paranoid, and maybe the priest was simply staring over his shoulder. But then Father Grimes nodded slightly at him as he turned and walked through the crowd. Howie had never attended church in his life—his dad thought the idea was ridiculous. The only time he recalled ever interacting with the holy man was at the grocery store in town. Howie shook off the strange feeling Grimes gave him and kept looking around.

Ryan's mom stood up front greeting people. She wore a wrinkled black dress and had matching black craters sunken beneath each eye. The poor woman lost her husband and son within the span of a few days. As much as Howie was hurting right now, at least he still *had* a family—albeit one that didn't exactly go out of their way to make him feel much better.

Howie walked up to the casket, continuing to stare blankly at it. What was even left of his friend inside the wooden box? Was that the smell of charred skin on Ryan's body, or was that just in his head? As hard as he tried to hold in the tears, they now came like a river breaking through a dam. It was just a weekend ago he was playing video games with them and making a movie in the woods. And now... He couldn't do this. He needed to get out of there before he had a complete mental breakdown.

Howie noticed someone approaching to the right in his peripheral vision.

"Hey, kiddo. Thanks for coming," Ryan's mom said, then put her arm around his shoulder.

She was also crying, which only added to Howie's heartache. She leaned her head on his shoulder as they stared at the pictures of Ryan hanging on the wall, a collage his mom must have put together for this occasion. There were a few pictures of the whole gang playing outside at younger ages, before life got so serious. Howie couldn't help but smile at a picture of Ryan, wearing his standard camouflage pants and Coke bottle glasses, staring at the camera with a toy gun pointed at it. He was obsessed with James Bond and spy movies as much as he was with horror. Howie's eyes moved to the next pic, one of Ryan and his dad standing back-to-back with their large bellies pushed out in exaggerated bumps. No matter how many people picked on Ryan's weight, he always tried to make it a joke instead of letting it bother him.

"I just wish we could have saved him, Mrs. Star. He tried to take her down himself, and I... I found him after she had attacked him," Howie said, though his words came out between sobs, making it hard to understand.

"Don't blame yourself, Howie. For any of this. Ryan told me how Jessica got free. You can't blame yourself for that. It was the generation before you who knew about all of this and let it go silent for twenty years. It was their fault. *My* fault. And now, now we're all paying for it. But please, Howie, promise me you and Cory won't carry this burden on your shoulders."

"Everyone keeps calling us heroes. It doesn't feel like that."

"Well, you are. You ended it, and while a lot of people died, think about how many more would have if you guys didn't stop her."

Howie turned to see that his mom was standing back, talking with someone else, giving him space to talk to Ryan's mom.

"Mrs. Star? Do we have anything to worry about? From the coven?" Howie whispered.

He felt her stiffen at the mention, and she lifted her head off his shoulder, glaring around the packed room.

"Let's not talk about that here, okay? It's best to just let that die. No need stirring that stuff back up."

"Okay."

"Well hon, I better go talk with some others. But I'll circle back and chat some more. I know this had to be hard, coming here so soon after everything. Ryan would've appreciated knowing you care so much."

"Of course. I know he'd have done the same for us. Have you seen Cory around at all?"

"Not yet. His mom said he was still feeling pretty sore, but they'd try to make it. If you see him, tell him to come say hi to me, k?"

"Will do. And Mrs. Star, I'm so sorry for your loss," Howie choked out.

She gave him one last hug and whispered, "Thank you." Then she was off into the sea of people. Howie looked around for any of his friends, spotting Bethany talking with a few people, mixed in with fellow students in the entryway. He debated going up to her, but she didn't give him a chance to avoid it, as she made eye contact with him and flagged him over with a smile.

It was a forced smile. One where even her dimples were sad. But she was still beautiful. Every time he had that thought, he felt ashamed. That was Cory's crush. His best friend's obsession, and most importantly, Bethany seemed to have the same feelings toward Cory. While they weren't technically dating, that was something you just didn't do, regardless of relationship status. After all they'd been through, Howie couldn't imagine losing his best friend because he had feelings for the same girl.

"Hey, Howie. I'm really sorry. I know this must be so hard for you," Bethany said.

"Thanks. How are you doing with everything?"

"You know, once the adrenaline faded, it really hit me. All of it. The friends we lost. The teachers and parents. And then it made me think of how close we all were to joining the victims. Ryan and Todd were good guys. They didn't deserve this. *Nobody* did."

Howie didn't know what to say in response. He just nodded in agreement, fighting back more tears. He had to say something to take his mind off crying.

"You really helped get so many people out of there, you know."

It was an awkward response, but he was just trying to deflect the attention back to her. Before she could reply, the back door opened again. Cory's mom, Sandy, walked in. At first, Howie thought Cory must have stayed home, still not feeling well enough to come. Sandy noticed Howie staring at her and gave a slight wave. She stepped to the side and Cory came into view behind her. He looked awful. The dark circles under his eyes made Mrs. Star look like a beauty queen. Howie stared at his best friend, hardly hearing the gasp from Bethany behind him.

Cory's eyes flitted left to right, taking in the room like a tweaker ready to jump at the first shadow. He scanned the funeral home until he noticed Howie and Bethany. Instead of a smile, Cory was grinding his teeth behind closed lips. He slowly approached Howie, walking almost robotic.

"Hey, Cory. How you feeling, man? I tried calling you, but your mom said you were in a lot of pain," Howie said.

Cory shrugged but didn't say anything. Instead, he gazed past Howie toward the casket. His eyes were completely bloodshot like he hadn't slept in days. Unlike the rest of the people around him, Cory didn't have a single tear in his eyes. He swallowed, then cleared his throat.

"I still can't believe it. Doesn't seem real..." he trailed off.

"Hi, Cory, I'm happy to see you...considering the circumstances," Bethany said.

He took his attention off his dead friend and focused on his living ones. He forced a fake smile of his own—a common occurrence for those in attendance—his mind still elsewhere.

"Hey, Bethany. What's up?"

"I'll be better once we're out of here— I'm sorry. That sounded rude. I just mean, it's so sad here. I want to go back home and hide in my room again. You know? There's so many more funerals to attend, too. I never thought I'd look forward to going back to school."

"I don't know if going back in that building would be much better. Not after all we saw," Cory said.

"Has your mom talked to any reporters yet? My parents keep getting rid of them, but they won't give up. Like a fly on shit, my dad says," Howie said.

"Yeah, my mom talked to them for a few. But just told them I wasn't up for talking. Any time I look out my window, they're all I see and it's starting to drive me nuts," Cory said.

Bethany blushed, then said, "My dad's been talking with them. I told him not to. But he's trying to force me to do a sit-down with one of the reporters from WMUR, saying he can get us on some stupid prime-time show that's offering a ton of money. He usually listens to me, but even my mom can't talk him out of it."

Howie realized he and Cory hadn't told her much about the coven and everything they'd discovered, but they really needed to fill her in. Now wasn't the time and place to talk about that, though.

"Maybe we can all meet up soon and hang? There's so much we didn't get a chance to tell you," Howie said.

"Yeah, I don't trust any of these people. Not even our families," Cory whispered.

"You two sound like the place is wiretapped or something, jeez. Everything okay?" Bethany asked.

Howie eyed Cory, then they both looked at her.

"There are...things we need to talk about. Jessica's gone, but she was only part of the problem," Howie said.

"Okay. Maybe we can all get together this weekend? Think your parents will let you out of the house so soon after everything?"

"As long as I feel better, my mom will be okay with it. Just has to be when she's home to take care of my gramp. He's pretty sick. We can only stay here for like an hour before we have to go back to him," Cory said.

"I think my parents will let me. My dad's actually been kinda nice—at least for him—since the Halloween homecoming. I know the bowling alley is opening back up this weekend. Maybe we can do some glow bowling?" Howie asked. "That way it's plenty loud enough and we won't have to worry about anyone eavesdropping."

"That sounds perfect. I'll message you guys on AIM to let you know for sure once I ask my parents. I think it'll be good for us to get out of our homes for something besides a funeral, too," Bethany said.

"Sounds good. Okay, I better go mingle with some of these people before everything starts," Cory said. Something behind his eyes was...*off*.

Howie watched his friend walk away, hoping it was just the events of the past week that were bothering Cory. Somehow, he felt it was more. He felt something was changing with his friend.

Father Grimes stood at the center of the room, pulling the microphone on the podium close so everyone could hear him. While it wasn't commonplace for him to give a eulogy without reading from Scripture, Ryan's mom had asked him to talk. He was well respected in town by everyone, not just church-going folk.

"We are here today not just to mourn the loss of this wonderful young man, but to also celebrate his life, his achievements, and the love he showed everyone he came into contact with. We are here today to remember not only what Ryan meant to his lovely family, but also to his friends and the entire town. For Ryan Star died trying to protect this town. This young man went through so much every single day, but he never let that get him down..."

Father Grimes continued talking, but Howie got distracted by Ryan's mom, who sat in the front row and was now crying so uncontrollably that the people around her surrounded her and attempted to console her. Father Grimes led a prayer—which Howie assumed Ryan's mom agreed to even though Ryan wasn't religious—and then he thanked everyone for their time and left the podium. He stared at Howie and Cory the entire way as he headed to the back of the room.

Howie watched the priest walk away, and as he did, he noticed someone else staring at him. Spunky. The barber wasn't smiling anymore, and Howie doubted very much it had anything to do with the threat of having to give him free haircuts. Could he be part of the coven? Had he heard anything they said to one another before the service started? Howie turned back around to face the front, hoping it wasn't obvious to anyone that he'd just been freaked out by the town barber.

CHAPTER 5

Cory got out of the car and headed into the house. The last few hours were not just emotionally tough on him but mentally draining as well. It had been so hard to keep the bad thoughts out of his head. Every time he talked with a friend or someone from town, the voice inside his head was saying terrible things to him. Sometimes, it was a simple insult toward the person he was talking to. For example, when he talked with Howie, the voice told him Howie deserved the beatings from his dad. That if anything, his dad wasn't hard *enough* on him. And then there were times when the voice told him to *do* things. Such as demanding he go up and open the casket so everyone could see what it had done to Ryan at the bonfire.

He'd somehow forced the voice from his head, ignoring the insults and demands. But it took everything out of him to do so, and he was glad to be home. He walked to the living room and dropped to the couch, closing his eyes for a minute. His mom shuffled in behind him, carrying bags from the car. She set them on the floor and went to the couch.

"Hey, hon. That was a lot, huh? You wanna talk about it?"

Cory sighed.

"No. I can't right now. I'm sorry, Mom. I just need to rest for a bit, if that's okay."

"Of course it is. I'll get dinner started, or we could call for takeout from Plaza Pizza if you want?"

"Pizza sounds good, actually. Mom, I wanted to ask something. Howie and Bethany were thinking it might be nice for us all to get out of the house this weekend. Would you be okay with me glow bowling with them on Saturday?"

She hesitated before speaking.

"We'll see how you feel by then, but I don't see why not. You think your body will be healed enough? The doc said no strenuous activity while the stitches heal."

"Yeah. Well, I don't even care if I just go to hang with them and not bowl. Just something to take my mind off all of this. I can play pinball or something."

"That sounds like a good idea. I'll be off work this weekend, so I can keep an eye on Gramp, and you can go have some fun. You deserve it. Speaking of Gramp, do you mind checking on him while I call the pizza in?"

Cory sighed again, feeling bad for allowing his annoyance to show when his mom literally did everything for him. As an only child, he was spoiled as much as his parents could afford to within their means. Once his dad had been deployed to Iraq, his mom made it even *more* of a point to spoil him in hopes of taking the sting out of his dad's absence by showering him with movies, junk food, and anything that would cheer him up. Including the movie camera he and the guys used to film their movies. The thought of showing his dad the cracked screen when he came home from deployment made Cory sick to his stomach.

"Yep, I need to go to the bathroom, anyway. Then I'll probably lay down until the pizza gets here."

His mom leaned over and kissed the top of his head, then headed out to the kitchen to unpack the bags she'd carried in.

Cory pushed himself up from the couch, feeling the skin stretching on his chest where the stitches held everything together. Jessica had torn right through his flesh, trying to get to his heart. He was lucky Howie saved him. But that's what best friends were for, right? He'd also sacrificed himself by jumping on Jessica's back so Howie could get the machete.

"And look where that got you, you little prick! You are mine now."

He squeezed his eyes shut, hoping the voice and the pain that came with it would go away. Was this what Todd had dealt with? He said it was Jessica in his head, but she was gone now. And this sure as hell wasn't the voice of a woman torturing him. Not that he could identify much about it. Each word that came felt like something had crawled inside his head and was carving the sentences into his brain with a chisel. Once the voice stopped, the pain softened, but it left his body exhausted.

At least the voice didn't hurt too bad at the funeral. He wasn't sure what he would've done had the sharp pain struck in front of everyone there. It felt as if the voice was taking its time with him, picking its moments when to present itself. Either that, or it wasn't strong enough to take control very often, at least not yet. He couldn't begin to imagine the pain getting worse. Or occurring more frequently, for that matter.

While at the funeral home, Cory had paid close attention to everyone there. He and Howie made a point to keep an eye on the adults, looking for any indication they were being watched. He didn't get a chance to talk with Howie about it before leaving, but he hadn't noticed anything out of the ordinary. Except for Father Grimes. The priest always seemed to be within earshot of one of them. Not that the funeral home was that big, but every time Cory turned around, Father Grimes was just turning away or shifting his gaze somewhere else. As if he didn't want to be caught staring at them. Could he have been listening for the coven? That wouldn't make any sense. But neither did the principal nor the police chief. The coven clearly didn't discriminate against certain occupations.

There was just no way someone of faith, of the church, could also be involved in such evil. So if he wasn't in the coven, why was Father Grimes paying such close attention to them?

Cory walked upstairs and quietly opened the door to his grandfather's room. The old man was sleeping, snoring so loud it sounded fake. A stream of drool slid down his wrinkled chin. Cory approached him and was overcome with the scent of piss. He gagged, then plugged his nose with his shirt and grabbed the facecloth on the nightstand. He carefully wiped away the drool from the old man's face and continued watching him sleep. It was something he tried not to think about but seeing his gramp like this really hit a nerve. A childhood full of memories that included a much healthier version of his grandfather replayed through his mind—going fishing every summer, listening to stories about his firefighting days, and even sitting together and watching the Red Sox on a nice summer day. Now they were all just counting down the days until he died, alone in his room with nobody by his side.

"So do him a favor and end his misery now."

"Stop it! I won't hurt him."

But he wanted to. He wanted to wrap his hands around that fragile windpipe and squeeze it until he felt the bones crush beneath his grip. He wanted to see the old man open his eyes in shock and discover his grandson standing over him, ending his life.

As quickly as the urge came, it was gone.

Cory staggered back and wiped tears away, disgusted with himself. How could he let this voice convince him that was a good thing to do?

"*Because it is. Grab that pillow and press down gently. Nobody will ever need to know. It will be our little secret.*"

"Who are you? What do you want?"

His grandfather murmured in his sleep and turned toward the wall.

"*You will know who I am in time. You'll have no choice but to do what I say. And what do I want? I think I've made that clear. Kill the old m an.*"

Cory tried to force the thought from his head, but it was getting harder and harder to do that. A dark shadow moved across the far wall, then stopped on the space over his grandfather. It was a tall shadow full of long, jagged limbs. It had no face, but that didn't stop Cory from sensing that it was watching him. And then, the shadow lifted an arm, the darkness somehow separating from the wall and pointed. It forced Cory's eyes to look at the pillow next to his grandfather. When he glanced back to the wall, the shadow was gone. But then he was hit with a sensation like the pull of a powerful magnet taking control of his body, and all he could do was let it happen.

He was moving. Walking toward the bed. He grabbed the pillow. While he couldn't control where his eyes traveled, he could see everything. He wanted to beg for it to stop, but now he couldn't even control his own voice.

"*Hey, old man. You're pathetic, you know that? I don't even want your decaying heart. I just want to watch you die, you fucking waste of life. Perditio misellus vos vitae!*"

Cory's mouth turned upward in a sick smile. Inside, he was crying, but on the outside, he loved every second of this. He squeezed the pillow tight, feeling the fabric stretch in his grip. Another step closer. He lifted the pillow, prepared to force it over his unsuspecting grandfather.

"Don't make me do it, *please.*"

The demon ignored the plea, closing within a few feet. That's what this was. A demon. Cory realized it wasn't Jessica Black invading his mind, it was the demon that had control of her, trapped in her body for decades. He needed to fight it, get it out of his head before it was too late. Instead, he placed the pillow over his grandfather's face, prepared to push down. He wasn't pressing hard enough for his grandfather to even notice yet, but slowly, he was cutting off the oxygen. The old man's arms twitched frantically, then grabbed the pillow, trying to pull it off. Cory noticed the grime of dead skin clinging to the inside of his gramps's yellowed fingernails.

"Cory, I ordered cheese. What are you doing, buddy?" his mom asked as she came into the room.

Cory's mind snapped out of his trance. He immediately pulled back on the pillow, relieved to see the old man still breathing. His grandfather was so drugged up, he didn't even wake through the commotion. Instead, he began to snore again with his mouth open wide. Cory's hands trembled, and he hugged the pillow tight to hide it. He turned to face his mom, hoping she didn't see what he had been attempting to do.

"He was drooling again. I was trying to elevate his head a little to help it," he lied. He felt awful lying about it. But he couldn't tell her the truth, she wouldn't understand. He gently lifted Gramp's head and placed the pillow beneath, then turned back to face his mother.

"You're such a good grandson, you know that? Thank you for helping. Why don't you come rest a bit until the pizza's delivered."

He gave one last look at his grandfather, forcing down the bile rising in his throat at the thought that he was just seconds away from killing him.

"Yeah. I think rest is a good idea."

CHAPTER 6

Howie awoke to his dad shaking him. He rubbed his eyes, opening them to glance at his alarm clock. It was only four in the morning. *What the hell?* He took a deep breath and looked up to his dad staring down at him. Was that guilt behind those eyes? This was all new territory to Howie. He hadn't gone more than a single day without some form of physical or mental abuse for at least the last five years. Why was his dad suddenly showing a more tender side—granted, the best his country-strong mentality could muster?

"Dad? Why are you waking me up so early?" Howie asked, immediately regretting the question. A simple clarification request often ended with a slap to the side of the head.

"Get up. You're coming to work with me today. If they're keeping you home from school over a month, I can't have you laying around the house the whole time feeling sorry for yourself."

There he is. The asshole I've grown up to despise. At least he didn't dump water on my head this time.

"Okay."

His dad left the room. Howie sat up in bed, yawning away some of the grogginess. His dad had one of the most boring jobs ever. He used to log in the woods when he was younger, but now he drove a logging truck to Massachusetts every day, leaving around four AM to beat the Boston traffic. The thought of being in a tractor-trailer truck for hours on end with only his dad to talk to wasn't exactly his idea of a fun-filled adventure. Especially with how weird his dad had been acting ever since the massacre. Even at the funeral, his dad wasn't just nicer to him but to others as well. At least nice compared to the standard he'd set in the past.

Howie heard his dad's truck already idling in the driveway, which meant they would be leaving any minute. He had no doubt he could survive a day of this, he just hoped this wasn't going to be a regular occurrence until school started back up. That would make for a tedious break.

They would drive through Boston, down to a small town in Massachusetts where someone would load logs onto the trailer his dad towed, then they would drive back to New Hampshire to the sawmill and have the logs unloaded. All in all, it was about a nine-hour day, with more than half of that spent driving. It wasn't ideal with how carsick Howie got. Anytime he went on a long ride, he always got a stomachache. His dad told him to man up and deal with it.

He threw on his *Good Burger* hoodie and thick sweatpants, then grabbed his winter jacket and hat. Not only were the temperatures starting to dip below freezing at night, but his dad was on the larger side, so he was always hot. Which meant he either left the heat off in the truck or on really low with his window cracked.

In the kitchen, his dad packed his cooler with a few large waters and snacks. Howie sat on the couch and put on his winter boots. As he tied them up, his dad came into the living room.

"I'll make a man out of you yet. It'll do you no good to stay home and think about all this shit, Howie. Believe me. I know you hate coming with me, but I'll keep you busy. Someday you'll thank me."

I can't imagine that ever happening.

They exited the house to a dark sky and frigid air. It was so early that the sun hadn't even woken yet. The log truck idled loudly next to the house, and Howie wondered how he slept through that sound every morning when his dad left for work. It was a good thing they didn't have neighbors within a half mile, or they would be sure to get some noise complaints. Howie climbed up the side steps and into the truck, which somehow felt colder than outside. *Yay.* His dad climbed in his side and checked the dashboard to make sure everything looked good. Howie had no idea what the hell his dad was looking at—it reminded him of a switchboard of a spaceship in some sci-fi movie. So many gauges and buttons to push.

His dad turned the radio on to the local classic rock station, and Howie was at least grateful he didn't have to listen to KIXX, the country music station his parents usually played in the car. Maybe his dad was trying to be nice in his own way. At least he wouldn't have to listen to the likes of Travis Tritt or Garth Brooks for a change.

Once they were on the road, Howie took off his winter hat and jacket, balled them up and placed them against the window, then leaned his head on them, trying to force himself to fall asleep. Howie tried to think happy thoughts, whatever those were these days, into his headspace. He thought of going bowling this weekend, something his parents were okay with, and hanging out with his friends again. He thought of Jessica Black, now gone for good. And then he started to doze off, but as he did, he had one more thought come. *If Jessica's gone, why do I feel like we're still in danger?*

Howie woke after the truck went over a rut in the highway, smacking his head on the window. He immediately tried to fall back asleep, thinking the longer he slept, the shorter his day would be. It was now daylight out, the clock on the radio said it was just past six AM. His dad kept his eyes focused on the highway, maneuvering the big rig through four lanes of I-93 traffic.

Howie closed his eyes again when the radio grabbed his attention. It was no longer rock music or even country. It was talk radio. Howard Stern was interviewing a porn star about her profession. As if Howie needed another reason to feel uncomfortable around his dad. He blocked MTV on Howie, but sure, why not let him listen to an adult film star talk about how she liked to take a dick?

He decided to pretend to be sleeping, at least until the uncomfortable stuff was done being discussed. Stern continued asking her questions that Howie couldn't believe they allowed on the radio. Not that he was complaining. He could picture what she looked like and exactly what she was talking about doing with her co-stars. There were even a few moments where Howie had to hold in a laugh at some of the ridiculous stories she told. It was easy to see why his dad enjoyed listening to the morning show.

When WBCN went to a commercial, Howie shifted in his seat, pretending to be waking up for the first time. He stared out his window as they drove by the FleetCenter, which reminded him of the prior summer when the old Boston Garden was smashed to pieces. One of the coolest things he'd ever seen while being forced to go to work with his dad was the inside of the arena when it was only half demolished. It was as if all the old yellow seats were memorials to some of the world's most famous sports moments. Like little yellow gravestones facing the highway as they drove through the Big Dig of Boston.

He looked over to his dad, who was spitting tobacco juice into an old Pepsi bottle. Was he really changing? Sure, some of his mean-spirited attitude had still been there, but he hadn't touched Howie in almost a week now.

Howie had a feeling when he arrived home after the massacre that things would be different for a while. That his parents would treat him a little better. But he never expected his dad to just stop the abuse cold turkey. He couldn't help but think it was just a ticking time bomb waiting to explode, and he'd eventually say something that brought the belt back out.

"What the hell are you looking at?"

"Sorry... I just, I don't know. Things seem different now. You've been nicer to me. I like it like this, is all."

The cab filled with awkward silence. Even if his dad agreed, he wasn't one to show any sort of emotion unless it was anger. Howie wasn't even sure why the statement came out of him in that moment, but it needed to be said. Otherwise, these good—or at least better moments—would be wasted. His dad focused straight ahead as the radio show came back on. Howie wasn't sure if he was going to say anything or not, but then he spoke.

"Kid… I know I'm tough on you. That'll probably never change, so don't go getting any thoughts of me going soft on your ass. But you're almost a man now. There's things you need to know. And when we got a call from the paramedics that you were okay after everything happened, let's just say it made me realize a few things. I'm not so sure I'm ready to talk about it all yet. Just know that I'm trying to be better now. I know I'm not perfect, and I know me talking this way sounds like some foreigner speaking English for the first time. My daddy beat the ever-living shit out of me every day of my life. I always told myself I wouldn't do the same to my kids. It's funny how some apples don't fall too far from the tree."

Howie didn't see the humor in that. He also felt completely blindsided by his dad's sudden burst of vulnerability. Who knew that a demonic witch could bring out a different side of an abusive asshole?

They rode on in silence for a while until his dad pulled off the exit to head toward the jobsite. Howie wanted to ask him more, but he was afraid to push too far. That was the rawest emotion his dad had ever shown, which was a repetitive thought these past few days.

"When we get there, I'll be swapping trailers to one already loaded, so we should get back a bit earlier today. I want you to tighten the straps when we get out. Think you can handle it? Or you too much of a wimp?"

Even though what he said wasn't nice, his dad had a smirk on his face, as if he was just ribbing one of the guys. Howie laughed. He didn't remember the last time his dad made him laugh. Had he ever? He must have one time or another. Tightening the straps required Howie to toss thick, heavy, yellow straps up over the top of the logs to the other side of the trailer, where they would ratchet them so tight you could strum the fabric like a guitar.

"Of course I can do it. Have you seen these muscles?" Howie flexed.

"Fucking toothpicks is what those are."

After they swapped trailers and got the straps in place, Howie climbed back in the cab of the truck and rubbed his hands together for warmth. Even with his dad being nicer, he didn't have the balls to ask him to turn the heat up. Old habits die hard, and he'd likely get a slap to the head just for asking.

When his dad was done talking with the guy he worked for, they pulled out of the jobsite and onto the main road, which was light on traffic this early in the morning. Howie waited for his dad to turn the radio back up, hoping Howard Stern was just talking about movies or something and not the firmness of breasts. But his dad didn't turn the radio up, he turned it down and cleared his throat.

"If I don't tell you this now, there's a good chance I never will. So here goes. Back in the late seventies, I was ready to marry someone else before I dated your mother. I was only a few years older than you are now, but my dad died, and I was left to fend for myself. Because I was of legal age, I didn't need to go to a foster home or anything. I was glad to see that peckerhead croak, but I wasn't so glad to be left on my own with no idea what to do with my life. I ended up working in the woods. I used his shitty old equipment to make a living; otherwise, I'd have starved to death. I was engaged to a girl named Sheila, and she was pregnant."

Holy shit, Howie thought, unsure of where the conversation was headed next.

"So one day I was out late working in the woods, minding my own fucking business. I start hearing screaming and shit, people running through the woods around the jobsite. I thought it was some druggies out smoking weed or drinking at first, but the closer they got, the more scared they sounded. Like they was running from something. I hopped in my truck and decided to wait it out, hoping they wouldn't see me. That was the worst decision I ever made," his dad said, then spit tobacco juice in his bottle again and continued. "I watched out the window, through the snow and darkness. People in black robes came running into the clearing, covered in blood. Then one of their friends came out behind them and I watched something rip through his chest. It was Jessica Black, Howie. She killed the man right in front of me, then ripped his heart out and fucking ate it."

"Holy crap. You saw her?"

"Shut up and listen."

Howie leaned closer to his window out of instinct, hoping to be far enough from his dad's reach.

"Not only did I see her, but I *knew* her, boy. She was Sheila's close friend. One of her best friends. I had no idea what was going on. Before I could think straight, a car pulled into the jobsite and lit up Jessica like a deer in their headlights. She took off out of sight. Then… Then I saw who had pulled in. It was Sheila. Before I could act, Jessica confronted her. Because they were friends, Sheila didn't try to run away. Christ, I wish she ran. Wish she got back in her car and left me for dead. But she didn't. She questioned why Jessica was in the woods covered in blood. Then Jessica pounced on her like a fox on a hen, tearing her apart before I could stop her. By the time Jessica got scared off by the others in robes, it was too late. She killed Sheila. She killed our unborn baby. She... she ripped the baby right out of her."

Howie didn't realize his dad was crying until he saw him wiping a tear away. His dad, who he'd never even seen so much as frown, who would take any ounce of sadness or fear and turn it into anger. Howie didn't know what to say. So he remained quiet, feeling tears of his own coming. Nothing would give his dad the excuse to treat anyone the way he did, but Howie could at least see why he had been such an angry person his whole life.

"I'm sorry, Dad."

His dad chuckled, although it was anything but a happy laugh.

"What the fuck do you have to be sorry for? It ain't your fault that happened. I've always had anger issues. Your grandfather gave that to me—not just from the beatings, but from genetics. Just like I can see that anger in *you* sometimes. I hope you don't grow up to be like me, boy. But I'm not telling you all this to give a life lesson, or to promise I won't lay a finger on you again because I can't promise that. I'm telling you this because... I don't know... maybe it'll help you realize why I'm the way I am. I suppose I took it out on you that I lost the wife and baby I was meant to have."

Howie wasn't sure if that was supposed to make him feel better or not, but the facts were facts. Had Jessica not killed his dad's first family, he would have never been born. Talk about a twisted spin. He was afraid to ask questions, but he needed to know things. Was his dad involved with the coven?

"How did you guys know Jessica?"

"Henry. When he and Jessica moved to Newport, Henry and I became friends. We used to watch the Pats games together and play cards on the weekend. He was only a few years older than me, and we had a lot in common. Jessica and Sheila hit it off, too, although it was more of a forced friendship at first. But they did things together. Jessica was going to be the godmother to our baby. *That's* how close we were. You wonder why every time those damn woods get brought up, I get pissed off? Now you have your answer."

"So did you know about—"

"I'm done talking about it, Howie. I just thought you should know, is all. Let's drop it, understand?"

"Okay, Dad."

They rode the rest of the way home in silence.

CHAPTER 7

"God damn it!" Jeffrey Carver slammed his fist down on the kitchen table, rattling the silverware in the cereal bowls of Bethany and her younger sister, Briana.

"I'm sorry, Jeff. But I'm not about to let you try to make money off our daughter's suffering. If you want to talk to the reporter, go right ahead and do it yourself. But I don't agree at all with having her sit down to do it. What good could actually come from it?" Bethany's mom asked.

"How many times do I need to say it, Erica? If we want them off our backs, the easiest thing to do is talk with them. And why not get some money toward the kids' college education while we're at it? Lord knows we could use the help."

Bethany knew that was a jab at her mom because her mom didn't have a well-paying job like her dad did. Her mom grew up in town, and she was the popular girl in school and captain of the cheerleading squad, just like Bethany. And what did that get her? A husband who moved into town with a fat wallet that slowly transitioned to a fat gut. Jeffrey Carver had his nose in everything that involved money in town. But his biggest claim to fame was leading the booster club and securing enough funds to get a massive scoreboard for the football field. While the town ate his personality up, it could be overbearing at home. Sometimes Bethany felt like he expected the same worshipping from his family that he got from the town officials.

"Real nice, Jeff. How many times are you going to throw it in my face that you pay most of our bills? I'll have you remember that I didn't want to stay in this town, but I had no choice. My family made sure of that. But we need to stop arguing in front of the kids. We're better than this."

"I know… I'm sorry. Sorry to you girls, too. We should be better role models in times of stress."

They continued breakfast in silence, and Bethany kept glancing at her sister to see if she saw any signs of emotion. Any cracks in her innocent youth. The poor little girl just ate her cereal quietly, but the glint of watery eyes was there. That brought Bethany's blood back to boiling and she stood from the table, pushing her chair back violently. Her parents gawked at her in shock. Bethany was never one to show much anger, even for a teenage girl who was full of hormones.

Earlier, Bethany envied her sister for being able to drown out the arguments while her parents got louder with each word. Meanwhile, Bethany was fuming on the inside. Listening to her parents disagree over her like she was some kind of object under their control. She'd had enough.

"I'm so sick of you guys fighting over me. Not just about the stupid reporters and what happened at the homecoming, but even before that. You act like you care so much about what happens to me, but you never ask *me* what *I* want. You won't even let me look at schools out of state, all so you can keep a close eye on me and make sure I grow up to be what you want me to be. What for? So I can end up stuck in this dump like you, Mom? I'm done listening to this. Briana, come with me."

Her parents sat in stunned silence, and Briana hesitantly got up from the table and walked to her sister, holding her stuffed dragon tight. Bethany grabbed her sister's hand and took her to the living room where they both sat on the couch.

"I'm sorry you had to hear all that, Bri. Are you okay?"

Her little sister nodded, but her eyes told another story.

"What would cheer you up right now? Want me to tickle you? Give you a raspberry on the tummy?"

Briana cracked a smile and instinctively covered her stomach, preparing for an incoming tickle attack. Bethany knew her sister blocking access only meant she wanted it that much more. She pretended as if she was getting up to leave, then lunged at her sister in a playful manner, tickling her stomach until Briana laughed so hard she lost her breath.

"I love you, little sis," Bethany said.

"I love you, too. I'm glad you didn't get hurt at the school with everyone. I was so scared."

"It was scary, for sure. But Mom and Dad raised us to be fighters, right?"

Again, Briana nodded, then said, "What if I was at the school when it happened? I'm not as strong as you. Do you think she would've got me?"

Bethany realized, as scared as she was through all of it, her sister was much younger. She could only imagine how terrifying it must be, even for someone who didn't live through it.

"Well, I'm your big sister. I'd never let anything happen to you."

"Promise?"

"I promise. I'm your protector!" Bethany said, puffing out her chest. "Let me put something on for you, okay? I need to take care of a few things. Want to watch Nickelodeon?"

"Okay. Can Smokey watch with me?"

Smokey was the name of her dragon. Briana never went anywhere without it, treating it like a security blanket.

"You bet. I love you, sis."

"I love you, too," Briana said in her sweet angelic voice.

Bethany retreated to her room, happy to put more distance between her and her parents. Her dad continued to chirp in her ear about doing the interview, while her mother wanted nothing to do with it. Her mom felt it was unnecessary for a young girl like Bethany to put herself in front of millions of people on TV. She was worried about it bringing more problems into their life than any sum of money was worth. Bethany's dad, however, was a businessman first, father second. He meant well, saying it would help set up her and her sister's college funds for the future, but it still felt like he had some selfish motives as well.

Briana went about her business, watching *Rugrats* and *Hey Arnold!*, playing with her dragon while their mom and dad continued to get louder and louder after promising just moments ago to stop. Instead of hiding in her room like Bethany, Briana just kept increasing the volume of the television to drown out the fighting.

Bethany looked around her room, realizing she really needed to clean it. Piles of dirty clothes littered the floor, including the shirt she wore to the Halloween homecoming as part of her *Scream* costume. The shirt was covered in red, and she could no longer tell whether it was the artificial blood she added to the costume, or the *real* blood of her friends who were lost in the massacre. She needed to get rid of it. Try and move past the horror. But she wasn't mentally there yet. Instead, she decided to continue ignoring it and distract herself by going on her computer.

She turned on the monitor and waited a moment while the dial-up connection brought her to the internet, then logged into Instant Messager to see if Cory or Howie had messaged her yet about bowling. There were three new messages. Both boys had, in fact, messaged her, saying they were good to go for bowling. That made her happy. Hanging with those guys brought a calm she could never get from the popular crowd she spent a good amount of time with. They were goofy, comfortable in their own skin, and most of all, they were nice to her and treated her like a normal person. She knew she was popular, but it wasn't something she ever sought out.

Her dad had some pull in town, owning the auto dealership in the center of Newport, but he was also the leading booster for the football program. He made sure his daughter was at the front of anything important for her class. Whether it be captain of the softball team, cheerleading, or president of her class, he made sure she was in the discussion, and people listened to Jeffrey Carver.

It all felt so overwhelming to her, and that was *before* the massacre. Now he found a new way to cash in on his daughter for the benefit of the family, and he was set on making sure it happened. Just the thought of a sit-down interview made her uneasy. She closed her eyes and took a deep breath. Then she opened the third unanswered message, assuming it was one of her girlfriends checking in on her to see how she was doing. The username wasn't one she was familiar with, and it was ominous, to say the least.

Liveinthedarkness101: *Hi, Bethany. How are you?*

The message had been sent only fifteen minutes ago. Maybe the person was still at their computer.

BethanyCarver1985: *Who's this?*

She waited a moment, almost shutting the monitor off when she didn't get a response, but then a new message popped up.

Liveinthedarkness101: *That's not very nice. I asked how you were. You know me, so don't worry, you're not talking to a stranger... Answer the question. How are you?*

Bethany's fingers hovered over the keyboard, afraid to respond.

BethanyCarver1985: *I'm fine. But who is this? How did you get my username?*

Bethany's heart rattled against her chest; something didn't feel right. Whoever this was, they were going out of their way to intimidate her. None of her friends would do something so cruel, especially after everything the town just went through.

> **Liveinthedarkness101:** *Small town. You will know who this is soon enough. We're going to need something from you soon.*

> **BethanyCarver1985:** *Need what? What are you even talking about?*

> **Liveinthedarkness101:** *We'll be in touch.*

Before she could respond, the user signed offline. Bethany's throat tightened up as fear wrapped its invisible hands around her. She checked to see if her friends were back online, but both were signed off. She decided it was best to act as if nothing was wrong, appear content to the rest of the world, so she put an away message up that stated, *Grateful for another day. Leave a message* with a big smiley face, then turned off the monitor.

A knock at her door almost forced a scream out of her, but she stifled it.

"Come in."

Her dad poked his head in, taking in the mess on the floor. Her white Persian cat, Belle, pranced into her room beneath her dad's feet and jumped onto her lap, purring softly, helping to calm her.

"Yikes, kiddo. I think with all this downtime, you should probably dedicate some of it to cleaning this disaster, huh?" Clearly trying to lighten the mood from breakfast.

"I know, Dad. I promise I will."

"I'm sorry you had to hear your mother and I argue like that in front of you guys. You shouldn't have to listen to that stuff. We both just want what's best for you, honey. We just don't agree on what *that* is. You know I've always looked out for you. In everything you do. This is no different. I know you don't want to talk with them about what happened, but I'm telling you, Beth, it's the right decision. It's therapeutic to get out in front of this stuff instead of burying it deep inside. Why not help set our futures up for success while doing that?"

Still shook from the messages on her computer, Bethany didn't have it in her to put up much of a fight. Instead, she slowly shook her head and sighed.

"I just want the news people to go away, Daddy. Talking to them just feels like it'll make more of them hang around longer. And why wouldn't I just talk to a therapist instead of a reporter if you really want me to talk about it with someone?"

"Because a therapist *costs* money. A lot of money, which our insurance doesn't cover. This conversation would *make* us money. A lot of money. How do you and your mother not see that?"

He was getting angry again, and she knew the discussion was going nowhere fast.

"I'll think about it, okay? If you leave me alone. That's the most I can offer right now," she said.

"Okay, honey. But really, think about it."

He shut the door behind him, leaving her in silence. She looked around the mess of a room, her eyes landing again on the Drew Barrymore sweater covered in blood. The first thing she planned to do was throw that thing in the damn trash. It was time to get over it. Before she did anything else, she decided to message Cory about what happened earlier. She couldn't stop thinking about what those messages said. Then she looked down at her cat, who was sound asleep.

"Let's clean this mess up, huh, Belle?"

The cat just laid on her lap and continued purring, not a care in the world. If only Bethany could feel the same way.

CHAPTER 8

Cory said goodbye to his mom as she left to work the second shift. He couldn't wait for her to get out of the house so he could be left alone. He watched out the window as she told off some reporter who tried to come into the driveway to question her. She got in her Jeep and backed out, almost hitting the cameraman who got a bit too close for comfort. Cory smirked at that, hoping it scared the bastard silly. That would teach him to trespass onto their property. At least the number of reporters hanging around the driveway seemed to be slowly diminishing with each passing day.

Once her Jeep was out of sight, Cory turned and headed back upstairs. He went to his room and sat at his computer. For a moment, he stared at the screen saver, watching a 3D ball bouncing back and forth off the walls of the screen. The lack of sleep was really getting to him. For a second, he thought he saw a face hidden within the blur trailing the ball, zigzagging every which way. It wasn't entirely visible, but enough that he could make out a smile beneath the two beady eyes staring back at him.

He moved the mouse, erasing the ball and black background and displaying his home screen. His AIM was blinking with a new message, so he opened it, expecting a message from Howie. His heart fluttered when he saw Bethany's name blinking instead. The warm feeling quickly evaporated once he read her message. Someone was threatening her. His mind went to anyone who could've heard their conversation at the funeral. It had to be Father Grimes, as he was the only one who Cory noticed watching them. But how the hell could he have heard what they were saying?

"Kill the devout old fuck!"

The voice caught Cory off guard, and he jumped back.

"Stop getting in my head!"

He found himself wanting to defend Bethany. Even though they hadn't clearly threatened yet, the intention seemed to be there. And she was terrified either way. Cory didn't think it was a coincidence that she got this message so soon after the funeral. There were just way too many people packed in like a can of sardines at the funeral home to have any idea who could've been eavesdropping on them. It was stupid of them to even think they could talk there without being heard. They really hadn't even said that much, but they'd said *enough*. Enough to let anyone listening to them know they weren't done trying to figure out what was going on in town.

He started to type a response to Bethany's message and decided against it. What if these people could find a way to read the messages sent back and forth? Could that even be done on the internet?

A sharp pain shot through Cory's head, down into his mouth. He cried out, grabbing at his face as the sensation continued to pulse through to his teeth.

"Do I have your attention now? I'm done playing games, you weak little shit."

"Please stop... Please."

The pain was unbearable, as if something with razor-sharp claws was digging into his gums. He jumped from his desk and ran to the bathroom. He had no idea what to expect when he stared into the mirror. He'd always hated going to the dentist, ever since he had his first cavity and they had to drill into his tooth. The dentist had accidentally given less Novocaine than needed, and he felt *everything*. The tool grinding into his teeth. The filling placed into the freshly carved space. This pain felt like that but amplified tenfold.

He turned on the light and approached the mirror, afraid of what he'd see staring back at him. He opened his mouth...and released a desperate groan.

His gums were turning black, with obsidian-like veins branching out from the roots of his teeth and spreading through his entire mouth. It hurt so damn much. Whatever was inside him was growing. He reached in and rubbed the roof of his mouth, jerking his hand back as a sharp jab stabbed beneath the surface. His eyes watered. Panic set in at the thought of some infection blasting rapidly through his body. He opened the medicine cabinet, throwing stuff to the floor as he sought out his toothbrush. He grabbed the toothpaste, loaded the bristles with a large clump, and shoved it into his mouth. Cory brushed through the agony, tears pouring down his face. He brushed so hard the bristles began to poke into his gums, drawing blood.

When he finished, he filled the small cup on the counter and rinsed water around inside his mouth before spitting it into the sink. The water splashed across the white surface in a mixture of red and black fluid. Again, he filled the cup and rinsed. He spat a second time, and something clinked off the porcelain interior of the sink. A tooth at the edge of the drain—black, stringy threads clung to the top of it like a reptilian tail.

"What the fuck!"

He slammed the medicine cabinet shut, ready to inspect the inside of his mouth some more.

The reflection staring back at him sent a swarm of gooseflesh across his body. It was his face, but the eyes staring back at him held a dim, orange glow. The face, *his* face, smiled with a sadistic grin.

"I've waited long enough. It's time we have some fun."

Cory pushed the door slowly open, listening to the hinges whine with age. The television was on, showing a late afternoon soap opera, but his grandfather was sleeping. The old man's chest rose and sank in slow repetition, his mouth agape once again. Cory walked in, no longer in control of his own body but watching behind his eyes like some virtual reality projector. He wanted to scream for his body to stop, but he couldn't even do *that*. Whatever this entity was—this demon—it currently held complete control over him.

"Hi, Gramps. How's it going?"

The old man moaned in his sleep.

Cory reached toward the bed. He feared his hands were reaching for the pillow, but instead, they went toward his grandfather's wrinkled, saggy throat. They hovered just above his neck, inches from squeezing the life out of him.

"No. I'm not ready for them to know I'm here."

Relief flooded Cory, knowing the demon wouldn't act yet. There was still time to try and stop it.

"*Which means, it needs to appear natural,*" the demon said. Cory felt his mouth creep upward in another smile.

He grabbed the pillow, begging himself to stop before it was too late. He was suffocating in his own body. The demon didn't listen. It gripped the cushion, pulling it taut. And then, it pressed down, burying the old man's face beneath the fabric. Just like before, the old man kicked desperately as his already narrow airways were blocked. Cory cried, but he didn't stop. He pressed harder. And harder. His grandfather pulled at the pillow, trying to break free to no avail. He gripped Cory's wrist and clawed with his bony fingers. His jagged fingernails broke through Cory's flesh, drawing blood, but that only pissed off the demon even more. Muffled whimpers escaped under the pillow, pleading with him to stop.

"I'm sorry, Gramp," Cory cried.

"*No, you're not. You love this as much as I do.*"

The moaning softened. The kicking slowed to a weak twitch. The old man's hands fell limply to the side. And then all movements stopped, Gramp's chest leveled off, no longer rising and falling. The only sounds were the *General Hospital* theme song coming from the TV and the ringing in Cory's ears.

Cory removed the pillow to see his dead grandfather staring back at him. His yellowed eyes frozen in panic. The demon reached out and closed Gramp's eyelids.

"*We can't have anyone thinking this was anything but a natural death yet, can we? I won't even eat this prune's pathetic heart. Didn't that feel wonderful, Cory? Don't you want to do it again?*"

Cory was trapped inside, wanting to cry out. He wanted to say no, it didn't feel good. It felt awful. The problem, beyond not being able to say that, was that it was a lie. It did feel good. He *did* want to do it again.

CHAPTER 9

Ken Kincade stubbed out his cigarette on the brick wall and went back into his motel room. He wasn't sure why he bothered going outside to smoke considering the room smelled like a wet ashtray, but he followed the shoddy-ass motel's rules anyway. He figured he stood a better chance of running into someone with information by hanging around outside instead of sitting in his room chatting with the bedbugs. He couldn't wait to get out of this town, but not until business was done. The longer he stayed, the dumber he felt. But he needed to push through it, hold out until the very end. Half the reporters who'd been hanging around for a story had already skipped town as things began to die down. Ken wouldn't be one of them.

He had spent the last few days biding his time, waiting for the right opportunity to catch one of the kids off guard and talk with them. Making the effort to dig into their lives and see what made them tick. For example, he knew Howie Burke was close with the dead film teacher. He could use that to his advantage. He also knew Cory Stevens's dad was stationed in Iraq and his mom worked second shift, which meant he was often left home alone. Those were things he planned to just keep in his back pocket for the time being. Because right now, he had Bethany Carver's dad by the balls. The moron actually believed Ken would get him a nationally televised interview for a large sum of money. Ken knew the first time he talked to the dad that it would be easy to bribe him. And he also had ways of getting in the daughter's head in hopes of getting more dirt as well.

Mr. Carver had just called him an hour ago to let him know Bethany would be at the bowling alley Saturday night with the other two "heroes." Ken planned to be there. There was no time for rest, though, as he needed to talk to some more of the locals about the town's history. Many of them were very secretive of the stories, but some were starting to crack. The town librarian, Belinda Wells, was a stereotypical gossip hound. Ken learned after sharing just a few beers with her that the town used to live in the shadows of a coven. It all sounded make-believe, but after the stories from the school event, he had no choice but to at least consider believing what the librarian told him. The town had since gone on to bury that secret over the last twenty years, to the point where even the mention of past events or going into the woods could land someone in serious hot water. How could something like that stay hidden for two decades only to come spewing out of the mouth of a local during Ken's first few days in town? Well, he had a few guesses. He liked to think that he was so damn good at his job that he was able to pry that information from Belinda, whereas others had tried and failed. But he knew that was only *partially* true.

That led to his next theory. Someone or multiple someones who were integral to the stories staying buried were now disposed of. It was easy to see that, considering almost forty people were killed in a single night. Maybe now, those who'd been eager to spill the beans all this time saw their chance to speak up. Ken knew one thing for certain. He was a shark, and he smelled the blood in the water.

He sat on the stiff motel bed and grabbed the folder he stored all his research material in. So far, he'd talked or *tried* to talk with someone associated with each family of the surviving kids involved. Putting the pieces of the puzzle together was half the fun for him. The rest of the reporters were so focused on these three kids and the victims who were lost. Ken saw bigger things beneath the surface that could expose Newport. He shuffled through the papers until he came to the list of the deceased from the Halloween homecoming.

Brian White, the school principal. Joshua Miller, the police chief. The entire Seymour family, including Todd, the friend of Howie and Cory. Most people would assume the murders were unrelated to those of the late seventies. But why would Jessica Black, who had vanished for twenty years, show up and kill again at random? No, these kills were calculated. Sure, there were likely some casualties who were just in the wrong place at the wrong time, but Ken was sure somewhere along the line there had to be a connection. If he could uncover that, cha-*fucking* ching. As long as the network let him stay in Newport, he planned to squeeze every single ounce of newsworthy information from the community until he had the pieces needed to get a headline-quality narrative together. He knew he could do it. The biggest challenge would be doing it while keeping the rest of the town, and even his fat slob of a cameraman, believing he was chasing the story of the local heroes.

He stood and admired himself in the mirror above the dresser. Beneath the smudges of fingerprints and grime, a handsome reflection stared back at him with a million-dollar smile.

"You're Ken fucking Kincade."

He grabbed his keys and left the hotel room. It was getting close to his time to go live for the evening news, so the network would be waiting for an update from him. Tonight, he decided he'd head to the ski jump to get some shots up in the woods behind the school. If any cops decided to show up and give him shit, he'd just play dumb and use his trademark charisma until they just slapped him on the hand and asked him to leave.

He knocked on the door of Brennan's room, hoping the piece of shit wasn't whacking his pud to the porn he was likely buying on the company's dime. While he waited for Brennan to get ready, he continued to think about how things could be connected. He couldn't wait until the weekend when he'd have the kids right where he wanted them, with no adults to stop him. It was time to get to the bottom of the Black Heart Killer.

CHAPTER 10

Howie's mom hung up the phone and walked to the living room. He knew by the frown on her face it wasn't going to be anything he wanted to talk about. A few days ago, Cory's grandfather was found dead, and Cory hadn't talked to Howie since. He'd gone radio silent.

"So Cory's mom said it was natural causes and that his grandfather is now at peace. Cory's shaken up a bit, but his mom said he still wants to go bowling tonight to take his mind off it. You think that's a good idea?"

"Yeah. Probably even more now. I doubt he wants to sit in his house where his grandpa just died."

"True. Make sure you give him our condolences. I'll give you twenty bucks for pizza and arcade games, too. Sound good?"

"Thanks, Mom."

After lounging around the house for a few more hours, they left for the bowling alley. Howie needed to talk to his mom about the story his dad told him the other day, but he didn't know how to bring it up. It was so hard to hold it in for this long after finding out, but this was the first chance he and his mom had been alone to discuss it. She had to know about it, right? There was no way his dad would tell him without her knowing. Unless he knew Howie was so scared of him that he'd keep his mouth shut no matter what.

When they pulled onto the main road, he convinced himself it was now or never.

"Mom... How come you guys never told me about Dad's past?" He figured it was best to start vague instead of going right for the kill.

She stared straight ahead, but he saw her swallow down her nerves.

"What do you mean, Howie? Do you think he was some special agent or something?" she asked in a half-assed attempt to deflect.

"He told me the other day. When I went to work with him. I just wish I knew when I was younger, at least it would have helped explain why he's so mean all the time."

"Howie, there's no excuse for the way he treats you, no matter what the hell happened to him in the past. Do you understand me? A child should never have to go through what you have."

"I know that. But at least it made me realize why he hates me so much. I wasn't even supposed to be born."

He was shocked at the words coming out of his own mouth. Until he said it, it hadn't even crossed his mind, at least not consciously. He bit down on his lip, trying to stop himself from crying.

"Don't you go saying stuff like that, Howie Burke. Everything happens for a reason. You're here because you're supposed to be. What happened to Sheila and the baby was horrible. But you had nothing to do with that."

"So you're saying they were supposed to die? You're saying an evil witch was *supposed* to rip them to pieces?"

"Howie... That's not what I meant. I'm sorry we didn't tell you earlier. Your dad said he never wanted to talk about it, and anytime I ever brought it up, well, I'm sure you can imagine how that went. It wasn't right for us to hide it from you."

They drove on in silence, and Howie was thankful for it. The last thing he wanted was to get all worked up before meeting his friends. Not that Cory hadn't seen it many times before. But Bethany hadn't, and he wasn't about to embarrass himself after all he'd been through. It was just that the more he thought about everything his dad revealed, the worse he felt. He and his mom were never supposed to be part of the picture. Recollections whipped through his mind, reminders of all the hateful things his dad said or did to him growing up. It was as if getting rid of Jessica lifted some burden off his dad's shoulders that allowed him to care again. But that wasn't fair to Howie or his mom. For his dad to channel that anger for years and direct it at his family was pure selfishness.

"So how did you guys meet and get married? If he had them before and had no plans to ever marry and have kids after? Was I just the mistake of a one-night stand that forced him to stay with you?"

"Howie! How dare you! I understand how upsetting this information is, I really do. But I'm your mother, and I will not be talked to that way. Do you understand?"

Howie didn't answer, continuing to stare out the window.

"Do you understand, Howie? Answer me right now, or so help me God, I'll turn the car around and go home."

"Fine. I'm sorry."

They pulled into the bowling alley parking lot a few minutes later and his mom parked the car in front of the main entrance. Howie started to get out without saying anything, but his mom stopped him.

"Howie. I'm so sorry about everything. I know how terrifying it must be for you and your friends to lose people so close to you, not to mention seeing it happen right in front of you. I know your dad and I don't say it enough, but we love you. Getting that phone call saying you were okay was both the scariest and happiest moment of my life. We thought we'd lost you. I told your father if he ever laid another finger on you, I'd leave him. I'm done seeing my kid suffer in life. I love you, Howie."

She said they didn't say that enough, but the fact was they *never* said it. Hearing her say it now made him uncomfortable when it should have warmed his heart. He climbed out of the car and looked back at her, noticing she was crying.

"Thanks, Mom," he said, then shut the door.

CHAPTER 11

Cory was the last one to arrive at the bowling alley, but he was okay with that. It was good to avoid any awkwardness of talking about his grandfather with his friends. He intentionally took his time getting ready and out of the house so that when he showed up, it was straight to bowling. If Howie or Bethany tried to talk about his gramp, he would just remind them why they were there in the first place—to talk about the coven and the threats.

The black lights were on, and the strobe lights put on a cheap laser show. Music thumped through the bowling alley as he walked toward the counter to get some shoes. He glanced around for his friends and saw them in the last lane, closest to the arcade. He didn't plan on bowling with his stitches still healing, but the owner, Larry Foreman, was strict about his "No Sneakers" policy in the bowling area. He waited for Larry to stop spraying a used pair of shoes before he turned around and spotted Cory waiting. The older man had a ginger handlebar mustache that was speckled with gray, along with a haircut that hinted at a mullet of years past.

"What size you need, Cory? Let me guess...size eight?" he asked with a smirk and sense of pride, somehow able to remember most of the kids' shoe sizes in town.

"Yep. Thanks, Larry."

Cory turned back and watched Bethany laughing at something Howie said and was struck with a hint of jealousy. What could they be talking about that would make her smile that way? Howie knew how much he liked her; how could he try to move in while Cory was grieving?

Stop being an idiot. He's just friends with her, Cory thought.

"Oh, you know that backstabber wants to pop her cherry. We can stop that from happening."

"Shut the fuck up!" Cory snapped.

"Excuse me? You got quite a mouth on you, huh?" Larry asked.

Cory felt his cheeks burn with embarrassment.

"Sorry. I was talking to my friend."

The owner looked around, seeing there was nobody near Cory and shook his head.

"Whatever, kid."

Cory grabbed his shoes and walked to the last lane, hoping the voice would at least hold off until the end of the night. He wasn't ready to tell them what was happening to his body. To his mind. He wasn't ready to admit how his grandfather *really* died.

The flashing lights and loud music were already starting to bring on another headache. The song ended, but the DJ announced, "Time to rub your lamp, because up next, we got 'Genie in a Bottle,' courtesy of new 'it' girl, Christina Aguilera!" Some of the younger girls screamed in excitement as the song began.

Bethany and Howie spotted Cory approaching and flagged him down.

"Hey, man! Glad to see you out and about. Sorry about your gramp!" Howie yelled over the music.

"It's all good. He was getting pretty old anyway."

Bethany hugged Cory, and the scent of her perfume relaxed him immediately.

"I'm glad you could come. I think we all needed a night out," she whispered in his ear. It sent gooseflesh across the back of his neck.

They made their way to the lane, and Howie typed in their names on the scoreboard. Cory assumed they were only doing the bowling as an excuse to get out and talk about things, but Howie obviously had other ideas. Every time a ball clattered against the pins, it was like a crack of thunder, making Cory cringe at the unbearable sound.

"Feels so weird seeing everyone from school again, doesn't it?" Howie asked.

"Yeah. I don't know if they should have opened back up so soon," Cory said.

"You really believe that? I was starting to go crazy in my house, listening to my dad and mom fight over the homecoming. My dad won't let up until I talk to the stupid reporter. I needed to get out of the house," Bethany said.

"I know. I don't mean to sound like a jerk. It just seems like there's still so many unanswered questions, I'm surprised they let it all go back to normal so quick, is all," Cory said.

"Well, the rest of the town thinks it's over. They don't realize we have people threatening us. To them, the killer's dead, and so is the fear," Howie said.

"Oh, they'll soon see the killer isn't dead at all, right Cory?"

"Are you okay, Cory?" asked Bethany. "You're pale."

"You should see him with his shirt off, his pale ass would blind you," Howie joked.

Cory knew his friend was trying to lighten the mood, but the jab toward him did anything but. He wanted to punch Howie in the mouth after embarrassing him in front of Bethany.

"We can show him pale. A knife to the stomach will drain the color from that little shit. He's trying to take your girl, our girl."

"Hey, man, I'm sorry. I was just messing around. You gonna bowl at all?" Howie asked.

"No. I don't think it's a good idea. I'm still really sore. I think we should talk about what's happening first. Bethany had someone threaten her because of what we knew. At least that's what we think they were getting at. When we were at the funeral home, the only person I noticed watching us was Father Grimes. Did either of you see that?" Cory asked.

"I did. I thought he was just worried about us after everything that happened. I've never been to church, but you both have, right? Have you ever noticed anything weird about him?" Howie asked.

"No. He's always been super nice to me and my family," Bethany said.

"Same. But I'm telling you, the way he was staring at me—" Cory started, freezing mid-sentence as the ringing amplified inside his head.

"He deserves to have his eyes gouged from their sockets."

Cory ignored the voice.

"So what is it they think you know? You guys only told me pieces of it at the homecoming. If Jessica's gone, why is someone threatening to come after us? And why would they specifically say they needed something from *me*?" Bethany asked.

Cory looked around, making sure there were no adults in sight. Larry was ringing up another family about to leave. The bar was off to the left of the main register, behind closed double doors that helped keep the music from the bowling alley blocked out as best as possible. The regular patrons hated glow bowling night because it messed with their normal routine of drinking and complaining to one another in peace and quiet, typically while whatever New England sports team was playing that time of year could be heard in the background.

The coast was clear, so Cory nodded for Howie to continue.

"Mr. B told us that before Jessica was possessed by a demon, she practiced witchcraft. She was part of a coven made up of residents in Newport. I know how ridiculous it sounds. But her husband, Henry, knew she was involved with the coven. When the demon possessed Jessica, it somehow used her witch abilities to get in Henry's head and make him kill for her," Howie said.

"What? I mean, obviously I know about the Black Heart Killer, but the rest of it? After what we saw at the bonfire, I'd believe almost anything. But witches? That just sounds silly. And if Jessica and Henry are gone, why would this coven still come after us?" Bethany asked.

Cory sat on the bench, overcome with nausea. The demon was trying like hell to take hold of his body right now, but he continued to fight it off. He needed to have this conversation with them. They *needed* to figure out what to do next.

"Well, some of the people who died at the massacre were members of that coven. Principal White, Chief Miller, and probably more. They knew we had found out about their secret. Not that they had much time to warn the others, but it would make sense if the remaining members found out. Principal White said they had gone years in hiding, afraid of getting connected to the murders tied to Jessica. I think there's still a bunch of them left in town, and now that they know we took down Jessica, they also probably know we could take them down, too," Howie said.

Cory jumped up, pushing past Howie. If he didn't get to the bathroom right now, he was going to throw up all over the bowling alley floor. Howie and Bethany watched him stagger by as he caught himself on the counter.

"Are you okay?" Bethany asked.

"Yeah. I just feel nauseous. I'll be right back."

They nodded hesitantly, but Cory didn't even wait around to hear their response. His eyes began to blur as he walked like Tommy, the town drunk, toward the back of the building where the bathroom was located.

"You shit-faced, kid?" Larry yelled after him.

Cory waved him away and continued down the hall.

He exploded through the bathroom door and rushed to the sink, immediately vomiting all over the counter. When he thought it was over, his stomach cramped even worse, and a blast of projectile vomit sprayed into the sink in a mixture of red and black fluids.

"What the fuck... What's happening to me?" he panted.

He stared at his reflection; a complexion that resembled a corpse after rotting in a dark basement for days stared back at him. His eyes were bloodshot, but the webbed veins were orange instead of red, and they were pulsating around his pupils. Every time they brightened, a sharp pain shot through his head. The sensation in his eyes reminded him of the time he had poison ivy in middle school, the itching so severe he wanted to claw the skin off his body. Only now, he wanted to rip his own eyeballs out and flush them down the toilet.

"Please leave me alone. *Please.*"

"*You think that hurts?*"

A sudden intensity unlike any he'd ever experienced ripped through his head, as if something was slicing down the center of his brain with a razor blade. Cory yelled, and when he did, he noticed the inside of his mouth was now completely black, like it had been slathered in tar. He rested his head on the counter, trying to fight through the pain. The overhead lights flickered a few times before settling in at a lower wattage, dimming the bathroom to a barely visible state. Cory shot back up, staring at the mirror once more. He knew that face glaring back at him. It wasn't him. It was the demon.

"*Time to shed some blood.*"

CHAPTER 12

"Should we go check on him?" Howie asked Bethany.

"I don't know, maybe wait a few. Something feels off, but it could just be that his grandfather died the other day. And mixed with everything that happened last weekend, it can't be easy. But when I hugged him, his body was stiff, and he was really warm, like maybe he had a fever."

"Yeah, I'll give him a few. We better get to bowling so we don't look like we're here just to tell town secrets," Howie said with a smirk.

Kids from the next lane over continued to laugh and have a good time. Howie noticed Bethany staring at them with a bit of envy and wondered if he was boring her. But then he realized one of the boys was her ex-boyfriend, Troy Weathers. Troy glanced over and caught her staring.

"Hey, Bethany, what's good? You glad to be out and about?"

"Yeah. Hope you guys are having fun," she replied.

Troy smirked, a cocky jock smirk that Howie had learned to despise over the years. A girl walked up to him and kissed him on the cheek. Amelia Evenson, one of the most popular girls in school. Along with Bethany, she was one of the cheerleaders for the football team, but unlike Bethany, one of the biggest bitches in Newport.

"You coming, Troy? You're up," she said, then glared at Howie and Bethany with a look of disgust.

"Yeah. I'll be right there," he said, and she scoffed and walked back to her friends. "I heard about all the shit you guys went through at the homecoming. Sorry you lost your best friends, Howie. It's really too bad Jessica ever came back to town, huh?"

Howie's heart sank. Nobody in town had any idea she had come back *because* of him and his friends, that he was the cause of all the suffering people were dealing with.

"Thanks, I appreciate it. Hope you guys are having fun," he said, trying to deflect the conversation in a different direction. Troy got the hint, nodding in confirmation, and turned back to his group.

"Ladies first!" Bethany said in an attempt to lighten the mood, then walked up to their lane and grabbed a ball.

The music and colorful lights continued to blast, somehow easing Howie's mood. It brought back a sense of nostalgia, of weekends past before everything changed in town. Bethany rolled her first ball, taking down eight pins. She came back to grab her second ball and smiled.

"Five bucks says I get the spare!"

"You're on!" Howie yelled over the repetitive bass of some techno song.

She grabbed a ball and lined up, double-checking her feet. Howie wasn't sure why he agreed to her bet, probably just for some fun banter. But he knew she was going to hit the pins. Bethany Carver was good at everything she did. Sure enough, she softened the speed of the second ball to allow more precision, the bowling ball just clipping the corner of the first pin which bounced to the right and took the last one down with it. She jumped up and down in celebration and walked back smiling.

God, she's so beautiful.

"Pay up, sir!"

Howie laughed and pulled a wrinkled five-dollar bill from his pocket and slapped it down in her hand. She squeezed his hand ever so slightly. They locked eyes, and something passed between them, whether it was anything more than a common feeling of relief to be here, finally having fun again, Howie wasn't sure. He couldn't let himself think it was more than that. It wouldn't be fair to Cory or Bethany.

The pop song ended, and the DJ came over the loudspeaker again.

"Okay, night owls, up next is the new joint from the doctor himself, Dr. Dre! This single just released this week, and it is *hot*! 'Still D.R.E.' coming at you now."

The blast of piano keys and bass killed the short silence and also broke the connection between Howie and Bethany's hands. Howie was thankful it was dark with the black lights on because he knew he was blushing hard right now.

"I feel really bad about the messages you got. Like it's somehow our fault you're involved in all this. I don't get why they'd threaten you and not Cory or me. We were the ones out in the woods," Howie said.

Bethany shrugged. "It's not your fault, Howie. Even though I wasn't out there with you guys that day, I would've done the same thing if I was. You were trying to stop something bad from happening. There's nothing wrong with that. Don't be so hard on yourself. Now get up there and bowl. Double or nothing says you don't knock more pins down than me," she said with a smile.

He walked up for his turn to bowl and grabbed a ball. Snoop Dogg sang out, "If you ain't up on thangs," as Howie sped toward the lane. The ball slammed off the polished wooden floor, picking up speed.

And then, as the ball reached the middle of the lane, the lights flickered out, sending the bowling alley into complete darkness.

Howie heard his ball smash off the pins, but that was the least of his concerns at the moment. The music abruptly stopped, allowing the screams of others to carry across the open space. They were in a black void of nothingness, full of terrified teens.

Howie faintly made out the seating area where Bethany sat and carefully walked toward her.

"Howie, what's happening?"

"I don't know. We need to find Cory!"

Larry attempted to shout from behind the main counter, but nobody listened as kids trampled one another heading toward the exit. He slammed his fist down on the glass countertop to get their attention, which stopped some of the shouting near him, but not all of it. He pulled a megaphone from behind the counter.

"Calm down! It's probably just a breaker! Don't run in the dark, you damn idiots, you'll kill each other!"

His firm tone got some of them to stop running. While Howie wanted to believe Larry, something told him it was far more than a blown fuse. He could tell by the fear in Bethany's eyes that she thought the same. While most of the kids had stopped trampling over one another, they still gravitated toward the exit, trying to get outside into the night where it was somehow lighter than it was inside. Howie wondered if the bar's power also went out, or if it was running on a different breaker. Could the adults hear the kids screaming next door?

"Let's wait here. We can't get out right now, anyway. But we need to find Cory and make sure he's okay," Howie repeated.

Bethany nodded without saying anything.

Larry walked around the counter with his megaphone in one hand and a flashlight in the other. He turned the flashlight on and aimed it toward the back of the bowling alley at a door that had a big red sign hanging that read *MAINTENANCE ROOM*. He pushed through groups of kids, telling them to move so he could get to the back. The door was in the opposite corner of the lane Howie and Bethany occupied, but Howie watched as the owner disappeared into the room, once again bringing the bowling alley to complete darkness.

Some of the remaining customers murmured amongst themselves, half-whispers mixed with panicked voices. The small windows on the double doors leading into the bar were filled with a murky blackness as well, so it *was* apparently the whole building that lost power, answering Howie's question. He assumed most of the bar patrons departed through the separate exit in the bar itself, as it was still mostly teens scattered throughout the bowling alley. Howie couldn't wait any longer. He grabbed Bethany by the hand to help guide her in the dark.

"Let's go back toward the bathroom and arcade area where he headed. We'll start there."

She squeezed his hand without a word and followed. There was no reason to be concerned, it was a shoddy old building with bad wiring. That's what he wanted to keep telling himself. But as they walked farther into the shadowy depths, he felt like he was entering the gates of Hell, and he knew something bad was about to happen.

Larry Foreman sat the megaphone down and walked to the back corner of the maintenance room, pissed at himself for not locking the door before he opened for the night. Any one of those punk kids could have snuck back here and busted something, and there was a good chance that's why the power went out. That, or something to do with the sketchy electrical work.

The building was due for some important maintenance, but he kept putting it off because money was tight. Owning a bowling alley wasn't a glamorous lifestyle by any means, but it paid the bills and he got to pop into the bar and catch a lot of the games on TV while sneaking some of the booze—the benefits of owning the place. Over the last few years, money coming in had slowly dwindled. Having to be closed for the past seven days was the last thing he could afford to do, but the town highly recommended that all local businesses deemed nonessential close for the week while they mourned the losses of all the victims. While he didn't want to close, he felt he had no choice if he wanted to keep future customers happy. Tonight was supposed to be his big reopening, and it was about to be ruined.

He walked past the lanes, instinctively checking to make sure the pins were properly lined up on the belt and double-checking the pinwheels to make sure they were all in working order. Not that a bad lane would trip the breaker, but it could have. He reached the breaker box and opened it, aiming the flashlight at all the different switches.

"What the fuck?"

Every single switch had been manually turned off.

Before he had a chance to flip any of them back on, a loud *thump* smacked off the floor behind him. He spun around, aiming the flashlight across the room.

"Jesus Christ. Who's there?"

He scanned the whole room with his light, but the cone of illumination only covered so much area. The boxes scattered around the room cast warped shadows along the walls, and he could have sworn one of the shadows moved. He froze, keeping the light focused on the spot when a movement on the floor startled him. He aimed the light down and saw a bowling ball slowly rolling toward him.

These pieces of shit machines were on their last leg. That might be the final straw that led to going out of business. There was no way he could afford to upgrade the equipment right now. Hell, the building didn't even pass the inspection codes needed to stay open, but Larry had dirt on the Fire Chief, Samuel Osborn. He'd caught the filthy scum trying to force himself on a young girl in the back alley when he went out for a smoke break a few months back. Osborn had already been threatening to shut the place down before the incident but had a change of heart and told Larry if he kept his mouth shut, he'd never fail another inspection again.

Larry crouched and picked up the bowling ball, then almost dropped it when something slick on its surface made it slip. He pointed the light at the ball and noticed red smeared across it.

"What in the *actual* fuck?"

Something moved in the shadows again and Larry snapped his attention toward the darkness, accidentally dropping the ball, which in turn landed on his shoe. The bones in his left foot crunched as the fifteen-pound ball landed firmly on top of his toes.

"Ah, shit!"

He fell to the floor, grabbing his foot. For a second, he'd forgotten about the movement. But then he saw it again. His flashlight had also dropped to the floor during all the commotion, but he was sure he saw a silhouette in the corner, watching him.

Two tiny orange dots glowed on the figure.

"Who's there? You're trespassing back here. If you don't want me calling the cops on you, I suggest you get the fuck out now before I get up from this floor!"

He hoped he sounded tougher than he felt. The figure didn't move. The orange dots remained in place, and just when Larry thought maybe they were lights he forgot existed, they blinked. And then he heard labored breathing from the gloomy figure. Fear gripped around Larry's throat and squeezed out any remaining confidence he had left.

"You were no better than any of them, Larry. You were there the night it happened. And you thought after all these years, you were in the clear, am I right?"

The voice sounded like a kid, but it was as if there was a second voice behind it, trying to force out the innocent youth.

"Wha-what in the hell are you talking about, kid?"

"Stop playing dumb, you pathetic cocksucker. You and the rest of the coven wanted to play with your magic potions and spells in the woods like a bunch of limp-dick wizards. You wanted to summon me. And then when you did, you sealed me inside that little slut's body. I spent twenty years buried out in those woods, and you all knew I was there, rotting with the maggots. I won't leave this shithole until every one of you are dead."

The figure stepped forward. It was the boy who had been acting strange earlier. One of the surviving kids from the massacre, Cory Stevens. His mouth was covered in blood as if he'd chomped down a raw steak with his bare hands. Larry had intentionally been keeping an eye on him and the Burke kid on orders from above him. While he wasn't the only one doing so, he needed to make sure the others knew the demon was still here, inside the Stevens kid.

"What the hell are you doing back here? And why are you talking like that?"

"I know you're an ignorant hick but stop playing the part so well. You know who I am."

Larry felt a lump rising in his throat that wouldn't go away. He let out a guttural groan. Yeah, he knew exactly who was talking to him, it just didn't feel real. After all these years. The rest of the coven had hoped that with Jessica disposed of, it would take care of their problem with the demon, but Larry knew that was a bunch of bullshit.

"If you know all this, demon, then you also know there were powers bigger than you that forced our hand. We did what we had to do to survive. You wanting to kill us off won't change anything. And besides, you act so self-righteous, like you're just going after us, but then you kill a bunch of innocent kids?"

The boy snarled and cackled a terrible laugh that sounded like hardened cement breaking free in his lungs.

"I never said I was just killing the rest of you. I need strength. I need fuel. I. Need. Hearts. *Unfortunately, I have to pass on yours for now while I adjust to this body, but that doesn't mean you get to live."*

And then the boy charged at him, but Larry was ready. He pushed the bowling ball with his good foot, watching it pick up speed as it rolled toward Cory. The ball slammed off the inside of Cory's ankle, and Larry was positive he heard a *crunch*. The boy stumbled slightly but kept coming like it was merely a plastic toy that struck him. But it bought Larry enough time to grab one of the pins from the machine next to him as the boy landed on him. He swung it like a club, cracking Cory in the temple.

Cory fell limply off him, and for a brief second, Larry was afraid he'd just killed the kid. But then he remembered the oath they had all taken those many years ago. If the demon ever came back, they needed to get rid of it by any means necessary. No matter who it possessed. Which meant if he didn't end it here right now, the others would try. A bowling pin wouldn't get rid of a demon, but if he could restrain the boy until the other members could join him in determining the next steps, he would be viewed with much more respect by the coven.

He attempted to stand and was greeted with an intense pain shooting through his broken foot. He cringed, then grabbed hold of one of the conveyor belts that carried the balls back to the lane and tried to pull himself up. Something struck him in the center of the back before he made it all the way to his feet, sending a jolt of pain up his spine. Larry fell back to the floor, then turned and saw the dark shadow of the boy, only dimly lit by the flashlight on the floor. He held the pin that Larry had dropped.

Cory lifted it and swung, connecting it with the side of Larry's neck.

"AH!"

He swung again, caving Larry's orbital bone. Over and over, the kid beat his face with the pin until Larry had no fight left in him. And then Larry faintly made out the club still striking him as his vision faded. He still heard the crunching of bone and cartilage as the pin connected again and again. The last thing Larry Foreman heard was the skin of his neck tearing apart as the boy twisted his head, snapping it from the spine.

CHAPTER 13

Howie and Bethany huddled close as they listened to muffled sounds in the back room. They made it to the arcade after blindly feeling along the old wood-panel wall until they reached the bathroom door. The back door at least had a lighted *EXIT* sign positioned above it, giving off a red glow at the end of the hall. Flashbacks of the dark school hallway came back to Howie. Running through the empty building while Jessica and Todd chased him and Cory down. Now, it was Cory they were searching for, but Howie wasn't so sure he wanted to find his friend anymore. Could all of this be his doing? Nothing happened until he left them for the bathroom.

"I'm going to check in here. Can you hold the door open so some of the light shines in?" he asked.

"Are you sure you should go in there? Maybe we should call for help."

"Half of the adults in town were just drinking in the bar next door and left with all the screaming kids. They probably thought it was a fire or something."

"Okay, but the first sign of something bad, we're running through this back exit, got it?"

Howie nodded and approached the bathroom door. He pushed in hesitantly, just a few inches at first.

"Cory? You in here, dude?"

Silence.

He pushed farther in, waiting for Bethany to hold the door so he could enter completely. As soon as he stepped foot in the bathroom, a rotten stench stung his nostrils. It didn't smell like normal vomit, it smelled like death. The red light hardly reached the first few feet of the bathroom, but it lit it enough for Howie to spot the vast puddle of fluid splashed across the countertop and sink. Not only did it smell of rot and decay, but it also looked like something had exploded into tiny fragments of gore.

He recalled how ill Cory appeared when he took off toward the bathroom and he started to feel sick himself. He grabbed hold of the counter to stop himself from falling, accidentally setting his hand into the puddle. The thick sludge felt disgusting beneath his fingers, as if it was trying to wrap around him like a slimy vine. He ran to the sink and gagged as he rinsed the phlegmy fluid away.

"He's not in here. We have to keep looking," Howie said.

"Maybe he came out the back exit to get some fresh air after being sick. Let's check out there first."

"I guess—"

Howie was interrupted by blasting music. "Pretty Fly (For a White Guy)" tore through the bowling alley, and he thought his heart was going to explode through his chest after adjusting to the last few minutes of complete silence. He left the bathroom, and they took off down the narrow hall back toward the bowling lanes. It was still dark until one lane lit up, the fluorescent lights flickering momentarily before they locked onto the polished wooden floor with a dim glow over lane thirteen.

They approached the lane, looking for any sign of their friend. The music was so loud that Howie struggled to think. The conveyor belt to the ball tray powered on, but for a moment it was just the belt moving. Howie froze, watching the belt travel like a well-oiled train making a nonstop trip to its destination. A large ball popped up through the black hole, rolling around until it came to a stop on the tray. Even in the dim light, streaks of blood on the ball stood out. Bethany squeezed his arm.

Where are you, Cory? Come on, man.

The belt jerked, skipping along as if something had caught inside the machine. And then another ball came into view as it jammed against the opening, trying to force itself out. Howie couldn't see it clearly, but then another ball pushed up behind it, forcing it through. That's when Howie realized it wasn't a *ball* at all. The round object rolled along the tray until it came to a stop.

It was Larry Foreman's head.

Bethany screamed, burying her face in Howie's chest. Larry's eyes were locked open in a permanent state of terror, staring up at the ceiling with his bottom jaw snapped violently to the side. The severed end of his spine poked out from the base of his neck in a jagged nub. They backed away from the lane, both unable to take their eyes off the grotesque scene. Howie continued backing up until he connected with something. *Someone.* He slowly turned, expecting it to be Cory. Instead, it was a man he didn't recognize. The man had frosted tips and a smile that reeked of a scumbag and liquor.

"Hey, kid. What's going on in here?"

"Who are you?" Howie asked.

"Name's Ken Kincade, WMUR News."

Ken glanced over Howie's shoulder and spotted what they were so scared of. Instead of sharing their concern, his eyes lit up with excitement.

"Where's Brennan when you need his damn camera? Looks like you kids got yourselves in quite the predicament, huh?" He paused, but not long enough for them to respond. "Here I was, minding my own business, when I found you two standing over a decapitated head. So I ask myself, what should we do about it? I'll cut you a deal. You give me your story from the massacre and everything you know about Jessica Black and the coven, and I'll tell the authorities you had nothing to do with that human bowling ball over there. You decline, and I tell them I saw you kill the innocent owner of Sunset Lanes, so scared and fucked-up in the head after the events last week that you were paranoid, worried he was trying to hurt you."

"Nobody would believe you," Bethany snapped.

"It's your story against mine. You think they'll believe a couple of kids who've been surrounded by death all week over a renowned anchor? Watch how quickly the mighty heroes fall."

"There's bigger problems than your stupid story. Larry's dead. We need to get help," Howie said.

"We'll do just that. After you tell me what I want to hear. Your daddy has worked long and hard to make sure you have a full scholarship to the best colleges in the area, little girl. You wouldn't want to mess that all up, would you? If, say, someone happened to leak that he was dropping some extra coin to certain schools to make sure you got accepted? And you, Howie Burke, right? What if someone reported your parents for abuse and you got taken away from your friends and family?"

"You don't know anything about me or my family," Howie snapped. He didn't dare look at Bethany, worried she would judge him.

"Kid. I know way more than you think I do. I know how close you were to Paul. Mr. B, as you called him. Well, guess what? I knew him, too. We worked together on a few documentary projects back in the day. Kept in touch over the years. If you don't think he told me about his prized protégé, this young boy whose dad beat the shit out of him, you're wrong."

Howie couldn't believe it. Mr. B would never tell anyone about Howie's home life, would he? A sudden rage filled Howie, but toward his dead teacher as much as this reporter. He felt betrayed and he could never tell Mr. B how he felt. He brought his attention back to this man who continued to smile like an asshole.

"What is it exactly that you want to know? People died. Jessica Black killed them. Then she died. You're treating this town like a story and not like we're living people," Howie said.

"Yeah, see, that's not true, is it? It's not that simple. I know it. You know it. The whole fucking town knows it. Yet, nobody will talk to me about the truth. I've picked up tidbits here and there, enough to put some pieces together. But I want more than that. I *need* more than that."

"Now's not the time for this. We have to get out of here. Please get out of the way," Bethany implored.

Howie felt his anger continue to rise inside. This cocky prick needed to give up already.

"Just leave us alone and move out of the way," Howie demanded.

"What's it going to be, kid? You going to talk with me, on the record, or am I going to have to get a little dirty to get what I want? I'm fine either way."

Howie started to move toward Ken, but Bethany gently pushed him to the side.

"You want to get dirty?" she asked angrily.

Ken arched his brow, uncertain what she meant. Then Bethany kicked him between the legs, her shoe making a loud *thump* that even the music couldn't drown out. Ken dropped to his knees, holding his crotch. He winced and muttered curses under his breath.

"Let's go, Howie." She grabbed his hand and led him toward the exit.

"You little shits! That was a huge mistake!"

After everything they had been through, Howie found himself smiling. He couldn't believe Bethany really just kicked Ken Kincade in the nuts. But then his smile faded, his thoughts returning to the decapitated head of Larry Foreman. Of Cory disappearing on them. As much as he didn't want to believe it, Howie knew his best friend had something to do with it.

CHAPTER 14

Cory didn't stop running until he was in the woods behind the shopping plaza. Tears pooled in his eyes as he looked back toward where he'd come from, seeing the back of Sunset Lanes lit up by the overhead lights of the rear parking lot. The demon laughed inside, but there was nothing funny about what had just happened. His own hands had ripped a man's head off his body and shoved it into the pinsetter machine. Flashing lights and sirens closed in from downtown. He had to leave before someone caught him.

Over the last few days, he had noticed the sickness putting a firm grip on him. Except when he killed. That was the only time he felt relief, the pain inside subsiding long enough for him to get his normal thoughts back. Even if he got this thing out of him, what would happen then? Would he get arrested for murder? Would the town want him dead to make sure the demon was gone for good? All he knew was that he couldn't go home. He had to find a spot to hide until he could figure something out.

"There's no need to figure anything out, little boy. I've done that for you. I will slowly grow inside you like a cancerous tumor until you are nothing more than a hollowed carcass. Until I no longer need your assistance. And

then? You will still be there, fading away in the recesses of your mind, watching me kill everyone and everything you love."

"I won't let you. I'll kill myself before I let you get my friends and mom."

"Please, boy. Don't waste my time. You don't have it in you to do such a thing. And if you did? I'd just take over someone else and do it all, anyway. It brings me great joy to watch people suffer."

Cory contemplated what to do. He heard the sirens closing in on the shopping plaza. He thought of places he could go, away from anyone he cared about. He considered the school, knowing it would be shut down for the foreseeable future, but it was too much of a risk. It was still a crime scene. Even though classes wouldn't resume for a while, there would likely be people coming and going regularly.

Then the idea came to him. Before his dad was redeployed, he used to work at the concrete plant that had since switched owners and reopened. The building just sat there on weekends, a deserted blip by the side of the road. And as far as Cory knew, it was one of the places that remained shut down temporarily after the massacre. It was only a few miles from his house.

A few years back, it had gone out of business, and all the equipment had been left inside. The bank owned the property for a while, but nobody wanted to buy it at first because of the reason it had shut down in the first place. The owner had killed his wife, dumping her in a block of liquid concrete. The employees had gone about their business, working every day like nothing had happened. The owner, Skip Fremont, told everyone she wanted a divorce and left town.

It wasn't until a group of employees had accidentally dropped a load of concrete slabs while moving them on a forklift that her body was discovered. The concrete block shattered, revealing her stiffened corpse inside. Skip then went on to kill himself in his home before authorities had the chance to take him in.

Cory knew the layout of the plant, not only because he visited his dad on his lunch break a few times, but also because during the transition between owners, he had snuck into the place with Howie, Todd, and Ryan after hearing stories of the place being haunted by Skip Fremont's wife. Instead of finding a ghost, they found a high school couple fucking in the back corner of the place and took off running after Todd giggled so hard he couldn't stop laughing and blew their cover. They laughed the entire way back to Cory's house.

It was the perfect place to hide. He wasn't sure what he would do to get rid of the demon, but at least he would make it harder for it to hurt anyone else.

With a destination now in mind, Cory took off through the woods, the light from the back alley now fading to a dim reminder of what he'd left behind. Now he was swallowed by the darkness of the forest. He didn't care. Getting scared in the woods no longer felt like a real-life fear after what he'd been through. The biggest threat now was *inside* of him, not out here lurking between the trees.

He needed to find a way to communicate with his mom without getting too close to her. He thought of all the pay phones around town. Which would be the easiest to reach? Offer the most coverage? There was one at the old laundromat connected to the convenience store on his way home. He wouldn't be able to use it right away, and his mom likely wouldn't be home yet anyway. After missing more work due to Cory's grandfather dying, she decided to pick up a weekend shift to make up the money lost. But that was the spot he'd call from. When he knew he had a chance to reach her, he'd make the call.

Cory thought of his poor mom. She'd just lost her dad. Her husband was stationed in Iraq in the middle of a war. And now her son—who literally just survived a massacre a week prior—was about to go missing. It broke his heart to think of the impact this would have on her, but he had no choice. He'd rather have her sad than dead.

The chilled air had no effect on him as he continued running through the trees, staying out of sight along the road. Eventually, there would be no forest left, and he would have to risk sneaking through part of town to get close to home. Or at least what would be his home until he figured out how to get rid of this disease infesting him.

The trees were thinning, making it harder to stay hidden. A police cruiser sped by with its lights on, heading toward the bowling alley.

"I killed someone," he whispered.

"Just wait until I rip out your friends' insides and spread them across this town. You will only be able to stop me for so long. Soon, I'll make sure every last person you love is dead. And then, I'll finish with you."

CHAPTER 15

Officer Ellis pulled his cruiser into the bowling alley parking lot to a mass of people all crowded around their vehicles. A mix of kids who'd left the bowling area and adults who were forced to leave the bar mid-drink all hung around like they were tailgating before a Patriots game. His lights flashed, lighting up the front of the building with red and blue. The new chief, Ron Mullin—who'd replaced Miller after he died during the massacre—was already on scene, pushing through the crowd to get closer to the building.

Ellis was brought in from the Keene PD to fill the lowest rung on the ladder vacancy, with Mullin moving up to chief. He had been hoping for a reason to move to another area of the state after he caught his girlfriend, now ex-girlfriend, cheating on him with a fellow officer. It wasn't ideal timing to leave, as he had just gotten used to his new partner—rookie cop Natasha Briggs. But he had no choice, he needed to get a fresh start. And while Newport wasn't a preferred landing spot, it was far enough away to get that fresh start.

He got out of his cruiser and pushed through the crowd, trying to reach the chief. Considering he'd arrived in town days after the school massacre, he could only imagine what these people were thinking now that they had another death on their hands after just losing so many the week before. Some of them looked terrified—mostly the teens—while others almost appeared numb to it. Ellis hadn't been in town long enough to become familiar with many of the locals, but he had been down to the bowling alley two times already to break up a bar fight and arrest a drug dealer trying to sell pot to an undercover cadet. He talked to Larry on both of those occasions, and the guy seemed nice enough.

"Chief! What can I do to help?" Ellis asked.

"Get inside and make sure there's no stragglers snooping around. We did a search, but there's too many people here to keep an eye on. I can keep the rest out, including these circus monkeys with the cameras."

"What about the body? Should we take pictures for evidence?"

"That's already done, rookie. This will be chalked up to an unfortunate accident. According to everyone who was inside, Larry went alone to the maintenance room to reset the breaker. He must've tried to fix a jam in the machine and the power came back on while he was up inside. Sucks, but at least that's all it was."

Ellis looked at his new chief, a middle-aged man with a flattop haircut and clean-shaven face. He showed enough confidence to fool most, but Ellis saw through it. There was no way in hell they had a chance to do a proper walk-through of the scene to determine the cause of Larry's death. Still, he bit his tongue and nodded, walking into the bowling alley.

The lights had been turned back on. Ellis scanned the lanes, then walked to the double doors that led to the bar and poked his head in. The room appeared empty, but he entered, anyway, checking behind the bar to make sure no scared kids were hiding out or trying to sneak booze. When he determined the room was clear, he exited the bar, went back to the bowling alley, and spotted the maintenance room in the far corner. He wanted to get a look at the scene before the others came back in.

The door remained halfway open, so he pushed it with his foot to avoid grabbing the knob and leaving fingerprints.

The room resembled a dungeon where a serial killer would hide his victims, with tools and spare parts to the bowling machines scattered about. And then he saw Larry's body, lying limply across the pinsetter with his neck propped up into the return hole.

Sure looks like a nice staged scene to me.

He circled the scene, careful not to get close enough that he'd leave footprints in the blood splashed across the floor. Could these machines even rip someone's head clean off like that? Seemed unlikely to him, but what did he know?

Ellis aimed his light at the body, scanning from head—or neck, to be more accurate—to toe for any other signs of a scuffle. He was about to leave when he glanced down at the puddle of blood on the floor. Another darker liquid appeared to be mixed in with the crimson, almost like motor oil.

"What the fuck is that?"

He kneeled, trying to make sense of the sludge commingling with the blood, when the front door to the bowling alley opened. Ellis heard the chatter of the crowd out front until the door shut again, followed by approaching footsteps.

"Ellis! Where you at?"

"In here, Chief."

"I thought I told you to search for kids. Why you back here messing with shit?" Mullin asked as he entered the doorway.

"I checked everywhere, Chief. Nobody inside. I even looked behind the bar and arcade area. Did you guys see this?" he asked, gesturing to the puddle in front of him.

"When someone has their head ripped clean off, there's usually blood, rookie. Of course we saw it."

Rookie. He wasn't sure how many times he could be called that without speaking his mind. Ellis had been a cop for almost a decade, and this asshole had the nerve to treat him like some recruit fresh out of training. One thing he learned over the years was that his mouth often got him in trouble. His mom had been a prideful woman, and that rubbed off on him growing up. If something seemed wrong, he had trouble keeping his mouth shut and moving on. But his old chief had made a point to include that in his reviews of Ellis, and it was one of the first things Mullin discussed when bringing him onto the force. Mullin had also made a point of letting Ellis know he didn't like the idea of bringing in an outsider over hiring someone within. But he had no say in it. The station was understaffed and had been issued the request to bring another officer on quickly.

"I know that. I'm talking about this black shit mixed in. I've never seen anything like it."

Mullin stepped forward and squinted, adding some theatrics to his so-called investigation.

"I mean, it's probably something that leaked out of the equipment. I'm sure ripping a head from the body requires a bit more than pulling up a bowling ball. Why don't you head on out for crowd control, and we'll finish up here. Just take some details from the witnesses so we can bring them in for questioning tomorrow, then send them on their way."

Ellis hesitated, not quite ready to just ignore the strange scene in the maintenance room. It was obvious Mullin didn't quite trust him yet, as he kept sending him off to do busy work and get him away from more important matters. He understood he had to earn that trust, but to be treated like a new cop was a bit of overkill. Still, he promised himself he'd attempt to make a good first impression and decided it was best to leave and do as he was told.

Mullin ignored Ellis as he walked by him and out the front door of the bowling alley. The crowd had thinned a bit, but some were still hanging around to see what was going on. Small-town gossip required keen eyes on scene to start spreading the word to those not in attendance. Ellis shook his head and approached the thickest part of the crowd, but he was cut off by a reporter with a cameraman trailing close behind.

"Officer! Just a minute of your time, please. Ken Kincade, WMUR News."

Fucking great, just what I needed right now.

He recognized Kincade from the evening news. The asshole's fake smile was even more repelling in person.

"We'll give a formal response to all of this soon, okay? We still need to talk with all the witnesses," he said, hoping Kincade would get the hint. But the guy didn't give off the vibe of someone who would be very understanding.

"Is it true you guys are calling it an accident? Is there any suspicion of it involving foul play?" Ken asked, ignoring Ellis's plea to leave him alone.

Ellis realized the camera was rolling, so he couldn't tell the guy what he really thought of him. Kincade was nothing more than a wannabe investigative journalist disguising himself as a news re-porter. He would be better suited working for a tabloid show like *Hard Copy*. Shit like that disgusted Ellis, but most of America ate it up.

"Talk to the chief if you don't like my answer. If that's what he said, then that's what I agree with. I just got here. Now, please, let me do my job."

He pushed past the reporter and headed toward the crowd of people. The cameraman lowered the camera and gave him an apologetic frown.

"Sorry, man."

Ellis nodded and kept moving. He had a feeling it was going to be a long night.

CHAPTER 16

Cory crept out of the shadows, scanning the area for any cars or pedestrians. The laundromat was open twenty-four hours a day, but at least this time of night didn't tend to be very busy. He snuck around the side of the building, worried about the fluorescent lights shining down from the gas pumps, and was relieved to see nobody using the pay phone. He walked quickly to it and dropped a quarter in, debating if he should call his mom or Howie. He decided on his mom and dreaded it, knowing it wouldn't be an easy conversation. But he had to toughen up, to let her know he would be okay and that he planned to find a solution to get rid of this monster inside him.

With each ring, Cory considered hanging up and running back to the woods. It wasn't that he was ashamed to tell her, it was more about knowing how crushed she'd be. He was an only child. His parents would do *anything* to take care of him. He couldn't risk his mom making a terrible decision that would get her in trouble, or worse, especially if the urge overcame him like it did with his grandfather. And Larry Foreman. Once again, the realization that he'd killed two people in the span of a few days set in.

Lost in his thoughts, Cory was blindsided when his mom answered the phone.

"Hello?"

He wanted to speak, but his mouth locked in place, unwilling to force out any words.

"Who's this? Why are you calling at this time of night?"

Cory sensed her getting ready to hang up the phone and spoke before it was too late, "Mom..."

"Cory? Hon? What's wrong?" Her voice immediately shifted from irritation to concern.

"I did something really bad... I can't control it." He wanted to say more, but his words came out in an uneven mess.

"You're scaring me, Cory. What did you do? Where are you? I'll come get you."

"I killed Gramp. It made me do it. And tonight—"

"Oh my God. Sweetie. Please don't put that on yourself. He passed away in his sleep. How could you think—"

"Mom! Listen to me. Whatever was in Jessica Black, it's in me now. It's trying to take over my body, but I keep fighting it. It... it wants me to hurt people. I know we didn't talk much about what happened at the school, but somehow, when we were trying to stop her, it came into my body. You have to believe me."

Silence filled the other end of the phone.

"Mom. Please, I need you to listen to me. I can't come home right now. It's too dangerous. I can still control it most of the time, at least right now. But sometimes it takes over and... I can't stop myself. I just wanted you to know. I need to find a way to get this out of me."

"Please come home. We'll figure it out together, baby. You don't have to face this alone."

His mom's voice cracked, and he knew she was crying. He wasn't even sure she believed what he was telling her, but either way, she knew her son wasn't coming home, and he was in danger. The tone in her voice was unequivocal defeat. At that moment, he didn't much care if she believed him or not. What mattered most, what he had to convince her of, was to make sure others thought he *was* home.

"I'm sorry... It's too dangerous. I need you to do something for me, though. We never talked much about the original murders and how Jessica became the way she did. But the more I learn, the more I realize most people who lived here back then know more than they admitted. So I'm figuring you do, too, and just didn't want to tell me about it. I'm not mad at you for it. I get why you hid it. But you must know that if *they* find out this thing is inside me, they'll come for me. I need you to act like I'm still home. I promise to call you and keep you updated. Can you do that for me?"

His mom was full-on sobbing now, no longer trying to contain it from him.

"I don't know. I can't lose you. Please, come back, Cory. I can't just sit back while you're out there scared and alone. What kind of mother would do that? A horrible one."

"You know that's not true. I need you to trust me. Can you do that?"

"Yes. Of course I trust you. But if anything ever happened to you... Cory, please be careful. *Please.*"

"I will, I promise," he said, knowing full well he couldn't guarantee such a thing with an actual demon festering inside him. He also knew if too much time passed, she would come looking for him one way or another. "One more thing. Please reach out to Howie. Tell him I'm sorry. For everything."

"Okay. Cory? Will you at least tell me where you are?"

"I... I can't do that. I can't risk you coming to look for me. Not until this is over."

A moment of silence came next, but then his mother blew her nose away from the phone and came back. "Please don't be too hard on yourself for what happened tonight. It's not you. And we will get you the help you need after all this is fixed—"

A sharp pain clawed its way from the front of Cory's face to the back of his skull.

"Oh, he loved it, you bitch. I just let him have some fun ripping that piece of shit's head off!"

Cory wanted to scream for it to stop, but he no longer had control of his body. His voice came out unnaturally deep, like a rabid dog guarding its meal. His mom cried uncontrollably on the other end, and all he could do was listen to it as the demon had its way with him. She started to say something, and he slammed the phone onto the receiver.

The door opened as someone exited the convenience store, and Cory didn't wait to see who it was. He forced himself to take off toward the trees, back into the shadows.

<h1 style="text-align:center">CHAPTER 17</h1>

Bethany just wanted to lay in her bed and cry. After a few hours of answering questions with the police, then answering *more* questions from her parents when she got home, she finally retreated to her room, shedding tears she'd forced to stay down in front of her family. It wasn't just the fact she had seen a headless body—that sight had unfortunately become quite normal over the past week—but more about how it happened. While the police were deeming the death an accident, she knew deep in her heart that Cory had been involved. Something was really wrong with him.

It was so hard to watch it happen to such a sweet boy. Cory had treated her differently than most guys, like an actual person with actual interests, focusing on more than just her beauty. Making movies with the guys was some of the most fun she'd ever had, even more than sleepovers with her best friends, Britt and Tanya. *They* usually just spent their nights talking gossip and listening to The Backstreet Boys and NSYNC. While Bethany had never been one to shy away from who she was, she still tried to limit how much she talked about the things that really made her happy in front of her friends. They would rather live the typical high school life, while she had dreams she wanted to chase, even at such a young age.

There was still no sign of Cory by the time they headed home. Howie had convinced her to hold off saying that he was missing if the police asked who else they were with. At first, she wasn't comfortable lying to the police, especially if she was blatantly withholding information about a murder. But Howie reminded her it wasn't Cory doing it, and if the authorities knew Cory was with them and took off, it would lead them right to him. Even though it appeared they were set on the death being accidental, Howie didn't want to give them any reason to believe otherwise. And the new chief didn't seem much better than Miller, so Howie wondered if he was mixed up with the coven as well.

Bethany booted up her computer, waiting for what felt like an eternity to connect to the internet and load the Instant Messenger app. She wanted to talk to Howie privately about everything once they got home. Unfortunately, he wasn't signed in. A message popped up before she got up from her desk.

It was the same username that had threatened her earlier.

Bethany hesitated but decided to open the message and see what it said.

Liveinthedarkness101: *It's almost time. Your friends are the reason it escaped, and you will be the reason we get it back under control.*

Her heart slammed against her chest and sweat glistened on her palms as she reread the message over and over. They had been so careful to talk quietly at the bowling alley. With the music cranked up, how the hell would anyone hear them talking?

She debated letting the message go unanswered, thinking if she ignored it, maybe the problem would go away. But then another message popped up.

> **Liveinthedarkness101:** *We are always watchi ng... Always listening.*

And with that, they were gone once more.

Bethany began to hyperventilate, the stress of everything hitting her at once. If she told her parents, they would insist on reading the messages and would see the other messages to her friends and start to question what was going on. If anyone found out about Cory, she knew nothing good would come of it.

She got up and peered out the window into the night, wondering where Cory could have possibly gone. As she went to turn back toward her bed, she spotted someone standing across the street at the edge of the woods.

They were looking at her house.

Watching her.

It was too dark to see who it was, but she didn't need to see to know she was being watched. She could feel it. The figure turned and headed into the forest, and that's when she saw what they were wearing. The unidentified person was draped in a black robe. Bethany screamed, then bolted downstairs to tell her parents.

CHAPTER 18

Howie awoke from a nightmare-infused stretch of sleep covered in sweat. He glanced over at his alarm clock and saw it was already eight in the morning. For as horrible as he slept, the time had passed rather quickly. It meant he would have another day without having to go to work with his dad, which he was thankful for. In all likelihood, his dad felt too awkward around Howie after telling him the story about Sheila and the baby. The fact he had cried, even if it was just a single, stubborn tear that refused to stay trapped inside, was more than his dad could handle. Howie wanted to tell him it's okay to cry, that it helps relieve some of the anger and sadness built up. But he would never dare say that to his dad, nor would his dad agree.

There was a soft knock at the door, then his mom popped her head in.

"Hey, buddy. How are you doing after the bowling alley incident last night? You can't catch a break, huh?"

"I'll be okay. I didn't really know him well."

"Cory's mom just called and asked for you to go see him today. She asked you to come a bit later. I guess he's taking all this a lot harder, and she thinks it would be good to be around his friends."

Howie didn't know what to say. When he fell asleep, there still hadn't been any indication that Cory had gone home. Howie had passed out before going online to chat with Bethany, but he assumed if Cory had reached out to her, he would have received a call. This was a good sign. If Cory was at home, maybe he wasn't involved after all. Maybe Howie was just losing his damn mind.

"Okay. You're cool if I ride my bike there to hang out later?"

"Sure. Just be safe. And be home before dinner. You know your dad hates it if you're not on time."

"Okay. Thanks, Mom."

Once she left, Howie stayed in bed for a few more minutes, rehashing the night before. Could he and Bethany have just been overthinking it? Was Larry's death really just an accident? He wouldn't know for sure until he talked with Cory. It was too early to head over there now, so he popped on the TV and skimmed through the channels. There wasn't much on at this time of day for someone his age, considering they were usually in school. He stopped on WMUR, remembering the reporter who had threatened them. It was currently a commercial break; Crash Bandicoot was yelling into a megaphone about Pizza Hut stuffed crust pizza. The sight of the melting cheese oozing out of the slice sent rumbles through Howie's stomach. He realized he'd never even eaten dinner with everything going on.

As he climbed out of bed, the commercial break ended, but instead of *Live! With Regis and Kathie Lee* coming back to chat with whatever celebrity guest was on to promote something, a *BREAKING NEWS* banner popped up on the screen, and Howie immediately recognized the building behind the scum, Ken Kincade. Howie sat on the edge of his bed and watched, interested in what the reporter had to say. He stood in front of the funeral home, the camera zooming out to show Burt Rollins standing next to him.

"Ken Kincade here, standing in front of the Newport Funeral Home with the home's director and owner, Burt Rollins. Thanks for speaking with us today, sir," Ken said, as Rollins nodded nervously with the camera spotlighted on him. "So we're experiencing unprecedented loss in the community. With a small town like this, how are you managing to keep things under control with the funeral arrangements? It must be very stressful trying to coordinate all of this in such a short time, am I right?"

Burt cleared his throat and loosened his collared shirt, and for the first time, Howie spotted a small neck tattoo on the director. The older man seemed so buttoned up that it surprised Howie to see anything out of the norm.

"Well, yes. It's been difficult, to say the least. But that's what I'm here for. As stressful as it's been here at the funeral home, I can't even begin to imagine what some of these families are going through. It's my job, and *our* job as a community, to try and lift their spirits. As for coordinating all the funerals, setting up the wakes with the families, even making sure we have enough caskets and headstones ready to go, it's all been tough. The families have been very understanding during this difficult time."

Howie couldn't help but think Ken appeared to be bored already. This wasn't headline-worthy enough for the attention whore. After a second of awkward silence, Ken tried to spice things up a bit.

"I'm sure all the families are thankful for what you do to help. We know pieces of what happened that awful night and that Jessica Black is gone for good. But after Larry Foreman's death last night, do you think this town is truly cursed like some of the locals say it is?"

Burt furrowed his brow, apparently caught off guard by such a question.

"I hope not. I'd like to think those cursed among us are a thing of the past. If we could get back to the matter at hand, though... You're interviewing me to talk about the schedule for the funerals. If I could, I'd like to focus on that," he said, but it was not all that confident a tone.

"Yes, of course," Ken responded.

"There will be a sheet not only on the front door of the funeral home but also at the town hall, police station, and the town common. It will list the dates and times of all the upcoming funerals for those who would like to attend. They'll be staggered over the next few weeks, and many of the victims will be stowed away until there is room for proper burials—"

Howie turned off the TV. He'd heard enough. To think there were so many deaths that the town had to spread out the funerals was horrible. When Burt said some of the victims would be "stowed away," what did he mean? That the bodies would sit in some frozen chamber until the cemetery had enough graves dug up to bury them? The thought of so many dead bodies—specifically of people Howie knew—packed away like junk in some old lady's storage unit made him sick. And why wouldn't Newport just reach out to surrounding towns for help? Was it the coven trying to hide something? It didn't add up.

After getting dressed for the day, Howie fixed himself some breakfast and sat at the table to eat. He debated telling Bethany that he was going to meet Cory but decided he'd hold off since Cory's mom only mentioned Howie coming over. Howie knew he would get more out of Cory if it was just him there, anyway. They told each other everything. He finished his bowl of Froot Loops, rinsed the bowl in the sink, then threw on his jacket and hat. The early November weather had bite and Cory's house wasn't the shortest bike ride for him.

After locking up the house, Howie hopped on his bike and headed toward town. The frigid air gave way to a cloud of warm breath every time he pedaled. It was odd riding through town in the middle of a workday, seeing the roads deserted as businesses went about their routine, at least those that were starting to open back up. When he passed the funeral home, he glanced over to see if Ken Kincade was still there, worried he'd give Howie a hard time if he spotted him. But the news van was gone, leaving Burt to deal with all those dead bodies. Howie noticed the list Burt referred to on the news, and even from the road, traveling at a decent speed, he saw how long it was.

He turned onto Laurel Street, riding up the steep hill until he reached the top. No matter how many times he made this trip, that hill was always the worst part. Panting, he passed the concrete plant that was still shut down after the murders, and the wool factory Cory's mom worked at. Up ahead, he saw Cory's house and noticed his mom was still home. He parked his bike in the backyard and walked up on the porch, ready to knock. Cory's mom opened the door before he got the chance.

She looked around skittishly, her eyes bloodshot.

"Please, come inside, Howie."

"Is everything okay, Sandy?"

She closed her eyes and sighed. "Please come in and I'll tell you everything I know."

Howie hesitated briefly, then followed Sandy inside. He'd never seen her acting this way, but then again, he had never seen her son acting this way either. The inside of the home was a mess, which was not like Cory's mother. She usually kept the house very tidy, something that rubbed off on Cory over the years. On sleepovers, Cory always made his guests help clean his room and the house before they left.

"Come, have a seat," she said, motioning toward the couch.

Howie sat, wondering why Cory wasn't there to greet him.

"Where's Cory?"

"He's not here, Howie," she said. "I'm sorry I lied to your mom about it."

An uneasy feeling came over Howie. Something wasn't right.

Sandy continued. "But he asked me to call you and apologize for everything. I'm scared, Howie. Trust me, I don't want to believe any of this myself. I begged him to come home, but he refused."

"Is it about last night at the bowling alley? Larry's death?"

"Yes and no. What I'm about to tell you, I'm only doing it because I want to save my boy. We all made a promise to bury this story as far down into the earth as we could twenty years ago, leave it to rot with Jessica, but to hell with those secrets now. Your parents would kill me for telling you this stuff, but I'm desperate, Howie. Cory's everything to me."

Howie realized his hands were trembling, not quite sure what she was about to tell him. After all these years, he was about to hear the secrets he and his friends had been dying to uncover. He found himself no longer excited, but terrified of the possibilities.

"Where to start... First off, Cory's in great danger. The stuff that started with Jessica didn't go away the other night. It's inside of him now. He's fighting it, and as strong as he is, I know he can only fight it for so long. This thing is powerful beyond anything you kids could imagine. There's a reason we kept it buried for so long. And now that it's inside my baby... If they find out it's in him, they *will* kill him, Howie. We can't let that happen."

Howie's heart rate accelerated, slamming against his chest. While he couldn't shake the feeling that something was wrong with Cory, he didn't understand how Cory could have gotten possessed. He thought back to the struggle on the ski jump. Reliving the events was something he tried avoiding, but he needed to know how it happened. The devil's star they had laid out was working on the platform. Jessica tried to go after them but couldn't move. Then Howie recalled the scuffle *inside* the star with Cory. He'd jumped on Jessica's back to hold her in place so that Howie could get the machete. Somehow, Jessica must have broken the seal while Cory was inside of it with her. But the demon had been trapped inside her body, so how did it switch over to him? It must have happened when her head came off, releasing the seal that locked it inside of her.

"How can we help him? We tried everything we could to stop her, Sandy. We thought we did it. Is there someone we can ask for help?" Howie was at a loss for ideas.

"There aren't many people in this town we can trust, Howie. The reason we kept this secret for so long isn't just because we wanted it to go away...but because we had no choice. We were *forced* to do so. Anyone who was caught even discussing the events faced severe punishment."

It didn't make any sense to Howie. How could an entire town be scared of a small group of people to the extent that they all agreed to hide a series of murders from the rest of the world?

"Why couldn't you guys just go to someone out of town? I get why you couldn't trust the cops here, but it's not like the entire world is in on the secret, right?"

"If only it was that simple." Sandy laughed. "Of course we would have done that if we could. After the first few murders, we held a town meeting. Most of us assumed it was just going to be the police giving instructions about staying safe, telling us to lock our doors at night, stuff like that. When we got there, Miller and a few other town figures stood at the podium with their faces as white as chalk. It was clear they didn't want to be up there talking with us. But it was a mandatory town meeting—something we'd never had before. They went on to tell us about the coven and the pact they'd made with a demon named Vorathor. It sounded absurd. Some of the real religious folk even got up and tried to walk out on them, but they were forced back into their seats. We had no choice but to listen to a story that sounded like it belonged in one of you boys' horror movies—but it was real life."

"So, we knew the coven summoned that demon. I still don't understand why you couldn't get help."

"Because the demon they called wasn't the one inside Jessica Black, Howie. It was far more powerful than the one that took over her body. They went on to tell us how the town was cursed. How they had made a pact with this entity to bring their coven strength. The demon offered it—but only if they were able to trap another demon in a sacrifice of their choosing and make sure it never escaped."

Howie's head was spinning. Multiple demons? Making deals with them? It all sounded far too crazy to be real. Even with everything he'd seen in the last week, it still felt impossible. Maybe it was just because he couldn't fathom something this big, beyond their scope of understanding. If they couldn't get rid of a demon, how the hell were they supposed to get rid of two? And where was this second one?

"What does all this mean? Are we screwed no matter what? Even if we *can* get it out of Cory?"

She closed her eyes, and a stray tear slid down her cheek. She looked at him and said, "We will have to worry about that after. Before I can worry about the rest of the town, I'll do whatever it takes to save my son. Do you understand that, Howie?"

"Yes. So now what?"

"The coven has always lived in secret. We knew a few of the members because they were the ones who talked to us at the meeting. But they were pawns in a much bigger game. And the ones we knew of are now dead. We still can't trust many people in town. I don't know who's in and who's not. To be honest, we always thought it was a much smaller group than it turned out to be. They were like a pack of vampires, recruiting members to join and growing by the day. If we're going to stop them, we need to stop *it* first. The only one in town I know we can trust, who will have any semblance of an idea what to do, is Father Grimes. We need to go to the church and ask for guidance."

"No way! I saw the way he was watching us at the funeral. I don't trust him. He was following me and Cory around the whole time, being really weird."

"I assure you, Father Grimes is not part of any coven, Howie. A priest believes in God, in Jesus Christ. The coven sure as hell believes in a higher power, but it isn't the same god church-going people follow. He's our best shot. Even if he can't do an exorcism, he might have some answers. The longer this thing stays in Cory... I can't even think about it. I *need* to talk to him."

"I don't know if that's the best idea. Don't you think they'll be watching you? If you go to Father Grimes, won't they think something's up?"

"They could be watching us *now*, Howie. There's no safe space in this town anymore."

Howie felt as if there were eyes burning into the back of his head. If she was this worried about them keeping tabs on her, why would she call him here and put him in danger? But she was right. And he knew if she was seen at the church, they would know something was up. As of right now, the only thing they had going for them was that nobody knew Cory was missing.

"Okay. I don't think you should go, Sandy. Let me do it. I can sneak behind the church on my bike and stand a much better chance of them not seeing me. I'll go talk with Father Grimes, tell him about Cory's situation and that he needs help. What if he says no?"

"He won't. I hate not being in control of this situation. But you're right. If I trust you to do this, I need you to tell him everything you know, even the stuff Cory won't tell me. Do you think you can do that? If they find out he's possessed, they will kill him."

Howie nodded, but felt an unbearable anxiety begin to crush his chest, making it hard to breathe. It was bad enough knowing this evil thing was inside his best friend. Knowing the coven would go out of their way to hurt, or worse, kill Cory to get rid of the demon added even more pressure.

"Can you think of any place he would hide? Any spot in the woods? Places around town you boys would sneak into?"

Howie thought it over, but his brain was too full of all this new information to concentrate.

"Nothing comes to mind, but I'll think about it."

Sandy thanked him and asked that he report back to her as soon as he talked to Father Grimes. Howie left, still trying to register what he'd just heard. He wanted to ask Sandy more about the coven, as she clearly knew more, but what mattered most right now was doing everything they possibly could to save Cory. He just hoped she was right about Father Grimes.

CHAPTER 19

Bethany thanked her friends for taking her out to lunch and got out of the car. She watched as they drove off in the distance and then walked toward her front door. Mr. Gould, her elderly neighbor across the street, trudged along toward his mailbox.

"Afternoon, little lady. How you doing these days?" The way he asked made Bethany realize he was clueless about what had been going on the past week.

"I'm fine. How're you doing, Mr. Gould?"

"Oh, you know. Back pain ain't getting any better. The most exciting part of my day is coming out here to check the mail!" he shouted, although he probably didn't realize it.

"Have a good day, Mr. Gould."

"You, too, Bethany!"

Her parents were both at work, and her sister was with her grandparents—their default babysitters, with school being shut down for the foreseeable future. Her mom told her to go out to lunch and then come right home and clean her room and do some chores before they arrived home from work. After telling her parents about the figure watching her from the woods, her parents freaked. Her dad ran out to investigate with a baseball bat, only to come back laughing. He said it was just a reporter watching their house to see if she would come out. He took the opportunity to say that was exactly why they should talk with the media... so this sort of thing wouldn't continue to happen. Bethany insisted she knew what she saw and that there was no way it could have been a reporter, but her dad shook it off.

Her mom wanted her to get out of the house and hang out with friends, do something to take her mind off all of the crap going on. Bethany was just happy to get the house to herself for most of the day and get some peace and quiet time.

She walked up her front steps and reached into her purse for her house keys. As she was pulling them out, Mr. Gould startled her with a barking cough while he checked his mail. She dropped her keys onto the porch and bent over to pick them up. The old man continued to cough, so she turned back to make sure he was okay. When his cough finally settled down, she turned back to her house and opened the door.

The house was silent, just the way she liked It. All she wanted to do was put on some music and read a book, take her mind off all the craziness. She tossed her keys on the counter and trudged upstairs to her room.

"Belle? Where you at, kitty?"

Bethany turned her boom box on to the radio and kicked her dirty clothes under the bed before lying down, taking a moment to rest. As she listened to a few songs, she thought of what the reporter said to Howie. How his dad abused him at home. How could anyone do that to their own kid? Sure, her dad wasn't the ideal role model, but he would never lay a finger on his family. Howie was one of the sweetest boys she'd ever met. So thoughtful and always offered to help with anything. She had never met his dad, but it was a miracle Howie turned out the way he did if his home life was really that tough.

Then she thought about what the reporter said about *her* dad. How he had been secretly paying state colleges to try and get her accepted. He remained insistent that she go to a nice school in New Hampshire. Bethany always wondered why, but maybe it was easier to use his power and money locally. She knew he was into some shady stuff with the booster club, but never in a million years would she have expected him to do something so dishonest. She hadn't built up the strength to ask him about it yet. But lately, she found it hard to look him in the eye.

When the radio station went to a commercial, Bethany's stream of thought was broken, and she looked around her room again. She spotted her diary on her desk, which she didn't recall leaving there. Whenever she wrote a new entry, she always stuffed it back into an old shoe box she kept in her closet. Not that she thought her parents would read it, but privacy was privacy, and even as she wrote in it, she always felt as if someone was watching over her shoulder, learning her deepest secrets.

Assuming it was on her desk because her mom decided to invade her privacy, she rolled out of bed and snatched it up. As soon as she opened it to the last page, she noticed handwriting that wasn't hers and knew something was wrong. She gripped the book tightly, cutting off the blood flow until the tips of her fingers turned white.

It's time. We left you a little gift to show how serious we are; maybe it will get the point across. We would hate to do anything worse. So let us be perfectly clear. Meet us tonight at the cemetery, behind the shed. Come alone. If you don't, we will kill your entire family.

Bethany struggled to read the last few lines as her hands were trembling. She set the diary on her desk.

They had entered her home. They had read everything she wrote, including her concerns about Cory and the possibility of him being possessed.

She thought back, realizing she'd never unlocked the front door after Mr. Gould's coughing fit.

It was already unlocked.

Are they still in the house? With me?

She froze, listening for any odd sounds through the second floor. The radio blocked out everything, so she turned it off and waited.

Nothing.

Then she realized she hadn't heard or seen her cat since coming home after instinctively calling for her, which wasn't like Belle. The cat was always the first to greet her when she walked in, rubbing her plush, white fur against Bethany's leg. It often left long strands clinging to her pants, annoying her to no end after she'd spent so much time putting her outfit together. She walked quietly out of her room, peering around the corner for any sign of an intruder.

"Belle?" she whispered.

Fear suffocated her, tightening around her throat like a python.

Down the hall, her sister's door was open. Something so minor, yet it told her someone had either been in there before she got home or was *still* in there. Every day, when her parents left for work, her mom shut the bedroom doors so Belle couldn't get in the rooms. She had a habit of going into the closets and pissing on the carpet unless her litter box was cleaned daily. Seeing the open door told Bethany to turn and run the other way. But she had to pass the room to get downstairs. She felt so stupid for not noticing the open door on her way up, but why would she pay attention to something like that with no initial cause for concern?

She inched closer to Briana's room, holding her breath. With the sunlight shining through her sister's window, a trail of light cast itself out to the hallway floor. Bethany stopped in her tracks.

A shadow crossed the light's path.

Bethany waited for any noise, movement, hell she'd even accept some masked attacker leaping out of Briana's room right now versus the anticipation of waiting.

But nothing came.

She kept her eyes locked on the floor when the shadow crossed again. Then back the other way, as if someone was slowly pacing back and forth. A cold gust escaped the open door, blowing against her cheeks. She let out the breath she had been holding, then peered into her sister's room. What she saw twisted her insides.

Belle hung upside down from the tail by a rope tied to the ceiling fan. Her feline body swayed back and forth, the open window inhaling a frigid breeze.

She screamed, her entire body shaking.

Blood dripped down to the carpet, forming a pool of crimson, staining the space below the dead cat. That beautiful white fur, now matted down with sticky maroon blotches. The smell of copper invaded her nose, and she felt the bile rise in the back of her throat. Yet, she couldn't take her eyes off the poor cat.

Why is the window open?

The thought came to her, and she couldn't help but think the bastard who did this escaped through the window when she got home, somehow jumping from the second story. Had she just missed them? She wanted to charge at the window and see if she spotted anyone fleeing. But she couldn't bring herself to pass Belle. The feline corpse slowly spun to face her. The insides were hanging out of an open wound in the stomach like strands of spaghetti saturated in pasta sauce. This time, Bethany couldn't hold the vomit down. She leaned over and threw up on the hallway floor, crying uncontrollably. She thought back to the message they left for her and the warning it contained. If they were really willing to do this to an animal, what would they do to her family?

CHAPTER 20

Howie pulled up to the church steps, intimidated by the large brick building. His family wasn't even the slightest bit religious, but the large cross towering over him still brought on a sense of power. It wasn't that he never wanted to go to church, he just didn't know anything about it, and his dad wouldn't be caught dead in a place like this.

He parked his bike around the side of the building so it wouldn't be out in the open. Once he had it in a safe spot, he walked back around and up the large concrete steps. He grabbed the wrought iron handle and pushed open the larger-than-life door, hoping there wasn't some sort of ceremony—or whatever they called it—going on inside. He was greeted with silence and the wafting smell of cleaning products and incense. Up front was a massive stage with a podium sitting in the center. Pews spread out on both sides of the carpeted aisle. In the corner of the stage, a large statue of Jesus Christ overlooked the empty rows with hands held open as if inviting everyone to come in and sit.

Howie had no idea where to go, so he scanned the room. To the left of the stage, he spotted what appeared to be an office in the back corner. His heart hammered with each step, unsure of what he'd say once coming face-to-face with Father Grimes. Part of him wanted the priest to laugh at his story, act as if he had no idea what Howie was talking about. That outcome felt far more realistic than the alternative.

The office door was closed, but there was a small rectangular window of stained glass in its center. Behind the cloudy surface, Howie spotted Father Grimes sitting at his desk, shuffling paperwork. Howie knocked, and the priest shifted his attention to the door. The old man smiled and rose to his feet.

Before Howie could change his mind and leave, the door opened. Father Grimes was short—shorter than Howie—but he still carried himself with confidence. He had shaggy white hair that reminded Howie of Doc Brown in *Back to the Future*, with bushy white eyebrows that resembled wiry caterpillars about to crawl off his face.

"Hello, young man. How can I help you today?"

It seemed a customary question, but Howie knew Grimes was familiar with his situation and who he was.

"Hi, Father Grimes. Sorry to bother you unannounced like this."

"Oh, don't apologize to me, son. I'm always here to talk. How can I help?"

Howie looked around the office, seeing stacks of Bibles, pictures of Jesus, and stuff that, while normal to many in town, was foreign to him.

"I know my family doesn't come to church, and I'm sorry for that," he said, thinking it was the right thing to lead the conversation with, "but I need your help. It's... it's about everything that's happened. With Jessica Black. With the coven." The last word came out barely above a whisper.

Father Grimes pursed his lips and lifted his brow.

"I've been waiting for you children to come to me, you know. Please shut the door and have a seat."

Howie hesitated, but he did as he was told and sat across from Grimes. He felt like he was about to be interrogated, not helped. Father Grimes lifted his hand, indicating for Howie to continue talking.

"I don't know how much you know about all of the stuff that's happened to us and to those people before us years ago. But we're all in danger, Father. I don't know what to do. Cory and I stopped Jessica, but that thing that was inside her is now inside my friend, and I need to help him get it out." He struggled to use the word demon in the presence of the priest.

"I see." .

Really? That's your response?

"His mom asked me to come see you. She told me some of the town's secrets about the coven and why it had remained hidden. She said you were the only one who might know how to help me with Cory before they find him. I... I really need your help, Father. He's the only friend I have left," Howie said, wiping away the tears as he talked. "Can you do an exorcism or something?"

"Hold on a moment, son. It'll be all right. Take a deep breath. She was right to send you to me, but I can't do an exorcism. I'm not trained to do so. And even if I was, I'd need approval from the church, which takes time. A lot of paperwork. But let's focus on what we *can* do. Yes, I'm aware of the coven, and of what they did to Jessica. And I knew as soon as she was free and terrorizing this poor town, they would come out of their slumber. I'm afraid we may not have that much time. You say he's hiding... Where?"

"That's the problem. I don't know. He won't tell anyone because he's afraid to hurt them. But if you can't do an exorcism, I don't know what else to do. Who else to go to..."

"Let's take a step back, okay? I haven't told anyone this outside of the Lord Himself, but I knew someday it would need to come out. There was never a good time when it was safe, and to be honest, right now may not be either. If anyone saw you come here, it could be bad news for both of us, Howie."

"Nobody saw me, I made sure of it. And I hid my bike around the side. Unless this coven has scouts in office buildings watching the town with binoculars, I think I'm okay."

"I wouldn't put it past them," Grimes smirked. "Back when this all started, we were just a normal small town. People came to church on Sunday, went to school or work during the week, and we all lived normal lives. The coven was here—don't get me wrong—but they dabbled in their own stuff and left everyone else alone. And then things changed. They became power hungry. They made a deal with a demon, one that would make them stronger than ever before as long as they held up their end of the bargain. If they didn't? Well, this place would be cursed for eternity. Not just them, but *all* of us. This town is consumed by evil, Howie. I do what I can to fend it off, but there's no way around it."

"The deal with the demon to trap another one, right?"

"How did you know that, boy?"

"Cory's mom told me. She said the town had a special meeting when Jessica killed people and a few of the coven members told the town about the pact. They forced everyone to keep quiet and threatened them if they didn't. She didn't tell me much more than that. What else do you know about the demon? And the coven?"

"More than I care to. It's not always angels against demons, Howie. Sometimes, demons want to eliminate other demons. He's called Vorathor. A powerful demon that seeks to eliminate others for his own benefit. Bear in mind, this is not the one you're dealing with. Vorathor is far more powerful than that. It's crucial that we stop this weaker demon before Vorathor returns to Earth and seeks to make those who failed him pay. But that doesn't mean we can take this other demon lightly. It may not be as powerful as Vorathor, but clearly, we've seen what it's capable of."

"Wouldn't Vorathor just come and kill the coven for us? Take care of our problems?"

"There are two things wrong with that, son. First, no matter how evil this coven might be, I can't, in good faith, sit back and watch them get killed. It's my duty to help all, whether they are good or bad. Secondly, you have to remember what Vorathor wants: to eliminate the demon trapped inside your friend. If he comes, and that evil is still festering inside Mr. Stevens, I'm afraid it will be too late. The coven will be the least of our concerns."

"Please help us, Father. This thing has ruined my life. It's destroyed this town. And... and it made my dad the way he is." Howie's eyes burned as tears welled up and slithered down his cheeks. Everything sounded so much bigger than anything he could have imagined. Jessica was bad enough. Then there was the coven. And now, they had an even more powerful demon on the verge of coming to make everything else look like a picnic in the park.

"As I said, I can't really help you myself. But... I do know someone who can. Someone who's been gone for most of the last two decades, hiding from the coven. Howie, do you recall the story of Henry Black and how he died in the state prison?"

Howie nodded.

"There's some truth to that. But there's also more to it than anyone else realizes. You see, he did die in that prison cell. He was brought to the funeral home and closed in a casket. But he wasn't *really* dead, Howie. No. Henry Black is still alive."

CHAPTER 21

The sun began to set behind the trees surrounding the concrete plant. Cory peered out the grime-coated window with a constant feeling of being watched gnawing at him. All he saw was the dirt parking lot that led around the building to a large gravel pit that ended where the trees eventually took over. He tried to force himself to sleep the previous night, hoping it would get rid of the evil thoughts lurking inside, but all that did was amplify the desire to give in to the demon. And then there were the few workers who stopped by for random quality control checks on the concrete slabs. He hid in a section of the factory where they wouldn't see him but the whole time, he was on edge, worried the demon would take action. He heard them discussing the slabs they were forming for the new dam down by the train track. While the plant was still technically closed, the slabs had to be monitored to ensure they would pass inspection. He considered finding another place to lay low, a spot where he didn't have to worry about surprise visits, but this still felt like the best option.

On multiple occasions, he had considered sneaking off to call his mom again on the pay phone, wanting the comfort of at least hearing her voice. The dark confines of the warehouse only added to the loneliness. He missed his mom. He missed his friends. All he wanted was to travel back in time to the bowling alley and hang out with Howie and Bethany again and force himself to leave before the voice convinced him to enter the maintenance room. While hiding here kept him a safe distance from those he cared about, it left him with his thoughts and the guilt that came with them. He hated being alone right now.

"You got me, pussy boy."

Cory winced, the demon's voice slamming through his head like a derailed train.

A sharp pain pulsed through his forearm. His veins were much darker than normal, swimming beneath the surface of his skin like any inky river. Evil was taking over his body and all he could do was hide out and hope the urge to cause more harm didn't come back before he figured this out. He knew he was running out of time. His body was changing, as if the demon didn't only plan to make him a conduit of death and carnage but wanted to make sure he looked the part.

He pulled away from the window and took in the dark space around him. The place could double as a playground for Freddy Krueger, full of tools and large equipment, everything remaining in place awaiting the crew to come back to work after the shutdown. Against the wall in the back corner was a large, empty, rectangle box, which Cory had used as a makeshift bed. He couldn't help but feel like a vampire sleeping in a coffin. A chute that looked like a narrow metal slide aimed diagonally toward the box, the top end connecting to some type of machine that Cory assumed filled the wooden frames with concrete when the business was fully operating. Next to the empty box he slept in, was another; that one full of liquid concrete that must have been in an advanced stage of curing, as it was starting to solidify. Above the main floor, a set of stairs went up to a second level catwalk that overlooked the main floor below.

He had considered sleeping up there so he could observe anyone from above who might show up again, but the metal grate platform was not ideal. The thought of going through all this, only to wake to another nightmare and accidentally roll off the edge to his death sounded all too fitting.

Cory couldn't handle the silence any longer. It was suffocating. He needed to get out of there and call his mom. If he stuck to the woods, he thought he could make it back to the pay phone without being spotted. He wasn't sure anyone would actually be searching for him yet, but he preferred to play it safe.

He opened the front door slightly, poking his head out and scanning the parking lot. It was empty. Again, he peeked behind the building toward the large gravel pit where the equipment and concrete trucks remained parked. He didn't expect anyone to be back there, but he double-checked anyway. When the coast was clear, he took off in a sprint toward the woods, all while trying to keep the unsettling feeling that was festering inside of him at bay.

Cory exited the woods and crouched behind an old dumpster. Before he went to the pay phone, he wanted to be certain there was nobody around he needed to worry about. While the sun was setting, allowing him to stick to the shadows, it was a lot more difficult to remain hidden from the public eye before complete nightfall arrived. A few customers entered and left the store, filling their vehicles with gas, buying thirty-packs of Budweiser, and going about their nightly routine like there was nothing wrong. And why wouldn't they? They had no idea the town was about to go through another nightmare. A nightmare *he* would be responsible for after he'd just worked so hard to save the town and his friends.

An elderly woman entered the laundromat with a basket full of clothes, but other than that, the coast was clear. Cory stood from his crouch and walked straight to the pay phone. He had two quarters, so he could make two calls if he wanted. He doubted very much his mom would be working when she was worried about his well-being. Knowing her, she was still out looking for him even though he told her to give him time to make this right. Instead of calling her first, he decided to try Howie's house, hoping he answered. Cory wanted to fill Howie in on what was happening. Maybe he could try to get help. Cory still wasn't comfortable telling anyone where he was hiding, afraid if they got too close the demon would take control and do something awful. Still, he wanted Howie to know. He owed him that.

He slid the quarter into the slot and dialed Howie's house.

The phone rang twice before someone picked up.

"Yello..."

Fuck!

It was Howie's dad. He always answered the phone that way. Cory always hated when he picked up, but never more than at this exact moment. He was about to hang up when Howie's dad spoke again.

"Who's this? If you're a bill collector, you can fuck right off."

Cory realized he was breathing heavily into the phone. He wanted to talk. To tell Howie's dad they were in danger. A jolt of pain stabbed into his eyes. It felt like something twisting the nerves behind his eyeballs and pulling on them. He cried out, and before he could hang up, Howie's dad spoke again.

"Cory? That you? What the fuck's wrong with you, kid? Howie isn't home right now, but his ass better get here before dinner if he knows what's good for him. Is he with you?"

"*I'm going to carve you up with my bare hands, just like I did your precious Sheila. Finish what I started. And then I'll gut your son for getting in my way!*" The demon now had full control of his body; he couldn't stop it from talking.

"You shit. You little *fucking* shit! I—"

Cory slammed the phone down on the receiver. He wiped tears away and hated himself for it. He knew the demon was loving every second of not only threatening others, but slowly taking over his body when there was nothing at all he could do about it. He wanted to force himself back to the woods, back into hiding, but he could sense that control leaving his body. Instead, he turned and walked toward town as nightfall settled in.

CHAPTER 22

Spunky flipped the barbershop sign to *CLOSED*, shut the blinds, then turned off the barber's pole. Not that he needed to turn the pole off. Everyone in town came to him for a cut and knew his hours—at least all the dads and sons of Newport. Their wives and daughters would go out of town to whatever salon they preferred. He was okay with that. It allowed shop talk to stick to the subjects he preferred—sports, booze, and town gossip.

He caught a glimpse of himself in the oversized mirror in front of his chair and cringed. Man, did it suck getting old. Back when he opened the place, all the ladies who brought their kids in used to flirt with him. His once flowing blond hair now receded to a white horseshoe wrapped around his glossy, hairless dome of a head. The puffy circles under his eyes added ten years, but they weren't the worst of it. His red, pockmarked nose was one shade shy of a clown's, screaming years of alcoholism.

After all he'd been through in the past twenty years, he couldn't blame himself for his appearance. For he had been one of the higher authority figures in the coven, one of the "Chosen." He lost his wife during the summoning at the hands of Jessica and had spent the last two decades as a widower who drank himself to sleep every night. Until Jessica resurfaced, the coven had remained dormant since the murders. They still met regularly—more so over the last handful of years once they were clear of any connections to the Black Heart Killer—but the massacre at the school had shaken them to their core. Jessica—and the demon inside her—were supposed to be buried forever.

Now the demon was somewhere out there, seeking a new host to come for them. If Bethany Carver's diary held any truth, there was a good chance it was Cory Stevens. She wrote about how he'd gone missing after Larry was killed. The pieces were adding up, and they needed to locate Cory before he got to any more of them. It was important that the Carver girl obey them and show up at the cemetery tonight. The reason they singled out Bethany was simple: she would be the final sacrifice for Vorathor. They would trap the demon inside her and make sure it was disposed of properly this time.

They would draw it in, seduce it with the body of a virgin who they knew it craved. The truth was that was why Jessica was singled out as well. She may have been married to Henry Black, but the coven had information about every family that came to Newport. They knew Jessica was waiting until marriage to have sex. Henry and Jessica moved to Newport while still engaged, eloping at the town hall shortly after moving to town. The coven made sure they disrupted the Black family before any act of sex could be completed, persuading her to join the coven, and then from there, it was easy work. Spunky, along with the others in power, brainwashed the weak woman.

Now they had a chance to make things right with Vorathor.

Spunky tossed his scissors and clipper guards into the Barbicide cleaning solution, then wiped down his chair. He grabbed the broom, sweeping the hair into a large mound, then used the dustpan to scoop up the pile. He looked above the mirror, locking eyes with the large twelve-point buck head he'd mounted on the wall the first summer he opened the barbershop. It was his biggest score in all his years of hunting, and the funniest part of it all was that he wasn't even *hunting* when he got it. They had a coven meeting in the woods one fall night, and he had just come across it, roaming around in a meadow on his way back from the meeting location.

Next to the mounted head, the backside of the deer was also displayed. It usually got a good chuckle from the kids when they came in for haircuts—the tail flagged up as if the animal was about to pepper the waiting area with deer shit.

He dumped the swept-up hair into the trash. Finally, he counted the money in the drawer to see how the day's business went. It sure as hell felt busy all day. Miller's replacement, Chief Mullin, had done a great job of covering up the murder as an accident to help avoid bringing more attention to the town, but he still had a lot to learn before the coven gave him an important role. It was one of the many things the coven did to ensure they maintained their strong grasp on the town. Every role, every person, had a backup plan if something was to go sideways. They made sure the next in line to Miller was also a member. After the massacre, their numbers were shrinking, and they knew they needed to build back the strength they'd had for decades.

Spunky walked to the back of the barbershop, tidying up along the way. He stopped at the bathroom and poked his head in to see if any customers left it a mess. It was clean enough. He'd just make sure to come in a little early tomorrow to mop the floor before he opened. Any other night, he would stop at the fridge in the back of the shop and crack open a beer before his drive home. Right now, though, he had to get ready to head out to the woods with the rest of the coven.

The front door jingled, but Spunky was positive he locked it after he flipped the sign to *CLOSED*.

"Sorry, we're closed!"

He exited the bathroom, turned off the light, then headed back down the narrow hall toward the main room to see who decided to ignore the sign.

The lights suddenly shut off, sending the hallway into darkness.

"Hey, this isn't funny. Get the hell out—"

Spunky stopped mid-sentence. A figure crouched in the entryway, shrouded in darkness. They hunched low, staring at him. Spunky's throat tightened, and his limbs froze. Whoever it was, they weren't talking, but heavy breaths escaped the stranger.

"Who the hell are you? Get out of my shop before I get you out of here myself."

The figure didn't move, just remained crouched as still as a statue. The initial fear that had overcome Spunky quickly turned to anger. Who the hell had the nerve to try and fuck with him? Out in the public eye, he worked hard to uphold a cheerful, friendly image. But this asshole didn't know the true Spunky. The things he'd done in the past to protect himself and the coven. He charged down the remainder of the hall to the edge of the main floor. With the remaining light trickling through the closed blinds, the figure became visible enough for him to recognize.

"*Cory*? Why are you here this time of night?"

He realized it was a stupid question. Of course Spunky knew why the kid was there. The speculation he and the rest of the members had about one of the kids at the school that night now being possessed just answered itself.

The kid was bent in a position as if he was about to play a game of leapfrog, ready to pounce at any second. His face, though, told another story. It was pain that contorted his features.

"Please... don't make me do it again," Cory pleaded.

"Do *what*, kid?"

"*Cory doesn't want me to slaughter you like I did your friend down at the bowling alley. I think you already knew that, though, didn't you, you pathetic drunk? Don't you want me to end your misery? Send you to that tiny corner of Hell where your wife resides while her saggy old corpse is raped by the demons?*"

Spunky couldn't talk. The mention of his wife completely deflated any strength he felt a moment ago. This demon killed his wife.

"Atahsaia. You took everything from me. You have no idea what you're dealing with. We're stronger than you. And if you leave here right now, we'll have another sacrifice for you tonight. A pretty, little virgin, just the way you like them."

The boy didn't respond, but tears began to pool in his eyes. He took sporadic breaths, keeping his eyes locked on Spunky.

"Please, I don't want to kill anyone else. I won't let you do it!" Cory said.

"That's right, boy, don't do anything stupid. Don't listen to it. Turn around and *leave*."

With the blinds drawn shut, nobody could see inside from the road. If the kid listened and turned to leave, Spunky had a chance to contain him and make the coven's job that much easier. He scanned the area close to him for any sort of weapon. His pistol was beneath the register, too far away to reach. He knew that wouldn't get rid of the demon, but it could at least slow the body down. His talisman remained hidden in a drawer to his right. It was the best chance he had to grab anything. He had to get over there without the demon realizing what he was doing, grab the talisman to ward this thing off, and get a chance to warn the others.

"Tell me, what is it you want from us? You seek revenge, yet you must know why we trapped you. We're faithful to Vorathor. You're nothing more than something that stands in his way. You're beneath him." Spunky sat in one of his barber chairs, keeping an eye on the drawer now within arm's length.

Get the talisman, scare him off, and warn the rest of the coven.

He turned back to Cory, who attempted to stand from his crouch, but his bones snapped and popped like a pack of firecrackers. He screamed in agony, standing straight and coming face-to-face with Spunky. Beneath the kid's pale skin, jagged bumps pressed taut as if fragments of bones had exploded beneath the surface and were trying to force their way out of his body.

"*There's* nothing *bigger than me. There is nothing that will stop me. And you sheep, you will come to a sad demise and be forgotten about. One by one. I will kill all of you. Just like your wife. Her heart tasted wonderful, if you were curious. I looked into her eyes as I tore it from her body, watched as the last glint of life drained from her with nothing but fear and defeat remaining. I was the last thing she saw before she died. How does that make you feel?*"

Spunky clenched his fists. He was overcome with pure hatred. It may have been the body of a child in front of him, but the voice belonged to something far more ancient. This demon—the cannibal demon—had done enough, and it was time the coven put a stop to it. Even with a demon inside him, Cory was still just a scrawny teenage boy. What were the odds he could overpower a grown man, even if that grown man was aging rapidly after years of alcohol abuse? Spunky stood from the barber chair and moved closer to the counter, all while keeping his attention on Cory.

Get the talisman. Force him to look at it.

"I think it's time we finished talking. That's how I feel," Spunky said.

He blindly reached for the drawer, remaining focused on the kid. When he felt the handle, he risked a glance to make sure he was gripping the right drawer. That was a mistake. Cory lunged from the doorway, pouncing on Spunky and driving him back against the counter. The mirror shattered as Spunky's back slammed into it, a container holding the dirty combs fell to the floor, sending shards of glass and liquid across the linoleum. The scent of cleaning solution wafted into the air, finding its way down the old man's throat as he took a deep breath.

His eyes watered, but not enough to block the horrific image of the deranged kid now standing inches from his face. Cory's teeth were rotting from his mouth, but beneath them, razor-sharp tips poked through the blackened gums. An orange glow surrounded his pupils, which were tiny obsidian dots in the center. Black veins bulged on his neck as he grabbed Spunky by the throat and squeezed, again slamming Spunky against the shelf and causing more equipment to fall to the floor.

Cory's head suddenly snapped back, cracking his neck and pushing his Adam's apple out so far that Spunky had a fleeting thought the kid's larynx might explode through his skin.

Cory cried, screaming "No" over and over, but his hands remained locked around the barber's throat. Spunky's vision was fading; the damn kid was stronger than he looked. Spunky turned to the side, partly because he couldn't stand staring into those demonic eyes anymore, but also to find anything that could help. The only thing in reach was a bottle of powder he used to dab onto the neck after using the straight razor to perfect the neckline. He grabbed the powder as Cory's sharp nails dug into his windpipe.

Cory looked to see what he had in his hands, and that bought Spunky enough time. He squeezed the bottle, shooting white powder into the orange eyes. Cory fell back, clawing at his face.

"*You cocksucker*!" It was Cory, but the voice was not that of a boy. It boomed in the tight space, sending a chill down Spunky's spine.

Spunky didn't waste any time, bending over and grabbing a pair of scissors that had fallen to the floor, ready to impale the bastard child in the eye.

He swung wildly, aiming the scissors for the face, but Cory instinctively lifted his right hand. The sharp tips shot through his palm and out the other side. It should have made him fall back. It *should* have caused him to collapse and clutch the wound. Instead, it was as if the pain fed the demon more power. Cory's fiery eyes opened wide, no longer worried about the powder irritating them. He snarled and again grabbed Spunky by the throat with his good hand. He squeezed and looked down at the scissors poking through the back of his other hand, blood oozing down his forearm.

"*That was a mistake, ol' Spunk.*"

The kid fucking smiled, again revealing his diseased mouth. His breath was revolting, and all Spunky could do was inhale it as he fought for air. Cory threw Spunky to the floor, and the barber's head smacked off the chair on the way down, clouding his vision. Cory jumped on his chest, mounting him in place, then observed at his ravaged hand once more.

"You know, this body is a lot more spry than that little whore you tried to trap me in. I don't much appreciate you damaging my new host, though," he said, focusing on the scissors.

Spunky coughed, finally able to take in air. He blinked away the fogginess and snapped back to the maniac on top of him. Cory was still admiring the scissors through his hand, smiling at the wound. With his other hand, he locked his fingers into the handles as if he was about to cut a sheet of wrapping paper. He began laughing.

"Snip, snip…"

He forced the scissors open and shut, open and shut, stretching the skin and forcing apart the muscles in his palm. Spunky wanted to vomit. The sound of metal cutting through the meat, tendons, and bone reminded him of when he gutted the deer that now hung on the wall, watching and getting the last laugh as his killer lay helpless on the floor. Cory pulled up on the scissors, forcing the hole in his hand to expand. Instead of pulling the blades free, he carved his way up through the top of his hand, splitting the webbing between the middle and ring finger, creating a permanent, bloody *V*.

Cory lifted the mangled hand to his face, resting it over his eye with the palm facing out. Spunky saw the orange eye through the opening, staring down at him.

"Peekaboo."

Then Cory drove the scissors down with force into Spunky's chest. The barber let out a gurgled cry as blood bubbled out of his mouth.

"Please…"

For a moment, Spunky thought his plea might actually work. Cory got off his chest and walked toward the far counter. If Spunky could just force himself up and make it into the street, he could yell for someone to help. But his legs were jelly, unable to move due to shock. He glanced down and spotted the scissors still sticking out of his chest. All that remained visible were the blue handles, the metal impaled all the way through his chest.

"I don't plan to let you off so easy, Spunk. I plan to make you suffer before I bleed you dry like that deer up there. Hell, maybe I'll put your head on the plaque next to it and your bare, wrinkly ass on the other. How's that sound?"

Spunky could only whimper in return.

Cory grabbed a jar of cleaning solution filled with razor blades on the counter next to the second booth. He walked over to Spunky and again sat on his chest. Slowly, the demon-child opened the jar, staring down into the unnaturally blue liquid.

"Phew! This shit stinks! How do you think it tastes, old man?"

Spunky groaned, the blood loss from his chest quickly depleting his will to fight.

"Let's find out, shall we?" Cory asked.

Cory grabbed hold of Spunky's jaw and pried his mouth open. His wounded hand shouldn't have maintained that level of strength, but the demon had control now. Pain was fuel. He held the barber's mouth open, slowly bringing the jar closer. Spunky tried to bite down on the bastard's fingers, but the strength was too overpowering. All he could do was groan a desperate plea. Instead of letting go, Cory pulled the bottom jaw lower, sending jolts of pain down each side of Spunky's face. He watched helplessly as the boy dumped some of the solution into his mouth. He kept his eyes locked on the jar, watching the razor blades float closer and closer to the edge of the glass like a bunch of hopeless boats about to plunge down a waterfall. Just as a blade was about to fall into his mouth, Cory lifted the jar and laughed. He forced Spunky's mouth shut and held it tight.

"Swallow, old man. Need to clean those insides of all the booze you drink every night."

Spunky began to choke, vomiting inside his closed mouth, the bile mixed with the solution to create a disgusting cocktail. He fought off swallowing, knowing the chemicals would likely poison him—not that it mattered at this point. He was bleeding out and even if he survived the stab wound, the demon would finish him off.

"Now, now. Swallow or I'll dump it all in."

Spunky complied, holding his breath as he gulped; the solution slid down his throat and into his stomach. A burning sensation worked its way through his body, sending sharp pains through his abdomen.

"See? You can listen. Which makes this next part important. Tell me what your pathetic pack of sheep has in mind. Where are the rest of you?"

"I won't tell you. Our bond is s-s-sacred!"

"Suit yourself..."

Cory grabbed Spunky's mouth, again ripping it open. The blood from the open wound on his hand dripped onto the barber's tongue, and that somehow tasted *worse* than the chemicals. Cory raised the jar again, but he was crying. The sinister grin that had exposed his mouth rot no longer glued on his face.

"I'm sorry, Spunky... I can't stop it." Cory shook his head violently, and his orange eyes bulged.

"He might be sorry, but I'm not," the deeper voice bellowed.

Spunky didn't even have a chance to react. The demon dumped the contents of the jar into his mouth; this time the razor blades poured in with the liquid. A few clinked off his teeth and bounced off his cheeks, but most landed in his mouth, cutting his tongue, gums, and finally his uvula. The liquid continued pouring in until the jar was empty. Blue streams slid down his face. Cory shoved Spunky's mouth shut, forcing the liquid and razor blades to float around behind closed teeth. Spunky coughed as some of it slid down his throat, sending a mixture of blue and red spray out of his nostrils. He muffled a scream, left with no choice but to swallow. His eyes went wide as the blades forced their way down his throat and into his digestive tract.

One blade went down sideways, pressing against the skin surrounding his Adam's apple as it dug its way deeper into his body. He continued to scream, and Cory just sat on top of him and smiled. When there was nothing left to swallow, Cory climbed off. Spunky's hands immediately shot to his throat, digging at the surface. He couldn't breathe. While some of the blades made it all the way down, others were stuck in his airways, cutting into his throat. He coughed, trying to jar them loose, but all that did was send another unbearable scraping sensation through his lungs. He ripped and clawed at his throat, knowing full well it wouldn't do any good, but he didn't care. If he could tear his own skin off to get to the blades, he would.

Cory grabbed the scissor handles and yanked them from Spunky's chest. Blood squirted out, soaking his barber shirt that he'd worn every day for the past forty years. His wife had bought it for him as a birthday gift when he first opened the shop. As he thought about his wife and how he hoped he'd be able to see her soon, his thoughts went to dark places, back to what the demon said about her.

He wept. It was as if the crying hurt Cory's ears because he bent over and drove the scissors into Spunky's chest. Again and again. The piercing jolts of pain shot through him every time the tips penetrated his flesh, but his body slowly numbed, no longer able to produce the undeniable pain. As Spunky faded, he realized the stabbing was concentrated on one single area.

His heart.

CHAPTER 23

Bethany sat in the corner of the Carver living room, hugging her knees. Her dad was on the porch yelling at a police officer, telling him their lives were in danger and that they needed to do something about it. Briana sat next to their mother, clinging to her stuffed dragon. After Bethany found the family cat gutted, she ran from her house screaming for help, knocking on Mr. Gould's door so hard her knuckles cracked. He called the police and then her parents, who both raced home from work.

"It's okay, hon," her mom said, rubbing Briana's back. And while she may have been rubbing Briana's back, her eyes remained locked on Bethany. And those eyes said everything. She was terrified.

Jeffrey Carver stormed in through the front door and slammed it shut behind him.

"I can't believe this bullshit! After everything I've done for this town... Sorry. I'm sorry. I know you're all scared right now. Listen to me, I won't let anything happen to you guys."

Bethany wanted to believe him. But between Belle being ripped apart and the message they left, she was having a hard time thinking her dad could do anything to stop the coven.

"Daddy. They want me to meet them tonight. I'm scared."

"Bethany, you're not going to the damn cemetery. I just talked to Officer Ellis outside. He's going to keep watch out front all night and send officers to the cemetery to track these assholes down. No way in hell I'm letting you out of my sight. Got it?"

Bethany hesitated, but she nodded, realizing it was a better bet than her going out there by herself. *But they said they would kill you guys if I didn't go.* Then she thought of Chief Miller and how he was part of the coven. What if she couldn't trust Officer Ellis? Was he in on this, too?

"But Dad, we don't know who we can trust. I—"

"Trust me. This guy is new to town, he has nothing to do with them. I've done my damn part in all of this. I've kept quiet like they asked. This wasn't supposed to happen. It's those fucking kids you hang around sticking their nose in places they don't belong. We stay here. We keep protection out front. And I don't want you talking with those boys anymore, do you understand?"

Bethany couldn't respond, the words caught in her throat. How could her dad blame her friends? It was the past generation that caused all of this. Howie and Cory just tried to stop it from killing everyone.

"I said, do you understand, Bethany Mae Carver?" His tone was not going to give her the chance to argue right now.

"Yes."

"Jeff, did you tell Ellis about the coven? Does he know what he's going up against?" Bethany's mom asked.

Bethany's dad hesitated, his eyes flitting to the left, "I told him all he needs to know to help us right now. I'm not about to get us all killed by blabbing about things we aren't supposed to."

"To hell with these secrets! They threatened our daughter. I think any courtesy they expect is gone at this point. I'm going to tell him, right now," Bethany's mom snapped.

"No! Sit the fuck down. We stay here. We stay safe."

The room filled with a thick sense of dread, the silence only adding to it. Bethany couldn't stand it anymore. She got up and pushed past him, running up the stairs to her room. On the way past Briana's room, she couldn't help but glance in, spotting the bloodstain on the carpet. As much as she wanted to believe her dad was making the best decision, she couldn't shake the feeling that they were making the *wrong* one. She shut her door and went to the window, peering out at the side of the road. A police cruiser sat parked along the sidewalk, a cloud of smoke floating out of its exhaust pipe. Was there really going to be a cop out there all hours of the night? It did make her feel a little safer, but not enough to let her guard down.

She wondered what Howie was doing and if he'd been in contact with Cory since the bowling alley. It was killing her not to talk with them. The only silver lining in the horrible day's events was that her dad finally stopped trying to get her to talk with the reporters. It appeared all it took for him to realize the seriousness of the situation was a literal death threat to her and the family.

Bethany left the window and went to her bed. She curled up in her blanket and closed her eyes, trying to forget about all the horrible things. But all she saw in the darkness of her mind was her dead cat, swinging back and forth from the ceiling.

Officer Ellis glanced at his watch and sighed. The night was bound to be a long one, sitting out front of the Carver home. Of course, as the new guy on the force he should have expected the grunt work. He'd rather be out searching for the sick fucks who did this to the poor family cat, but Jeffrey Carver insisted he be the one to stay. He watched the older daughter stare out the window at him, and he couldn't imagine what was going through the girl's head. She stated she had come home to find the animal as well as the note threatening the entire family. Ellis couldn't help but feel he wasn't getting the entire story from the dad. The letter was pretty vague, but it was written as if it wasn't the first threat. Carver insisted it was the only letter and they weren't sure who the threats were coming from. He even said it could just be a prank, but Ellis thought that was a bit far-fetched. People don't break into homes and leave a note like that for a damn prank.

Ellis turned on the radio and popped it over to Rock 101. If he was going to be sitting here for hours, he wanted to listen to music that would wake his ass up. "Bawitdaba" by Kid Rock had just kicked off and Ellis couldn't help but smile. The song was dumb as hell, but it was catchy, he had to give it that. He finger-drummed on the steering wheel to the music while continuing to scan the area for any sign of intruders. And then he saw a teenage boy riding his bike toward the Carver house. He considered stopping the boy and telling him to go home, that now wasn't a good time. But he wasn't here to stop a kid from visiting the family, he was here to make sure the threat didn't return. He continued listening to the music as the boy walked up the front porch and knocked.

Bethany heard a knock at the front door, followed by her parents whispering in sharp tones. She figured it was the cop checking on them. She poked her head out her door and listened.

"Troy? How you doing, buddy?" her dad asked.

"Good. It's great to see you, Mr. Carver. I hope I'm not intruding on anything."

"No, no. Come on in."

What the hell, Dad? Is now the time to play catch-up with my ex-boyfriend?

The front door shut, and Bethany didn't want to be caught snooping, so she popped back into her room and tried to listen from there. Why would Troy come over randomly? They broke up months ago and rarely talked anymore.

"Yeah, she's upstairs in her room if you wanna go chat. Again, good to see you, buddy," her dad said.

She missed what Troy said before that. But as his footsteps came up the stairs, she heard her mom saying it was stupid to let anyone in the house right now, and her dad arguing back that it was better to make things appear normal.

Troy knocked on her door softly, then poked his head in.

"Hey. Sorry to come over unannounced, mind if I come in?"

"Hey. Sure. What's up?"

Troy stepped into the room, looking around at the familiar space they'd spent so much time in while dating. Bethany felt uncomfortable, remembering the last time they were in here they were making out on her bed.

"What's up with the cop parked out front? Everything okay?"

"Yeah, my parents are overprotective. They're just nervous after everything that's happened lately," Bethany lied. She hoped he bought it.

"I hear that. Can't be too safe. I just wanted to see how you were doing after the bowling alley. That was pretty fucked, huh?"

"Yeah. I'm doing okay, though. How about you?"

He shrugged his shoulders. "I'll be fine. I know I play up this big tough guy image for sports, but that stuff really gets to me. I was up on the stage at homecoming when she attacked. It could have easily been me who was ripped apart. And then to see another death so soon . . ."

"We all could use a break from this crap," Bethany said.

"I know it. Hey, the other thing I wanted to apologize for was how Ameilia was acting the other night. She can get pretty jealous. Especially when it's someone I dated."

"Ha! She's . . . I won't say anything. Just that you can do better. I'm fine. It's not like you and I just broke up, it was months ago. But thanks for coming by to check on me. My parents love you, if you couldn't tell," she said with a smirk.

"Big Jeff Carver! I miss your family. I'm sorry for everything," he said, though she thought he was being a bit overdramatic. They had a clean breakup, there was nothing to apologize for.

"I should get back to cleaning, though. I promised my parents I'd clean my room a bit more since I'm stuck at home."

"No worries. It was good seeing you," he said as he started to exit the room. He turned back. "Hey, what was up with Cory? He was acting really strange. He okay?"

The question caught her off guard. She wasn't sure how to answer, so she went with the default answer she'd been giving everyone.

"Yeah, he's just taking all this really hard. Between the school, his grandfather, and the injuries he had, it's been tough on him."

"Have you seen him at all? Word is he's been missing ever since the bowling alley. My dad said the cops are looking for him."

Bethany tensed up. Were the cops really after him? What did they know?

"I haven't talked with him since, but I hope he's okay."

"Yeah, hope so. Anyway, have a good night."

With that, she watched Troy go downstairs and say goodbye to her parents, then she shut her door and took a deep breath. She really hoped Cory was okay.

Ellis watched the kid exit the house, staring directly at his cruiser and waving. He gave a wave back and kept his eyes locked on the kid as he got back on his bike and took off toward town.

A knock on his window startled him.

He turned to see Chief Mullin standing there and rolled it down.

"Jesus, Chief. You trying to scare the shit out of me?"

"Kid, if a tap on the window scares you, what good will you be if trouble actually shows up at their doorstep?"

There he goes again, calling me kid. I'd love to smack his smug grin right off his face.

"Why are you here, Chief? Thought you were out looking for the culprits."

"Change of plans, Ellis. I'll relieve you of your duties here. Why don't you go back out on patrol and leave this to me?"

Confused, Ellis didn't respond right away. Ellis was the responding officer, which was why he now sat out here. But the chief apparently had a different plan in mind.

"I mean, I don't mind keeping an eye on the family, Chief. Mr. Carver seemed pretty set on me staying here. He said whoever this gang of thugs was that did this to them was dangerous and he didn't know who to trust."

Strangely, Mullin looked relieved at that statement.

"Well, he can trust me. I'm the chief, for Christ's sake. Just follow orders, Ellis. I'll let them know I'm out here."

"Shouldn't I go provide backup at the cemetery?"

"I got men on it. But I'm light on patrol because of it. So go downtown and hand out some speeding tickets by McDonald's. The kids are always driving like morons down there doing that damn McDonald's 500."

"Okay. Let me know if you need me," Ellis said.

"Will do. Thanks for responding to them so quickly, Ellis. You might just be a good cop yet."

Yeah, I'm a good cop, all right. Enough to know you're full of shit and something's up.

He put his cruiser into drive and drove off, watching his new chief in the rearview as he went. Why the hell wasn't the chief's car parked behind him? It was as if Mullin appeared out of thin air, sneaking out of the woods or something.

Ellis would follow orders, but he wasn't happy about it. His new chief was either really bad at his job, or he was hiding something. And Ellis was determined to get to the bottom of it.

CHAPTER 24

Howie exhaled and walked in the front door of his house. He hoped his dad's newfound "softer" side was still in effect because he was late for dinner, which was one of the big no-nos in the Burke household. Being late for dinner was up there with murdering a baby and fornicating with your sibling to Bill Burke. Howie never understood why his dad was so strict about the dinner rule when they typically spent most of the time eating in complete silence unless his dad decided to insult his mom's cooking.

When he walked in, the living room was empty. He could smell the Shake 'n Bake chicken in the oven, which either meant dinner was starting late or his parents had already eaten, and he was smelling the leftovers. For a second, he thought maybe his parents weren't even home, which didn't make any sense considering their vehicles were parked in the garage. And it's not like they went for a walk—Howie's dad had said on many occasions that the only time he'd walk was to get from point A to point B. He didn't understand the concept of cardio for recreation.

"Mom? Dad?"

Howie continued walking through the house, listening for his parents. He hoped he would run into his mom first to get an idea of what state of mind his dad was in before confronting him. He knew he had to sit his parents down and tell them everything. About visiting the priest, about what was happening to Cory, and most of all, about Henry Black. What would his dad do when he found out? He had been friends with Henry.

As he approached the hallway toward his parent's bedroom, he heard a sniffling cry coming from behind their door. Hesitantly, he walked to it and pressed his ear to the exterior. His mom was crying in bed. If his dad hit her, Howie wasn't so sure he could forgive him. It was one thing to put his hands on his son, but he had *never* touched Howie's mom. All that goodwill his dad had earned the past week could've all been for nothing.

"Mom?" Howie whispered.

She stopped sniffling.

"Howie? Come in."

He pushed open the door, prepared for anything. He *thought* he was prepared for anything. What he saw was more confusing than anything he'd seen in the last few weeks, and that was saying a lot.

His mom was crying in bed, as expected, but she wasn't alone. His dad was next to her, curled in almost a fetal position and facing the opposite wall.

"What's happening? Is everything okay?" Howie asked.

"Come sit with us, Howie," she said.

In a house where nobody showed one iota of feelings other than anger, this was foreign territory for Howie. He knew he should sit on the edge of the bed, but the whole situation was making things extremely awkward. He pushed through the unease and sat at the foot of the bed. His dad didn't move, as if he had passed out asleep and nothing could wake him from his slumber. But his eyes were open, staring blankly at the wall.

"Cory called the house, Howie. Your dad answered."

Howie felt his insides twist into a pretzel. For Cory to do or say anything that made his dad act like this... it couldn't have been good.

"Did something happen? Is he okay?" Howie asked.

"He... No, he's not. He threatened our family. You need to stay away from him starting right now. We don't want you going out of our sight anymore, okay?"

Tears burned the corner of Howie's eyes. He had to tell them everything and hope they changed their mind. Still, his dad reacting this way wasn't like him, even if he *had* been threatened by Cory. If anything, it would piss his dad off and he'd take it out on Howie for being friends with Cory. He was nervous to bring his dad into the conversation, but the concern of helping Cory outweighed the stressfulness of giving his dad a chance to lash out.

"Dad? Are you okay?"

His mom tried to smile but it was forced. She rubbed her husband's back and then spoke for him.

"When Cory called, he tried to warn your father. But then he switched, his voice sounded awful, not human. And he brought up the past. The things this demon did to..." she trailed off, but Howie knew exactly what she was talking about. This might be the only chance for him to bring up what Father Grimes told him.

"I left to see Cory like you said this morning, but when I got there it was just his mom. She was really worried about Cory. He hadn't been home in a few days, and she wanted help finding him. Then we started talking about getting him help if we found him. She was trying to go to Father Grimes about what was happening, but I told her I didn't think it was safe for her to go. So I went there and told Father Grimes everything.

About Jessica's grave, what happened on top of the ski jump, and how Cory was acting. He told me they can't do an exorcism, but he said he knew of a way to help. A way Cory might have a chance at getting saved before the coven gets to him, or before Cory gets to others in town."

Talking about Jessica and the coven like it was just part of the daily routine felt so odd. Howie had gone his entire life without mentioning the deaths and the Black Heart Killer in anything more than a passing comment to his parents. And it usually ended with a date with his dad's belt. His dad didn't want to hear anything to do with it under his roof. Now Howie knew why. But it was also his only chance to save his best friend.

"You went to the church? What did he say?" his mom asked.

Still sitting on the edge of the bed, Howie let his eyes wander around his parents' bedroom. He wanted to tell them everything, but he needed to make sure he chose his words carefully.

"He said doing an exorcism would take too long to get approved, and that the coven would track Cory down before it happened. He told me Henry Black could help."

Howie's dad shifted ever so slightly in the bed, but he kept his eyes locked on the wall. What did Cory say to make him act this disconnected from the world? Howie shivered at the thought of it.

"What? Howie... Henry Black died years ago. What are you saying?" his mom asked.

"Henry Black is still alive. And he's been in hiding since faking his death. To stay safe from the coven."

His mom furrowed her brow, obviously confused. But his dad sat up and stared at Howie like someone had just poured salt into an open wound.

"What the fuck did you just say? This isn't funny, boy. What do you mean he's *alive*?" He got out of bed, grabbed Howie by the collar and shoved him against the wall. Howie flinched, ready for the forthcoming blow, and his dad didn't let him down. He slapped Howie across the face, the sting of his callused hands bringing more tears to Howie.

"Bill! *Stop* it," Howie's mom spat.

Howie felt his collar, which had been pulled tight, loosen at his mom's demand. He'd never heard her raise her voice like that to his dad—she would've never dared before.

"Yeah... I know. Sorry. Fuck! Tell me everything, boy. What happened? What did Grimes say?"

Howie cleared his throat, rubbed his cheek, and adjusted his shirt.

"He said back when Henry Black supposedly died, he had snuck him something to make him appear dead. And that once he was out of prison and back at the funeral home, he helped Henry escape. We need to go see him, Dad. Please. He's the only one who could save Cory."

His dad was breathing heavy, and Howie couldn't tell if it was because he was still mad at him, or if he was having some form of a panic attack after being blindsided about one of his close friends being alive after years of assuming he was long dead.

"Why would they go through all that? He was safe in prison from those evil fucks," his dad finally managed to get out.

"I don't know. I didn't ask that. I'm sorry. When Father Grimes told me, I didn't know if he was telling the truth. But his story made sense. I'm not sure where he is yet, though. I told him I didn't want to go there without you, because I knew you were friends with him."

His dad closed his eyes, and Howie saw a single tear force its way down his bearded face.

"Thank you. I'll go talk with Grimes. But Howie, it's too late for Cory. I heard it in his voice. It was the same fucking way Jessica sounded before she... Fuck! I'm sorry, kid. We can't save your friend. But we can take that goddamn thing down once and for all."

"No... *Please*, Dad. We have to try and save Cory. I promised him."

"I don't give a shit what you promised, Howie. That's not your friend anymore. All that is, is a danger to all of us and a fucking disease. It ruined my life once before and I'm not going to let it happen again."

"But Dad..."

"Shut the fuck up."

"What are you going to do to him?" Howie asked.

"First thing I'm going to do is talk with Grimes and demand he take me to Henry. Then I'll deal with that evil little shit."

"Bill. It's too late to go out there tonight. Let's sleep it off and make sure we don't make any stupid decisions, k?" Howie's mom reasoned.

"The longer we wait, the more powerful that thing gets. We don't have much time. And if we want to keep this fucking coven off our back, we need to take care of this before it's too late."

"Why didn't you leave? After the murders. I don't get why the entire town just listened to the coven all these years and didn't do something about it or get as far away as possible," Howie said. He was trying to rationalize it in his head, but all he could think about was Cory and what was going to happen to him. They had been through everything together. And he partly blamed himself for Cory getting possessed. If Howie hadn't made them keep the gravesite a secret when they discovered it, there was a good chance none of this would have ever happened. All so he wouldn't get in trouble.

He knew he couldn't debate with his dad anymore, but that didn't mean he was going to give up.

"We couldn't leave. We're all tied to this curse. Whether we were part of their cult or not. Those selfish assholes made a deal that put us all in danger. With Jessica buried, that deal had been satisfied, but the curse was here to stay. And then she was let loose, creating a massive clusterfuck," his dad said while glaring at Howie. "And it *is* a damn curse. The longer anyone remains away from town, the worse things get for them. Some get sick. Some die. Hell, some just have awful luck until their life completely crumbles. Many have tried to leave, and they always end up coming back. At the town meeting when they told us, Officer Miller called it 'karmic retribution.' The bottom line is, we're all stuck here."

Howie couldn't believe what he was hearing. An invisible cinder block pressed against his chest as he felt the onset of a panic attack coming. He ran to the master bathroom and threw up into the toilet. He clung to the porcelain, forcing up more vomit. How could they hide this from him all these years? He thought back to any time he left town for sporting events or went to the movies in Claremont. Even going to Boston with his dad for his job. What he had always assumed was motion sickness on the car rides or anxiety for big games, it all came crashing down on him at once. Not only did they hide it from him, but they also let him do all these things and feel sick to his stomach while doing them. *All* the parents did.

A gentle hand rubbed his back as he hunched over the toilet. He shot up and whirled around to face his mom, wiping the vomit from his chin.

"How could you do this to me? Lie to me my entire life. What about when I go to college? Move away? Were you planning to just lock me in a room my entire life?" His vision blurred with a mix of tears and rage.

"Howie... I'm so sorry. We wanted to tell you. We weren't allowed to. Not until you graduated. That's the pact in place, and if we break it, this whole town will unravel. Don't you get that?"

Howie's thoughts swirled around. It didn't make any sense. How the hell could an entire town keep this a secret for so long without someone slipping? Without someone leaving and saying fuck the stupid curse?

"This... This makes no sense. If nobody could leave, we would have way more people in this town than we do. This whole idea is crazy," he said, but he knew there was more to it.

"Yeah. Well, that's the worst part of it. It doesn't affect everyone in town. It only applies to the families that have ties to the coven. If someone new came to town? They could leave whenever they wanted. If it was someone who never had anything to do with them, the same. It's a set group of us that are stuck here," his mom said. She was crying with him now.

With everything being dropped on him like an atomic bomb, it took Howie a moment to realize what his mom's last sentence really meant.

"How... How are we linked to the coven?"

His mom just stared at him with glossed eyes, unable to speak, but his dad finally spoke up, "Your great-grandmother. My gram. She was a founding member of that fucking cancer. She used to torture my dad. Most of them are sadistic assholes. I can barely do my damn day job, driving to Boston and back, without feeling sick to my stomach. But I still do it because I won't let them set the boundaries of what I can and cannot do. And besides, I'd never want to work for any of those bastards in town not knowing who's involved."

His dad's statements were all over the place, but the more he said, the more Howie realized how hard a life his dad had experienced. Stuck in

Newport. Abused by his dad. Losing the woman and unborn child he loved so much. All because of the coven. And then to be forced to hold that secret for so long.

Howie walked numbly past his mom and sat on the bed. Was he really trapped here his entire life? He thought back to all those who graduated ahead of him. Not of the obvious choices who wouldn't leave their comfort zone if they were paid a king's ransom to do so, but of the kids who seemed destined to go on to bigger and better things. Things Howie and his friends dreamed of their entire childhood. This meant they could never truly go make movies in Hollywood someday. As far-fetched as that sounded, there was always a certain level of hope. And that was now pulled out from under him.

"So what's next? Is there any chance of us getting rid of this curse forever?" Howie asked, knowing the answer.

"What's next is, we go talk with Grimes. Get to the bottom of Henry's situation. Then, I'm sorry, Howie, but you need to stay out of it after that. I can't let you get in your own way to try and save something that isn't worth saving. What matters most is us. You have to accept that there's nothing we can do for Cory. Do you understand me, boy?"

Howie dug his nails into his palms, furious on the inside. But he would tell his dad what he wanted to hear.

"Yeah, Dad. But I want to go with you to see Father Grimes tomorrow. I think I've earned that after what I've dealt with the past few weeks."

"Okay, fine. First thing tomorrow morning, we will go see him and end this shit before it's too late."

Howie got up and walked out of his parents' bedroom, forcing himself to wait until he got to his own room before he let himself unravel.

He shut his door and screamed into his pillow, crying uncontrollably. No matter what, he couldn't bring himself to let the thought go that he needed to do whatever he could for Cory.

CHAPTER 25

The clock ticked away, minute by minute, as Bethany tried to fall asleep. Before Troy showed up, she found herself continuously getting out of bed to check the window and make sure the police cruiser was still parked there, but also to make sure some hooded figure *wasn't* there. After he left, the house settled down, but she was still on edge.

Every sound in the house startled her. Her dad carried Briana to her room after she passed out on their bed. Even though he had ripped out the carpet where the blood had soaked through, the empty square with the *slightly* stained plywood was almost worse. Like they were trying to erase what happened to poor Belle.

As desperate as she was to fall asleep, every time Bethany closed her eyes, she saw flashes of the shadow swaying back and forth in her sister's room. The threat she had read in her diary traveled across the blank space behind closed eyelids like a teleprompter.

Meet us tonight at the cemetery, behind the shed. Come alone. If you don't, we will kill your entire family.

She couldn't sleep. It was pointless. Bethany got out of bed again and went to the window. One last look to make sure things were okay, then she would force herself to sleep. She pulled back the curtain... and the police cruiser was gone. Just an empty road with no sign of protection. And then she saw it. Movement in the tree line.

It has to be the trees moving with the wind. It's in your head again.

Only this time, she couldn't blink them away. They were really there. Not just one figure, but multiple figures, all exiting the woods in black robes.

Bethany ran from her room, almost tripping over her dirty clothes on the way out. She darted down the hallway toward her parents' room. Why didn't they listen to her? Why did they feel it was safe enough to just stay at home and think that a cop out front would protect them?

She barged through their door, feeling her heartbeat thrum through her ears.

"Mom! Dad! They're coming! Wake up!"

Her dad rolled over, groggy from a deep sleep (must be nice) and checked his alarm clock.

"Honey, what? What's wrong?"

"The coven, they're here! We need to go—*now!*"

He jumped out of bed, startling his wife awake.

"Oh God, what is it?" her mom asked.

"The cop. Ellis, he'll see them and help. We just—" Bethany's dad started to say, but she didn't let him finish.

"No, he's gone. The car isn't there anymore."

"Honey, go get Briana. We need to get these kids somewhere safe," Jeffrey Carver instructed.

His wife did so without hesitation, running out of the bedroom.

"Dad, I'm scared."

"We won't let anything happen—"

The front door jiggled violently, but the lock held firm. But then the lock clicked, and the door opened slowly. The intruders had picked the lock or found their spare key on the porch. Jeffrey ran to the window in the master bedroom, looking out to the driveway.

"Go to the attic. *Now!*" He grabbed the baseball bat from under the bed and pushed her toward the door.

Bethany went into the hallway, ready to make a run for the drop-down door in the ceiling leading to the attic. Her ears rang with nerves, but not enough to stop her from hearing footsteps downstairs, scuffling along the tile floor. Briana came out of her room with their mom, her eyes wide with shock. She hugged her stuffed dragon tight, a security blanket that offered no real protection.

Their mom lifted her finger to her lips, reminding them to be quiet. Even if they *could* make it to the attic door, there was no possible way to let the ladder down without making a ton of noise. The metal groaned every time the ladder was extended to full length. One time when Bethany was younger, she'd tried sneaking up to the attic to get an early glimpse of her Christmas presents, hoping she would spot the Barbie Dreamhouse she wanted so badly. Her parents had been sleeping and she thought she would be able to open the door without them realizing. Her ignorant youth got the better of her and as soon as she had the ladder down to climb, her parents walked out of their room and caught her in the act.

She wasn't about to make that same mistake. Her mother walked ahead of her, taking the lead. They could still hear multiple people walking through the house beneath them, whispering something to one another. Not knowing what they were saying somehow made it even worse for Bethany. With the cop gone, it was clear they were in on it, and this was all planned.

Her mother also knew the attic was a lost cause, so she directed her daughters into Bethany's room, silently shutting the door behind them.

"Girls… you have to remain quiet, no matter what. Bethany, get under your bed. Briana, come with me," she whispered.

Bethany did as she was told, crouching low and shimmying beneath her bed. She grabbed the pile of her clothes and blocked herself from view, hoping the mound of dirty shirts and pants would hide her if anyone looked.

Her mother and sister went to the closet and shut themselves in. Not being able to see them twisted Bethany's insides. She was alone, with nothing but a pile of clothes to protect her. She held her breath and listened. With the bedroom door shut, it was difficult to hear, but she could still make out the faint movements somewhere in the house. On any other night, she would have convinced herself it was just the pipes forcing hot water through to heat the home.

She knew their hiding spots felt very cliché, like something out of a bad horror movie. But where else were they supposed to go? It wasn't like they could climb out a window and cling to the side of the house like Spider-Man or try to run by the intruders and out into the streets. Maybe if it was one hooded figure—not three or four like she saw exiting the woods—as a family, they might attempt to restrain the intruder until help arrived. As sad as their hiding spots were, they were the best option.

The stairs creaked.

Someone was coming.

Bethany's entire body trembled, making it much tougher to remain still. She took a deep breath, then let it out. Over and over until she thought the coven members were within hearing distance.

What about Dad?

Lost in all the commotion, she'd forgotten all about him deeper in the house somewhere with only a baseball bat to defend himself. And then she heard the all-too-familiar groan of the top step leading to the hallway, right outside Briana's door.

Briana sniffled from the closet. Bethany could only imagine what was going through the poor girl's head. Or her mother's, for that matter. Trying to control the fear of a kid not much older than a toddler had to be impossible.

Bethany covered her face with a dirty sweater, leaving just enough space to peek through.

The footsteps got closer.

The sniffling from the closet stopped, and Bethany imagined her mom was squeezing her hand over Briana's mouth, begging her to stop making noise.

The doorknob turned, followed by the door being pushed in slowly.

Without shifting her position, Bethany moved her eyes enough to see a set of black boots enter her room, taking one slow step at a time. Once the first person was far enough into the room, a second followed close behind. This figure wore a pair of Nike shoes, like they were just casually going out for a jog and decided it was a good time to break into someone's home.

It was nearly impossible for Bethany to stop herself from trembling. She bit her bottom lip, hoping, praying that something came to distract these killers. That's what they were, she had no doubt about it. They were here to kill, just like they had promised.

"Check the closet," a man whispered.

Mom. Briana. Please, no.

As the first hooded figure approached the closet, something shattered deeper in the house, near her parents' bedroom.

Dad.

"Shit, go see what that was. We can't let them escape. You know what we have to do."

Nike Man exited the room, leaving just one intruder in the bedroom with them. Could she crawl out and take him by surprise? It was too much of a risk. She knew there were at least three of them in the house, and she was pretty sure she saw a fourth before she ran to tell her parents they were coming.

Everything that came next happened so fast. A struggle in the hallway. Something cracking, like a tree snapping. *Dad's bat?* The wall vibrated as something in the hall slammed against the other side, sending a picture to Bethany's floor. Glass shattered from the frame—a picture of her and her friends at Lake Sunapee, sunbathing on the beach. The remaining intruder ran to the hall to see what was causing the commotion. There was choking. Someone was choking or being choked.

"She should've listened, Jeff. This didn't have to happen," a voice said.

"Leave...us alone," her dad said, forcing it out.

And then the sound of a knife slicing into fabric, followed by a gurgling cry. A body dropped to the hallway floor.

Bethany held her hand over her mouth, fighting back cries.

"Where are they hiding, Jeff? The harder you make this, the more you suffer."

Instead of responding with words, her dad groaned. It sounded like he was on the floor on the other side of the wall from where Bethany was lying. She wanted to reach out for him, tear through the Sheetrock and pull him to safety. Instead, she listened as someone stabbed him repeatedly, metal entering flesh, as her dad slowly dragged himself across the floor.

Eventually, the crawling stopped. Her dad no longer laboring through pained breaths. Bethany buried her face into the dirty sweater and cried, soaking the wool fabric. She didn't get long to mourn, as the intruders came back to the doorway.

CHAPTER 26

"Go check the master bedroom where he came from; they might still be in there," the man with black boots said.

Bethany swallowed, a dry gulp of terror burning its way down her throat. There were only so many places for them to search; it was only a matter of time before the rest of them were discovered.

The man walked to the center of the room, and each thud of his combat boot brought another shot of dread to Bethany.

What is he doing? Why is he standing in the same spot for so long? He's listening.

His boots were pointed toward the closet. She thought he must be watching the door, waiting. But then more of his legs lowered into view as he slowly dropped to the floor and rested on his knees. Bethany squeezed her eyes shut, as if erasing him from her view would somehow erase *her* from his. She risked a peek, opening her eyes.

She stifled a scream. The man was now in an army crawl position, staring right under the bed. Bethany couldn't see his eyes but thought that he must not be able to see her, or he would already be grabbing for her. The room was dark. Beneath the bed was even darker, and the pile of clothes appeared to be doing its job, for now. With the black hood hiding his face, he was a Ghostface mask away from looking like he was straight out of *Scream*.

And then he moved toward her bed, reaching out for the pile of clothes. A cry from the closet took his focus away from Bethany's position. *Briana, no*!

He jumped to his feet and stormed to the closet, ripping the door open. Bethany's mom screamed, but it was more of a war cry as she lunged out of the closet and slammed into the intruder. His knife dropped from his hand, bouncing off the floor close to Bethany's head. It was close enough that she noticed the crimson slathering the shiny metal. Her dad's blood.

Her mom and the intruder fell to the floor, rolling around as they fought for leverage. The man punched Bethany's mom in the face, the force behind it so powerful she fell to the side, her head smacking off the floor.

"You stupid bitch," he muttered as he got to his feet. Bethany's mom attempted to crawl away, but the blow to the head made her disoriented. She mumbled incoherently, and Bethany thought she heard something about not hurting her kids. The man grabbed her by the hair and yanked her to her feet, obscuring Bethany's view so she could only see their legs again.

Briana whimpered from the closet. The man dropped Bethany's mom to the floor, then kicked her square in the nose. The sound of a steel toe connecting with cartilage was sickening. Her mom lay motionless on the floor, either unconscious or dead. But now the man was approaching the closet once more.

"It's okay, sweetheart. I don't want to hurt you. Why don't you come on out of there?"

Bethany wanted to help, but she found herself frozen in fear, watching everything unfold. She couldn't see her sister, only the back of the man's legs as he got closer to the closet. Briana cried louder, and then the man had her, pulling her out of the closet by the arm as she screeched for help.

I have to help her. She's going to die.

But you can't get out. There's too many of them. Plus, they won't hurt a kid, will they?

She wanted to believe that. But they had shown no indication that they gave two shits whether it was a man, woman, or a child that they hurt. They cared about one thing: getting Bethany. She had to give herself up. To save her sister. And hopefully her mom. She focused on her mom, who still lay motionless, although Bethany thought she saw her mother's chest rising and falling, but it was too dark to know for sure.

Briana's scream snapped Bethany's attention back to the struggle. Briana stomped on the man's foot, but he laughed at her.

"Steel toe, you brat."

Then her sister's feet were elevating, and she was gasping for breath. The man was lifting her by the throat. Bethany prepared to crawl out, to help, give herself up, whatever it took. Before she made it a few feet, something bounced off the floor near her face. Almost screamed, but she held it in. She was staring back at Smokey, the purple dragon, its large cartoonlike eyes locked on her judgingly. Her sister continued to fight for air, ripping and clawing at the intruder. Bethany couldn't see it, but she could hear it. She could hear *everything*.

"Let me go!" Briana yelled, followed by a clawed swipe at the man's face.

"Bitch!"

And then Bethany's worst fears became a reality. The same sound she heard from the hall when they attacked her dad, stabbing him over and over until he stopped moving, happened a few feet from the bed.

Blood splashed across the carpet, spraying the purple dragon and staining it red.

Briana's body dropped to the floor. The mound of clothes blocked her body, something Bethany was thankful for at the moment. Her little sister wasn't moving. Bethany lost control, crying so hard there was no way the man didn't hear her. But she didn't care anymore. Her sister meant everything to her. Briana looked up to Bethany. Saw her as her protector. Her hero. Bethany had promised her she wouldn't let anything happen to her. And all she did was hide beneath the bed while this evil bastard stabbed her.

The man just killed a little girl, and he didn't even seem to care. He was *laughing*. Bethany was numb, unable to move. She wanted to throw up, claw out her own eyes so she didn't have to see the horrific scene in her room. She wanted to curl into a ball and never move again.

Tears masked her vision so she couldn't see more than a few feet in front of her now. She wiped the tears away and looked out, but instead of seeing the man standing there, he was gone. It was just her mother, who was beginning to stir, and her sister's little feet remaining completely still. *She's dead. My little sister is dead.*

Something clamped around her ankle, sending a shot of pain through her leg. And then she was dragged out from under the foot of her bed. She attempted to grab hold of the floor, hoping to stop the intruder from pulling her all the way out. She dug her nails into the carpet, desperate for something to grab hold of, but there was nothing. Instead, she was yanked all the way out, then raised up by the neck.

"I thought I heard you under there," the man said with a hint of humor.

He flung her on the bed and walked around the side with his knife in hand. He was going to kill her right now. Stab her like he did her dad and let her bleed out all over her room. The man pinned her down, his hood hiding his face in the darkness. He brought the knife to her throat, poking the tip into her skin. Bethany winced, preparing for him to push until the blade sliced her jugular.

"You fucking kids. We had things taken care of. We had it good, and so did the town. Now we have to clean up your goddamn mess. That starts with you, little girl."

She slapped at his hands, trying to knock the knife from his grip. But he had it firmly in his grasp and was not going to let it go. When that didn't work, she clawed at his face, digging her nails into his cheek and swiping down. He loosened his grip and brought his hand to his face.

"You bitch!" he snarled, then slapped her across the face. His voice... she recognized his voice. She ripped the hood back...and stared at the man in confusion.

"Burt?"

The funeral home director, Burt Rollins, stared back at her with eyes full of hatred.

"Darling, if you only knew how badly I wanted to shove you three kids in one of my wooden boxes and bury you alive for the shitstorm you've created. Some things are better left undisturbed. You see, Brian White ran things a bit differently than I intend to. He was too skittish, stuck in his ways. The old bastard forced us to lay low far longer than many of us wanted to. The only silver lining to your boyfriend freeing that demon is that she took care of Brian for me. Now I'm in charge and you can expect things to be run a bit differently."

Bethany stared at him, speechless. She had talked with Burt countless times in her life, and he was always really nice to her. When she worked at Ames department store as a cashier the last few summers, he would regularly come in and buy stuff and chat it up with the workers. She never in a million years would have expected him to be involved with the coven.

"What's the matter, cat got your tongue? Oh, sorry... Too soon to bring up your cat. Don't act so surprised, kid. While there aren't many of us left, there's enough to finish the job Brian couldn't accomplish with his kinder, gentler approach. That old softie thought it would be enough if we buried her in the woods, carried around a talisman in the slim chance she escaped, and remained out of the public eye after we framed Henry for the murders."

"Why would you do this? My fam—" She couldn't continue, choking on any words that wanted to come out.

"We're all pawns to Vorathor, hon. It's nothing personal. But I wouldn't expect you to know that."

Bethany wanted to jump from the bed and gouge his eyes out. How could someone do something like this? And then to talk as if it was just a matter-of-fact situation, it somehow made it even worse. Part of her wanted to just curl up in the bed and cry until he did whatever he had to do to her. But she couldn't let her family die for nothing.

"You're pathetic."

"Ha. Pathetic is your dad trying to crawl for his life while his intestines dragged across your floor. *Pathetic,* is your mom trying to save your little sister only to get knocked the fuck out while I slit her tiny little throat.

What I am is far from pathetic. And what you are, is the answer to get this demon contained for good. But I'm done talking about it with you."

I'm the answer? What does he mean?

Without warning, Burt reached down and grabbed her by the hair, pulling her off the bed. Bethany cried out as his hands twisted her blonde locks and yanked.

"Let me go!"

She kicked frantically, connecting with his shin, momentarily breaking free. But she didn't make it more than a few feet before he punched her in the stomach, taking any last-ditch escape effort away. Bethany dropped to the floor, clutching her stomach. She struggled for breath, suffocating on the last bit of hope she had. Burt stalked toward her with his bottom teeth biting into his upper lip. His beard looked like a snake about to thrust out at her. But worst of all, the look in his eyes. He was no longer the nice old man who helped so many families get through tough times after losing a loved one. He was now the one creating the loss. And he loved every second of it.

Bethany backed up in a crab walk, reaching the far wall with nowhere else to go. This was it. The place she'd take her last breath. But if he was going to kill her, why hadn't he already? Maybe there was still a chance. As Burt inched closer, Bethany caught a flash of movement behind him. *Mom.* Bethany tried to keep her eyes on Burt to not give up her mother's position, while in her peripheral vision, her mom grabbed her state championship cheerleading trophy off the shelf.

Burt was too focused on getting his prize. He crouched in front of Bethany, the familiar smell of mothballs from the funeral home wafting between them. He smiled, but there was no happiness in those eyes. The smile stopped at the corner of his lips.

"Honey, this is what has to be done. Don't make it any more difficult than—"

Her mom cracked the trophy over the back of Burt's head. His eyes rolled up as the fake marble base connected with his temple. He dropped to the side, leaving only her mother remaining in her view. As happy as Bethany was to see her, the happiness vanished within seconds. Her mother was hurt. Badly. Bethany didn't see it while she hid under the bed, but somewhere in the scuffle, Burt stabbed her, and there was a large gash in her abdomen. Her skin was sickly pale, and every breath appeared labored.

"Mom..." Bethany whispered, once again crying.

"It's... it's okay, hon." She winced, then spotted Briana on the floor and lost any control she had left. She dropped to her knees, crawling to her youngest daughter's lifeless body.

"No... No! Briana! Please... My girl, my girl," she sobbed hysterically, clutching her baby. Snot bubbled from her nose onto her upper lip. She lost all self-control, a delusional mess on the brink of completely snapping. Bethany needed to do something, or they were going to die.

"We need to get out of here, Mom. I'm sorry..." she said softly.

Her mother shook her head, refusing to budge. She buried her face in Briana's chest and let the tears flow, oblivious to anything else around her. "No. I can't leave her. Go without me, Bethany. Get help. Maybe... maybe I can save her."

"You're bleeding. We need to get you to a doctor, Mom."

Bethany got to her feet, the pain in her stomach now an afterthought. Burt was beginning to stir on the floor. They needed to get to safety fast. She put her arm around her mother, attempting to guide her toward the door, but it was like trying to move a boulder with her bare hands.

And then the floor creaked in the hallway. Multiple sets of footsteps approached quickly. With all the commotion, she had completely forgotten there were more members of the coven in the house.

"You need to get out of here, honey. Save yourself and don't worry about me," her mother said.

"Mom, I can't leave you. You'll die."

Her mom was too weak to argue, but Bethany still had to tug on her to break her away from Briana. Her mom kept her eyes locked on her dead daughter as she got to her feet, making inhuman sounds as she was forced to distance herself. Bethany felt awful, but it had to be done. They made it to the door and into the hallway, where they came face-to-face with two coven members.

"Where do you think you're going, little girl?" a hooded, stocky-framed man asked. He had a gun aimed at them.

Bethany didn't even need to see his face to recognize who it was. Chief Mullin blocked the hallway leading to the stairs. Her mother stiffened at the sight of him. There was nowhere to go. Back in her room, Burt groaned, pulling himself to his feet.

"Please. Leave my daughter alone, she's just a kid," Bethany's mom cried.

"Which is why we want her, you dumb bitch. Vorathor will be very pleased. It's the least we can do considering your daughter's ignorant friends helped free Jessica. So why don't you stop fighting it and just make it easier on all of us tonight?"

"Our town trusts you. How can you do this to us?" Bethany's mother asked.

"Please. This shithole is a breeding ground for evil. I took over as chief to keep it in line, but that doesn't mean getting rid of it. It means controlling it and making sure nobody else knows what goes on here. There's no escaping it, only containing it. So I'll say it again. Just give up and give us your daughter so we don't have to gut you like your husband," Mullin spat.

The mention of her dad brought Bethany's eyes to the unmoving corpse of Jeffrey Carver. A trail of blood soaked the floor behind him, displaying his attempted exit that led right up to his final breath.

Behind them, Burt staggered toward the door, breathing heavily. He had to be concussed after the blow from the trophy.

"Nowhere to go, girls. What's it going to be? A bullet to the head for Momma Carver? Or a peaceful transfer of the girl?"

Bethany looked around, but in the narrow hall, she didn't see any possible way to get out of this. She had to give herself up. She kissed her mom on the cheek and whispered, "I love you. I have to do this."

She released her mother and walked toward Mullin.

"No! Bethany, what are you doing?" her mom shouted.

"She's being a good girl, that's what she's doing."

Bethany turned back to her mom, but Mullin grabbed her by the wrist and yanked her close with a smile on his face. Behind her mom, Bethany saw Burt exiting the bedroom, holding his head as he approached them. The knife gleamed in his hand as if trying to warn Bethany of what was about to happen next. Mullin held her tight and all she could do was watch.

"Mom! Look out!"

Mullin threw his hand over her mouth to stop the shouting as her mom turned a second too late. Burt drove the knife into her jugular and pulled back, a fountain of blood sprayed across the wall. Her mother dropped to her knees, face-planting at Burt's feet.

Bethany bit down on Mullin's fingers and he shouted angrily, loosening his grip. She turned and hammered her knee into him, hoping to connect with his groin but hitting his stomach. Still, it bought her time. She pushed him against the wall and ran around him. She had to get help, wherever that might be. Burt shouted for someone to grab her as she reached the stairs, ready to take them two at a time. But the third member of the coven, Nike Man, cut her off. She got a quick glimpse of his eyes before she saw his fist flying, and then came the pain for a fraction of a second before she blacked out.

CHAPTER 27

Howie's dad shook him awake. After a night full of sleepless hours with a few nightmare-fueled stretches, Howie found it hard to open his eyes. But then he remembered what they were doing. Today was the day Father Grimes would take them to see Henry Black. Howie's dad had his own agenda, but Howie fully intended to try and get the help Cory needed to free him from the demon and the coven. He still couldn't believe Henry was alive after all these years. How did he remain undetected? Where was he hiding out? And why the hell didn't he help when Jessica escaped?

The fact was, Henry was the only chance Cory had. Grimes made it abundantly clear that he would not and could not perform an exorcism. If Henry couldn't help extracting the demon, Cory would die with that thing inside him. And if the coven found Cory before they helped him— Howie couldn't allow his thoughts to go to those dark corners of his mind.

"Wake the fuck up, Howie. I swear you'd sleep through a nuclear bomb exploding. We need to get to the church before any of the religious quacks get in there to pray or whatever the hell they do."

Howie sat up and blinked away the morning grogginess. His dad left the room, satisfied to see Howie finally moving. It was killing Howie that he couldn't touch base with Cory to see how he was doing. He also wanted to reach out to Bethany and fill her in. There wasn't enough time to do the things that needed to be done. One thing Howie couldn't shake was how set his dad was on not being able to save Cory. Would he really do something to hurt Cory? Bill Burke was a very stubborn man, and once he stated an opinion on something, it was all but impossible to dislodge it from him.

Howie got dressed quickly and met his dad in the living room. His dad sat in his recliner and started lacing his work boots.

"Dad, what will you do when you see Henry?" It was a question that had been bugging Howie since Father Grimes revealed the truth. It was his dad's close friend, but also the man married to the witch who ruined his dad's life.

"Who knows? First thing I need to do is see it with my own eyes. None of this makes a lick of fucking sense to me. If it's true, it means he hid like a coward for years while the town was left to deal with the bullshit these coven assholes brought all of us. I need answers. And then, well shit…" he trailed off, scratching the scruff of his beard. He grabbed his truck keys and stood from his chair. "Let's go."

"Bill, please be careful," Howie's mom said from the kitchen where she was washing dishes. Howie noticed she'd been crying before she turned back to the sink. He wanted to go hug her. It couldn't be easy watching her husband and only child leave, knowing they were likely to confront a demon. But she would never question his dad's decisions, so as soon as he said they were going, she had no choice but to accept it.

Howie followed his dad out the door, ready to get help.

They pulled into the back parking lot of the church and Howie's dad killed the engine. He stared at the old brick building and shook his head.

"Of all things to get me to step foot in this place…"

Instead of going around to the front door, his dad approached the back door and knocked. A moment later, the door opened and Father Grimes nodded, motioning them inside.

"Thank you for coming, Mr. Burke. I'm sure what Howie has told you came as a bit of a shock."

"That's one way to put it. What the hell's going on, Father? I need answers."

"Right this way, let's head to my office and talk. Don't need anyone to come in and hear us conversing. I'm sure you have many questions, and I'll do my best to answer them."

They walked down a long hallway toward the front of the church, passing by many hanging pictures and crosses. A sign above the entryway to the main floor read "*May the Lord bless you and keep you; may the Lord make his face shine upon you and be gracious unto you; may the Lord lift up his countenance upon you, and give you peace.*" (Numbers 6:24-26) Howie wondered what it even meant.

Seeing his dad in a church was the equivalent of watching a grizzly bear walk down the Vegas strip.

Father Grimes led them into the office and shut the door, gesturing to the seats in front of his desk like he'd done with Howie the day before.

"Before you ask your questions, all I ask is that you let me explain the best I can how this all came to be. I told your son to fill you in on what I've already told him, but he also insisted I wait to go visit Henry until you were with him. You have a smart young man here," Grimes said, smiling at Howie. "So, here's the situation, Mr. Burke. Yes, Henry Black is alive.

And yes, he remains in hiding after all these years. I want to take Henry to Cory Stevens, as I feel he's the only one who could possibly help save the young man. First, we need to figure out where Cory is hiding. Henry is also the only shot we have at stopping the coven. But before we go see him and ask for assistance, I need you to understand a few things. Henry Black is not the same man you once knew. After years of having Jessica warping his mind—even after he'd buried her and went to prison—well, let's just say it left a lasting impact on him. He can still function, but he's had a few wires crossed and is a bit more of a loose cannon."

"What do you mean? Is he fucking crazy now?" Howie's dad asked.

"No. Not crazy. He just has a hard time differentiating his nightmares from reality. He's always looking over his shoulder, and rightfully so. He has...episodes. I've been able to keep him hidden from the coven all this time, but that doesn't mean I don't worry about them discovering what I've done. I vowed to never tell another soul outside of the Lord Himself, but these are desperate times, I'm afraid. We need to come together for the greater good of this town."

"How did you do it? Not just fake his death but keep him hidden. And we know Jessica was in his head, making him kill. Why would you help him escape prison knowing he could kill again? You just said she was still in his head while he was locked up."

Howie realized in that moment his dad was smarter than he'd ever given him credit for. Unanswered questions usually just upset his dad, so Howie always assumed it was because he lacked the proper education and that feeling stupid made him angry. But he was thinking of questions that never crossed Howie's mind. On the contrary, he also saw that trademark stubbornness showing its ugly face. It was black-and-white to Bill Burke: if Henry Black could kill again, he shouldn't have had the chance to live his life outside of a cell. This further backed his dad's intention of disposing of Cory, not helping him. Get rid of the threat instead of trying to help fix it.

"Yes, and that's where this all comes together. You see, Henry buried his wife alive, knowing the demon was trapped in her body. Knowing that as long as it was inside her, she would still be in his head as well. He sacrificed himself in a way, understanding that she would haunt him from the grave. But he did it, anyway. He did it because as long as the demon was trapped, it couldn't infest someone else and continue to kill. He did it because even though it made the coven stronger, it also kept them happy—which meant that while the town was still under the curse, they were at least safe. After he went to prison, the voice wouldn't stop inside his head. She tried to convince him to kill himself. And believe it or not, it was her threats and constant barrage of sinister thoughts that gave him an idea. I went to visit him regularly, tried to give him a sense of good versus evil and a reason to want to live. On my last visit, he told me he wanted to kill himself. Of course, I immediately jumped in and refused to hear him talk that way. He smiled at me and said that if he could die, stop breathing for even just a few minutes, he believed it would break the connection of Jessica having control over his thoughts."

"Jesus Christ. Like a broken link," Howie's dad said to himself.

Father Grimes looked to the statue of Jesus in his office and made the sign of the cross. Howie cringed at his dad's lack of respect. His dad didn't care that he was in a church. He spoke the way he spoke, plain and simple.

"Yes. A broken link. And it worked. On that last visit, we talked about his plan as discreetly as we could in a maximum-security prison. Sometimes it helps to be a man of the cloth, as they didn't pay much attention to me on my visits. I told him I'd get him what he needed, then see to it that he was brought home for a proper burial next to his wife's grave—even though her grave was empty. He took tetrodotoxin, a poison that gives the appearance of death. The guards assumed he killed himself because he tied a sheet around his neck to give the impression that he hanged himself. They just wanted to get rid of the body as soon as possible, so when they transported him to the funeral home here, the second part of our plan went into action. It all felt horribly wrong, but you must understand I knew the severity of our situation in Newport. There was no funeral, no open casket for loved ones to say their goodbyes. They skipped the embalming stage just to get his body in the ground. This town wanted to forget Henry Black, for they were led to believe he was the killer, all so the coven could bury the story."

"Help me try to understand this," Bill said. "All this shit, as crazy as it sounds, makes enough sense, I suppose. But why the hell did you go through all that just to hide him away like someone in witness protection for so long? I know the coven framed him as the Black Heart Killer, so they couldn't afford to see him free or alive. But I also know—or knew—Henry very well. He wouldn't have just lived in some bunker all this time without trying to take down those responsible for what happened to Jessica."

"Well, as I've said, Henry struggles to keep his focus these days. He still has stretches of genius, only to see it followed up by him going off the rails a bit. But before his mind slipped to its current state, he had done extensive research on the coven, as well as the demons they're involved with. This is why we must try to get through to him. Make him understand what's at stake. We can use what's left of his brain to put a stop to all of this. If we can stop the demons, we can stop the coven.

Because this curse, this awful, evil thing that keeps us trapped in this place, would be lifted if we can get rid of these demons."

Howie's dad sighed, then stood from his chair. "So what the fuck are we waiting for?"

CHAPTER 28

Bethany opened her eyes to a searing pain in her face, a swift reminder of being punched in the face. It took her a moment to realize she was tied up. Her hands had been wrapped in front of her tightly with duct tape, and as if that wasn't enough, they'd decided to also put a chain clamp around her ankle. The coven had killed her entire family. What could they possibly have planned for her? Bethany was a fighter, and although her spirit was crushed, she was thankful to still be alive. For however long that lasted. She needed to find a way out of this situation. She squinted through the black eye and invading light, taking in the scenery.

She found herself in a small room, not much bigger than her walk-in closet at home. A window high up out of her reach proved to be the culprit of the sunshine blasting in on her. The walls were made of stone, but the surface had been smoothed as if to make sure there was no way to climb up to the window. She tried to get to her feet, and that's when she felt the throbbing soreness spreading through her core. Burt had kicked her so hard that she'd heard her ribs crack. Now that the adrenaline had subsided, she was feeling the full effects of the beating.

The room reminded her of a place where a psychopath in a straitjacket would be held, not a teenage girl. Was there a place in town with rooms like this? She couldn't recall. Her throat was parched, her head hurt, and all she wanted to do was scream for help. But she knew that wouldn't help. If she was going to escape these monsters, she needed to do what they said long enough to catch them off guard. The door was directly across from her, a small window with three metal bars protecting it. She fought off the pain and pushed herself the rest of the way to her feet, then shuffled her way to it. The chain connected to her ankle pulled, rattling as it reached the last link's length. As small as the room was, the chain was even smaller, shorter. They had made sure to block any possible escape.

She leaned toward the door, extending her fingers as far as she could, only to come up just short.

"Damn it."

She stretched her abdomen, hoping that would help relieve some of the pain. It was a terrible mistake, as an intense throbbing jutted through her. Bethany sat and hugged her knees, letting the emotions she'd been stuffing down finally come to her. She cried some more, thinking about her poor sister who put false security in a stuffed dragon to protect her. Who was so excited to take part in the upcoming talent show for her class and show off her gymnastics moves, only to have the show canceled thanks to the massacre. And now, she'd never get to do gymnastics again. She wouldn't live her life and grow up to become the amazing girl Bethany knew she could be.

As much as she wanted to mourn the loss of her family, she realized she had to do everything possible to push that to the back of her mind right now. The coven needed to pay for what they did, and she'd be no good if she continued sitting here feeling sorry for herself. There was always a way, and she just hadn't found it yet.

There was a noise outside the door. Someone was approaching. The doorknob clicked, then opened. She made a mental note: *it pushes out-*

ward. One of the hooded figures walked in with a tray that contained a glass of water and a few breakfast biscuits. She hated herself for wanting to jump up and grab the tray from the coven member. It wasn't until the member was all the way in that Bethany noticed it was a kid, close to her age.

"Please. Help me get out of here."

The member continued to stare down, hiding his face in shadow. He didn't talk, only shook his head as he knelt and set the tray on the floor. Bethany observed him and recognized the Nike shoes from her house. This was the person who knocked her out.

"How could you do that to us? I hope you rot in Hell!" She knew saying stuff like that would only make matters worse, but she couldn't help it.

"I'm sorry."

She didn't expect a response at all, let alone an apology. But she recognized the voice. She just couldn't put a face on it.

"If you're sorry, then help me out of here. *Please*. I didn't do anything. Why do you guys want me so bad?"

The hooded figure lifted his head and removed the hood.

Bethany wanted to vomit.

"Troy?"

Troy had acted a bit strange at the bowling alley, but she assumed it was because he was with another girl and felt awkward around his ex. And then when he came to see her at home... It all started to click. Seeing his face beneath the hood still sent a shock through her. She always assumed the coven members were older people who were slowly dying off. But seeing someone she knew, in her own grade, wearing the robe changed everything. It meant the coven was still adding members, still growing.

Howie and Cory were under the impression there weren't many of the coven left. This was a huge blow to any hope of ridding Newport of a group that had plagued them for decades.

"I know. You're probably surprised to see me under the hood. Hell, I'm still surprised to be with them. It wasn't until Mr. White died and Burt took over that changes started to happen."

"Troy, that was a fucking week ago. How the hell did he have time to make this many changes? And why would you ever want to be part of something so horrible?"

Troy scoffed, furrowing his acne-covered brow. "Horrible? You have no idea what we're all about, Bethany. And me joining isn't some spur-of-the-moment decision. It's something that's been in my family for years, and I've wanted to be part of it my whole life. The elder members had a rule that we must remain nameless to the public, that anyone who wasn't part of the group was never to know about us unless they joined. That all changed when Jessica escaped their trap and murdered so many people. A select few were chosen to come public and inform the town of the dangers. Do you think if we didn't care about the people of Newport that we would have warned them about her? And now, here we are again, like déjà vu. The murders are back, the demon is back. And it's up to us to put a stop to it and bring this town back to what it should be."

"Which is what? A prison none of us can leave? What exactly are you doing for us that wouldn't make us hate you?" Bethany seethed, grinding her teeth as she thought of all the trouble they had caused her family.

"Just be thankful we're here to help, no matter what it takes."

"You killed my family! How—" She couldn't even finish her sentence as she choked down the tears. She didn't want to show any of them the impact it had on her, but how could she hide it?

"I said I'm sorry about that. Believe me, I wish there was another way. Your parents were always good to me. Your dad even snuck me my first beer. But if certain things don't happen, it would be much, much worse than anything we've seen before. I'm not even supposed to be talking to you about this stuff. I have to go before I get in trouble."

"Wait! Please don't leave me here alone. I know you're a good kid. I know you see how wrong this is. Let me go, please?"

"You're mistaking my generosity for weakness. *I'm* the one who stabbed your dad over and over. I'll do whatever the coven asks of me. Nothing is more important than what we stand for. Goodbye, Bethany," Troy said, then he turned and walked out, slamming the door shut behind him.

Bethany backed against the wall crying, sliding down until she was sitting next to the food tray. She had just seen Troy at school before the massacre. Sat next to him in history class as he made stupid jokes with his friends about George Washington's wooden teeth. Then at the bowling alley, hanging out with his friends and on a date. And when he came to her house to apologize. Like Burt Rollins, there had been no indication that he had any ties to this group. After a few more minutes of crying, her parched throat won out over her stubbornness. She grabbed the glass of water and chugged it down, disgusted with herself for doing it. But if she was going to escape, she needed to be hydrated. She needed to come up with a plan to get herself out of this situation and get help.

CHAPTER 29

After sneaking Father Grimes into the back of their truck, Howie's dad drove mostly in silence, following Father Grimes's directions. They had been driving for close to fifteen minutes when his dad couldn't take it anymore and broke the silence.

"What type of place can you actually hide someone for so long and get away with it?"

Howie sat shotgun, Grimes in the back seat directly behind him. He couldn't see the priest's facial expression, but he could tell by his tone he was very uncomfortable.

"Well… years back, before I even took over as head priest, the church bought a place at the edge of town. The plan was to open a private school, but we never received proper funding. The house had been unoccupied for years, but the church never sold it. After sitting so long without proper maintenance, the place was condemned by the town. The hope was someday the church would tear the place down and build a new school on the property. That never happened. And nobody had any reason to worry about the place as it was just an old, shoddy home like half the places in town. It's right up here off Pine Street."

Howie realized the house Grimes was referring to and his eyes lit up.

"My friends and I used to ride our bikes by there and thought it was haunted. We used to make up stories about it and even talked about making a movie based on it. Henry Black has been living there this whole time?"

He couldn't believe it. All these years, the stories they had told, the discussions about the Black Heart Killer, and Henry Black was within feet of them where they rode their bikes. The thought gave him chills. *Was he ever watching us out the window when we passed by?*

"Enough, Howie. Nobody wants to hear about your stupid movies," his dad snapped. The stress of everything brought out the impatience Howie grew up seeing most days, only it was amplified significantly. Howie wouldn't have been shocked had his dad reached out and smacked him right in front of Father Grimes.

"But yes, I believe we are talking about the same house, son. It's up here on the right," Grimes said, ignoring his dad as he gestured toward a long dirt driveway where darkness suffocated the trees. It was part of what led Howie and the guys to think the place was haunted. No matter what time of the day or how sunny it might be, the narrow dirt road always appeared to be a few minutes short of nightfall. His dad turned into the shadows, the tires rumbling over packed gravel. Overgrown grass grew in the center of the tire tracks, showing years of neglect. The crumbling home came into view, creating an out-of-place eyesore in the center of a scenic background full of trees. It reminded Howie of the saying his dad always used, "You can't polish a turd."

Howie's dad turned the vehicle off and went to get out, but Father Grimes reached out and put his hand on his shoulder to stop him. Howie's dad glared at the hand like he'd just been puked on.

"I think it's best I lead the way. You two wait here for a moment so I can talk with him. You have to remember he hasn't spoken with anyone besides me in years."

"Yeah, well… if he doesn't remember me, then he's too far gone. We were like brothers."

Howie noticed his voice crack, but the stubborn man held back tears. He tried to picture if it was Cory who was gone, left for dead, only to find out that after years of accepting it, he was still alive. He couldn't even imagine Cory dying—let alone coming back from the dead—which was why this visit was so important.

Grimes exited the vehicle and walked up the front steps, now covered by the front porch shade. Howie's dad sat in the driver's seat with his door open, but Howie could tell he wanted to get out and push past Grimes.

After a moment, the front door opened, but it was too dark inside for Howie to see anyone. Father Grimes talked quietly—too quietly for Howie to make out what he was saying. The old priest gestured to the vehicle, then continued, and the front door shut. Father Grimes came down the steps looking defeated, shaking his head as he approached the passenger door.

"Well?" Howie's dad asked.

"We can go in, but Henry said he'd have to check you for the mark before you could enter. I hope that's not a problem."

"For fuck's sake. Does he really think I'd be tied to them?"

"The mark? What are you guys talking about?" Howie asked.

"Don't worry about it, Howie," his dad said.

Father Grimes looked at Howie, then his dad. "I think he needs to know, Bill. We've come this far, no point in holding back anymore."

Howie's dad shook his head and sighed. "The coven members all have a tattoo on them; it's how they pledge themselves to the group."

Howie's eyes lit up, immediately remembering Burt Rollins on the news, and the tattoo on his neck. He wanted to say something, but the words lodged in his throat. He'd lost his chance as his dad got out of the vehicle and followed Father Grimes to the door. *Burt is in the coven. He was around us through the entire funeral, probably listening to everything we talked about.* He shook the thought and quickly followed his dad up the porch to the front door.

The door opened and Howie locked eyes with the man standing inside. After all the pictures he'd seen, all the articles he'd read, he was finally face-to-face with Henry Black. Henry appeared much different than he had back then, having aged to a great degree. Dark bags drooped below his eyes. Red scratch marks lined his hairline as if he had spent time aggressively digging at his scalp. Howie pictured him trying to rip his own skin off to get Jessica out of his head.

"Holy fuck, it's true," Howie's dad muttered to himself.

"Henry, this is—"

"I know who they are. Get in here, quickly," he said in a raspy voice, his eyes flitting east to west, scanning the tree line for any sign of them being followed.

They all walked into the house, and Howie clung close to his dad's side. He never could have imagined a world where he depended on his dad for safety, but here he was. Henry locked the door, working his way down a few more installed locks for extra measure. The home smelled like stale cigar smoke and mildew—an odd combination.

"Henry... I never thought I'd see this day," Howie's dad said.

The two men stared at each other for an uncomfortable moment, and Howie wasn't sure if either was going to talk or throw fists. But then something changed behind Henry's eyes. As if he decided to let his guard down, just a little bit. His hard eyes softened, and his lips quivered. He embraced Howie's dad in a hug, something Howie had never even been on the receiving end of from his dad.

"I'm so sorry, Bill. About everything." He pulled away. "I wish you had come to see me in prison, so I could've told you everything. But I get why you wanted nothing to do with me. Hell, *I* wanted nothing to do with me."

Father Grimes walked around them and stood near Howie. He leaned down and whispered, "The Lord works in mysterious ways, son."

Howie had no idea what he meant. Why would it take so many people dying for two long-lost friends to rekindle their relationship?

"I'm also sorry I gotta do this, but I'm gonna need you to prove you're not one of them, Bill."

"Are you fucking serious? They're the reason Sheila was killed, Henry. You know that," Howie's dad said.

"Listen. I just need to know, okay?"

An awkward stare down followed, but finally, Howie's dad pulled down his shirt collar to reveal no sign of the coven mark. When Henry was satisfied, he backed off and nodded. Howie's dad tugged his collar up aggressively. Father Grimes warned them that he was a bit of a loose cannon, but so far, he seemed normal for the most part.

"Okay. I'm sure you have plenty of questions for me, as I do for you."

"You're damn right, I do," Howie's dad snapped. "For starters, why go through so much trouble just to hide all these years? Why not try to get rid of these fucks before all this happened?"

Henry cackled, an unsettling laugh that sounded more like loose phlegm in his throat, and said, "You think it's that easy, huh? I lost everything. I buried the love of my life alive, just so she couldn't kill others anymore. And I did it knowing she'd still be in my head. The things she said to me when I was in prison, the things she tried to get me to do... I thought I hit rock bottom when I buried her and got arrested. But imagine... imagine the person you love most, planting a seed in the back of your mind that continues to grow and grow, until it takes up more space than your normal thoughts. Imagine that seed telling you she never loved you, that you should just kill yourself. I considered it many times in that prison, which is when it finally clicked to me how to get rid of her. But you know what the worst part is? I didn't *want* to get rid of her. Because once she was gone from my headspace, she'd truly be dead to me. I had to lie to the world about her, refuse to tell them where she was buried.

"I know I'm rambling, sorry. Please bear with me, as it's been quite some time since I've talked to anyone besides Father Grimes. There are reasons I haven't shown my face since my death. The easiest answer is that they'll send me back to jail, or worse. If you recall, I was serving life in prison. As I should. I killed for her. I hid her from people when I knew what she was doing. I accept that I deserve to live the rest of my days a miserable, lonely old man. But I need to know that when I do, they'll go down with me."

"Right, so why wait so long?" Howie's dad spat.

Howie looked around the house, observing the dark stains spreading across the ceiling. The house smelled of mildew, and with no upkeep to speak of, it wasn't surprising. There was minimal furniture—a chair here or there, an old kitchen table in the corner of the dining room with chipped paint on the legs. Howie assumed Father Grimes brought Henry this stuff. But he couldn't imagine such a deflating existence, especially after everything Henry had done and seen.

"I'm getting to that. I see you're still as impatient as ever," he smirked. Howie noticed his teeth stained a dark yellow and unintentionally cringed. Henry focused on him and turned up the smile even more. "Is this your boy, Bill? He's the spitting image. What's your name, kid?"

"His name's Howie. And as much as I'd like to play catch-up, I came for answers," Howie's dad said.

"I know, I know. Well, nice to meet you, Howie," Henry said, turning his attention back to Howie's dad and Father Grimes. "Bill, if anyone understands why I couldn't do anything, it's you. I know your family has ties to them, and what have you done? There is one shot and one shot only to end this coven, this curse, for good. I've spent twenty years figuring this all out. And I think you'll want to see this. Follow me," he said, and walked ahead of everyone before they could resist.

Father Grimes nodded, and they followed him deeper into the house, the shadows now overtaking the minimal light trying to force itself through the windows. Had Howie not been with grownups, he would have hightailed it out of the house at this point, telling his friends, "At least we tried."

The floorboards groaned beneath them, giving off a spongy softness with each step. Howie couldn't imagine how anyone would be able to sleep a single night here, let alone live in this dungeon for years.

They rounded a corner and came to the basement door. Henry again unlocked multiple padlocks before opening the door. Based on what he'd seen of the rest of the house so far, Howie expected it to be an entryway into a rat-infested black hole but was shocked to see a bright light shining below, illuminating the surrounding area.

"Where the hell are you taking us?" Howie's dad asked.

"Just come," Henry said.

Howie trailed behind, again scanning the first floor before heading down, shocked by the dilapidated state of the house. Leatherface wouldn't even feel comfortable living in a house this grimy. As he got to the bottom step, his mouth opened in awe. The basement looked like a completely different house, like something out of a spy movie, full of maps, charts, and a whiteboard with writing that Howie couldn't read from the stairs. Stacks of books and newspapers were scattered about on every surface. In the corner of the room was a small twin-sized bed out of place, an afterthought to Henry's real purpose—taking down the coven.

"Holy shit..." Howie's dad trailed off, walking up to the corkboard on the far wall.

Howie walked to his side and inspected at it as well. The board was full of names, starting with a single name at the top and branching out toward the bottom like a sadistic pyramid scheme. While the writing was messy, reminding Howie of how Todd used to write with his opposite hand just to piss off the teachers, he could still make out some of the names. At the top of the board, written in large letters, were the words *COVEN CULT.*

"Cult?" Howie asked.

"Yeah, kid. There's a fine line between a coven and a cult, and these monsters crossed that line long ago. Don't let their identification as a coven fool you. Covens don't do shit like this. They keep to themselves. Don't have a power hierarchy. And while both can believe in something that brings them together, only a damn cult would do anything it took to make whatever god or demon they worship remain happy."

"Which is why this town is in such danger, men. For years, they remained peaceful. After the horrible events at the school, it seems a new power regime has taken over the coven, and any rules they had in place are a thing of the past," Father Grimes said.

CHAPTER 30

Howie read the list of names, starting from the top. Some of the papers were wrinkled and aged as if they had been on the board since before Howie was born, whereas others were recently added. It was clear Henry had been at this for years. *Is Burt really in charge of them? Spunky?* He'd been getting his hair cut by Spunky since he was fresh out of diapers. And all this time, he was inches from one of the highest-ranking coven members. He recognized other names, some obvious, some not as much. Larry from the bowling alley. The new chief, Mullin. Mr. White and the previous chief, Miller, were crossed off, which meant Henry knew they were dead. And then his eyes fell upon the bottom of the chart. What he saw made his heart skip a few beats. There, Henry had listed a few kids close to Howie's age. Kids he went to school with. There were question marks next to their names. The fact that Henry even thought there was a possibility of kids he grew up with joining the coven changed everything. It meant anytime they talked, speculated, gossiped, someone could have been listening to what they said. At school, the bowling alley, even at Ryan's funeral.

"You think there are kids with them?" Howie asked.

Henry turned to see Howie staring at the board and walked over, scratching at his scalp.

"I have no proof of it yet, but the sad truth is, I do think so."

"How could you even know that being holed up in this shithole? You didn't even show your face when your own wife came back and killed half the town," Howie's dad said.

He was still upset, but Howie now realized this was how his dad got when he was scared. He got defensive, said mean things. Every little thing agitated him.

"Bill, please. It's not that simple. That all happened so fast, I didn't even know about it until it was all over. She wasn't in my head anymore, not after I died for a short time. By the time Father Grimes filled me in, everything was over."

"It's true. I wasn't at the school. I heard about it the next day and at that point, Howie and his friends had already stopped her. Any time I have new information, I come out here to give Henry whatever I've gathered, whether it be overhearing people talk on Sundays at church or somewhere else in town. I'm always listening for things that could help him. And I bring him food and supplies."

"You did good work, Howie. I'm sorry you lost some friends," Henry said.

Howie wanted to say thank you, but he couldn't get the words out. Mention of his friends not only reminded him of those he lost, but of Cory, who was on his own, hiding himself to protect everyone else.

"Can we save Cory?"

It didn't matter what words came out of his mouth next, his eyes said it all. Henry didn't think there was any shot at helping Cory.

"This thing... It isn't something to take lightly. I don't know, kid. All I can do is promise to try. I've learned a lot in the days since Jessica's been gone, different methods to try and extract demons. But it's one thing to read about it and another to attempt it. We have many issues on our hands here. Your friend is possessed. A more powerful demon is threatening to tear this town apart. And the coven worships this more powerful demon. Saving your friend will do us no good if we can't stop the other problems."

"I've been through this shit once before, and it caused me to lose everything. There's no saving this damn kid, Henry, and you know it. We need to get rid of him," Howie's dad said.

Howie couldn't help himself anymore. Whatever consequences came, he'd accept them.

"Dad, I'm sorry you lost everything before me. I'm sorry I wasn't the kid you wanted and that Mom wasn't the wife you wanted. But I'm here. I'm your son. And no matter how mean you are, you're still my dad. Cory's my best friend. If there's even a small chance of saving him, I have to try. And whatever you decide to do to me, whether it's punishing me, hitting me, grounding me for life, I don't care anymore. I'm going to save Cory, with or without you."

The room went silent, with everyone waiting for Bill's reaction. Howie immediately regretted the outburst, knowing full well that the moment of stepping up would fade and he'd wished he had kept his mouth shut. His dad stared at him, ice-cold eyes locking onto Howie. Even his nostrils flared, which only happened when he got *really* mad. It wasn't so much that Howie was worried about what his dad would do here, it was later when they were back home in his dad's comfort zone—his recliner with the leather belt resting on the arm. His dad stepped forward, now only a few feet from Howie. Howie forced himself to stand his ground—any sign of weakness now might make his dad reconsider waiting until they got home.

"Please, now is not the time for this. Everyone is stressed right now, and we have work to do," Father Grimes said.

Howie's dad ignored the priest, stepping closer to his son.

"Boy, you know not to talk to me that way. I need you to understand one thing right now. Yes, I lost my first love and the baby I was supposed to have. But that doesn't mean I didn't want you or your mother. I'm a miserable prick, I know that. But if you think for a second that I'm going to let that happen to me again... I can't lose another family to that thing. I won't."

A shelf rattled against the back wall, followed by something slamming to the floor, and they both turned to see the cause. Henry writhed on the floor, convulsing. He clawed at his scalp as an unnatural groan escaped from his chest. His jaw locked tight, and his eyes rolled into the back of his head as his body went rigid. It was as if something was forcing his mouth shut, with panicked screams trying to batter through his teeth.

"He's having a seizure! Get over here and help!" Father Grimes shouted as he ran to Henry's side. "Quickly, hand me your jacket, son."

Howie unzipped his jacket and ripped it off, handing it to Grimes. The priest set it under Henry's head, talking calmly to him.

"It's okay, Henry. It will pass."

Howie and his dad stood over Father Grimes's shoulder staring down in shock. Henry continued to tremble, the whites of his eyes going bloodshot. Somehow, Father Grimes remained calm through the ordeal, as if he'd been through this before with Henry. And Grimes was right, it did pass. Eventually Henry stopped convulsing, his once stiff body loosened, and his eyes no longer rolled into the back of his head. He took heavy, long breaths, his eyes closed like he was in a deep sleep.

"What the fuck just happened?" Howie's dad asked.

"Ever since he got Jessica out of his head, he's been having these seizures randomly. They pass, but as you can see, it can be quite terrifying. We need to let him rest."

Howie noticed the scratches on Henry's forehead now had fresh blood seeping out through the old wounds. *Is that how those scratches got there? He digs at his head while he's having seizures?*

"So, we just sit here and wait? Then what? We don't exactly have a lot of time here," Howie's dad said.

"Well, the thing is, after these episodes, Henry… He has visions. Much of this information you see here plastered all over the wall, about the coven, the demons, he got from these visions. This is how we get our answers to end this thing once and for all."

CHAPTER 31

Cory sat in the dark corner of the concrete plant, burying his face in his palms. The open wound on his hand throbbed like hell every time he touched it, but the light was hurting his eyes, and he needed to keep it out. After eating Spunky's heart—he couldn't believe that was even a memory of something that actually happened—he'd taken one of the barber's neck towels and wrapped it tightly around his hand, tying a knot to keep it firmly in place. Within minutes, the white towel had transitioned to a dark maroon, soaking the fabric in copper-scented dampness.

His body continued to change, the demon taking its hold on him more and more by the second. While he had attempted to clean most of the barber's blood from his face, the crusted remains cracked and stretched every time he moved his mouth. And he needed to brush his damn teeth—however many of them remained—as the viscera and gore from the organ he had devoured settled in between the gaps, leaving a constant metallic taste in his mouth. He rubbed his tongue along the roof of his mouth, sliding it across the now bumpy surface. It was as if there were tiny sharp teeth growing through his entire mouth, replacing the normal human teeth that continued to drop out one at a time.

Each passing minute brought on more strength for the demon, and now that he had eaten a heart, Cory sensed the demon seizing every nerve, muscle, and bone in his body, digging in with razor-sharp hunger. One heart only made it want more hearts—which meant more killing. Cory wasn't sure he could handle another situation like the barbershop.

It had now been a few days since he saw his mom. Since he murdered Larry Foreman at the bowling alley. As more time passed, he wondered if he had actually made the right choice to distance himself from his loved ones. All it had done was leave him lonely and depressed, wallowing in his thoughts about all the horrible things the demon had made him do. Was Howie even worried about him? Or was he taking the opportunity to move in on Bethany and win her over? And maybe his mom was leaving him for dead, accepting that she had lost her boy to the evil force, deciding to let him rot alone.

"Now you're thinking. They don't want to help you. We need to teach them a lesson."

"No! She's staying away because I told her to. She doesn't even know where I am!"

"But Howie could figure it out if he really thought about it, couldn't he? You guys talked about how easy it was to break in here after you caught that horny couple fucking in the corner. Why hasn't he helped you? Because he's fucking your girl, that's why. He's too busy licking her body from head to toe, laughing the whole time while you sit here like a bitch."

Cory wanted to shout at the top of his lungs. The demon was having way too much fun getting in his head, poisoning his thoughts. He walked over to the industrial sink in the corner, blasting the cold water. It sputtered for a few seconds before a full stream powered through, and he lowered his face, scooping the cold water onto his cheeks to cool off. Even though it was late fall, the last leaves dropping from the stubborn branches that refused to let them go, and the temperatures rarely hit above the low forties, he felt like he was on fire. Sweat glistened on every inch of his body, creating an uncomfortable stickiness beneath his clothes. Not only that, but he needed to get the rest of the blood off his face and hands.

The water quickly filled the stainless-steel sink, an apparent clogged pipe blocking the water from draining fast enough to keep the sink empty. Cory stared at the pool of water forming, zoned out in his thoughts. The sink was more than half full by the time he realized what was happening, and he quickly turned the faucet off. He continued staring at his reflection as he splashed his forearms and scrubbed away the dried blood with a sponge that must have been used to clean dishes during the workday. The ripples slowed, bringing the water back to complete stillness.

The outline of a figure standing over him reflected off the water's surface.

Cory jolted up and turned around, leaning against the sink, hoping his eyes were playing tricks on him in the dark space. But he was wrong. Undeniably wrong. In front of him, a charred body stared back, its blackened head twitching side to side. There were no facial features, just a solid black face that resembled overcooked meat. The figure towered over him with long, narrow arms that almost reached the floor. He didn't dare move, afraid any sudden motion would trigger this thing to attack him. Instead, he remained in place and held his breath, hoping it would disappear. Hoping it was just his eyes seeing things as he attempted to fight off the fever taking hold of his body.

The thing exhaled, from where, Cory had no idea because there was no mouth. No nose. Just a blank canvas of absolute evil.

"*Cooooory... Feeeed meee...*"

The familiar scent of sulfur stifled his senses. It was the same smell he'd picked up right before he killed his grandfather. And then at the bowling alley and barbershop. But it was the first time he had an image to associate with the smell. This had to be the demon, finally strong enough to show itself to him. The shadow that had been following him wherever he went.

"Please. Leave my body. I didn't ask for this. Just go," he demanded, closing his eyes to wash away the horrible sight. With his eyes glued shut, his hearing intensified, and the cracking of burnt skin moved closer. "You're not real. You're not real. Go away!"

The movement stopped and the sounds muted. Somehow, the silence of the open industrial space was as sharp as fangs latching onto him. He opened his eyes, hoping the demon was gone, back to the deepest part of his mind until it got the strength to show itself again.

Instead, the ink-black figure was mere inches from his face, leaning down to be eye level with him. Cory tried to back up, but he was trapped against the sink with nowhere to go. The blank face inched closer, and then the space where a face *should* sit began to split; a raw, pink line of muscle traveled down the center of its head, like a crack in the asphalt after years of shifting. Flecks of blackened flesh popped off, revealing streaks of a half-melted mouth beneath. Cory froze in terror as the mouth expanded, cracking more of the charred exterior. A large, wormlike tongue slithered out of its mouth, swaying with a life of its own as it stretched beyond anything possible for a normal tongue.

Cory attempted to run, but the demon latched its long limbs around his wrists and tightened until they dug into his skin like barbed wire. Every attempt to resist was met with more of its thorny mass digging in. The tongue stopped, floating in front of Cory's face. And then it shot out, forcing itself into his mouth, pushing down into his throat.

He couldn't breathe. The tongue traveled deeper, and Cory sensed it expanding inside of him, traveling in different directions at the same time and attempting to tear him apart. His eyes bulged as he tried to take air through his nose. The rancid smell of the burned corpse would've gagged him had he not already been choking from the snakelike member penetrating his airways.

As its mouth opened wider, beyond the range it had any right to, the raw cracks expanded up the center of its face, settling where a set of eyes should reside. And then the cracking skin melted, oozing down its cheeks. A pair of dark orbs burned through, staring into his soul, sucking away any ounce of hope he had left. He wanted to die, to never see another thing again. His vision began to fade. Cory realized he was losing consciousness. Before he passed out, multiple car doors shut in the parking lot. Was it workers here to check on the curing status of the concrete again? Was it his mom who finally figured out where he was hiding? The demon disappeared, dropping Cory to the floor. Voices approached outside.

The front door opened, but Cory couldn't move. He wasn't visible to whoever had entered, but he could hear them talking, their words now crystal clear.

"Doesn't look like the kid's here. Let's do a quick sweep and move on to the next property. When Mullin found Spunky, he said the trail of blood started off in this direction, so the kid couldn't have gone too far."

"Wait a sec, what's this over here? Come take a look," a second voice said, followed by quickening steps. Cory sensed them standing over him, but he was too weak to do or say anything.

"Holy shit. It's him. Go phone this in from the office, let them know we found him, and ask what they want us to do with him," the first voice said.

As the first man approached, Cory felt the demon taking hold. It was only a matter of time until it had the strength it needed to take care of these men. With that thought, Cory blacked out.

CHAPTER 32

Patrick Ellis sat with his cruiser hidden behind the Newport shopping plaza sign, numbly waiting for the next stupid teen to come flying out of the McDonald's parking lot. It was boring work, but it's what he was instructed to do...again. He couldn't help but continue feeling as if he was being cast aside, forced to distance himself from the regular crew that Mullin was comfortable working with.

He wanted to question the Carver family after he left their house per Mullin's instructions. But the chief forbade him from doing so, saying he had it taken care of and the family wanted their peace. But that didn't mean Ellis couldn't talk to others in town. It had been a bit since anyone had heard from the Stevens family. The kid had a rough go of it after the school massacre and was still missing. Mullin painted the situation as a threat, saying the kid was dangerous and if anyone found him to let him know. He didn't want Cory simply getting put in the holding cell overnight and let go. Mullin insisted the boy needed to be treated more dangerously than Tommy, the town drunk. Ellis decided it was time to take a trip out to their house and see how the mother was doing. Maybe get a little more information from her now that she'd had some time to think things over. Maybe she had some more ideas as to his whereabouts.

Anything would beat sitting here all day. If he could get any indication of where the Stevens boy had run off to, maybe he could help. He started the cruiser, pulled out from his designated speed trap, and drove in the direction of the Stevens's home. Mullin might chew him out later, but if Ellis obtained any helpful information, his chief would have no choice but to back off and see that he had a good cop on his hands. But deep down, inside his core, Ellis knew it was more than that. Something was off about this entire town, and he wished he'd gone with his instinct sooner. It felt like more than just Mullin trying to contain the problems. That was it. He wasn't containing a problem; he was covering it up. What the fuck could he possibly want to hide?

Within a few minutes, the home came into view. Ellis was thankful there were no reporters surrounding the house, the news crews seemingly on to their next scoop. Still, Ellis scanned the bushes surrounding the house, making sure there weren't any hidden surprises ready to get more dirt on the murders. While Mullin had officers out searching for Cory, saying the kid was a danger to the town, Ellis worried it was much bigger than that. After all the boy had gone through, it was easy to see how a fragile mind could snap. But Mullin had given instructions to contain the kid by any means necessary, including violence. Ellis wasn't about to watch a kid who'd been to hell and back, who just a week ago had put his life on the line to help stop the massacre, get beaten in the streets like he was Michael Myers.

He pulled into the driveway and walked around the back of the home where the porch was located. As he approached the steps, he noticed the curtain sway shut. He climbed the porch and knocked, instinctively taking in his surroundings. If the boy was, in fact, home, and he was as dangerous as Mullin made him out to be, Ellis wanted to be ready.

Nobody came to the door, so he knocked again, this time louder. Finally, Sandy Stevens appeared in the door window, a nasty expression etched on her face. She flung the door open.

"I already told you guys, I don't know where my son is, okay? I've looked everywhere. They searched my entire house and left it a huge mess, thinking that I was hiding him. Please, leave me alone."

"Ma'am, please. I'm only here to help you. I just wanted to ask a few questions that might help us find Cory. I'd like to locate your son before anything bad happens to him, okay?"

She stared at him, and Ellis couldn't tell if she was going to crack and let him in or chase him off the porch with a damn broom. Her eyes softened, just slightly, but he knew he had created a window of chance as long as he didn't push too much.

"I know it's hard to trust anyone these days. This whole case doesn't sit right with me, though. Your son goes missing, and you don't even file a missing persons report. Before you get defensive, I don't think you avoided it because you had anything to do with his disappearance. I think you're scared of something. And whatever that is, I'm not part of it. I need you to trust me if you want help finding Cory."

"You're new here, right? Let me ask you, Officer..."

"Officer Ellis, ma'am."

"How much do you really know about this town?"

"What are you getting at?"

"You know, after all these years, the secrets we were forced to keep, it was all for nothing. And now, my son's life is in danger because of it. Had we done something about this back then, maybe none of this would have ever happened."

Ellis had figured out enough to know the town had a past. Hell, he remembered reading about the murders when he was a kid and all about the Black Heart Killer. It was stories like that which made him want to become a cop in the first place. But he sensed that she was talking about something deeper than that.

"If you really want to help me find my boy, I suppose it's best you hear what got us into this whole mess."

"I'd love to hear it. But I must ask, why aren't you out there trying to find your son? Why is there no sense of urgency, ma'am? I don't have any kids, but I have to imagine if I did, and I was in your shoes, I wouldn't stop until I found him."

Sandy's expression hardened once more, and Ellis regretted pushing too far before gaining her full trust. But he couldn't understand why she was sitting inside watching out her window while her son was missing. He didn't think she was guilty of anything; he thought she was scared and that she knew more than she was letting on.

"Before you judge my parenting, why don't you come inside and hear what I have to say? It's freezing out here, and I don't want anyone seeing me talking to you."

Ellis checked his watch, debating whether he had enough time to go inside when he was supposed to be out on patrol. Hesitantly, he followed her inside the house, unprepared for the story he was about to hear.

Troy watched from the woods as Officer Ellis talked with Sandy Stevens. He couldn't pick up on much of what they said, but it was clear by her demeanor that she was opening up to him. If that bitch told him, an outsider, about the coven's past, she'd suffer greatly. Troy was the newest member of the coven, and he wanted to prove himself. From the stories his dad had told him over the years, the coven used to be a lot tamer, just dabbling in silly witchcraft and creating a small community to support their beliefs. As the years passed, there was a shift in the group, an attempt to bring more power to their members. Slowly, the women were phased out, and the men who sought undeniable strength took charge. It was when the group started communicating with Vorathor that things really ramped up. The demon viewed females as having only two roles: to be sacrificed and to bring new potential members into the world through birth. Larry White was the first to adopt the newer ways, although even he was far from the leader Burt had become. As horrifying as the massacre was, it brought the coven new life. New leadership. In the old structure, there was *no* leadership, only an equal split of power.

Troy had begged his dad to join, promising to keep the secrets that the coven held so intimately. It wasn't until his mom died unexpectedly that Troy finally convinced his dad. Troy owed Burt his life. He was the one who wanted to expand the coven, get some youth in the mix as many of the elders died off.

So yes. He would do anything for the coven. And it would start today with him not only catching Cory's mom babbling about the town secrets, but also making sure Mullin knew the new cop in town was sticking his nose where it didn't belong. This was his chance to make a good first impression. He'd hoped that he would get more information from Bethany about Cory's whereabouts before they took her, but she either really didn't know where he was, or she didn't plan to tell anyone.

Troy waited, crouching so long he became lightheaded when he stood to stretch his legs. From his hiding spot, he had quick access to the parking lot at the clothing store behind the small wall of trees bordering the property. The store remained closed since the murders, just like many of the town's small businesses.

He wondered what they were talking about in the house, and if he should sneak to get a closer look. But instead, he convinced himself to remain hidden—he couldn't blow his cover. Finally, after close to twenty minutes, the front door opened. Officer Ellis walked out, his eyes in a lost gaze. *She definitely told him everything.*

Sandy followed him out, her face puffy and red. She wiped tears away beneath her glasses and trailed Ellis down the steps. Troy assumed she was just coming out to say goodbye, but she approached the cruiser with Ellis. *What the hell is she doing?* She pulled her jacket tightly around her and opened the passenger door. Ellis scanned the area again, and Troy was almost too late, but he dropped down out of sight before being spotted. When he peeked out again, the cruiser was backing out of the driveway. Troy bolted back through the woods to the store parking lot and hopped in his beat-up Chevy Cavalier. By the time he got around the parking lot back to the main road, the police car was almost out of sight. That was okay. As long as he had sight of them, he'd see where they were headed. And he'd tell Burt and his dad, then he'd get back to dealing with Bethany.

Howie stood behind his dad and Father Grimes, who were tending to Henry. After the seizure, Henry remained unresponsive for a while, but Father Grimes said that was normal after each episode. It felt like they were wasting too much time, that Cory was in greater danger with every passing minute.

Howie spoke up, "Father Grimes?"

The priest turned around to face him, and thankfully, Howie's dad didn't. He remained near Henry, waiting for him to wake up so he could talk.

"Yes, son?"

Howie couldn't find the words he wanted but forced down the anxiety and continued.

"Is it going to be too late to save Cory? Is this thing going to be stuck in him? Like it was Jessica?"

"Well... the demon was trapped inside her because of Henry. He carved a seal onto her skin to keep the demon imprisoned in her body. The demon isn't sealed in Cory like it was in Jessica, so if it wanted to find another host, it could do that. But you have to understand, the longer it remains in Cory's body, the more powerful it becomes. I know you watch a lot of those horror movies, Howie. The thing is, real demons don't work that way. They take their time. Are you familiar with the four stages of possession?"

Howie shook his head.

"Ah. Well, it's not as simple as a snap of one's fingers and all of a sudden, a demon controls the body. It likely started back when you were in the woods with Jessica. He probably began to experience odd occurrences at first. Seeing things, hearing voices. And then gradually, over time, it intensified. Messing with his thoughts, telling him to do awful things to others and himself. Making it so he didn't dare sleep due to the nightmares that came. Part of why I kept an eye on him at the funeral was because his appearance was extremely...sallow. Eventually, it gets to the point where the demon can control him at will. But I need you to listen to me. When we see him, there's no telling who will be in control, and if the demon is advanced enough—as I suspect—we may not be able to tell right away. Demons love to manipulate. Whatever he tells you to do, do *not* do it. Do you understand me?"

Howie nodded. He felt so stupid. He saw the early signs. Yet he did nothing about it. Not that he knew the stages of possession, but he knew his best friend, and it was obvious for days now that Cory wasn't right.

Henry started to make strange noises, a mix of moans and wheezing.

"Grimes, get over here, now. I don't know what the fuck he's doing," Howie's dad said.

Father Grimes turned away from Howie and went back to the bed.

"It's okay. This is normal after an episode. It's as if his brain is recalibrating." He felt Henry's forehead and talked softly to him. "Henry, it's okay. We put you in bed. You've had a seizure."

Henry's eyes shot open, darting around the room. He looked like a nutcase who thought they were strapped down inside an alien spacecraft.

"We have to go! It's going to be too late! They have the girl, and they're going for Cory next. Let me up!" Henry shouted incoherently.

"Settle down, Henry. You need to let your body adjust. It's not safe to leave until we know you're back to normal."

Henry shot up, grabbing the priest by the collar as strings of saliva flew from his mouth.

"You don't understand, Father. If they find the boy, they'll tempt him with the girl, and if their sacrifice works, the curse will remain on this town. We need to stop them before it's too late."

Fear trickled up Howie's spine. But the coven had no way of knowing where Cory was hiding, so they should have more time. *Henry must still have a few screws loose after just waking up,* Howie thought. Regardless, Howie didn't like the conviction behind those words. Even in his crazy state, Henry believed every word he told them. Henry turned away from Father Grimes and over toward the wall of names. He pushed himself up and past Howie's dad, stumbling on his feet.

"Slow the fuck down, Henry. You're going to be no good to us if you fall and break your damn neck," Howie's dad muttered.

"No...time. We need to hurry," Henry slurred as he reached the wall and started scanning the list of coven members.

"What are you looking for?" Father Grimes asked.

"It's something I didn't see before. All these members, they have connections to one man. I don't think Burt Rollins is the true leader. Look..." he said, pointing to a few of the names. "Burt Rollins owns the funeral home. Spunky owns the barbershop. Larry Foreman owns...ow ned the bowling alley. Do you see it?"

"A bunch of middle-aged assholes?" Howie's dad asked.

"They all own businesses in town. But it's not just that. The buildings they have their businesses in...they're all owned by the same man. Felix Ruger. He has to be connected to the coven! I think he's the true leader of the group. How did I not see this before?"

"Because he owns half the buildings in this town? That's a bit of a stretch. You telling me everyone in Newport has joined the damn coven now?" Howie's dad asked.

"Not all of them. Stop with the sarcasm, Bill. It's not helping anyone. I'd guarantee there are more businesses and people in high places here who are either with them or helping them. Keep in mind, the strictest of rules in this town for the last twenty years has been to stay out of those woods, and to keep the demon trapped. All so they could satisfy their deal with Vorathor."

"Who the fuck's Vorathor?"

"The demon that the coven worships," Howie said, unable to help himself.

"Jesus, my damn kid knows about this? What've you been filling his head with Grimes?"

"Please, Bill, listen to what Henry has to say," Father Grimes urged.

"The coven *wants* the town to remain cursed. With the curse in place, they hold all the power. By keeping the demon that was inside my wife trapped, they get everything they want. They could care less about the rest of the town being stuck here. If we can take down Ruger, I think it would not only save Howie's friend, but it would save this town. It would end the curse."

Howie was trying to follow the logic. A lot of what Henry said made sense, but there was plenty that didn't fit. Even if Mr. Ruger was in charge of the coven, how would getting rid of him also take care of the demon? The demon was in Cory, not Mr. Ruger. Unless...

"Wait, do you think Vorathor is inside Mr. Ruger?" Howie asked.

Henry's eyes lit up.

"Exactly! Maybe not possessing him, but at least connected to him somehow. Bill, how did someone as dumb as you raise such a smart boy?"

Howie tried to stop the laugh from escaping, but it was too late. His dad glared at him, then back to Henry.

"Hell if I know. Must have got it from his mother," he said. And then his dad did the unfathomable. He laughed along with them.

"I don't know how much time I have before another episode comes. We have to act now, save Cory before they complete that part of their plan. That has to come first."

"What's it like? When you have the seizures?" Howie asked.

Henry sighed, then rubbed at the claw marks on his head.

"Well, son, I don't wish that on anyone. When Jessica was in my head, I thought that was the worst thing I'd ever go through. Her visions, her thoughts. And hell, maybe these are brought on by her still having a tiny fragment of my brain. Her way of somehow trying to help me. They come without much warning, just a blast of pain in my forehead, then I black out. I see things. It's like I'm in another world, wandering around Hell itself."

"Before we go anywhere, I need answers, Henry. I came to confront you after thinking you were dead for half my life. You were like a big brother to me. And you knew Jessica was part of the coven, yet you never said a goddamn word to me? Before we go any further, I need to know. Why?" Howie's dad asked.

"Bill... we don't have time to get into this right now. You know the coven wasn't like this back in the day. When we moved to town, they might have lived in secret, but they weren't violent people. They accepted us into the town with open arms. Granted, we didn't know who they were at the time. But they slowly brainwashed Jessica. I had no control over her joining. Once I saw what it was doing to her, it was too late. They tricked her. When she was possessed, it wasn't something she volunteered for. That wasn't her who killed your family, just like it's not Howie's friend out there killing now. I'm so sorry. I never thought I'd get the chance to say that to your face."

"It's in the past..." Howie's dad said, but the words sounded forced.

"No. I killed for them. The shit the demon made me do... I don't deserve to live. The only thing keeping me going is knowing I can end this for good. And this is our chance to do it. We can avenge Jessica. We can get revenge for Sheila and the baby. We *can* make this right," Henry said, choking on the last few words, his eyes glistening.

"You know... we were going to name him Henry. After you."

The room filled with a dreadful silence. Howie felt as if he'd been punched in the gut. To hear that his dad's would-be-son had such an important name, and he got Howard. Which quickly became Howie to anyone who knew him. There was no meaning to the name at all.

"I... I'm sorry. Really. But look at you now. You've got a wonderful young boy here, and he helped put an end to what they did to my Jessica. Now it's my turn to return the favor to him and save his friend. I know you don't think it can be done, but we have to try."

Biting his bottom lip and shaking his head, Bill glared at Howie. Without a word, he stormed out of the basement.

Father Grimes rested a hand on Howie's shoulder before saying, "Son, I'll go have a talk with him. Why don't you help Henry get stuff ready to go." Grimes followed Bill and exited the basement.

"He'll be okay. Let's get a move on. We need to pack supplies and be prepared for any situation. Then we need to find Cory and contain him until we can extract this demon from him. We can do this, Howie," Henry said.

Howie wanted to believe him.

"I need you to think hard about where Cory could be hiding. Look at the map, are there any locations that stand out over others? We can go around searching for him from place to place, but if we can narrow it down, it would give us a leg up on finding him before the coven," Henry said.

Howie walked over to the map, reading the names of Newport's streets and businesses. He started at Cory's house, but he already knew Cory wasn't there. He scanned the surrounding areas, including the wool factory where Cory's mom worked and the motel, among others. None of them made sense for Cory to hide in because there were too many people around. That led him to the concrete plant. He thought of the time they had snuck in after the rumors of it being haunted spread around town. The place was huge, and there were plenty of spots where Cory could lay low. It was the best option.

"The concrete plant. That's gotta be it. It's near his home, it's away from the main part of town, and it's huge. We have to check there," Howie said excitedly.

"Okay. Good work, kid. It's a start. I'll tell your dad to go there first. I need to ask you something, though. Are you ready for any possible outcome, Howie? What we're about to face doesn't just endanger your friend, it's dangerous for all of us. For you, your dad, the whole town. If there's even a chance Cory will harm us, I have to take action. But I promise, I'll do everything I can to save him."

Howie nodded but didn't say anything.

Henry opened a metal bin that looked like a large toolbox and started taking objects out of it. A blowtorch, a long metal rod with some circular design on the end, a large cross, a green amulet that contained a foggy haze in its center, and finally, a sharp dagger with an ivory handle. The sight of the sharp blade concerned Howie.

"What is the dagger for? Are you going to use it on Cory?" Howie asked, not sure he wanted to hear the answer.

"I have no intention of it. But we need to be ready for everything. If… if he's too far gone, we may need it. It's ancient. It's said that it possesses the power to permanently kill or at least greatly harm most demons. I've yet to try it, obviously, but this goes back to the days of the Kurds. Apparently, the blade is infused with magic that can banish them. The handle is said to be carved from Satan's bones."

"So why didn't you use it on Jessica? Why not get rid of the demon back then?" Howie asked.

"I know what you're thinking, Howie. It's not fair that I wouldn't kill my wife when she was possessed, but I'd do it to your friend. I assure you, I would've done what needed to be done. I knew if I killed her, and the knife didn't work, the demon could find a new host. By trapping it in her body, it guaranteed that the demon would remain buried forever. Clearly, I was wrong. So now, I'll leave no scenario out of the question.

But we have to go before it's too late. There's a good chance they already know where he is. We must get to him first."

CHAPTER 34

Ken Kincade was too excited to sit still for so long. But he felt his patience was finally about to pay off. After countless attempts to reach Jeffrey Carver to see if he'd convinced his dimwit daughter to take the interview had come up empty-handed, he decided to drive out to their home and take business into his own hands. Brennan didn't understand why he had to pack up his camera gear and drive Ken to the Carver residence, but he did as he was told. Ken had been set on getting the interview one way or another, and he was ready to call out Jeffrey in front of his family to get it.

When they arrived, nobody was home. The cars were gone, the lights were out. Ken circled the house, peering through each window for any sign of the family. What he saw instead left a permanent smirk on his face. There was no luggage packed, and the home appeared as if a gang of angry looters had ransacked the downstairs trying to find the Holy Grail. Something happened here, and it wasn't good.

"We need to get a look inside," Ken said.

"Are you serious, man? I'm not about to break into someone's fucking house. I've gone along with your bullshit this entire trip, but that's crossing the line," Brennan snapped.

Ken shook his head and sighed. He'd take control as he always did, whether this slob wanted to help or not. He tried the windows, which were all locked, as expected. He went around the back of the house next, and the bulkhead appeared to be unlocked, so he grabbed hold of the doors and pulled up. They swung open with a rusty whine, and he let them fall to the ground, revealing the concrete stairs.

"No way. Nope. I'm going to wait in the van. This is too much, even for you, Ken."

"Listen, dummy. If we discover something in here, nobody will be talking about us breaking in. They'll remember the evening news, and everybody will be saying, 'Ken fucking Kincade.' If you're too much of a Sally to come down here with me, go do what you gotta do. But if and when I need a camera, you better get your ass down here."

Brennan shook his head and walked off, leaving Ken to himself. Ken was okay with that. He took the stairs, hoping the basement door below was also unlocked. Unfortunately, the knob didn't budge.

"Fuck."

He glanced over his shoulder, making sure Brennan was gone, then turned back to the door. With a quick strike, he drove the elbow of his jacket through the windowpane closest to the lock, sending small shards of glass to the floor inside. When he determined nobody was within earshot, he carefully reached in and unlocked the door. It opened to a dark room, only lit slightly by the fading daylight seeping in behind him. Careful not to step on any of the larger pieces of glass, Ken walked in on his toes, dodging the mess on the floor.

"Hello?"

He'd rather get busted right away instead of in the middle of snooping through their belongings. Nobody answered, so he shut the basement door behind him and turned on the light, bringing the room to life. Nothing out of the ordinary as far as he could see. The adrenaline pumping through him filled him with a high that the world's best drugs couldn't touch.

Once he determined there was nothing of use in the basement, he went upstairs to the first floor, again calling out to make sure nobody answered. The house was deathly silent. Someone had left here in a hurry, not concerned with cleaning up the mess before they did. Which meant the family was either on the run from someone, or something had already happened to them. This story was only getting better by the minute.

He searched the entire first floor, only to find more of the same. Shit tossed from counters, drawers open, and nobody around to blame. As soon as he reached the top step to the second floor, he spotted bloodstains traveling down the hall toward a bedroom.

"Holy shit. *What* did you people do?"

Ken kneeled, determining the blood had mostly dried. This wasn't recent. He got up and followed the trail to a bedroom, careful to avoid stepping in the blood. Anything could be on the other side of the door. Whatever it was, it was bound to be newsworthy. He reached out with his foot and pushed the door open, then stepped over the stains. He thought he was prepared for the worst-case scenario. But the scene displayed in front of him was far worse than anything he could imagine. Ken's legs turned to jelly, and he reached out for the bed frame to hold himself up. In the far corner of the room, Jeffrey Carver lay sprawled out with his stomach cut open. His intestines lying beside his body, shriveled and putrid. Next to him, the wife and younger daughter hugged each other in a frozen embrace, their eyes open.

The dead family had been moved to the corner of the room like a pile of dirty laundry that had yet to be washed. For the first time in recent memory, Ken had no idea what to do. He knew he should call the police and report everything he'd discovered. But he also realized that he had broken into this house, and even though these bodies had clearly been here for a while, his prints were everywhere.

Ken couldn't take his eyes off the little girl, and the stench that permeated the room smelled like rotten meat. Flies buzzed around them, and Ken saw one land on Jeffrey Carver's eyeball. He closed his eyes, trying to erase the images from his head, but the outlines of the victims were burned into his retinas like a faulty television. He slapped himself in the face.

"Think, damn it, think!"

He knew he couldn't say anything to Brennan yet. He wasn't ready to call the cops. This had to remain between him and whoever did it, at least for now, because he planned on discovering who was behind it. Why did someone do this to the Carver family? Could Jeffrey have owed some loan shark money and got into so much debt that he couldn't repay it? None of the reasons he thought of carried enough weight to bring any sense of clarity to the situation. But then he realized there was one family member missing. Bethany Carver wasn't here. Was it possible this had something to do with the school massacre? And the so-called accidental death at the bowling alley?

Ken wasn't stupid. He knew he wasn't the only one attempting to talk with the family. Which meant there was likely more than just reporters attempting to get information out of them. All of this pointed to something far bigger in the town, something he could have never imagined when he came to the dump to research the school massacre.

He checked his watch, realizing he'd been in the house for a good twenty minutes already. If he didn't get out soon, Brennan would likely come looking for him, and that was something he couldn't afford. He forced himself to forget about the lives lost, instead remembering he was here to serve a purpose. He was here to uncover the secrets Newport had been hiding for years. Whoever did this left the bodies, but they also thought enough to move them all to one room and lock the doors when they left. Which told Ken they could have been short on time, planning to come back and clean up the mess later on. With that thought, he left the room, racing back down the stairs and through the basement. When he got back to the news van, Brennan was smoking a cigarette and leaning against the driver's side door, still shaking his head at Ken as if disgusted by his colleague. *If only you knew, buddy.*

"Let's get out of here. Head toward town. Something big is happening, and we need to catch it," Ken said.

Without a word, Brennan threw his cigarette to the asphalt and ground it with his shoe, then he hopped in the driver's seat. As Ken gave one last glance back to the house, they sped off, leaving it in the rearview.

CHAPTER 35

Cory stood over the dead bodies whose hearts he'd just devoured. It wasn't his fault. He purposely hid in a place where he didn't expect people to come, trying his best to keep the demon from harming anyone. It wasn't his fault that a few coven members decided to drop by the shop and look for him. It wasn't his fault they entered the plant and gave the demon a chance to smell blood. All the hard work he had done to distance himself from people and it was all for nothing.

When he woke from his blackout, the two men were standing over him, attempting to lift him off the floor. Then he recalled them talking, one of them telling the other to call and say they found him. Did the guy make the call before he woke? What were they going to do with him? The demon didn't give them the chance to see their plan through. Now their shredded remains could be mistaken as roadkill. With each passing victim, Cory couldn't help but sense the overpowering strength of the demon growing inside him like a rotten fetus. Whatever he saw before he passed out, it had to be fake. That thing was far more terrifying than all of his nightmares combined.

He knew he needed to do something with the bodies, but would that make him more guilty than he already was? Killing them may not have been his fault, but hiding the evidence was all his idea.

"It's a great idea. Drag them to the concrete retainers and throw them in just like Skip Fremont did to his wife. Nobody will ever know."

Cory hated himself for agreeing with the inner voice. In the far corner of the concrete plant, there were multiple molds in different stages of curing. The plant had been hired to produce precast concrete slabs to restore the dam in town, as without it, the train track would flood, and most of the businesses in Newport still used the train for imports and exports. The slabs on the far end were mostly solid, like hardened clay that was never sealed back in its container. They had curing blankets set on top of them to help them dry. But the molds closest to him were in a much earlier stage of drying, reminding Cory of the mud soup he used to make for his parents as a toddler. If he could lift the bodies—a feat that wouldn't be easy considering they were both grown men—he could hide them from being discovered and hope the blocks hardened before anyone had a chance to search for them.

He grabbed the first man, a heavyset guy he'd never seen in town, and attempted to drag him by the pant leg. It was slow going, but eventually he got the body close enough to the concrete molds and dropped the feet. After taking a moment to regain his breath, he searched for a way to lift the stocky frame up and over the retaining wall and into the sludge. It was hard enough dragging the body; there was no way in hell he could lift the corpse that high. The wall had to be at least six feet tall.

Cory searched the area and found a long chain, but that still wouldn't make lifting the body any easier. The concrete plant was massive, a huge open-concept space with loads of equipment he didn't know the purpose of. Then he remembered there was a forklift near the front entrance. If the keys were in it, he could tie the chain to the fork and lift the body in that way. He hurried toward the entrance, relieved to find the keys in the forklift. He had no idea how to drive one, but it was better than attempting to drag the dead weight himself. The gash on his hand continued to throb every time he touched something, and after dragging the first body to the containers, he noticed the previously maroon bandage was now soaked again.

After a few attempts to get the forklift turned around, Cory felt he had control of it enough to drive to the other end of the floor. He sped up, wanting to get it over with so he didn't have to see the bodies anymore. Approaching the first body, he tried to slow the forklift down, but he couldn't figure it out right away. Panic laced his concentration with scattered commands. He swerved in time to avoid the large container holding the liquid concrete, but not quick enough to avoid the body. The forklift crushed the skull of body number one, crunching bones and brain matter in its wake and leaving behind a trail of gore.

He finally got the machine to come to a stop and looked back at the mess he'd created. It was becoming abundantly clear there was no way out of this situation without something bad happening to him. Everywhere he went, he left a path of death and destruction. It was only a matter of time before he hurt someone else he cared about. The most important people in his life right now were his mom, dad, Howie, and Bethany. The thought of his dad being the "safest" of them all—stationed in the middle of an actual war—was absurd to think, but it was true.

Cory forced himself to focus. He hopped off the forklift and tied the chain to one of the forks, then dragged the other end and wrapped it around the man's ankles. Once he felt he had it snug, he jumped back in the forklift and debated which of the levers to push. The first lever he tried only tilted the forks, but the second lever raised the forks up in the air until the chain extended all the way and lifted the body off the floor. Blood poured down the man's caved-in head, pooling on the floor below. Cory tried not to gag at the grotesque sight. When the body was high enough to dangle over the concrete container, Cory carefully pulled forward until the man hung over the center of the mix. The dead man slowly spun on the chain, his arms dangling below. With a soft touch of the lever, Cory lowered the body into the liquid concrete, watching as the man slowly disappeared into the gray abyss.

Now he just needed to figure out a way to get the chain off the foot so he could complete the process all over again with the second body.

He backed the forklift up, pulling the chain tight once more until the man's leg broke the surface again, then stopped the forklift and jumped off. He climbed up the side of the container, careful not to put too much pressure on his injured hand, and reached out for the leg, pulling the chain like an ice fishing line to drag the body closer. Finally, he pulled the chain free, then watched the body again sink to the center. Small bubbles gurgled up where the body had just been seconds before.

He completed the whole process a second time and did so with improved efficiency. Still, he found himself exhausted, and all he wanted to do was return home to ask his mom for help. The men had likely called whoever they reported to and let them know they had found him. They were trying to move him to their vehicle when he became alert. And all they got in return for their extra effort was a hole in their chests and concrete coffins. Cory wondered if this sense of grief would ever lighten. Over the past few days, he had now killed five people, and each time it brought on another layer of depression. He had never considered killing himself, never understood how people could mentally get that low to think it was the only remaining solution. Now, as he navigated through the bloody trail leading back to the main entrance, he envisioned that scenario playing out. His mom would be safe. His friends would be safe. As more time passed, he started to accept that this was his new reality.

If he had one thing going for him, it was that the bouts where the demon gained control of his actions were brief, and they came with a warning. Each time it happened, though, he found it more difficult to fight it.

The days were bleeding into one another, making it impossible to know what day of the week it was. When did he talk to his mom on the phone? Two days ago? Three? He hadn't slept more than thirty minutes straight since the bowling alley, and it was only adding to the confusion. Somehow, he had been able to contain the demon in the concrete plant most of the time, even when a few workers came to check on the slabs drying. In a moment of weakness, he allowed himself to leave, and it led to Spunky getting a mouthful of razor blades. He wouldn't let it happen again, not if he had anything to say about it. But if his strength continued to weaken, he knew he needed to do more than just stay locked up in this place. If the demon forced the issue, it could easily demand that he leave and seek out more blood.

Cory scoured the building, checking over the tools and equipment, hoping he'd find something that could force him to stay, even if—more like *when*—the urge came to kill again. For now, he just wanted to sleep. His body was battered, beaten, transforming by the second. The inside of his mouth had a constant needlelike sensation jabbing into his gums, and his tongue hurt anytime it accidentally touched one of the new teeth protruding through with their spiky tips. As much as he had fought off sleep, afraid of what he'd see when he closed his eyes, his body was insisting he rest. So that's what he did. He found a spot in the corner office and propped up a few coats left behind on the coatrack as a pillow. As soon as his head landed on the makeshift pillow, sleep took him. But not before the image of the faceless demon burned itself into his brain.

CHAPTER 36

Bethany had given up on her attempts to escape. Not that she was done trying, but she realized she was wasting energy trying to find a way out of a room the coven had clearly taken extra measures to make sure couldn't be escaped. She needed to preserve what little gas she had left in the tank. On more than one occasion, different members had come in to check on her and given her small amounts of food. She hadn't seen Troy since the morning, and while it disgusted her that he was part of all this, and she hated his guts for taking part in killing her family, she still thought maybe there was a chance she could get in his head to help her.

With the sun shifting outside, her space had darkened substantially over the last hour, leaving her unable to see much. Instead of wasting energy trying to get out, she killed the time thinking of any weaknesses she'd seen in the group. While she wasn't coming up with much, it sure beat thinking about her family.

If they were bringing kids into the coven, it meant one scenario was likely: they were trying to expand to become much bigger than they had ever been, so desperate after the last few weeks that they needed to bring on new members to beef up their roster. There wasn't any logic in attempting to expand if they were actively adding only male members.

There was no bloodline, nothing that could keep the legacy going after they were gone.

Even if she did escape, she had no idea where to go. It was obvious she couldn't go to the cops. Not only was the chief of police with them, but the last chief was as well. She couldn't go to anyone in town besides Howie.

She leaned her head against the wall and closed her eyes. The ankle chain was so heavy that it sapped her energy; it took every ounce of strength she had left just to lift her arms for normal gestures. How the hell was she supposed to fight if she couldn't even scratch her head without needing to catch her breath?

The door to the room opened, sending in a blast of light from the hallway. Bethany opened her eyes and was hoping to see Troy in the entryway but instead, she saw three coven members in full attire. The one in front held a mound of cloth, and it wasn't until he entered that Bethany realized it was a sack. She didn't recognize the man, but his snarly expression told her he was not one to look to for sympathy.

"It's time," he said. Those two words, they could mean anything. But Bethany knew they couldn't possibly mean anything good.

"What are you doing with me?"

"You'll see soon enough, girlie. He sent us for you, and now it's time we bring you to him. We found your scrawny boyfriend."

Cory? She hadn't seen him since the bowling alley. But if they found him, what would they do with him? If she didn't find a way to escape, she knew she would die tonight. But the coven came prepared, as the three men flanked her like she was some kind of wild beast about to pounce on them. The one who spoke approached her with the bag.

"Please don't hurt me, I'm not going to fight," she said, praying they would take it easy on her. Her entire body hurt from the attack at the house, and if she had to endure another episode like that, she wasn't sure she could make it out of this holding room, let alone live to see another day.

"Yeah, right. You think we were born yesterday? Get on your knees and don't move. The first sign of fighting, I'll knock your ass out again. Got it?"

Tears streamed down her face as she nodded.

"Good. I'm going to put this bag over your head. Can't let you be seeing where we are and have a chance to blab about it to anyone."

The man nodded to his helpers, who went to each side of Bethany and held her arms firmly. Once they had her in their grip, the man in front shoved the cloth bag over her head, immediately cutting off her sight. The fabric smelled earthy, like something that had been hidden in the back corner of a shed for years until this very moment. Bethany concentrated on slow, deep breaths, but the bag filled her open mouth every time she inhaled. The fabric was thin enough that she could see a light blur on the other side but not enough to grasp what was in front of her.

"Get to your feet. No funny business," the man said.

Bethany stood as the men holding her arms unlocked the chain around her ankle. She was grateful to shed the weight on her leg. They then removed the duct tape and bound her hands with a metal zip tie.

"Where are you taking me?"

"None of your business. It's time you served your purpose in all of this. We don't ask questions. He told us to bring you, so we bring you."

She had no idea who "he" was, but she assumed it was the leader of the coven. The men at her sides grabbed hold of her arms and squeezed tightly, guiding her toward the exit. With the bag over her head, trying to escape was too risky. She knew there would only be one shot to get away, and if she wasted it now, she wouldn't get another chance.

They entered a hallway, and while she couldn't see the walls, she could sense the narrow space they moved through. After a moment of walking, they came to a stop, and the sound of a heavy metal door being forced open scraped the floor in front of her. A cold breeze seeped in through the sack, chilling her face. She tried to use her other senses to take in her surroundings, knowing it could later help to determine where they had taken her. It was asphalt, not dirt beneath her feet. While the scent of the cloth hogged her sense of smell, there was still a hint of nature sneaking into her airways. There were no cars driving in the distance, indicating they must not be too close to a main road. Besides the men breathing, the only sounds she could pick up were the trickling of water and an occasional bird.

This had to be somewhere along the Sugar River, on the edge of town. And it had to be a place that wasn't isolated enough that it would be located on a dirt road. As she walked, she thought of where the river traveled far enough away from the main road. The first place to come to mind was somewhere down near the train track, maybe the parking lot where cars used to park when the trains actually brought people to their destinations. Now the only purpose of the track was for shipping goods to and from town to other locations. That was the answer. If she wasn't on the verge of being killed, she would have been proud that she figured all that out without seeing anything.

She heard a van door slide open and sensed their pace was slowing.

"Toss her in the back and tie her ankles again. Don't need her trying anything on the way there," said the man in charge of the other two.

Someone grabbed ahold of her neck and pushed her into the back of the van with force. Her shins banged off the bottom of the door, sending a jolt of pain through both legs as she fell into an open space in the back. One of the men wrapped something around her ankles. The door slammed shut, then the men climbed into the van and shut their doors.

As they drove off, Bethany had a million thoughts fighting for her attention. The one that kept coming back the most, that ate away at her ever since they had dragged her from her home, was that they needed her for something. They killed her family and they kept her alive and fed her. No matter what it was, she could only imagine it was far worse than a quick death.

CHAPTER 37

Sometimes things just don't make sense. Howie had come to understand that in life. It didn't make sense that his dad beat him. It didn't make sense that the town covered up the murders and blamed Henry Black. These were subjects he debated internally ad nauseum. But here he was, seeing firsthand that even those things that don't make sense have their reasons. He just never expected it all to be related. And now, he sat in a car with his abusive dad, a convicted serial killer, and a priest, and they were on their way to try and extract a demon from his best friend before a coven, who worshiped another demon, got to him first. The fact was, he was a kid who grew up watching horror movies and wanted to have the creative imagination to come up with stories to wow audiences someday, and *still* couldn't see any possible scenario where this story made an ounce of sense. It was crazy.

They rode on in silence, with Father Grimes in the back seat next to Howie, Henry in the passenger seat. It had been a decade since Henry had left the old church home, and Howie sensed he was taking in the town, in awe of all the changes that slipped by him after all these years. Everything looked the same to Howie, but that was because the gradual day-to-day changes went unnoticed. But he couldn't imagine what it must look like to see the same familiar spaces after so long. Some homes might have a different color paint, whereas some stores had replaced old signs with new ones. To Henry Black, it must have felt like stepping into a time machine and fast-forwarding ten years. Even the cars driving by were different.

"And you're confident the concrete plant is the best place to check?" Father Grimes asked.

Howie nodded, but he didn't feel confident. They were putting their faith in a teenager and a guy who, just earlier in the day, Father Grimes basically told them was crazy. While he did seem a bit more normal than Howie expected him to, it didn't mean he trusted the guy. Howie's dad, who usually put up his guard a bit more, uncharacteristically followed along with what they were doing. Howie realized saving Cory was the last thing on his dad's mind. Bill Burke wanted to tear down the coven for good. Twenty years of hate built up, and he finally had a chance to do something about it.

If Felix Ruger was indeed the leader of the coven, and he held powers he'd obtained from Vorathor, it meant they were going up against something they might not be able to defeat. Mr. Ruger was an enigma in town. Everyone knew the name, they knew he was wealthy and owned many of the properties in town, but nobody really ever saw him. Howie recalled seeing a picture in the Eagle Times, the town newspaper, of Ruger standing in front of the gun factory in town, his thick gray hair combed to the side with a big smile on his long face and strong jaw. In the photo, he stared into the camera, posing for an article promoting the workforce he had created in Newport.

Ruger wasn't someone who ever went to the local restaurants or had a night out with friends at the bar. For all Howie knew, the business mogul didn't even have friends. Howie and the boys would often ride their bikes by the large mansion up on the hillside near the golf course Ruger owned. It always reminded them of the house in *Salem's Lot,* but they never expected it to be home to an actual evil bastard.

Howie's nerves kicked into overdrive as they closed in on the concrete plant. All this time, he wanted to save Cory, but now, as they approached that moment, he wasn't so sure he wanted to see Cory. It had been a few days since he'd seen him, and even then, Cory had the look of someone who could snap at a moment's notice. Who knew what they were about to get themselves into? Not just with Cory, but what if the coven beat them to him?

The concrete plant was just around the corner now. Howie glanced down at the bag of supplies between him and Father Grimes, focusing on the end of the metal rod poking out and the symbol that decorated its end.

"What's this metal rod for?"

Henry turned from the passenger seat to meet his eyes.

"That's a brand, son. That symbol there, that's the seal that can trap the demon inside something if we need to. The blowtorch is to heat the end of it. It's a hell of a lot easier than sitting there trying to carve the seal with an inhuman strength resisting you."

Howie thought about it for a second, then realized what that meant.

"So... So you're going to trap the demon inside Cory?"

Henry was clearly uncomfortable, but to his credit, he remained honest.

"If we need to. Like I said, I don't want to leave any scenario out of the question. We'll do everything we can to avoid that, I promise."

The plant came into view, and Howie's heart sank. There were other vehicles already in the parking lot. They were too late.

CHAPTER 38

Officer Ellis and Sandy Stevens had spent the last few hours driving around Newport, searching for her son. Ellis was about to give up and tell her they would have to go back out tomorrow to look for him, but then he thought of something.

"We've been driving all over town for a few hours to places not even close to your home. Most runaways don't stray too far from home. They want to feel they're on their own but want the comfort of knowing their parents are still close. We should have been searching for places closer to your house, Sandy. Can you think of any places he might consider? Any spots that could be easy to hide without worrying about a lot of people?"

"There are so many places to consider. There's the motel, but I don't think he'd dare go there. The factory I work at, but he didn't want to come home because he was so scared he'd hurt me, so I can't imagine him going there either. He wouldn't hide in the woods, not with it getting this cold at night. I just don't know. I guess you can head back to my house and drop me off, Officer. I'm sorry I've wasted so much of your time," Sandy said, and the defeat in her voice was heartbreaking. Ellis didn't want to give up, but he was running out of ideas. So he didn't say anything. Instead, he drove toward her house in silence, hoping that for once, he'd catch a break on a case.

Troy was getting impatient. He'd been following the cruiser around for the last few hours, but he was determined to see what these two were up to. They had made stops at the cemetery and the school, among other locations, surely trying to find her demonic son. And if they found him, Troy wanted to be the first to do something about it. A few moments ago, Ellis pulled a U-turn and headed back toward the Stevens's home. Troy feared the cop spotted him, but he had no reason to worry. Ellis didn't even know much, if anything, about the coven, outside of what the bitch told him over the past few hours, and nobody would expect a teen to be part of the coven, anyway.

If there had been time, Troy would have stopped and used a pay phone and checked in with the others to see if they had discovered where Cory was hiding. He couldn't afford to lose their trail, though. They drove through the center of town, which was all but deserted now. With half the businesses still shut down, nobody had an incentive to be out and about. Troy wished there were more vehicles on the road so he didn't stick out like a sore thumb behind the cruiser. He made a point to hang back enough that he wouldn't be right up on the bumper and give Ellis a reason to spot him.

They passed the town hall, with its vast clock lit up from above, indicating it was now past seven PM. As they exited the belly of the town, they took a hard right toward the west end of Newport. They headed toward the industrial section, where the gun factory, wool factory, and concrete plant were located. There wasn't much else out this way, so Troy wasn't sure why they were wasting their time going in this direction. Was he taking her back home? What a waste of time. If he had to, he'd wait until Ellis left her house and then surprise her with a knife to the throat after she told him what the cop knew.

Ellis couldn't help but feel a bit down in the dumps, like a failure of a cop. Realistically, he knew finding the kid wouldn't be easy, not unless Cory wanted to be found, which he obviously didn't. But Sandy Stevens deserved answers. The ride back toward her home dragged along, ten minutes that felt like an hour. And then, as if the police gods were listening, Sandy sat upright in the passenger seat, staring out her window. The concrete plant appeared dark, but she wasn't focusing at the building itself, she was looking at the vehicles parked out front.

"What is it?" Ellis asked.

"That's Bill Burke's truck. Howie's dad. He has no reason to be at the plant, especially when it's not even open right now. Oh, please, dear God. Pull in," she said, but Ellis was already cutting the wheel before she spoke.

The concrete plant came into view. The first thing Troy noticed was one of the coven's vans parked around the side. Then he spotted another vehicle, a truck parked right up front. As the cruiser pulled into the parking lot, a door on the idle truck opened, and a few people exited the vehicle.

Shit! Who else is here?

This threw a wrench in everything. He felt confident enough to sneak up on two of them, but now there was a whole group of people. Instead of pulling in behind them, Troy continued driving. As he passed, he spotted Howie Burke and his dad, along with...Father Grimes? And some other man he'd never seen before.

Troy drove up around the bend, then pulled off on the side of the road. If he was going to stop them, he had to catch them by surprise. One thing that was clear as day was that this had to be where Cory Stevens was hiding out. And the fact he noticed one of the coven's vehicles in the parking lot meant that at least a few of the others knew about it as well. Troy got out of his car and entered the woods surrounding the plant. It didn't take long to reach the clearing leading to the space where concrete equipment was stored. He felt around in his pocket, locating his Swiss Army knife. Once he had it in his grasp, he made his way closer, prepared to help his coven complete their sacrifice.

CHAPTER 39

Howie stared up at the concrete plant with his heart in his throat. Cory was in there. Not just him, but the demon that occupied his body. The last time he saw his best friend was the start of his downward spiral, moments before he killed Larry Foreman. Who knew how much worse he was now? Could they even save him? If they extracted the demon, would Cory ever get back to normal? And then there was Howie's dad, who had already made it clear he wouldn't waste a second thought to save Cory if he thought it put them in danger. Howie already held unlimited resentment for his dad for his upbringing. If his dad did anything to harm Cory, Howie wasn't sure he'd ever forgive him.

"Listen to everything I say in here. He'll try to get in your head. Talk to you in ways that break you. Never give in, men," Henry Black said. He grabbed his bag of supplies from the back seat and shut the door.

Father Grimes looked fearful, giving the sign of the cross as he scanned the surrounding area. Howie's dad walked over to him and for a second, Howie thought his dad was going to grab him by the shirt like he'd done so many times, but he again surprised Howie and gave a half smile.

"Kid, I don't suppose I can convince you to stay back in the car, can I?"

Howie didn't talk, just shook his head slowly, fighting back tears.

"Yeah, I didn't think so. You know, if we make it out of this, you're grounded after the way you talked to me in front of them, got it?"

Howie almost laughed. Their lives were on the line, and his dad still found the time to reprimand him for his disobedience. The tone his dad said it in was softer than normal, though. An awkward moment of silence fell over them until Henry walked up.

A police cruiser pulled around the side of the building, parking behind them. At first, Howie assumed it was Mullin, here to stop them before they even got started. And then he spotted Sandy in the passenger seat as she opened the door. It was the new cop, Ellis, with her.

"Howie. Is he okay? Did you guys find him yet?" Sandy asked, speeding toward them. Then she spotted Henry Black, and she froze. She stared at him for a moment, and the realization of who was in front of her clicked. "Henry? What's going on here?"

"Long story that we don't have time for right now. Short answer is: he's alive because he faked his death in prison and remained hidden the last ten years. And why the hell did you bring *him*? We can't trust the police," Howie's dad snapped.

"I assure you, I'm here to help, sir. Whatever threat is inside, I think it's best I lead the way. Or better yet, you should all wait out here while I check the place. Whatever this group...coven is up to, they're dangerous."

Howie's dad glared at Sandy. "You told him? What are you trying to do exactly, Sandy? If this gets out, we're all dead and you know it."

"What I'm doing, Bill, is trying to save my damn son. I don't give a shit about the town's secrets anymore. Don't you get that? Not that I'd expect you to understand, considering how you treat your boy."

The words were a gut punch to Howie. Had Cory told her what he'd seen? That he witnessed Howie's dad hit him and abuse him? That was supposed to be a secret between the two. He tried to force the thought from his head, not willing to get upset with Cory while they were in the middle of trying to save his life. If—*when*—they saved him, then he could give Cory shit for opening his mouth. He probably meant well by it, but that wasn't the point. Or maybe his secret wasn't so secret after all. Maybe the whole town knew how bad his dad treated him all these years.

"What I do with my family is no concern of yours," Howie's dad said with a snarl.

"Enough! We are here with a purpose, and if you can't help with that, you can leave or wait out here. Sandy is trying to save her boy, Bill. For God's sake!" Father Grimes said.

"Yeah, and that little shit is the one threatening to kill my family, Grimes."

"If anyone should understand the situation, it's you. You know that's not Cory in there. But that doesn't mean Cory isn't *somewhere* inside that body, begging for help," Father Grimes said.

Howie's dad didn't respond. Instead, he just shook his head and walked back toward the truck. Howie thought maybe he was second-guessing coming here and was about to call for him to get in so they could leave. Instead, he reached into the passenger side and grabbed something from the glove box. Whatever it was, he stuck it in his pocket and shut the door.

Henry was already closing in on the entrance, ready to get inside. He turned on a flashlight, then faced the group.

"Stay close, and like I said, don't listen to a word he says until we get this demon out of him."

With that, they followed him through the door into the dark space of the concrete plant.

The plant smelled of industrial machinery. Large pieces of equipment were scattered around. Howie thought a football field could fit from one wall to the next. With as many times as he'd driven by the place growing up, he never realized just how big the place was. It was impossible to see more than a few feet, so he stayed close to Henry and Officer Ellis, the only two with flashlights.

Father Grimes, Sandy, and Howie's dad walked quietly, scanning the shadows for any sign of Cory. Henry had insisted they not yell out to him because even though there was a good chance he heard them come in, they didn't want to put a target on themselves or trigger the demon.

Something skittered up ahead, freezing them all in place. Henry held up a hand for them to remain still. Howie wasn't sure if his eyes were deceived or not, but he thought he saw movement behind one of the large containers to their right. And then a scraping sound, muffled by the smothering darkness. Henry stepped forward, aiming the light toward the sound.

Scrawny limbs exposed themselves, reaching out across the floor from behind the container. If they were Cory's arms, they sure as hell didn't look normal. Pale white skin covered raised black veins branching out across the arms. Jagged nails on the end of each finger clawing at the ground.

What is he doing? Howie wondered.

"*Heeelp meee... Mooom?*"

Officer Ellis tried to reach out and stop her, but Sandy blew by him, the desperation in her son's voice too much to take. She reached the corner and looked down. Then she gasped and backed away.

"Cory... Oh, honey. I'm so sorry. I brought you help."

Howie wanted to run to her side to see his best friend, but before he could move, Cory lunged out of the darkness, flying toward his mom. The sharp nails on his fingers extended a few inches, ready to tear apart her flesh. But then his body jerked backward and fell flat to the floor. He snarled at his mother, exposing blackened teeth sharp enough they could cut through concrete. A fiery glow burned behind his shrunken black pupils. Those eyes darted left to right, rapidly taking in the threats.

The flashlight shone off something on the ground, and Howie realized it was a chain wrapped around Cory's ankle. He was chained in place like a rabid dog, his mother just out of his reach.

"Come here, you useless cunt! Your son tells you not to go looking for him, and you listen? Misellus excusatio matris!"

He lashed out, falling just inches short, driving Sandy back farther.

"Cory... I tried. I tried to find you," she whispered, reaching her hand out to him as if begging her real son to break through and come to her.

Either someone had trapped Cory in place, or he did it to himself to prevent the demon from attacking others. While it was admirable of him to do so, Howie couldn't help but think if this was the same demon that possessed Jessica, there was a good chance that chain wouldn't be enough to hold him back if he really wanted to attack. Knowing Cory was possessed was one thing, seeing it in the flesh brought a sense of reality to the situation that crushed any ounce of hope Howie had left. There was no way they could save his friend.

Cory moved his sinister eyes over Howie's body, right through to his terrified core. He wasn't staring at Howie, but *into* him, searching for weakness, smelling the fear. Howie shivered and instinctively backed up near his dad.

"Aww, so cute. You look to that monster for protection? He gives me the warm and fuzzies. Just picturing him punching you across your backstabbing face gets my cock hard," Cory spit the words out like they were venom.

Howie couldn't help but take the insults personally, even though he knew deep down it wasn't Cory saying it. But was the demon just saying what Cory was thinking all this time? And what did he mean by "backstabbing"? As if Cory could read his mind, he decided to answer for him.

"I got sick. I needed your help. And you took that opportunity to try and mount Bethany like a horny Chihuahua? I should rip your nuts off and stuff them down your throat!" Cory again tried to lunge toward them, only to have the chain tighten, holding him steady.

Officer Ellis went for his gun, but Father Grimes held the cop's hand down.

"Let me try something," Father Grimes whispered. He pulled a large cross from beneath his cloth and held it up toward Cory.

"Atque haec de ancilla! Deus tuus non respondet," Cory said.

Howie couldn't believe what he was hearing from Cory's mouth. Not just the foreign words, but the voice he delivered them in. He'd read books about demons seizing the vocal cords of the possessed. Hearing it up close and personal was disturbing. Whatever he said, it threw doubt into Father Grimes and his effort to fend off the demon.

Sandy had seen enough. She approached her son, her face soaked with tears. There was a glimmer of the real Cory behind the insanity, and for a second, Howie thought maybe she would be able to get through to him. But then Cory flashed his rotted mouth upward in a sick smile. If Sandy took one more step forward, she was going to die.

"Sandy, don't do it!" Officer Ellis yelled.

She ignored him, inching closer to her son as if she was about to tame a wild animal. Everyone was so focused on the shrinking distance between her and Cory that they didn't see the figure approaching over her shoulder. Howie took his eyes off Cory just in time to see someone coming up behind Sandy. He attempted to yell but it was too late. The figure had something in their hand. A knife. They were draped in a black robe, blending with the darkness.

No, the coven is here.

Before anyone could warn her, the coven member thrust the knife into the side of Sandy's neck, repeatedly stabbing her exposed skin over and over. Her eyes went wide as the blade penetrated all the way in and back out, squirting blood across the floor. She reached for her neck, instinctively attempting to cover the wounds. Blood pumped between her fingers, and she looked down in shock.

Ellis raised his gun and fired, sending a bullet into the chest of the hooded member. The sound echoed through the open space, ringing through Howie's ears. He couldn't hear the shouting that followed. Both Ellis and Howie's dad ran toward the downed coven member. Father Grimes walked to Sandy, who fell to the ground in a pool of her own blood. She was still breathing, but barely, as she drained out rapidly.

"No! Mom!"

Howie turned to Cory, who had transitioned back to himself, the orange in his eyes diminished, the attack on his mom momentarily allowing him to overpower the demon's hold. He dropped to his knees and cried, reaching out for her, only this time he wasn't trying to rip her apart. Henry realized Cory had fended off the demon for the moment and took advantage. He carefully stepped around Sandy and kneeled in front of Cory.

"Boy, listen to me. We may not have enough time before it's back. Let me help you get this thing out of you for good, then we can get you unchained."

"Mom..." Cory ignored Henry, staring beyond him with his eyes still glued to her dead body.

"Please, Cory. I'm sorry about her, I really am. But I need you to listen to everything I say right now," Henry pleaded.

"It's all my fault. She's dead because of me," Cory said, shaking uncontrollably.

Howie stepped closer, careful to stay out of reach. He noticed the end of the chain connected to Cory's ankle had a padlock on it, holding it firmly in place. The only thing that would break him free besides locating the key, would be if Cory himself snapped his own damn ankle or the chain.

"Hey... I'm really sorry. Sandy was like a second mom to me. Whatever we need to do, you know I'm here for you. Henry's right, though. If we don't get you fixed before it's back, we may not be able to get out of here and make sure they pay for what they did to your mom."

Howie had no idea what to say to Cory, but everything he said was the truth. Sandy was a second mom to him. Every time he slept over at Cory's house, the cold, angry atmosphere of his own home could be forgotten about for a night. And after what Sandy said to his dad tonight, it was clear she knew, at least somewhat, how his dad treated him. She always went out of her way to make him feel comfortable, buying his favorite snacks and renting extra movies. He couldn't begin to imagine how soul-crushing it was to Cory to not only see his mother dead, but to have watched her repeatedly stabbed while he was chained up and unable to do anything about it.

Cory whispered something to himself, now staring down at the concrete floor in front of him. Howie couldn't make out what he was saying, but it sounded like he was talking to himself. Father Grimes and Henry exchanged concerned looks, while Howie's dad shook his head and walked up to Ellis.

"Shoot him, Ellis! He's going to turn again, and he'll kill all of us."

Officer Ellis pried his eyes off the dead coven member and looked at Howie's dad.

"No. I'm not about to shoot a kid who's chained up, man. We need to get him help."

Henry unzipped his bag, digging through its contents. He set some stuff on the ground as he sought out whatever he needed. As he rummaged through his items, Cory's crying intensified. Howie wanted to run to him and tell him it would be all right. That they would get him out of here and cure him of this terrible affliction. Cory sat hunched, with his head buried in his hands. The sobs sounded inhuman, more like an animal who'd been shot and was attempting to get away before the hunter came for the final blow. And then Cory slowly lifted his head, the cackling sobs proving to be nothing but theatrics. Instead of normal tears sliding down his cheeks, it was instead a black substance, like the ink from an exploding pen. Cory smiled, again showing off the plague festering inside his mouth.

"Mommy, I'll miss you... Say hi to Gramp for me. Be sure to ask him how that pillow tasted when I throat fucked him with it."

Henry shot a glance up from his bag, realizing the demon was back. He was about to retrieve something when his eyes rolled back into his head. His throat muscles bulged as he began to force out desperate groans. It sounded like he was trying to push his tongue up through the roof of his mouth. He dropped to the floor and began to convulse.

"Father, he's having another seizure!" Howie yelled.

Cory bellowed, a demonic laugh exploding from deep within his chest.

Howie's dad and Father Grimes ran to Henry's side, and Officer Ellis kept his eyes trained on Cory.

With all the commotion, the group hadn't heard the approaching vehicles. It wasn't until the sound of multiple car doors shutting peppered the parking lot that Howie realized someone else was there. The coven had found them, and it couldn't have happened at a worse time.

CHAPTER 40

Bethany felt the cold night air smack her in the face the moment someone ripped the bag off her head. It was nightfall, but after her sight was blocked by the bag for so long, her eyes didn't take long to adjust to the scene in front of her. Two members of the coven dragged her with force away from the vehicle toward...the concrete plant? What the hell were they doing here? She glanced back, trying to see how many of them were with her, and she noticed at least three of them before the man to her left forced her head forward.

"Don't be a nosy bitch. You're here to serve your purpose, little girl."

It was Burt Rollins, and to the other side of her she recognized Chief Mullin. From what she'd gathered, they were two of the highest-ranking members. If they were the ones doing the dirty work, who was the taller figure trailing behind?

The moon cast a blue shade over the brick building, making the dirt parking lot appear white as snow. They were heading toward the plant, and while she had anticipated the woods, this was somehow far more horrifying. It brought back memories of the previous owner killing his wife and hiding her body. But that couldn't be their plan, right? Why butcher her family only to go out of their way to *carefully* kill her? That wasn't it. Whatever it was, she knew she wouldn't have to wait much longer to find out. Her wrists throbbed, the metal zip tie cutting into her skin.

An unnatural screeching sound came from somewhere in the building, and it chilled Bethany to the marrow. *What the hell was that?* The two men forcing her toward the front door stopped, and she sensed their concern as their bodies stiffened.

"Go. This is why we are here," a voice she'd never heard said calmly from behind. The composure in the man's tone somehow made it worse. That inhuman call didn't frighten him in the slightest. He had a deep voice that carried the confidence of a leader who would stop at nothing to make sure he got what he wanted.

"Sir, you sure about this? That thing sounded pretty pissed off," Burt said.

"I said...*go*. Now."

Bethany had the sudden urge to break free. She didn't know what was inside, but she knew she didn't want to go anywhere near it. With the men caught off guard, now might be her only chance. The woods lining the property could hide her long enough to find a way to town and get help. Who she could trust for help was another question. She would worry about that later.

With all the power she could pull from within, she turned and kicked Burt's knee, feeling it buckle beneath her foot. Burt grimaced, his grip on her arm breaking free as he growled in pain. Mullin tried to tighten his own hold, but Bethany swiped him across the face with her nails, drawing blood along his cheek.

She took off in a sprint toward the woods, but her hands were still tied together in front of her, making her strides awkward. The leader yelled at the coven members behind her, but she had already put enough distance between them so that she couldn't hear what he said. She passed the building and came to all the concrete trucks and equipment. As badly as she wanted to reach the woods, her legs were already beginning to weaken. She glanced over her shoulder and determined she had a good enough distance between her and the men to try and find a hiding spot before they caught up to her.

The first truck she came to was a large cement truck. She climbed the side step and tried to open the door, only to find it locked. The odds were that all the vehicles back here would be locked. She was wasting time. There was a commotion coming from inside the building, reminding her of another problem waiting for them. The members were getting closer, their agitated voices now audible.

Bethany jumped down off the truck step and ran to the next vehicle, a red dump truck. There was no time to check the door. She climbed up the tailgate, searching for a place to lift herself. Again, her tied hands made things much more difficult, but thankfully after years of gymnastics, her upper body strength aided her. She found a thin ridge to plant her foot, then pushed herself up, just able to reach the top. As the voices closed in, she lifted herself up and over, falling into the bed of the truck. Thankfully, it was full of finely crushed stone, softening the blow somewhat. Had it been empty, her landing wouldn't only have hurt, it would have echoed across the parking lot and given away her location.

She prayed the cement truck had blocked her from their view long enough that the coven members didn't see her climb into the back of the dump truck. If they saw her, she was a sitting duck with nowhere to go. The voices of Mullin and Burt closed in on the area, now sounding like they were right alongside the truck. Bethany remained still, staring up at the dark blue sky as the moon spotlighted the ground below. She wished she had more time before they were close so she could bury herself in the stone.

"Did she go into the woods?" Mullin asked.

"How the hell should I know? The little bitch fucked up my knee or I woulda caught her," Burt said.

"I can't imagine you catching anything except a disease from those dead corpses you play around with."

"Fuck you."

"Go search the entrance to the forest. I'll check around here. If we don't find her, he won't forgive us this time."

The fear in Mullin's voice, a man who appeared as cold and stern as a serial killer, sent chills through Bethany. What kind of man could scare Mullin this much?

Bethany waited, listening as the footsteps faded on the packed gravel. She considered getting out of the truck and making a run for it again, but with her hands tied, she wasn't sure she could climb out safely, especially in a timely manner. The parking lot returned to silence. Inside the concrete plant, another guttural cry erupted.

What's happening in there?

Tree branches snapped and cracked as someone approached from the woods.

"There's no way she's out there right now! Mullin, where you at?"

Again, the footsteps slapped across the gravel until they faded to nothing. With both of them gone, she saw her chance to escape. She sat up and crawled to the edge of the dump bed, slowly lifting her head to peek over the side. There was no sign of them. Bethany stood on the uneven surface, fighting through the crushed rocks to get to the back. Loose pebbles fell into her shoes, stabbing her feet. She turned onto her stomach and put one of her legs over the side. Gripping the edge of the dump bed, she brought her other leg over and felt for the same place she'd used to climb in.

The metal zip tie around her wrists was pressing tightly against her skin and drawing blood, sending sharp pains every time she moved her hands. She pushed the pain aside, gripping the edge of the dump bed and lowering herself to the ground. After a few deep breaths, she prepared to take off through the woods—when she sensed someone behind her.

Bethany turned around and stared up at a towering figure in a black robe. The man wore an obsidian mask beneath his hood, but she could still sense the sinister intention beneath. He stepped forward, closing the distance in two quick strides, and grabbed her by the hair. The eyes staring back at her were glowing orbs of crimson rage.

"We've worked too hard to lose it for a stubborn girl who doesn't know her place," the muffled voice said.

As soon as he spoke, Bethany recognized it as the man who'd been giving the instructions to Mullin and Burt. This was their leader, the man who was responsible for them bringing her here to do whatever it was they had planned. He yanked on her hair, dragging her back toward the concrete plant.

"No! Let me go!" Bethany tried to claw at the man's arm, but he was too powerful.

"That is not in the plans, girl. You're here to serve a purpose. To be the sacrifice Jessica was supposed to be. And how fitting that your friends are the ones who ruined our plans with her, and now you get to take her place, buried alive with Atahsaia caged in your soul—at least what is left of it when we're done with you."

She had no idea what he was referring to, or who. The name sounded made up, but the thought of them trying to do to her whatever they did to Jessica Black, weakened any fight she had left. She was going to die tonight. Unless…

"I won't consent to anything you try to do with me. Anything you need me to take part in for this…sacrifice, I'll fight it!" She knew he didn't care whether she would consent or not. She was just trying to distract him long enough to strike.

The man laughed, but instead of distracting him, he stopped walking, then ripped her hair to the side so she had no choice but to face him. The mask melted her confidence. Its lack of features drew her to his eyes, and those eyes were no longer crazed. They were calm. Dead. And inside them, she noticed a scarlet river swimming around the pupils.

"*Hora est jam nos de somno,*" he said in an octave so low it rattled her heart in her chest.

Before she could do anything else, he tugged her hair down at the same time he drove his knee up, connecting with her cheekbone and nose. She felt the right side of her face crack inward, and then everything went black.

CHAPTER 41

Ken sat in the passenger seat, demanding Brennan continue driving around town until they found something, anything, that would help break more of this story. They'd spent the last few hours circling the main route they had become accustomed to over the last week, but it appeared nobody was around tonight. After Larry Foreman died, the bar shut down with nobody to run it. Between losing the bar and Jeffrey Carver, his sources dried up. Which only meant he had to take matters into his own hands even more than he already had been doing.

"Take a ride out of town a bit, something's not adding up here. It's a fucking ghost town. Where is everyone?" Ken snapped.

"Jesus, man. We've been driving around forever. I gotta call my wife and say goodnight to the kids before they're sleeping. How much longer we need to do this?" Brennan asked.

"Your kids have years ahead of them for nighty-night time. We may only have another night or two left to get a story before the station gets bored with it and forces me to go report on the Y2K shit again. I'm not about to waste my one shot."

"You're such a prick, you know that? I'd say I can't wait for you to have kids, so you know what it's like, but the thought of little Ken Kincades running around is scarier than these murders."

"Real funny. Take this right and head up toward the Stevens's home again. I want to see if that little rat bastard is home yet," Ken said.

Brennan did as he was told, throwing on the turn signal and leaving downtown behind. Ken scanned the passing locations like a hawk, desperate to find anything that would lead to news.

Ken thought back to the dead bodies piled up in the Carver home, wondering what state of decomposition they were now in. The scent of death came back to him at the thought, and he almost made an audible gag before catching himself. He opened his notepad, flipping through the notes he'd taken over the last week.

What do we know so far?

For one, Ken knew Larry Foreman's death was no accident. What kind of moron—even in a redneck town like Newport—would stick their fucking head up a machine to make sure it was working properly? Especially a moron who owned the bowling alley and knew how the equipment worked?

Secondly, the missing kid, originally deemed one of the heroes during the massacre, conveniently disappeared right after Larry died. Cory Stevens was at the bowling alley that night, and then he wasn't with his friends when the little bitch, Bethany Carver, kicked Ken in the nuts. Cory was linked to Larry Foreman's death, and Ken knew it. But he also knew it was much bigger than that. Bethany's entire family was brutally murdered, and there was no way Cory could have done that himself. Was he the reason for it? Did he have help? Ken thought it unlikely.

Everything felt like it was tied back to the Black Heart Killer murders from the seventies, and the plot holes that seemed to go overlooked by the town or anyone who investigated that case.

Brennan flicked his high beams on as they traveled through the windy back roads. And then, as if a sign from God himself, Ken saw it. Up ahead, in the parking lot of the concrete plant, someone ran across the lot toward the back of the building. While it was hard to see much, the person appeared to be wearing a black robe or cape, and they weren't alone. Many vehicles were scattered across the parking lot, including a police cruiser.

"There! Kill the lights and pull in. Something big is happening."

The momentary doubt he had just minutes ago had vanished, and Ken felt an overwhelming sense of excitement course through his body at the thought of what they were uncovering. Brennan sighed and cut the headlights as they turned into the parking lot entrance.

"Park here. Grab the camera and I'll get the rest. We need to be quiet, so leave the doors cracked and don't shut them."

"Dude... this is ridiculous. Is this even legal? What do you want me to film?"

"You didn't see it, Brennan. There were hooded nutjobs running toward the building. There's a cop car here. Something's up."

"If we get in trouble for this, I'm not taking the damn blame. You want me to park way back here? The fucking camera cords will be a pain in the ass to get from the van to the building."

"You can use the exercise," Ken said without taking his eyes off the large brick building.

Brennan turned the van off and started to get out, then Ken put an arm on his shoulder.

"Remember, be quiet."

Brennan shook his head and got out of the van, walking around the back to grab the equipment. Ken got out and scanned the parking lot, noting all the other vehicles. While he no longer saw anyone outside, he heard a disturbing sound coming from inside the building. The plan would be to get some footage of whatever was going down inside, then he'd have to voice over the shots. It wasn't ideal—his face would bring the ratings—but it would have to be good enough. He wanted to rush Brennan along, as every second wasted felt like another piece of great material getting tossed away. He couldn't risk making too much noise, though.

Once Brennan had the camera equipment all set up, he fed the cord along the ground, getting closer to the building. Ken passed him, taking the lead. The closer they got to the building, the louder the sounds were from within. Gooseflesh spread across his arms as he listened to the painful signals of a monster, something that could only be described as an unholy presence, full of malicious intent.

"Go around the side, we need a good view in the window," Ken whispered.

"The cord doesn't have much slack left, man. We can't go much farther unless we move the van."

"Will it reach that window up ahead?"

"Barely."

"Then let's go. Start filming as soon as we get close," Ken said, smiling the whole way. Regardless of how scared he was right now, he was equally excited. When he peered into the window, he stifled a scream. The scene made the Carver home look like a cozy Thanksgiving dinner.

CHAPTER 42

Cory knew he was losing the last bit of control of himself he had left. He had all but given up until he saw his mom killed right in front of him. As the shock set in, he found himself momentarily himself. But the demon, Atahsaia, ripped and clawed inside, demanding to come back to the surface. It wasn't done unleashing its wrath on anyone it could get its hands on. While he battled with himself, he half paid attention to everyone around him. Howie watched Cory with fear cemented in his eyes. Henry Black lay on the ground as he babbled something under his breath that sounded like a prayer, command, or spell. While Cory couldn't hear or understand the words, whatever Henry said was sending lightning bolts of pain through Cory's stomach.

The famed serial killer had collapsed to the ground moments before, his eyes rolling into the back of his head. Cory assumed the demon was doing something to Henry. It wasn't until he heard the others mentioning seizures that he realized this wasn't the first time.

Father Grimes stood over Henry, talking calmly. Cory's ears buzzed as the unbearable pain continued its rampage through his insides. With all the commotion, he hadn't heard the car doors shutting outside. It wasn't until he spotted multiple figures standing at the main entrance that he remembered. Nobody else saw the coven coming behind them.

Howie's dad stared down at the two dead bodies in shock. Howie followed Cory's eyes to the main door.

"*Free me so I can rip out their fucking hearts!*" Cory yelled in the deep growl of the demon.

Poor Howie. Cory knew he had no idea what to do right now. He alternated his attention from Cory to his dad, waiting for someone to instruct him.

Cory wanted someone to help free him, but he also realized the whole reason he had chained himself and tossed the key out of reach was so he wouldn't hurt anyone else. The demon had already attempted to kill his own mother earlier. Thank God she didn't get close enough for it to get ahold of her. Not that it mattered anymore. She was dead. He'd never get another embrace from her again. No more home-cooked meals. She did everything for him and helped raise him to be the young man he'd become.

The figures in the doorway came closer, into the blue-tinted light burning through the windows above. Three hooded coven members, wearing white, expressionless masks moved with confidence, heading right for Cory and the rest of them. The masks reminded him of the one they'd used in their slasher movie—minus the blood they had added to the eyes. Just the sight of the robes and masks sent the demon into a frenzy. Cory dropped to his knees, clutching at his chest as his heart battered against his ribs.

He didn't know who these members were, but the demon's rage took over. He wanted to kill them. To rip them to shreds and tear their hearts from their chests.

"*Pascam et custodiam pecora tua!*" the demon spat.

Officer Ellis pulled his gun again, ready to aim. The new cop couldn't hide the confusion; even though Cory's mom had told him the story of the coven, it was his first time seeing them in the flesh.

Cory tore at the chain, trying to break free, but all that did was dig the metal into his flesh even more, pressing just between his ankle and the start of his shin bone. He kept his eyes on the coven, watching their every move. They stopped their approach, spreading out to be three wide, now only twenty feet from the rest of them. The middle member stepped to the side, clearing a path. From behind them, a large man in a matching black robe strode forward. He wore an obsidian black mask, making only his eyes visible in the shadows, looming over them like a tower of darkness.

Cory heard a faint cry, and that's when he noticed the tall man wasn't alone. He was dragging someone behind him by the hair.

No. No, no, no...

The tall man dropped her in the center of the floor. Cory thought he was going to be sick. Bethany was barely conscious, moving lethargically with her hands tied together. Her face was covered in blood and there was a large bruise spreading from her cheek to her nose.

"Let her go! She has nothing to do with this," Cory said.

The tall man chuckled beneath the mask, the faceless expression adding to the eeriness of the laugh.

"She has everything to do with this... *Atahsaia.*"

Something wet and warm seeped out of Cory's nose on both sides. He wiped it with the back of his palm, looking down to see more of the black and red sludge that filled his insides right now. The mention of the demon's name did something to his body. An intense pinching sensation blasted across his skin, and he stared at his arms to see tiny, needlelike points forcing their way out of his pores.

"*You dare speak my name... What do you want?*"

"To make an offering, of course. We know how you like to inhabit the innocent. What's more innocent than a young virgin?"

When Cory realized what the tall man was saying, panic set in. Only he no longer had control of his thoughts or words. He was once again a prisoner in his own body. Bethany continued to regain consciousness, attempting to force herself up into a sitting position, but fell back over. While Cory wanted to do anything he could to help her, the demon had other plans. He felt his cock stiffen, his teeth extending. He wanted to take her body and ravage her insides with sin.

"Stay back! I'll fire. Put your damn hands up, now!" Ellis demanded, aiming his firearm.

One of the men came forward, standing next to the tall man. He removed his mask, and Ellis opened his mouth to speak, but no words came out. Chief Mullin smirked, staring at Ellis.

"Ellis, you'll do nothing of the sort. Put the gun down and you can get out of this alive. We need good men to keep the balance in line. You're either with us or you're not."

A silent standoff followed, with both police officers waiting for the other to make the first move. One of the masked men spotted the dead coven member on the ground and ran over to the body. He kneeled and pulled back the hood, revealing Troy's face.

"No! Troy! They killed my fucking son!" He held Troy in his arms, staring down at him. If he backed up just another foot or two, Cory would snap the fucker's neck.

"We all know the dangers when we commit to the cause. He won't be lost in vain," the tall man said.

"Let me kill them. All of them!"

"You'll do nothing of the sort. We have a purpose here tonight, and we will see it through, do you understand?" the tall man asked.

An awkward silence followed, but eventually Troy's dad nodded without another word. As they all stood around Bethany, something smacked off the window in the far corner. The tall man snapped his head in the direction of the sound, lifting his mask to get a better view, and everyone else turned to look as well. A camera stared back at them, filming the entire scene.

"Make sure they don't do anything stupid," the tall man ordered, pulling the mask back down before Cory got a good look at him, then he took off toward the exit while the rest of them remained in place. Officer Ellis kept his gun trained on the three coven members, but they didn't seem the slightest bit concerned.

"So... what's it going to be, Atahsaia? The girl? Or the boy you already possess? Vorathor won't ask again," Burt said.

Cory realized something in that moment. They needed the demon to take Bethany. Otherwise, why wouldn't they just trap it in his body with him already chained up? For the pact to work, there had to be a sacrifice. Cory was not a sacrifice, just a body in the wrong place at the wrong time. He knew, whatever happened, he had to prevent them from letting the demon take hold of Bethany.

CHAPTER 43

"You fucking idiot! They heard that. We got enough footage anyway, so let's get the hell out of here," Ken said.

Brennan, while great at his job, was a damn klutz. He'd stepped forward in an attempt to get a better shot and bumped his camera against the glass. When the hooded figures all turned toward the window, Ken's limbs trembled as fear gripped him. Who the fuck were these people? This material was gold. He just needed to make sure they got out of there alive to air it.

Ken took off toward the parking lot, focused on making it to the news van. Brennan lagged behind, rolling up the camera cord as he went. Ken knew if he helped, they could get back sooner, but as important as the footage was, his life was *more* important. Never in his wildest dreams did he anticipate a group of hooded figures in masks would show up. He expected Cory and a few others involved to paint a picture for him. This... This was bigger than anything he could have dreamed of.

"Come on, you're fucking slowing us down! Just unplug the damn wire!" Ken yelled over his shoulder.

He glanced back, only to see Brennan hadn't made it around the corner of the building yet.

Jesus Christ, he's going to get us killed.

Quickening footsteps slapped off the packed gravel around the front of the plant. Not only had they been spotted, but whatever was going on inside had been put on hold to come take care of them. The van came into view, but Ken was worried whoever had come out the front door would see him before he made it there. He leaned against the building and peered around the corner toward the entrance. He didn't see anyone. After scanning the parking lot, allowing his eyes to adjust to nightfall, he made a run for it. He almost tripped over the camera cord but caught his footing, making it to the van. Again, he turned back but still saw no sign of Brennan.

"For God's sake, man. Where the fuck are you?" Ken whispered.

He hopped in the passenger side, keeping his eyes glued on the front of the building as he did. For the moment, he held off shutting the door completely, determined to make as little noise as possible. Finally, Brennan appeared, the camera in one hand and rolled up cable in the other. The slob moved so damn slow, yet his face would've made someone think he was cranking into overdrive. Part of Ken wanted to tell Brennan, "Fuck the camera, let's go," but he hadn't come this far to lose that footage.

Brennan continued to roll up the camera wire as he went, picking up speed as he got into a rhythm. He was halfway back to the van when a tall, dark figure appeared behind him. One second, the figure wasn't there, then they were, blending with the night itself. Ken wanted to yell a warning, but he wasn't about to give up his spot to do so. Instead, he hopped over to the driver's side seat and prepared to make an escape himself. But the keys weren't in the ignition.

"Fuck!"

Ken checked above the visor, then in the center console. The keys were nowhere to be found. Which meant Brennan had them in his pocket. Ken had no choice but to either hide until the giant was done with Brennan or hope the useless bum somehow got away. When he looked back to Brennan, it was clear getting away wasn't in the cards. The man with the black hood was now only a few feet behind him.

"Look behind you, you son of a bitch!"

Even with the window up, Brennan must have heard the warning because he turned around and spotted his pursuer. He back peddled toward the van, tripping over the camera wire, and landed on his ass, sending the camera to the ground. *Not the fucking camera!* The figure picked up speed, giving Brennan no time to get up. He turned over and attempted to get to his feet, but the tall man grabbed him by the back of the head and pulled his hair. Then he grabbed the camera wire that had unraveled after Brennan dropped it and wrapped it around his exposed throat. Ken saw the keys glisten on Brennan's belt, as if the moon was spotlighting his only chance of escape. He wanted to do something, but there was no way he was putting his own life on the line right now. He would hide in the van, hoping the evil son of bitch went elsewhere, then he'd grab the keys from Brennan and get the hell out of this town. Whoever it was, he had to be their leader, as Ken noticed the others following his orders earlier. His black mask gave him the appearance of a walking shadow.

The leader pulled back the thick wire, choking Brennan, sinking the cord into Brennan's throat. He was pulling so tight that Brennan's face quickly turned a bright shade of red. Desperate to survive, Brennan pulled at the man's hands, trying to loosen the wire before he was stran-gled to death. He kicked frantically, trying to get his footing. The leader drove his knee into Brennan's stomach, dropping him to the ground. Brennan continued clawing at the cord, but it was so deep into his skin that there was nothing to grasp.

Then the masked man turned around, going back-to-back with Brennan while still pulling tightly on the wire. He leaned forward, putting all his force into it and pulling Brennan off his feet. Brennan gurgled and his eyes widened. He reached out, grasping at the air in front of him toward the van. Toward Ken. Ken didn't wait to watch Brennan's eyes fade to nothing. Instead, he dropped low, crawled to the back of the news van, and lay low, out of sight.

After Brennan's last exasperated breath, the parking lot returned to silence. Ken couldn't hear the attacker anymore. If he had to lay in this position until dawn, he'd damn well do it. There was no chance he was risking getting out unless he heard the guy leave the area. He didn't think he was spotted getting in the van, but there was a chance the leader heard him yell to Brennan. Ken swallowed a dry gulp of air, wiping the perspiration away from his face.

Please, just get the hell out of here. Let me go. I'll get out of this town before they realize I was even here.

A few moments passed before he heard movement, but it sounded like the footsteps were getting closer to the van, not farther away. Ken searched around frantically for something to defend himself with, finding a boom mic pole that sat in the van collecting dust without a third person on hand to hold it during live feeds. He grabbed hold of it and realized the light weight of it may not do much damage but felt a little safer knowing he had something to strike with if needed.

The attacker approached the van. Ken squeezed the boom mic tight. He remained hidden behind the passenger seat, so as long as the attacker didn't open the back door, there was a good chance he wouldn't see Ken. The faint moonlight in the front of the van suddenly darkened as the figure stood at the passenger door, peering in for his second victim.

Don't open the door, don't open the door…

Then Ken remembered he hadn't even shut the door all the way, afraid to create too much noise. All the man had to do was realize the door wasn't closed and he'd know someone was there. Ken's heart thrummed through his eardrums, pumping him full of fear. The door began to open, and Ken pressed himself tightly to the side wall, pressing so hard he thought he might burst into a puddle of gore and bodily fluids.

He could hear the heavy breaths coming from beneath the man's mask. If the attacker leaned in, he'd see Ken.

An agonizing cry came from inside the concrete plant.

The moonlight returned to the front seat.

Relief flooded through Ken, even more so when he heard the footsteps retreating farther away. He'd made it. Whatever freak show had taken place inside just saved his damn life. The irony of it wasn't lost on him. He waited long enough to be sure he was alone, then slowly sat up and climbed to the front. Sure enough, there was no sign of the attacker. Cautiously, Ken opened the van door with the boom mic in hand and walked at a brisk but quiet pace to Brennan's body. He couldn't help but stare at the cameraman's face, still frozen in shock. A bloody trail traveled across his neck, with bursting veins branching out from each side of the camera cord.

"Jesus, man, you were too slow. I tried to warn you."

Ken reached down, grabbed the keys, and let out a sigh of relief. He tossed the boom mic pole to the ground and turned to head back to the van, ready to make his escape. Something inside urged him to stop. He glanced down at the camera next to Brennan, still fully intact. The work Brennan had done to make sure the cord was rolled up neatly was all for nothing, as it was now spread across the ground once more.

At this point, why would he *not* grab the camera and bring it with him? He could live and still get the footage he needed. It would only become an even bigger story once the country found out what happened to his cameraman on the scene. Without hesitation, he grabbed the camera off the ground, inspecting it to make sure everything was in working condition. Once he determined it was fine, he headed back toward the van. The first thing he noticed was how heavy the camera was. Maybe he didn't give Brennan enough credit.

Halfway back to the van he stopped to exchange the camera over to his other hand. As he did, the camera wire tightened like a fishing line getting a fresh bite. The wire cracked like a whip, lifting a few feet off the ground behind him, remaining as snug as a trip wire. Ken turned and followed the cord with his eyes until he saw what had done it. Who had done it. The tall man with the black mask stood a ways back, his silhouette tall and ominous. It was as if the moon itself didn't want to spotlight him, leaving the sky above him a malevolent shade of darkness. The man had the cord in his gloved hand, just staring silently at Ken.

"Oh, fuck this!" Ken said, then dropped the camera to the ground, running toward the van without looking back.

The van was now only five feet away. He was going to make it out of there. The passenger door remained open, so all he had to do was jump in, start it up, and get the fuck out of Newport forever. There were no sounds coming from behind him. Was the tall man just watching him escape without doing anything?

And then, as if the man could read his mind, something shot through his hamstring, forcing its way out the front of his leg. Ken screamed and dropped to the ground. He looked down and was shocked to see the snapped end of the boom mic impaled completely through.

How the fuck is that even possible?

The tall man was at least ten feet away. The force it would have needed to complete such a feat, to throw the piece of equipment like a javelin, was inhuman. Supernatural. This man was no *man* but something far more sinister. The initial shock faded, and an extreme stabbing pain replaced it, bringing tears to Ken's eyes. He crawled, reaching for the van. He was so damn close. The jagged edge of the boom mic scraped against the ground as Ken army crawled. He did everything he could to ignore the pain.

Footsteps approached behind him. Ken stretched his arm as far as it could reach, relieved to feel the bottom of the van beneath his touch. He pulled himself up to his knees, grimacing as the metal pole tore through more muscle, and he collapsed forward. The footsteps stopped and were followed by a *woosh*. A sudden thump on the ground directly behind Ken startled him, and he realized the tall man had just leaped almost ten feet to land next to the van.

Ken peered over his shoulder, afraid of what he'd see. Blocking the beautiful night sky, the tall man with the black mask towered over him. Large black pupils, surrounded by smoldering embers of crimson stared at him with only one thing in mind. Murder. Ken realized he wouldn't make it out of this alive. But he wouldn't stop trying. He started to climb into the van when an oversized hand clamped down on his ankle, crushing the bone beneath its force. Ken was pulled back, landing hard on the ground and knocking the wind out of him. With his other leg, he kicked at the man's hand, but the grip was impenetrable.

The tall man planted his foot onto the center of Ken's back, pushing down with such force that Ken was sure his spine snapped.

"Please... Don't do it!" Ken begged with blood dripping from his mouth.

He pulled himself back up, making a half-assed attempt toward the van. His head and shoulders landed inside the vehicle, inches away from a crumpled-up McDonald's bag that Brennan must have tossed to the floor.

The tall man let go of his leg. Was he having second thoughts? Was he letting Ken go?

Ken knew that wish was desperate thinking. The leader of the coven grabbed hold of the passenger door, watching as Ken tried to pull himself the rest of the way inside. And then the man swung the door, driving it into Ken's ribs. Bones snapped on impact, sending flashes of light into Ken's vision. Again, the door opened and rammed into his side. Something warm released inside Ken's stomach. He slid down to his knees, falling mostly to the ground. *Mostly*. His head still rested on the edge of the doorway. He rolled over, now staring directly up at the man.

"Why? Wh-why are you doing this?"

"For getting in our way."

Before Ken could comprehend, the door swung shut again, crushing his skull beneath its force. Ken just wanted to die. But the tall man slammed the door onto his face, over and over, until his features were unrecognizable. His cheek, nose, and mouth caved inward, and he felt his right eye trying to force its way out of the socket. The man stopped, panting heavily. Ken's body involuntarily twitched, his bowels released, and he accepted death.

Please kill me.

The man grabbed the door one more time, throwing it against Ken's mangled head. The sickening *crunch* was the last sound Ken Kincade ever heard.

CHAPTER 44

Everything happened so fast. One minute, everyone was surrounding Bethany as she seemed to be stuck between consciousness and unconsciousness. The next, something bumped against the window and the tall man rushed outside to take care of it. When the rest of the coven approached Bethany, Cory screamed, only it wasn't just Cory. The force behind the scream rattled the windows, shook the foundation of the brick building.

Howie wasn't sure if it was Cory trying to protect Bethany, or the demon wanting to feast on her. Either way, it was now clear why they had brought Bethany. She was going to be sacrificed to the demon currently living inside of Cory. And Howie knew how that ended for Jessica Black. Cory had screamed a second time, clawing at the cement floor to try and break through the chain. The coven members just laughed at him, knowing they had him right where they wanted him.

So now, here they all were, back where they started. A standoff with Bethany in the middle of the floor. Howie looked at his dad, wanting protection, help, anything. But instead, his dad stared at the coven with hatred and rage.

"Why the hell would you three join this cult? That's what it is, a damn cult. This isn't a coven. You guys worship a demon. You're nothing but a bunch of fucking cowards," Howie's dad said.

"Look at the little priest over there behind you, trembling in the corner. And you want to call us cowards? Following a man like that for faith? We do what needs to be done. To restore the balance of power in this world. If anything, you should all feel honored to meet our leader. He doesn't make many...public appearances," Mullin said.

"If I break free from this chain, we'll see who the fucking cowards are!" the demon bellowed. The black veins in his neck bulged as he pulled at the metal links.

"Mullin, I knew something was up with you when I came to town. I should have gone with my gut sooner. Everything you had me do, something felt off. The Carver family"—he paused, taking in the damage done to Bethany—"what did you do to them?" He hadn't stopped aiming his firearm at them, making sure they kept their distance.

Mullin scoffed. "Like I said, we do what has to be done. That's all you need to know. And I see you're making the wrong choice. Picking the wrong side."

"There are no fucking sides! What the hell is wrong with you people? Mullin, there is still time to fix this. I'm not sure what you're involved in, but I know enough to know that you backed yourself into a corner by joining these people. We can—"

Troy's dad yelled, sending a painful cry echoing through the plant. They all turned to see Cory digging his razor-like nails into the meat of the unsuspecting coven member, using the flesh to latch on and pull Troy's dad closer. Within seconds, Cory shredded his face and throat, leaving a bloody mess at his feet. Nobody dared approach, but Father

Grimes said a prayer while Howie turned away, unable to watch his friend savagely murder someone before his eyes.

Howie turned back just in time to see Cory breaking free from the chain, ripping it from the concrete, and then leaping out of sight.

"Burt, go get him! I'll keep an eye on them until He's back."

Burt took off toward the darkness, grabbing hold of a green necklace that had been beneath his robe.

Ellis and Mullin stared each other down, while Father Grimes continued to try and get Henry Black fully alert. This second seizure appeared to take a bigger toll on Henry. He was awake, but speaking in a foreign tongue that Howie couldn't make out.

Howie's dad was the forgotten man in the scene, and he realized it. With Mullin focused on Ellis and Burt off chasing Cory, Howie's dad saw an opening and took it. He charged at Mullin, who attempted to draw his firearm in the process, but the chief wasn't quick enough. Howie's dad slammed the police chief into a concrete molding, ramming his back into the rebar beams. Mullin yelled out, dropping his gun. Howie's dad drove him into the bar again, dropping the chief to his knees. Howie remained frozen in place as his dad powered fist after fist into Mullin's face, bloodying the police chief.

"Bill, stop! You're going to kill him," Ellis said.

Howie's dad turned back to Ellis, heaving a lungful of breath. Howie had seen those eyes before, only he was on the receiving end of the beating. When his dad appeared this way, there was no reasoning with him.

"And? This son of a bitch deserves to die. They all do!" He turned to punch him again when Ellis stepped forward and pulled him back by the shoulder.

"Stand down, Bill. Don't make me cuff you. I'll cuff him to that rebar, then we can figure out what to do next. That tall man, he'll be back in here soon, and we need to have a plan," Ellis said, looking over at Henry and Father Grimes, who sensed the statement directed toward them.

"Henry's almost back with us. We can't rush this situation, or it could bring dire consequences. You must trust me on this," Grimes said.

"Take his gun and go search for the other one while I get Mullin taken care of. Then I'll try to get Henry somewhere safe until he's alert enough to help. But don't fire unless you have no choice, Bill. You don't want that weight on your shoulders, believe me. Howie, you'll stay with them until this is all over. We aren't about to lose another kid if I have anything to say about it."

"What about Bethany?" Howie asked.

Ellis sighed, apparently realizing he'd forgotten all about her during all the turmoil.

"That's how you can help. Why don't you take her to the office and lock the door, keep the lights off and don't make any noise. Can you do that?"

Howie stared at Bethany on the ground, her eyes still closed. Then he glanced back at his dad, who was picking up Mullin's gun off the ground. His dad nodded his approval, and that was all Howie needed. He didn't want to leave his dad's side, and he didn't want to abandon Cory. But if he could get Bethany to safety, then he could come back out and try to help Cory after. The adults wouldn't be happy, but he wouldn't stop until his friend was safe.

Howie kneeled next to Bethany and tried to lift her up carefully. He was afraid she had a concussion, or worse, something broken, and he didn't want to aggravate it. Her wrists were still bound. Howie spotted

Troy's knife on the ground, the one that was responsible for killing Cory's mom, and grabbed it. He sliced the zip tie, breaking it into two pieces and freeing her hands, then he threw the knife to the floor and wiped his hands on his pants.

"Bethany, can you hear me? We need to go—*now*," Howie said softly.

She groaned in return, her eyes fluttering. He placed his hand beneath her neck and lifted her to a sitting position, but she cried out with the movement.

"I'm sorry. I don't know what to do. Where does it hurt?"

She opened her eyes, squinting as if the sun was shining in them, even though the building was dimly lit at best.

"My head, my face. I can't see out of my eye."

Her cheek was so swollen that her right eye was practically sealed shut. Howie tried to hide his concern, but Bethany saw right through it.

"Is it bad?"

"You're alive, right? That's what matters right now," Howie said.

Bethany forced a smile, revealing a bloodied mouth. The tall man really did a number on her. But if Howie's theory was correct, they wouldn't kill her. Not until it was time to do what they came for. And as long as they didn't have Cory, they had no use for Bethany.

"Where is he? That man? He's not normal," she said, looking around frantically for the leader.

"I know... He went outside to chase down the news crew that followed us, but he's been gone awhile. He'll be back. We need to get to the office and lock the door. Can you walk?"

Bethany tried to get to her feet, but the pain in her face conveyed that she was far worse than she was letting on. She clutched at her ribs, wincing upon touch. Howie carefully put her arm over his shoulder and walked slowly toward the office in the far back corner. He wanted to move faster, as it was only a matter of time before Ruger was back. As they got closer to the office, Howie turned back to see if his dad was still okay, but he was nowhere to be seen, already off searching for Burt Rollins. Ellis was standing over Chief Mullin, locking handcuffs around his superior's wrist.

"In here. We have to be quiet, okay?" Howie said as they entered the office.

There was a desk with an expensive-looking office chair in the corner closest to the window that overlooked the workplace. In the back of the room there was a beat-up couch, well-worn from years of factory workers coming to clock in for the day or take their breaks. Howie guided Bethany to the couch and helped her sit. She rested her head against the cushion like she'd just climbed Mount Washington when, in reality, they had traveled maybe a hundred feet. Then Howie went back to the door, shutting and locking it. He closed the blinds, completely hiding them from the outside world.

"They got my entire family. My parents. My...my little sister. Even my cat," Bethany said, then broke down crying.

Howie felt sick to his stomach. Her sister was so young. How could they kill a little kid? Or anyone, for that matter? Bethany's family had nothing to do with the coven or their problems. He sat next to her and rubbed her shoulder.

"I'm so sorry. I can't even imagine."

After a few minutes of silence while Bethany cried on his shoulder, she surprised Howie, sitting up and staring at him with eyes that would intimidate anyone who dared stare at her.

"We have to stop them. No matter what."

CHAPTER 45

Ellis stared down at Chief Mullin, wondering how anyone could ever get involved in something so sinister. Seeing the police chief with a black robe on like he was about to attend a late Halloween party wasn't something he could get used to. And Mullin's bloodied face only added to it. The chief was still conscious, but he was far from alert. He tried to lift his head as Ellis handcuffed him to the rebar structure but lacked the strength to do it and eventually just conceded, allowing his head to drop to his chest as blood dripped from his split lip.

"Who else is involved, Mullin? I don't dare call this in. Do you have the entire department working with them? Huh? Answer me!"

Over the years, Ellis had dealt with many horrendous cases. Child murders. Rape victims. Murder for hires. But he had never seen anything this elaborate. This sadistic. Not only that, but until the last few days, he'd never even believed in anything supernatural or demonic. Now, he was given no choice but to believe. The way Cory Stevens looked, and the abnormal strength he displayed to break a chain clear off a concrete block, that wasn't normal. Everything Sandy Stevens told him was true.

Ellis hated himself for not reacting in time to save her. The kid from the coven had come out of nowhere, and while Ellis didn't have a good shot either way, it was the fact that he wasn't prepared that bothered him. He allowed himself to get too caught up in everything going on.

Instead of answering, Mullin just mumbled through his swollen lips, spitting blood on Ellis's boot. With Mullin contained and Howie and Bethany safe in the office for now, Ellis turned his attention to Father Grimes and Henry. Henry was now sitting up, but his eyes were glossed over like he had just finished a week-long bender, and he was staring at the ceiling. He spoke in what Ellis assumed was Latin, but he couldn't be sure. Father Grimes eyed Ellis with concern.

"He usually comes to by now. I'm afraid he may not be back with us in time to do what needs to be done."

"What the hell is he saying?"

"*Ad finem omnia, sacrificium dandum est*," Grimes repeated to himself more than to Ellis.

"Yeah, thanks. I got that part. What does it mean?"

"He's saying to end it all, a sacrifice must be given."

"Sacrifice? He sounds like one of them. Clearly, you can't take anything this nutjob says serious...*right*?" Ellis asked.

"I assure you, while he may seem a bit off, he's never wrong with these visions."

"So, what? We have to sacrifice someone to the coven? I'd just as soon take down their leader and stop them that way. I'm not going to watch you guys give up a young girl to them. Is that what you're saying?"

"No. The girl is who *they* are trying to use to attract the demon, then they can trap it inside her like they had done with Jessica. As soon as the demon was free from her, Vorathor came back, set on making it right again. It will help them maintain the power they desire. We must make sure the girl is safe."

"I really need answers, not a riddle."

The large window overlooking the main floor shattered, sending shards of glass raining down around them. Startled, Ellis looked up, expecting Cory Stevens. Instead, the man with the black mask sat perched on the window frame, staring down at them.

Bill Burke was glancing around the corner of a concrete container when the glass shattered. From where he stood, he couldn't see what caused the window explosion, and he didn't want to lose focus on what he was there for. He still hadn't found Burt, or Cory for that matter, but he knew they'd headed in this direction. One thing he made clear to Howie was that if he came across Cory, he wouldn't hesitate to do whatever he needed to stop the kid. Because he knew it wasn't really the kid inside, and he *knew* that there was no getting the kid Howie considered a brother back. Bill had lost people close to him because of the same demon, and he'd been forced to eventually move on. Howie would, too. His son was stronger than he ever was, and someday he'd realize it was the right thing to do. He was proud of the kid Howie turned out to be, in spite of the way he was raised, not because of it. Bill just couldn't bring himself to tell the boy. He needed to right that wrong, but that would have to wait.

He held the gun, something he hadn't done in years, and the firearm felt foreign. He'd never fired at another person before. The last time he was put in a situation to save someone, he froze and watched the love of his life get ripped open. Bill wouldn't let that happen again. He already regretted letting Howie come with him. Admittedly, he never truly loved Howie's mother. She was there when he needed someone, and that branched out into an unenthusiastic proposal, followed by an even less enthusiastic marriage. When Howie was born, Bill resented the kid. He wasn't supposed to be the one Bill raised. He knew he took things—that nobody should ever get away with—out on an innocent child. He hated himself for it every day. But that didn't help make it easy to stop. Not when Bill himself grew up abused by a dad who went far more extreme than Bill ever had on Howie. Not that he thought that made him any better than his dad, but he did set out to be a better father than he grew up with, and for that, he at least thought he succeeded.

As Bill grew older, he understood his dad more. The reasons he was so violent. Bill's grandmother was an early member of the coven, and while the coven was much more peaceful back in the day, she was still a nasty lady. She would often use her witch abilities to fuck with Bill's dad, getting in his head and making him think inappropriate thoughts. The physical abuse Bill suffered was nothing compared to the *mental* abuse his dad dealt with on a daily basis.

Although Bill wanted to stop the abuse, and he wanted to love his wife the way a husband was supposed to, the anger was ingrained in him from an early age and only intensified after the horrific events out in the woods. There wasn't a night that went by where he didn't see flashes of Sheila's torn insides, the unborn baby savagely shoved to the side by a demon set on getting to her heart. Bill would always hate himself—that was a given. But if he could end this whole thing, bring down the demon and the coven all in the same night, he truly thought he could be at peace.

A flash of movement shot around the corner of the next container, snapping him from his thoughts. It was an illusion of black-on-black movement, the robed figure sneaking stealthily through the shadows.

Bill raised the gun, afraid to fire and miss. He didn't want to give his spot away or attract any more attention from others. Instead, he attempted to keep the distance between them short, making as little noise as possible. Where the hell was Cory? After he broke free, he darted away into the darkness.

The main floor came to an end, leading to a narrow hall on the left that was absent of any light, and Bill thought he heard something coming from the abyss. Heavy breathing. Or was that crying? Then there were whispers. His hands shook, rattling the gun in his grip. He wasn't sure what to expect down the hall, but he forced himself to move forward. Any sign of light had been sucked out of the hallway as if trying to warn Bill not to proceed. He did so anyway, and at first, he struggled to comprehend what he was looking at. He expected to find Burt hiding in the corner waiting to attack him. But it was Cory in front of him, crouched low on all fours. His eyes glowed orange, faintly displaying his facial features. Bill wished he didn't see anything at all on the kid's face. This wasn't his son's best friend—he'd as much stated that fact to Howie—but deep down, Bill had hoped there was a chance to save him.

Cory bared his razor teeth toward Bill like a rabid dog.

"Hey, Billy! Think your daddy is treating your dead baby the way he treated you?"

Bill aimed the gun with his trembling hand, his finger hovering over the trigger. He wanted to fire, to put a bullet right between this little shit's eyes. But he couldn't bring himself to do it.

Cory stood from his crouch, and that's when Bill spotted the thornlike spikes poking through his pants and shirt. It was as if Cory's entire body grew a defense system to keep the demon safe.

"What's the matter, Bill? First time seeing a demon? You look like you're about to piss yourself."

"You little shit. I should shoot you right here!"

"Do it. It won't kill me, but you know that already. And hell, if you get rid of this body, maybe I'll just take yours. Better yet, I'll take your son's. He'd love to get some payback on you after all these years."

Bill stepped forward, his finger inching closer to the trigger. Cory's disfigured body became more visible the closer he got. Those orange eyes, they were the same ones Jessica had the night she took everything from him. Memories flashed through Bill's mind of freezing in his truck while Sheila had her insides ravaged. Of Sheila staring up at him with her drained complexion, telling him to save their boy. He'd been too late to save the baby. He'd been too late to stop the demon from killing his family. He wasn't going to let that happen again.

With the barrel of the gun aimed as steady as possible, Bill pulled the trigger.

CHAPTER 46

Howie didn't dare open the door, but he had to know what was happening. Just minutes after the glass shattering, the sound of a gunshot exploded like a stick of dynamite. He observed Bethany, who was doing her best to hold it together, but after everything she'd been through over the last twenty-four hours, she didn't have much left in the tank.

"We have to go out and help," she said.

"I know… But we need to know what we're getting ourselves into first. We know there were at least three coven members here tonight, and Cory broke free. That tall man, it's Felix Ruger, the guy who owns a ton of property in town. Henry said he's the leader, and he's possessed by another demon. He could be back any minute. We have to have a plan first," he said. Then he realized she had no idea about what had gone down before she got there. "That man with us, that's Henry Black."

"What? What are you talking about?"

"He's alive, Bethany. He thinks he can get the demon out of Cory and save him. But we need to stop the coven first. They… They want to sacrifice you to the demon that's inside Cory. It's what they tried with Jessica, and until we found her grave, their deal was still in place. Henry thinks the leader of the coven, the tall man, made a deal with a more powerful demon. If they can get the demon from Cory into you and trap it, their sacrifice will be in good order again. Does any of this make sense?"

She shook her head, confused by it all.

"No. Henry's alive? There's more than one demon? What the hell are we supposed to do? I guess it all makes sense why they kept me alive…" The realization hit her that her family was murdered so they could take her. Sadness infiltrated her eyes as she put the pieces together.

"You stay here. I'll go check on them," Howie said, starting to unlock the door.

"No way. I sat back and did what you asked at the school and look where that got you guys. Cory is possessed right now. I'm not hiding out again while you go do all the macho man stuff and try to save the day, Howie."

"I… But they want you, Bethany. If they can't find you, they can't take you," Howie said, trying to choke down the tears. He couldn't lose another friend, and he and Bethany had grown much closer over the past week.

"I appreciate you being considerate, I really do. But they killed my entire family. They're the reason Cory's possessed, and they're trying to not only use me to trap this thing but to kill Cory in the process. So, no, I don't think I'll sit back and watch it all happen."

"Well, that's that, I suppose. Are you okay to move now, though?"

"I feel a little better now that I've rested. My ribs really hurt, but that's the least of my worries right now."

"Can you see okay out of that eye? It looks pretty rough."

"Wow, thanks for the compliment," she said, but then a smirk followed.

Howie felt his cheeks burn, hopeful the dark room hid the embarrassment.

"Okay, then. Let's go."

If his dad saw him walking around, he'd be pissed. But right now, after hearing a gunshot and something breaking a window, he would almost prefer to see his dad give him that glare that sent fear down his spine growing up. Because the alternative was far worse.

Father Grimes was relieved to see Henry getting to his feet. He wasn't sure if it was safe for Henry to move around yet, but they were on borrowed time. When Henry spotted Ruger perched on the window, his eyes drained any ounce of confidence they had before the seizure. His suspicion of Ruger leading the coven was all but confirmed, as well as Ruger somehow being connected with Vorathor. At that moment, Ruger continued to stare down at the scene, and Grimes wasn't sure what he was doing. It reminded him of a hawk waiting for the right moment to attack its prey.

"Henry, are you sure you're okay enough to move?"

"I have no choice. I need to get the brand ready, Father. I'm not sure we can save the boy, but none of that will matter if we don't stop Ruger."

Grimes looked to Officer Ellis, then at Henry's bag on the ground next to him, spotting the iron rod and blowtorch. Were they really going to seal a demon in Cory's body? It would be a great sacrifice to the town, but it wasn't something Grimes was comfortable proceeding with. He'd promised Howie they would do everything in their power to extract the demon from his friend, yet the first sign of trouble and they were ready to lock it in place and be done with it.

"So what's the plan? Do we try to save him first, or not? And what of Vorathor?" Grimes asked.

"I told you, I'm not willing to intentionally give them a kid, and I'm not about to shoot Cory either. I promised his mom I'd try to help him, and I intend to honor that promise. There has to be another way," Ellis said.

"If we can find the boy first, I can try to get the demon inside the amulet. But I need time, not only to speak to him and convince him, but enough time to make sure the binding spell is in place. We need to extract Atahsaia, then seal him in."

Grimes glanced back up at Ruger. The demon locked eyes with him, and even from his height, the priest could still see his ruby eyes—more like balls of a raging inferno—as the leader watched him in disgust.

What is he doing up there?

But it didn't take long for Grimes to figure it out. The reason Ruger wasn't attacking was because he was hunting. He was searching for Bethany. She was the final piece they needed. Father Grimes wasn't about to let that happen.

It was time he helped get rid of the evil in this town.

"I can help, Henry. I'll distract Ruger while you go find Cory and work your magic. I can hold him off long enough for you if you get a move on."

"Father, no offense, but I'm not going to leave an old man to a sure death. I'll wait here with you while Henry searches for Cory," Officer Ellis said.

Henry furrowed his brow in uncertainty. It didn't matter if he thought Grimes and Ellis could get the job done or not, they had no other options. So Henry grabbed his bag and rushed off into the body of the concrete plant.

CHAPTER 47

Bill wasn't sure if he'd hit Cory with the shot or not. As he was pulling the trigger, a sharp pain pierced his lower back, dropping him to his knees. He stared over his shoulder to see Burt holding a bloody knife. It took a second to register, but he realized the blood was his own. He'd been stabbed in the lower back.

"Sorry, Bill. We need the boy alive. Can't let you be killing him without the sacrifice. Nothing personal."

"Motherfucker," Bill said through gritted teeth.

Burt Rollins lifted the knife, prepared to bury it in Bill's flesh again, and all Bill could do was prepare for the killing blow. Everything next happened so quickly that he only got a glimpse of it. Something flew over his head, landing on Burt's chest, driving him to the floor. Bill didn't realize it was Cory until the funeral home director let out a bloodcurdling cry.

The sound was horrible. And all too familiar. Bill recognized it as the same sound he heard when Sheila was torn to shreds. Cory was on top of Burt's chest, ripping and clawing. Blood sprayed across the concrete floor with each swipe of his clawed hands. Tiny spikes traveled across the back of Cory's neck like thorny goose bumps.

It's too late to save him. Shoot him while he's not looking, Bill thought.

He raised the gun once more, ignoring the numbing sensation spreading along his back. Ignoring every memory of this very boy being like a brother to his own son, attending all the birthday parties, sleepovers, and wrestling out back on the trampoline like they were WWF superstars.

Cory drove his hand into Burt's chest, leading to one final cry for help before his life ended. Cory ripped out the heart of the funeral home director, squeezing it in his hand. The squishy sound of the organ was the most disgusting sound Bill had ever heard. And then Cory raised it to his mouth, opening wide. Bill couldn't watch him eat it. He stepped forward, now only a few feet behind Cory. *It'll be like putting a sick animal out of its misery—pull the trigger before you have to make eye contact.*

"I'm sorry," Bill whispered.

"Bill, don't do it!"

Bill followed the voice and saw Henry speeding toward them with his duffle bag over his shoulder. He held an iron rod in one hand, the end of it was glowing orange with an intricate design that Bill had seen before. He spotted the blowtorch in Henry's other hand.

Cory looked up, yet to bite into the bloody heart. He saw Henry approaching, saw the symbol glowing in the darkness. Bill assumed the boy was about to jump off and attack Henry, and he was prepared to shoot him at the first movement. Instead of attacking, Cory froze as if he was afraid of the symbol.

"Demon, it's time we had a talk," Henry said.

"Henry, how could you do this to me?" It came from Cory's mouth, but it was a female voice. Bill knew it all too well. Jessica. The demon was trying to get in Henry's head.

"Don't listen to it, Henry!"

"Bill, we were like family. Sheila didn't deserve what happened to her. Neither did the baby," she said. The way the light hit Cory's face in the shadows, it was so strange. Not only was the voice Jessica's, but the boy's features shifted slightly, and the expressions were that of Henry's dead wife.

"Jessica..." Henry whispered.

"You know it's not her. Stop letting it get in your head," Bill snapped.

Bill walked over to Henry, grimacing with each step. He knew he was likely bleeding out as something felt off, like a warm mass spreading through his insides. Henry didn't even see him coming, his eyes were glued to Cory. Bill grabbed him by the shoulders and shook him.

"Snap the fuck out of it!"

Henry shifted his attention to Bill, shaking his head as if he'd just been in a trance. He reached into the bag and pulled out the amulet, which now had a green glow to it. Bill didn't recall seeing the bright light before, but he hadn't been paying much attention when Henry explained everything he'd packed. Cory's face mutated back to normal—as normal as one could appear while possessed by a demon.

"Quid est?" the demon spat.

"You know what this is, Atahsaia. It contains the hearts of the fallen. An endless supply of what you crave, demon. You can smell it, can't you?"

Bill watched in shock as Cory climbed off the limp body of Burt Rollins, his orange eyes staring at the amulet with a craving fit for a starving beast discovering the biggest meal it could ever eat. Black drool slid down his mouth as he slowly stepped forward, and he dropped Burt's heart to the floor. His nostrils flared, smelling the aroma he desired.

"*Give it to me... Give me the amulet,* now!" The voice came out like a pack of rats clawing at his vocal cords.

"There's only one way to attain it. You must enter the amulet. You must swim through a sea of organs, and you'll have what you desire," Henry said in a commanding voice that carried much more confidence than Bill felt at the moment.

Cory continued moving forward, his back hunched as the tiny thorns continued to grow through his skin, forcing pus through open wounds. He licked the black spit leaking down his chin, breathing heavily.

This is actually going to work, Bill thought.

He wanted to feel relief. He wanted to feel hope. But he couldn't shake the feeling of something bad happening. Henry still held the metal rod in his other hand, a backup plan to trap the demon in Cory's body if the amulet didn't work. As Cory got within a few feet of Henry, something briefly covered the moonlight coming in through the windows above, followed by a *woosh*. Bill looked up, and fear prickled his skin.

The tall man, Felix Ruger, was gliding down from his perch. He appeared even larger than he had up close, with his wingspan so wide it had to be over ten feet. Bill realized they weren't actual wings but the coven leader's robe, torn apart at the back, making it more like a makeshift cape. Ruger landed somewhere out of sight, behind one of the large concrete containers.

Father Grimes tried to contain the terror that now smothered his thoughts. Ruger was bigger than he was before he went outside after the news crew. Angrier. The red in his eyes melted any faith Grimes had committed to his entire life. Ruger landed ten feet from them, cracking the floor beneath his feet. He ripped off his mask and threw it to the floor, displaying a hideous face that shifted rapidly, skin stretching and tearing, revealing raw meat beneath. He focused on Grimes, ignoring Ellis and walking straight toward the priest. He wasn't just taller, his limbs had extended, both in length and radius, tearing at the cloth. Something swam beneath his skin under the hood, and Grimes momentarily froze, unsure what to even do.

"Priest, your faith has no power over me. You are only getting in my way."

"Don't move! Stand down!" Ellis yelled.

Ruger paused his attention on Grimes and slowly turned his head until he was facing Officer Ellis. He looked at the gun and laughed. Ruger made a sudden movement toward Ellis, and the cop fired, the shot connecting in Ruger's chest. The tall man jerked back, then narrowed his eyes and rubbed away the liquid oozing from the wound.

"Really... You really are that stupid, aren't you?"

Then he brought his insidious eyes back to Ellis, who attempted to fire again, but Ruger backhanded the gun from his grip, sending it across the floor. Ellis reached for his baton, but Ruger was on him in a flash. He grabbed the cop by the hair and swiped across his face, snapping Ellis's jaw and sending him through the air. Ellis crunched against the concrete container and dropped to the ground. His body wasn't moving.

Grimes backed up slowly, squeezing the cross in his hand. He couldn't even get the prayers out, couldn't bring himself to hold the cross up in front of him. Instead, he hugged it to his chest and hoped it was all just a horrible nightmare. Ruger smiled as if he knew Grimes's spirit was diminished to nothing more than dust particles floating around the concrete plant.

"What's wrong? Your God not answering you anymore?"

"Vorathor... Go back to Hell where you belong. In the name of God, I command you, foul creature of darkness, to depart from this vessel and return to the abyss from whence you came! By the power vested in me as a servant of the Divine, I banish you! Begone, and trouble this soul no more!"

Ruger just laughed as he continued closing the distance.

"I'm not troubling any soul, priest. He *invited* me in. We have a mutual agreement, a partnership, if you will. So I'll say it again, your power is useless over me."

Grimes took another step back, but this time his back pressed against something. He realized he was backed up against the same concrete mold that Ellis slammed into with nowhere to go. Finally, he remembered to raise the cross, preparing to give another command. Ruger stared at the cross, disgusted, but it didn't stop him from approaching. His arm shot out, the extended limb reaching well beyond its normal range. Grimes had no time to react; the cross was thrown from his hands, and before he realized what was happening, Ruger had a firm grip on his throat, squeezing tightly.

The force was unlike any Grimes had ever felt. Squeezing around his neck so tightly that he thought the base of his spine was about to snap in half. His eyes bulged, breath fighting to enter his lungs. Ruger lifted him off the ground with ease, pressing him against the container behind him.

"This...all could have been avoided if you had just let us handle it. Now you, along with the rest of them, will suffer," Ruger said, his rancid breath permeating Grimes's sense of smell.

The priest closed his eyes, accepting that his death was coming. Accepting that he would soon be with his Heavenly Father. He just hoped he had bought enough time for Henry to do his part. When Grimes opened his eyes, Ruger had his free hand raised near his head as if he was about to throw a punch. Only he didn't keep his fist closed; he opened it and extended his elongated fingers, sharp nails pointing directly at Grimes's face. And then he drove the fingers into Grimes's eyes, plowing them through to the back of his skull. Grimes began to twitch, his thoughts fading away. Ruger squeezed inside of his head and tore down, ripping everything from the eyes to the mouth clean off the priest's face as if it was simply old wallpaper.

When Ruger pulled his hand from the new cavity, he now stared at a canvas full of gore and shattered bone. He dropped the priest to the ground, glaring down at the lump of flesh. Then he walked in the direction he'd spotted the girl and boy sneaking out of the office. It was time to make the sacrifice.

CHAPTER 48

Howie held Bethany close, helping her limp along in the dark. They made their way toward the back, away from where the tall man had landed when he jumped. He had heard multiple gunshots in different locations of the building, so he wasn't sure where to go. He wanted to get to Henry and make sure they could at least get the demon out of Cory before it was too late. He hoped Henry also had a plan for Ruger. Otherwise, it would all be for nothing.

They leaned against the back wall, moving along slowly, avoiding making too much noise. Howie prayed the gunshots didn't kill anyone he cared about. He'd seen enough death over the last few weeks. He heard shouting up ahead and tried to pick up the pace as best he could with Bethany hurting. When they got past some of the large equipment, Howie stopped in his tracks. His dad was on the ground but moving. Howie spotted blood beneath him. His heart sped up at the sight, wondering if his dad was on the verge of dying.

Next to him, Henry held the amulet he'd packed in his bag, only now it was glowing green. He was speaking in another language while Cory inched closer to him, reaching out for the amulet. The skin on Cory's face was stretching as if something was trying to tear through the flesh. Whatever was in the amulet, the demon wanted it. Henry backed up, continuing his chant while Cory became increasingly impatient to get to it.

"*Give it what it wants, my dear Henry,*" Cory said, but the voice came out female. Judging by Henry's face Howie assumed it was the voice of Jessica.

"My wife is dead. Your tricks won't work on me, Atahsaia!"

With Cory distracted, Howie went to his dad.

"Dad, are you okay?"

His dad winced, baring his tobacco-stained teeth.

"I'll be okay. I'm not dead. Fucker stabbed me in the back. What are you doing out of the office, boy?"

"I heard gunshots and was worried something happened to you. I'm scared..."

"Don't be a pussy. You need to get back in the office now. We got this."

Bethany squeezed Howie's arm, and he turned to see why. The towering figure of Felix Ruger approached, and he was getting close. Howie glanced back to Cory, making sure he wasn't going to get a surprise attack from behind. Henry was leading him somewhere, but Howie wasn't sure where. Whatever was in the amulet, it was working, leading the demon like a farmer herding sheep.

"Howie, go *now*. Let us handle this," his dad said. It was the first time Howie recalled hearing fear in his dad's tone, but he couldn't blame him. Ruger was intimidating enough as it was. Now, he was transitioning into something far worse. Behind his hood, the red eyes lit his hideous facial expression now that the mask was removed from his face.

Howie had no intention of going anywhere until this was over, though. His dad slowly got to his feet to stand side by side with him. They needed to slow Ruger down. Howie wasn't sure how long the demon trap took to work, but based on Cory's appearance, he thought it might be close to done. Cory continued his march toward Henry.

Without warning, Ruger stopped, and Howie wasn't sure if he was going to stand there and watch them or not. But then the tall man's limbs cracked and snapped, his face expanded, revealing a mouthful of blackened teeth similar to Cory's mouth. Howie watched in horror as Ruger's fingers extended to be a foot long, knifelike claws protruding from his fingernails. His head twitched to the side, cracking his neck.

"Atahsaia, look at me when I'm talking to you. The hearts of the fallen await you," Henry snapped.

Howie was so focused on Ruger, he didn't notice Cory had turned to watch the tall man as he transitioned into a full-blown monster. Cory shifted back to Henry, again focusing on the amulet. Howie had even more respect for Bethany than he did before. She knew the coven wanted her, that Ruger wasn't just coming for all of them, that his intentions were set on her, yet she stood her ground next to him. The three of them blocked Ruger from getting to Henry.

"You fools. I will tear you all to pieces and make the girl watch it. You dare get in my way?"

"You almost done back there, Henry?" Howie's dad asked without taking his eyes off Ruger.

Henry didn't answer and instead continued his chants as the green glow intensified. Vorathor took complete control of Ruger, his inhuman abilities on full display. The coven leader leaped over their heads, clearing them with ease and landing near Henry, who stopped his chant and turned in time to see Ruger swinging his arm down like a mallet toward his head. Henry dove to the side, avoiding the brunt of contact, but he was still hit hard enough to drop the amulet; Cory's eyes went wide as he watched it slide across the floor.

Howie's dad aimed the gun and fired multiple shots, hitting Ruger in the back. He whipped around, coming face-to-face with Howie's dad. The demon's eyes glowed with rage. Ruger raised his clawed hand and lunged at him, driving the daggers into flesh.

"Dad, no!" Howie yelled.

Howie's dad focused on the wound just above his collarbone. Blood poured out of the holes down his shirt. Ruger pulled back, retracting his claws to strike again. Then he bellowed so loud that glass shattered, exploding the windows around them. At first, Howie wasn't sure why, until he spotted Henry standing behind him, a cloud of smoke sizzling around them. Henry backed up, revealing the iron brand.

Ruger's eyes opened wide as the realization of what Henry just did set in. He had trapped Vorathor inside of Ruger, who snarled and grabbed Henry by the neck.

"You fucking scum!" Ruger snapped.

And then, with one quick strike, he sliced his claws across Henry's neck with such force that Henry's head snapped back, most of his throat and neck disintegrated. Henry's head fell to the side, clinging to his body by a thread of skin and muscle. His dead eyes moved one last time to meet Howie's dad, as if to give one last apology for everything he'd done to Bill's family, then Henry fell to the floor.

With everyone distracted, Cory took the opportunity to go for the amulet. As he reached for it, Ruger stomped on the glass piece, shattering it beneath his boot. Cory and Ruger came face-to-face, staring each other down. A malevolent thickness surrounded them. Howie shook off the shock and grabbed Bethany by the arm.

"I don't know what to do anymore. Henry was the only one who knew what to say. I'm not sure how to stop it now," Howie admitted.

Bethany trembled, knowing exactly what that meant. If they couldn't stop Cory, the demon would come for her. Ruger took in his surroundings, spotting Bethany and Howie.

"I told you, I come offering a gift. The heart of a virgin, your favorite kind. The amulet didn't carry half the power her body does, and you know it."

Howie shuddered when Cory zoned in on Bethany, his eyes eating her up from head to toe. Cory took a step in her direction.

"Cory, don't do it, man. She's your friend. Don't listen to the thing inside you. It's Bethany it wants; don't let it take her."

Cory clenched his fists and kept moving. Howie wasn't sure what to do without the amulet or Henry. He was trying to think of a way to save his friend while protecting Bethany at the same time. They needed a new plan, and they weren't going to come up with one in this situation. Without another word, Howie nudged Bethany to move. They took off in a sprint, back toward the direction they had come from. Behind them, he heard movement. The demons were coming for them.

CHAPTER 49

They took the stairs to the second level, to a catwalk that lined the perimeter of the building, overlooking the main floor. Bethany was in so much pain, but she knew if they didn't move, Ruger would get her. Their steps echoed off the metal platform with a loud *gong*. Howie stopped and peered down through the metal grate, where they could see everything beneath. The main floor had to be close to twenty feet down. The demons were nowhere to be seen.

"We need to be quiet. I'm not sure if they saw us come up here," Howie said.

"What are we going to do? He's too powerful, Howie. We should have gone for the exit."

He knew she was right, but if they had run, not only would Howie's dad be left for dead, but Cory would still be possessed, and Ruger would still be alive. Bethany walked to the edge of the catwalk, looking down over the side of the railing. They were right over the top of the liquid concrete slabs. She could see bodies scattered about. Cory's mom and Troy, what was left of Father Grimes. Mullin appeared to be alive, but he was handcuffed the way Ellis left him. Speaking of Ellis, Bethany didn't spot him anywhere. Hopefully he was still alive. Howie's dad appeared to not be moving. And then there was Henry, with his head hanging on by a strand of flesh, collapsed in a dead heap. But Ruger and Cory were missing.

Something moved beneath them so quickly she would've missed it had she blinked. A clinking noise, like nails tapping on steel, started quietly and picked up in volume. She realized it was Cory, climbing up the metal structure to reach them.

The only way down was to go back the way they came. Bethany turned back toward the stairs and stopped, seeing Ruger was halfway up the stairs now, slowly closing in on his sacrifice. There was nowhere for them to go.

"If we have to jump, will you do it?" Howie asked.

"Jump? That far down?"

The thought terrified her, although not nearly as much as what was approaching on each side.

"Yes. If we can land in that liquid concrete, I think it will be deep enough that we won't hit the bottom. I can't be sure, but there's nowhere else to go."

"I don't know if I can do it…"

They got closer to the railing as Ruger reached the top of the platform.

"Girl, you're making this far more difficult than it needs to be. Don't you want to join the rest of your family?" Ruger asked.

She hated him. Everything he stood for. And she knew even if she did give up, she wouldn't be dying, but trapped forever with something inside her, eating at her insides and making her a monster. Ruger took one long step across the metal grate platform, and even a soft step by him rattled the whole floor beneath them. Howie stood next to her but turned in the opposite direction as the *tick-tick-tick* on the metal was now much closer. She didn't dare take her eyes off Ruger.

Howie heard it before he saw it. At first, it almost sounded like pipes expanding, and then he realized something was climbing up to the second level. Staring down below and hearing an approaching sound brought back images of the ski jump. And just like Jessica climbing over the edge to come face-to-face with them, Cory appeared, leaping over the guardrail and landing a few feet from Howie. Bethany gasped but kept her back to Howie. They were cornered by two different demons with similar intentions.

"Oh, I can smell that virgin heart beating, girl." The words slithered out of Cory's mouth.

"Atahsaia, you know how this works. We sacrifice the girl, you get her body, her heart, and anything else you could ever dream of. In return, we get back control of this space. You no longer get in our way. You move on somewhere else. For if we ever see you here again, we will banish you for eternity. Do you understand?"

"Yes. Give her to me. I'll do horrible things to her body before I'm done with it."

Howie wasn't sure if Vorathor was attempting to trick Atahsaia or truly intended to let them go their separate ways. Either way, it ended with Bethany dying. And he wouldn't let that happen.

"Cory, I know you're still in there. Don't give in to it. *Please.* We can get this thing out of you," Howie said.

"Oh, that's where you're wrong, little bitch boy. He loves it. He's fully surrendered his body to me, and every time he thinks of getting his hands on her, he gets stiff. Even if it is just a little prick between his legs," Cory

said, but this time in a different voice than Howie had heard come from the demon.

Any hope Howie had of saving his friend vanished. Up until now, it at least seemed Cory still had some control, that he could fight and stop the demon from taking hold entirely. With his attention stuck on his best friend, Howie didn't see Ruger until he was on them. A sudden crack in his ribs was followed by a burning pain. Howie dropped to the platform and rolled over, staring up at the coven leader as he grabbed Bethany by the hair and dragged her away.

"Let her go!" Howie yelled, and with each word, another burst of agony shot through his back and into his lungs.

Ruger pulled Bethany to the railing, and Howie thought he was going to throw her over the side. Instead, he tore cloth from his tattered robe, then forced a struggling Bethany to remain still as he tied the cloth around her wrists one at a time, leaving her in a crucifix position overlooking the floor below. She screamed, fighting to break free. When Ruger leaned close to inspect his knots, she spit in his face. Ruger snarled, but it slowly transitioned into a smile. He wiped the spit away, admiring his glistening finger. Then he licked the saliva, and his red eyes rolled back into his head.

"Yes, I see why Atahsaia wants you so bad."

Before she could respond, Ruger struck her across the face. Bethany's head whipped to the side and then slumped down. He had knocked her out for the second time tonight. Howie tried to get up, but Cory held him down. Cory grabbed Howie by the hair and yanked his head back.

"Cory knows you want to steal his girl. To fuck her brains out and leave him for dead. Sadly, for you, that will never happen," the demon said.

Then he pulled back more on Howie's hair, his mouth now inches from Howie's ear. "Trust me..." he whispered.

Howie didn't dare look, but he knew in his heart it was really Cory. He wasn't sure what his plan was, but if Ruger believed it was Atahsaia and not Cory talking, they might stand a chance. Ruger remained focused on Bethany, lifting her head up and pushing it back, watching as it fell limp and exposed her bare throat. He then pulled a blade from his pocket and pressed the tip to her neck. Howie could only watch as he dug into the skin, carving a design. Cory tensed but remained in character.

Behind Ruger, someone was quietly coming up the stairs.

Dad.

Ruger turned as Howie's dad charged at him, the scalding rod that Henry had branded Ruger with earlier in his hand. His dad moved at full speed, but even with Ruger distracted, his supernatural abilities still allowed him to react quickly enough to avoid the blow as the rod came swinging down. Ruger let go of Bethany and turned to face Howie's dad.

"Now you're just pissing me off," Ruger snapped.

Howie's dad didn't wait for him to retaliate. He drove the brand up into Ruger's face, pressing it just below his eye. The skin sizzled as smoke emitted from the wound. Howie smelled the burning flesh and gagged. Ruger stumbled back, falling to one knee. Howie's dad pulled back and drove the scorching iron into Ruger's open mouth. Ruger growled deep from within, choking on the end of the rod. Howie's dad pushed it further in, and the sounds that escaped Ruger were made of nightmares.

"You've tortured this town long enough. Choke on it, fuck face!" Howie's dad said. He then reached into his pocket and pulled something out. Howie recognized the dagger that Henry had packed. His dad prepared to stab the dagger into Ruger's heart.

Ruger's eyes bulged, and Howie thought he saw smoke behind the red. The coven leader opened his mouth wide, expanding his jaw and cracking bones. His jaw unhinged, and another set of razor teeth expanded behind the first set. He grabbed hold of the metal rod, burning his palms, but he didn't even react to it. He pulled the rod from his throat, and Howie's dad dropped the dagger, again focusing on the rod and trying to force it back down with all the strength he had in him. And then the end of the rod came free from his mouth, and he snapped the wrist of Howie's dad. Bill groaned, dropping the scalding bar to the ground as his wrist dangled limply, the bone forcing its way through the flesh. Ruger bit down on the mangled hand, tearing it completely free and then spit it on the floor. Howie's dad looked at his arm, now only a jagged bone and loose muscle dangling from where the hand used to be.

Ruger grabbed Howie's dad by the head and drove it down, driving it off the metal railing. Howie heard his dad's neck snap as the railing shattered his teeth and nose. Ruger pulled back and rammed his head down, again and again, until all that was left was mush. Bill Burke's lifeless body dropped to the floor.

Howie burst into tears, reaching for his dad, but he couldn't reach the dead body. The pressure of Cory pressing down on him vanished and he found himself crawling to his dad, or what was left of him. He reached the body and lay on top of it, crying into his chest. After everything they had been through, the abuse, the insults, the lack of love, it seemed as if they were finally turning a corner, the start of a real relationship forming. Now, he'd never get to see it play out.

As he lay on his dad, a hand grabbed him by the neck and jerked him up. It was Ruger, his face now a burned wreck. Blisters had already begun to ooze pus around his lips and on his tongue. The bottom of his eyelid had burned completely off, exposing the entire eyeball in a storm of violent red. Ruger lifted his hand, the claws extracting once more. Howie had seen this exact thing happen to Henry moments ago. But then Ruger glared over Howie's shoulder and loosened his grip.

"No! Don't... You'll ruin everything!" Ruger said.

He dropped Howie to the floor and stepped over him. Howie turned over and saw Cory holding the metal branding rod. The orange glow of the symbol had faded since his dad burned it into Ruger, but it was still carrying significant heat. Howie wasn't sure why Ruger was concerned until Cory raised the end of the rod close to his own face. Ruger lunged at him, but Cory drove the symbol onto his own neck, screaming as it singed his flesh.

"No!" Ruger snapped.

The two demons grasped one another, struggling to gain control. They slammed against the railing, only a few feet from where Bethany remained tied up. She lifted her head, her eyes dazed.

Ruger pushed Cory against the rail, trying to force him over the bar. Howie crawled over to the dagger his dad dropped and picked it up. He jumped to his feet and ran up behind Ruger, driving it into his back. Ruger stiffened, bellowing out as the dagger sunk into his flesh. He exhaled sporadically, reaching for the weapon but unable to grab it. His face began to sink inward, the red in his eyes slowly fading.

Cory snarled, then lifted both his hands and drove the jagged tips of all his fingers into Ruger's skull. Ruger tried to shake them free, but the thorny digits were locked in. And then Cory launched himself backward, over the railing, pulling Ruger with him. They both plunged twenty feet, and Howie glanced over the side just as their bodies smacked off the edge of the concrete mold, then fell into the pool of liquid concrete. The slab wasn't fully dry, but it was cured enough that the texture was more like quicksand than pure liquid. Ruger—Vorathor—fought to break free. Cory held on tight as their bodies slowly sank, consumed by the concrete.

Howie watched, still standing next to his dead dad, as his best friend disappeared beneath the surface. His instinct was to get up and try to save Cory. But Cory had just sealed the demon into his own body. He had sacrificed himself to save the rest of them. The top of the concrete shimmered, but nothing came to the surface. Howie understood now that he would never see his best friend again.

CHAPTER 50

Bethany didn't know what to say. She was still tied up, and the lack of blood flow to her hands had forced them to go numb. She wanted to console Howie. To tell him everything would be okay. She had lost her dad as well. She had lost Cory as well. But that didn't feel like the right thing to say. And she wasn't so sure things *would* be okay. Instead, she cried silently while he sat with his dad. He held his dad's remaining hand, staring blankly at the concrete mold below, as if he expected Cory to come up and say he was fine.

"Howie..."

He looked up at her, noticing she was still tied to the railing and climbed to his feet. She stared at his face, into his heartbroken expression as he carefully untied her. Even in a moment where his world was falling apart, he was still thoughtful enough to be gentle with her. As soon as her hands were free, she wrapped her arms around him and hugged him tightly. He flinched, and she realized he was in pain. Somehow, he found a way to laugh.

"What's funny?" Bethany asked.

"When you hugged me, I felt you tighten up and remembered you have sore ribs too. This is probably the most painful hug in history."

He pulled back, and she noticed he was crying again. So was she. They held each other and walked to the stairs, but Howie paused to look down at his dad again. He closed his eyes and shook his head.

"You know, I hated him my whole life. It wasn't until the massacre that we actually started to get along. He was still an asshole, but I finally started to understand him more. I just wish I had more time with that version of him."

"I'm sorry. Just try to remember that you ended things on a good note with him. That's all we can do."

He wiped away another tear and they walked downstairs. The main floor was a war zone. As they stepped around the dead bodies of Troy and Cory's mom, someone coughed behind them. Bethany spun, startled by the break in silence, and spotted Chief Mullin, still handcuffed to the equipment. His breathing was labored, but he was staring at them with hatred in his eyes.

"You little shits ruined everything. The coven had been around for decades, staying out of the way of all you sheep that just go about your day like there's nothing bigger out there. You brought the massacre onto the town. You brought death into your own homes. If you had just let us be, none of this would have ever happened."

Howie let go of Bethany's hand and approached Mullin.

"Howie..." Bethany said, but realized he had to do this.

"We didn't ruin anything. You selfish assholes trapped half the town here for your own gain. That's over now. The coven is gone. And with it, my best friends. My dad. Bethany's entire family. You guys said it was all about a balance of good and evil, but that was just bullshit. You called us sheep and yet you followed Ruger like he was a god. Now he's rotting in Hell where he belongs."

"I'll kill you, kid. Both of you. If you think this coven is dead, you have another thing coming."

Howie turned his back on Mullin and walked back to Bethany. They headed for the exit.

Howie wasn't sure who they would go to for help, but the first thing he wanted to do was call his mom. She had begged them not to go, and now he had the unfortunate job of letting her know his dad wouldn't be coming home with him.

Footsteps scraped along from somewhere out of sight, and Howie turned, prepared to see Ruger coming back for one final kill. Instead, he saw Officer Ellis, limping slowly. Ellis saw Mullin and stopped.

"Uncuff me right now, Ellis. If you want to keep your job, you better fucking do it," Mullin said.

"Oh, I'm doing my job, all right. You wait there. I'll be sure to come back for you in a minute, you piece of shit." Ellis walked to Howie and Bethany. "Are you guys okay?"

They both nodded and the three of them exited the building together. Ellis walked toward his police cruiser.

"We still can't trust the other cops, can we? There were only four coven members here tonight. There has to be more," Howie said.

"I'm going to call in a few friends out of town from my old department. Why don't you both go sit over there and rest while I do that. You kids did good in there. Saved a lot of people. Your families would be proud," Ellis said, giving a sympathetic smile.

"The place they kept me, I think it was down by the river, at the old train station. I think that's where they meet," Bethany said.

"I'll be sure we check down there. Thank you for the info," Ellis said.

Howie found a soft pile of dirt and they sat on it. He could hear Ellis talking on his radio, and hoped whatever help he had come to the scene would believe their story. They were done hiding from the world. Holding secrets that kept the town in the grasp of a malicious leader. Ruger was gone. The coven was gone. There were concerns about surviving members and what they would do, but Howie knew in his heart that without their leader, they would crumble.

"The curse is over," Howie whispered to himself.

"What?"

"Without either demon tormenting us, it's over. We can leave Newport and never look back. I hope my mom will leave," he said.

"Yeah... I don't know where I'll go, or who I'll live with. But I really hope it's far away from this place."

Howie had lost his dad and all of his friends. He couldn't imagine what Bethany was going through after losing her entire family. She had no mom or dad, no sister. She would likely get stuck in a foster home or adopted until she went to college. Howie hoped his mom would sell the house and move away. There wasn't anywhere in town that didn't remind him of adventures with the guys. He thought of Todd and how he was the class clown. Always tried to make people laugh, even if he annoyed them in the process. Howie never thought he'd miss that pestering, but it had only been a few weeks and it felt like part of him was missing without it. He thought of Ryan, and how over-the-top he was at trying to make his friends happy so that they liked him. All Ryan ever wanted was to be accepted. And then Howie thought of Cory. No matter what Howie went through, Cory was there for him. His first girlfriend. First breakup. Most importantly, Cory was there when Howie needed someone to talk to about the relationship with his dad.

Speaking of dads, Howie wondered who would reach out to Cory's dad overseas and let him know. He was working so hard to fight for and protect the country; all the while, his family was home in a place far more dangerous.

"Howie?"

"Yeah?"

"No matter what happens to us, will you promise to always keep in touch? We've lost enough, there's no reason we need to lose each other."

He looked at Bethany, who was wiping away more tears.

"Of course."

She was right. They had lost a lot. But one thing they would never lose was the bond they shared. With each other, with their friends. Cory, Ryan, and Todd would live on in their memories. Howie realized how lucky he'd had it growing up, to have such a close group of friends that did everything together. Whatever Howie did from here, he promised to never let their memory fade.

EPILOGUE

Officer Ellis remained behind to help search the scene for any survivors and evidence. Once he got the kids to safety, he explained the events that had occurred throughout the night. The only thing he left out was the missing bodies of Felix Ruger and Cory Stevens. After talking with Sandy Stevens earlier in the night and then Howie and Bethany before anyone else showed up to check them for injuries, it was clear nobody could know about what resided in the concrete mold. Seeing as it was a murder scene, the place would be shut down indefinitely until the case was closed, which would give him time to find a way to move the concrete coffin somewhere safe.

"Officer Ellis..."

He turned to see another officer quickly walking toward him.

"Yeah?"

"You need to come check this out. We checked the news camera to see if there was any footage on it. It's... it's disturbing, to say the least."

"I'll be right there."

He finished up the area he was searching and headed around the side of the plant to where the camera was left. It had been carefully placed back near the news van, and someone had hooked it up to the monitors inside. He nodded to a female officer sitting at the controls and she hit **<PLAY>**.

If he didn't know he was watching footage from the news crew, he would have thought he was watching some Serbian snuff film. The lighting was grainy, closing in on a window. He realized it was footage inside the concrete plant. He watched everything they recorded from the conversation Ellis had with Sandy and everyone involved, all the way until the coven members came in and Ruger spotted the camera. The officer running the controls paused the feed, a grainy image of Felix Ruger locked in place after he had just briefly removed his mask. While it was blurry, it was obvious who they were looking at. His face was undeniable to those in town who knew who he was.

"Why was Felix Ruger here, and where is he now?" she asked.

Ellis shook his head slowly, wondering why, after everything that happened tonight, there had to be one more piece of evidence that made it even more of a headache.

"He was with them. He took off when things got dangerous, and I don't know where he went."

"We have to reach out to his next of kin, make sure they're aware he's missing," she said.

"Felix Ruger has a family?" Ellis asked.

"His wife and daughter died tragically years ago. But he has two adult sons, and they live on the edge of town."

About the Author

John Durgin is a proud active HWA member and lifelong horror fan. Growing up in New Hampshire, he discovered Stephen King much younger than most probably should have, reading *IT* before he reached high school—and knew from that moment on he wanted to write horror. He had his first story accepted in the summer of 2021. His debut novel, *The Cursed Among Us*, appeared on June 3, 2022, and went on to become an Amazon best-seller. His sophomore novel titled *Inside The Devil's Nest* released in January 2023 followed by his debut collection, *Sleeping In The Fire*, in June 2023. His 2024 novel, *Kosa*, released to stellar reviews.

www.johndurginauthor.com
X: @jdurgin1084
Instagram: @durginpencildrawings
TikTok: @johndurgin_author

A Special Thanks to John Durgin's Patreon Members

Rebecca Rogers

Mari Pittelman

Sophia McIntyre

Trina Thompson

Allia Kennedy

Andrea Johnson

Gage Greenwood

Kevin Feeback

Meredith Livingston

Molly Mix

TripleAre

Alicia Toothman

Jay Bower

Jyl Glenn

Megan Stockton

Nick Roberts

THE END?

Not if you want to dive into more of Crystal Lake Publishing's Tales from the Darkest Depths!

Check out our amazing website and online store or download our latest catalog here.

https://geni.us/CLPCatalog

We always have great new projects and content on the website to dive into, as well as a newsletter, behind the scenes options, social media platforms, our own dark fiction shared-world series and our very own webstore. Our webstore even has categories specifically for KU books, non-fiction, anthologies, and of course more novels and novellas.

Readers...

Thank you for reading *Consumed by Evil*. We hope you enjoyed this novel. If you have a moment, please review *Consumed by Evil* at the store where you bought it.

Help other readers by telling them why you enjoyed this book. No need to write an in-depth discussion. Even a single sentence will be greatly appreciated. Reviews go a long way to helping a book sell, and is great for an author's career. It will also help us to continue publishing quality books.

Thank you again for taking the time to journey with
Crystal Lake Publishing.

You will find links to all our social media platforms on our Linktree page.
https://linktr.ee/CrystalLakePublishing
Follow us on Amazon:

MISSION STATEMENT

Since its founding in August 2012, Crystal Lake has quickly become one of the world's leading publishers of Dark Fiction and Horror books. In 2023, Crystal Lake officially transitioned into an entertainment company, joining several other divisions, genres, and imprints, including Torrid Waters, Crystal Lake Comics, Crystal Lake Games, Crystal Lake Kids, and many more.

While we strive to present only the highest quality fiction and entertainment, we also endeavour to support authors along their writing journey. We offer our time and experience in non-fiction projects, as well as author mentoring and services, at competitive prices.

With several Bram Stoker Award wins and many other wins and nominations (including the HWA's Specialty Press Award), Crystal Lake Publishing puts integrity, honor, and respect at the forefront of our publishing operations.

We strive for each book and outreach program we spearhead to not only entertain and touch or comment on issues that affect our readers, but also to strengthen and support the Dark Fiction field and its authors.

Not only do we find and publish authors we believe are destined for greatness, but we strive to work with men and women who endeavour to be decent human beings who care more for others than themselves, while still being hard working, driven, and passionate artists and storytellers.

Crystal Lake Publishing is and will always be a beacon of what passion and dedication, combined with overwhelming teamwork and respect, can accomplish. We endeavour to know each and every one of our readers, while building personal relationships with our authors, reviewers, bloggers, podcasters, bookstores, and libraries.

We will be as trustworthy, forthright, and transparent as any business can be, while also keeping most of the headaches away from our authors, since it's our job to solve the problems so they can stay in a creative mind. Which of course also means paying our authors.

We do not just publish books, we present to you worlds within your world, doors within your mind, from talented authors who sacrifice so much for a moment of your time.

There are some amazing small presses out there, and through collaboration and open forums we will continue to support other presses in the goal of helping authors and showing the world what quality small presses are capable of accomplishing. No one wins when a small press goes down, so we will always be there to support hardworking, legitimate presses and their authors. We don't see Crystal Lake as the best press out there, but we will always strive to be the best, strive to be the most interactive and grateful, and even blessed press around. No matter what happens over time, we will also take our mission very seriously while appreciating where we are and enjoying the journey.

What do we offer our authors that they can't do for themselves through self-publishing?

We are big supporters of self-publishing (especially hybrid publishing), if done with care, patience, and planning. However, not every author has the time or inclination to do market research, advertise, and set up book launch strategies. Although a lot of authors are successful in doing it all, strong small presses will always be there for the authors who just want to do what they do best: write.

What we offer is experience, industry knowledge, contacts and trust built up over years. And due to our strong brand and trusting fanbase, every Crystal Lake Publishing book comes with weight of respect. In time our fans begin to trust our judgment and will try a new author purely based on our support of said author.

With each launch we strive to fine-tune our approach, learn from our mistakes, and increase our reach. We continue to assure our authors that we're here for them and that we'll carry the weight of the launch and dealing with third parties while they focus on their strengths—be it writing, interviews, blogs, signings, etc.

We also offer several mentoring packages to authors that include knowledge and skills they can use in both traditional and self-publishing endeavours.

We look forward to launching many new careers.

This is what we believe in. What we stand for. This will be our legacy.

Welcome to Crystal Lake Publishing—Tales from the Darkest Depths.